THE FINAL FORMULA

BECCA ANDRE

The Final Formula
Copyright © 2013 by Becca Andre. All rights reserved.
Third Print Edition: 2018

Editor: Shelley Holloway
Cover and Formatting: Streetlight Graphics

No part of this book may be reproduced, scanned, or distributed in any printed or electronic form without permission. Please do not participate in or encourage piracy of copyrighted materials in violation of the author's rights. Thank you for respecting the hard work of this author.

This is a work of fiction. Names, characters, places, and incidents either are the product of the author's imagination or are used fictitiously, and any resemblance to locales, events, business establishments, or actual persons—living or dead—is entirely coincidental.

CHAPTER 1

THE COVERED CRUCIBLE RATTLED AGAINST the glowing red support ring. When it took a little hop, I stepped back. No need to risk my eyebrows. Again. It's not that I'm vain, but a gal needs her eyebrows to communicate. And here at Master Boris's Alchemical Academy, a nonverbal response kept me out of trouble—most of the time.

I tweaked the Bunsen burner and cast a quick glance at Boris's office door. He'd have another fit if he caught me deviating from his lesson plan, but I needed to dry this last ingredient. Unfortunately, his lab lacked an oven, so I'd had to make my own.

An oven wasn't the only thing the lab lacked. The small room barely had enough space for the three laboratory workbenches and mismatched bookcases he'd crammed inside. Every horizontal surface held the well-used equipment of the trade: extra ring stands, chipped Erlenmeyer flasks, a gravity-defying tower of black rubber stoppers—just to name a few. Most of it looked like it'd been around since the 1950s.

The screech of steel on tile alerted me that my lab partner had once again moved her stool to the other end of the bench. I offered the woman a reassuring smile and got a frown in return. No surprise. Like most of the other students, she knew nothing about alchemy. When magic returned two decades ago, these so-called academies had sprung up in community centers across the country. A mecca for bored housewives and magical wannabes, they offered more in entertainment than true instruction. The self-taught alchemists who ran them varied in skill level, from the completely inept to the terminally clueless. I hadn't decided where Boris fell on the scale, but then, I wasn't here for instruction. I needed a lab and for the moment, I had one. It was the best I could hope for in Portsmouth, Ohio.

The crucible began to dance, clattering against the support ring. Perhaps I shouldn't have taped down the cover. I reached for my tongs, but before my fingers closed over the grip, the crucible shot straight up in the air. I gave up all pretense of professional indifference and ducked under the bench. The heavy porcelain dish smashed into the ceiling fourteen feet overhead—or at least I assumed it was the ceiling. My view was limited to stool legs and fleeing feet, but the following rain of porcelain supported my assumption.

"Addie!" Master Boris's voice drowned out the muttered curses of my fellow students. How had he known it was me? He hadn't even been in the room.

"What the hell was that?" His scuffed Wolverine boots came to a stop in front of me.

"Sir?" I crawled out from under the bench and dusted my knees. Master Boris stood a few inches shy of six feet, with a width nearly equal to his height, but his mass didn't intimidate me. He'd need a little something between the ears for that.

"Today's lab was a simple distillation. None of the ingredients were volatile!" He must have missed the smell of burnt rosemary, otherwise he'd realize that I hadn't been performing his simple distillation.

"I'll clean it up, sir." I bowed my head in an effort to look contrite and glanced at the bench top. A fine red powder covered the slate surface. Not bad. My crude oven had been a success, though next time, I'd find a way to vent it.

"You're the worst damn alchemist I've ever had the displeasure of teaching." His thick-jowled face moved a shade closer to purple.

"Master Boris?" My buddy James left his workspace to join me. Tall and lanky, and just out of high school, he was easily the youngest person in the class.

"Stay out of this, Huntsman." Boris spared James a frown before turning back to me. "I can't afford your ineptitude. Clean this up and get out." He wheeled around with a porcelain crunch and stormed off.

I took an involuntary step after him, ready to protest, and stopped. No, I wouldn't beg. I could find another lab. I pulled a clean brush from my bag. With practiced strokes, I began to sweep the fine powder into a mound closer to the edge of the bench.

"About damn time." The young man at the workspace across from mine flicked a piece of crucible in my direction. It emitted a faint tink when it struck the scarred tile at my feet. "You're a menace."

I gave the Neanderthal the appropriate eyebrow arch before I pulled a clean vial from my bag.

James moved to my side, exchanging a glare with the other man before turning his attention to me. "What's that?" He jerked his chin toward the red powder.

"Remembrance Dust. Chemically, it's similar to rosmarinic acid, but with an alchemic twist." A bent scrap of paper made a temporary funnel, and I gently swept the powder into the vial. "Not the classic preparation, but it works. My next *master* will have a muffle furnace."

James snorted, well aware that Master Boris was anything

but. "And where will you find a man who can call himself your master?"

"I'd settle for one I could call my equal." A pen loop inside the front pocket of my backpack provided secure storage for the vial. With a grunt, I swung the bag over my shoulder. Time to go.

"Addie, wait up," James said.

"Finish what you're doing." No need for him to miss out on the lesson.

I left the lab and pulled the door closed behind me. The slamming door echoed in the empty hall, rattling a glass case that held lop-sided clay pots from the pottery class a few doors down. Community center learning at its finest.

I knew I was being too critical, but getting kicked out of Boris's academy stung. Of course, if my current potion worked, my laboratory needs might prove irrelevant. Hitching my pack higher on my shoulder, I shoved open the front door.

"Addie!" James caught up with me before I'd even left the block. "Hey, why didn't you wait?" He slowed to a walk beside me, still cinching his bag.

I glanced over at my sidekick, one-time rescuer and only friend. With dark hair, bright green eyes, and a smile that caught the attention of every teenage girl around, I couldn't understand why he chose to hang with me. "You better not have quit," I said.

"No. Not yet." He slung his bag over his shoulder. "Let me talk to Boris."

"No need. If this doesn't work…" I wasn't sure how to finish that sentence. I tried not to think beyond the potion I had brewing at home. It wasn't the end of the road, but what my future held beyond it was as obscure as my past.

"It'll work," he said. "You didn't receive those bands for—"

I swatted him in the stomach and glanced around to see if

anyone was eavesdropping. A couple of late-model cars drove down Ninth Street, but the only pedestrian close enough to overhear bobbed his head to whatever played on his iPod.

Beneath my shirt sleeves, five tattooed bands encircled my right biceps and four decorated the left. A symbol of rank at the Alchemica, each band represented a discipline mastered. No one except James knew about my tattoos, and I intended to keep it that way.

"You don't even know if they're legitimate," I whispered.

"And neither do you."

I gave him a frown and picked up my pace. The earliest memory I had was James pulling me out from behind a dumpster, blocks away from the burning ruin of the Alchemica in Cincinnati. I couldn't remember how I'd gotten there or how I'd escaped the explosion that killed all the others. All I remembered was alchemy. Every formula. Every ingredient. Every technique.

"Addie, come on." He matched my stride with ease. "I'm saying that you're a good alchemist. The best. With or without your memory, that won't change."

I didn't feel like arguing, so I let it go. "Thanks."

We rounded the corner, and the Huntsman Gun Shop came into view. They carried everything your avid hunter could ever need—or so they claimed. Guns, bows, ammo, clothing and assorted paraphernalia I knew little about. They were family owned and operated, local but modern. They had even hired an alchemist. Me. Magic bullets were all the rage, and I helped the Huntsman keep pace with the times.

"We're not due back at the shop for another hour," I said. "I'd rather not tell your brothers I flunked out."

"Then don't." James turned down the alley beside the shop, leading me to the side entrance rather than the front. A decade-old black Buick sat near one wall, blocking most of the narrow space. James slowed as he eyed the car.

"Anyone you know?" I asked.

"No." He gestured at the back end of the car. "Hamilton County plates."

I grunted. "You think word of the shop's bullets has spread as far as Cincinnati?" The city was over a hundred miles away.

"Your bullets." He flashed me a grin and climbed the three steps to the side door. "And I'm surprised it took this long."

Shaking my head, I followed James inside and up the back stairs. After today's experiences, it was nice to have someone on my side.

The attic room over the shop served as both my workshop and my bedroom. I'd shoved a twin bed into one corner along with a couple of milk crates to use as a nightstand. Three folding tables occupied the rest of the room, each cluttered with an assortment of makeshift lab equipment. The shop paid for the things I needed to make bullets, but the rest I'd acquired panhandling at local high schools. My take included a nice assortment of cracked beakers, volumetric flasks without stoppers, and stained stir bars. If I could have found better equipment, I wouldn't have had to attend Boris's academy.

I set down my pack and shrugged off my jacket.

"Are you sure you want to do this?" James asked.

"Yes." I gave him a frown. I'd been working up to this for weeks; he knew that. "If you're staying, close the door." I waved a hand toward the door and unzipped my pack. Removing what I needed, I walked to the table where I'd cobbled together some of my better pieces of equipment. The product of the complicated set-up had filled one tiny vial. It sat in a rare clear space on the table, majestic in its solitude.

The door closed with a soft snap of the latch, but I didn't look over. I sprinkled the Remembrance Dust into the vial, and the clear liquid turned a deep ruby red. Burnt rosemary momentarily overpowered the usual odor of gunpowder in the room. A month's worth of work in a 20mL vial. Perfect. Would it prove to be the perfect solution? I had my doubts, but until I knew what potion had stolen my memories, I could do no better.

James stopped beside me. "It could be dangerous."

I capped the vial and gave it a shake. "Are you afraid the potion is toxic, or do you fear it will work? You know what they say about Alchemica alchemists."

He shifted his weight from foot to foot. "I've heard the rumors. You know, about the ingredients they used?"

"Blood, body parts, decaying flesh…"

"Yeah. You think it's true?"

"I can tell you the alchemical effect of each of those ingredients—and then some." Which, come to think of it, was a bit disturbing.

"So? You can do that for anything. Even for things I would never suspect could be used as ingredients." He folded his arms across his chest. "It really pisses me off the way Boris treated you."

I tried not to smile at his righteous anger on my behalf. "I did blow up a lot of his equipment."

"Still, you're brilliant." James scowled at the vial I held.

I studied his youthful face. Where did the kid get such faith in me? I had no idea what I'd done to deserve it. "You don't want me to take this potion, do you?"

He looked up, the anger replaced by uncertainty. "It could be toxic."

"It isn't, and if you truly believe I'm as good as you claim, you'd listen." I held up a hand to stop his protest. "You're afraid it'll work and I'll turn out to be the Alchemica Master these bands declare me to be. That I really did earn them through blood—or worse."

"Addie."

"Tell me the truth."

His brows lowered, shadowing his eyes, and I got a glimpse of the man he would be. My sidekick was going to be someone to be reckoned with. His expression softened. "You're not evil."

I gave him a fond smile and uncapped the vial. "Shall we find out?"

His brow wrinkled further, and he opened his mouth, but I didn't wait for his comment. I downed the potion in a single swallow.

Familiar shadows surrounded me. I didn't turn my head, but I knew that if I did, I'd see a battered nightstand to my right and an overflowing bookshelf to my left. The mattress beneath my back poked and bulged in the usual places. My bed, my room at the Alchemica—and I wasn't alone.

The mattress shifted to bear the weight of an old man in split-sleeved robes of white: the Grand Master. He leaned forward to brace one hand beside my pillow and brushed back the hair from my forehead with the other. The movement exposed his upper arms and the black bands encircling each—four on the left, five on the right. Like me: a master alchemist lacking only the elusive final band. The final band for the Final Formula.

I caught his scent, a mixture of Old Spice and acetic acid, and felt a twinge of déjà vu. Before I could analyze the feeling, he spoke. Pain splintered my head at the sound, making it impossible to follow the words. The dim lights went dark.

Garbled voices and darkness reigned for a period of time I couldn't judge. It could have been minutes or hours, maybe even days. Suddenly someone pulled me upright and in the same motion, threw me over his shoulder. The Grand Master? Too confused to protest, I simply hung there as my head pounded in rhythm with my heart.

He carried me from my room into the brighter light of the hall. Through pain-narrowed eyes, I looked down his back.

The Final Formula

What the hell? The man carrying me didn't wear the robes of my Grand Master; he wore black fatigues. Had the military decided they needed an alchemist?

I tried to cry for help, but shouted a list of ingredients instead. I snapped my mouth shut, too stunned to be afraid. Oddly, the pain lessened. It seemed as if speaking the words had released the pressure clamped around my head. That scared me even more.

My captor stopped at the intersection of two corridors. I tried to get my bearings, but I wasn't used to viewing the hallways upside down.

"Check out the tattoos," he said.

Another pair of black boots and matching fatigues came into my line of sight. "Nice work. He'll be pleased."

I took a breath to try another shout, but the words never left my lips. The world exploded in light and sound. My captor screamed and released me. The stone floor rushed toward my face, and I threw out my hands.

I woke to darkness, facedown on an uneven surface. My hips and legs on one level, while my upper body rested on a sloping decline. The position didn't help my pounding head. I shifted and sucked in a gasp of smoke-scented air. I ached all over.

A glimpse through slitted eyes revealed distant fire and mounds of rubble. The Alchemica—or what was left of it. What hadn't been reduced to jagged piles of stone was burning. Dear God, how had I survived that? Had anyone else?

"Over here!" The loud voice sent bolts of pain rocketing through my skull.

I lifted my head to turn it in the other direction and the muscles in my neck and shoulders screamed in protest. Gritting my teeth against the pain, I pushed my dark hair out of my eyes and searched for the speaker. A man stood a few feet away, his back to me. He wore robes, but even in the faint light I could see that they were the wrong color for an alchemist. His robes were dark gray, trimmed in small black triangles: the alchemical symbol for fire.

My heart tried to escape my chest. An Element. No, The Element. The Lord of Flames himself. What the hell was he doing here?

Elements didn't like alchemists. Since magic had returned, those with magic and those without had waged a cold war to see who would claim this new world. The alchemists fit in neither category. We were a hybrid: mundane humans who dared to wield power we didn't innately possess. No one with magic could stand us, and the Elements were the most magical of them all.

"Your Grace." Running footsteps halted nearby. "I pulled the car around."

"Good. Let us go." The deep commanding tone made me want to slip off my slab and hide in the rubble. I didn't breathe until the pair moved away.

I don't know how I went unnoticed. Perhaps my black robes blended with the shadows. Once they were gone, I pushed myself up to my hands and knees. I had to chew my lip to stay silent. Fine grit coated the slab, biting into my scraped palms. My stomach threatened to heave, and I slumped forward, pressing my forehead to the stone until it passed.

"There!" a voice shouted from close by.

I pushed myself back up and saw two men in black fatigues only yards away. The same two men? If they'd survived the blast as well, perhaps it'd been our location within the building that saved us.

"I found her!" the same man shouted.

I didn't know who they were or what they wanted with me, but I wasn't going to sit here and find out.

With a grunt, I pushed myself to my feet. The world swam around me, and I stumbled off the stone slab using a partially standing wall to catch myself. No way I could outrun these guys. It'd have to be a potion then.

I slipped a hand along my ribs to the vials I kept hidden among the folds of my robes. The bodice fit close, the gathered fabric forming a multitude of little pockets, the perfect size for a potion vial. I found nothing.

The two men advanced toward me. My head clearer now, I noticed that neither moved well. They hadn't come through the explosion unscathed. Maybe I could make a run for it. I shifted sideways, back to the wall. An opening gaped a few feet away.

"Stay right there," the more agile of the pair told me. He picked his way through the rubble, cursing when a loose stone nearly felled him.

I slipped through the gap and ran.

At first, I didn't think I'd escape the debris-laden remains of the Alchemica. I nearly went down twice, but once I reached the street, I did much better. Running warmed my sore muscles, and I stumbled less with each block I put between me and the Alchemica.

My head pounded, but I couldn't stop to rest. A block back, the men were still following. They kept up better than I expected. I darted across the street. When I reached the curb opposite, I glanced back. Now three men in dark clothing were following me. Three? Had they picked up a recruit along the way? I increased my pace and turned the corner before they caught up.

An alley too narrow for cars branched off to my right. A dumpster blocked the far end, but enough space remained for me to squeeze through to the street beyond. I turned and jogged toward the gap, hoping it'd be too small for my pursuers to crawl through.

The sickening sweet odor of rotting garbage grew stronger the closer I got. Breathing through my mouth helped. I glanced over my shoulder, and my foot slipped in one of the iridescent puddles beside the dumpster. I staggered to the side and smacked into the wall, somehow managing not to land on my butt in the putrid slime.

"I told you she took this alley."

My stumble had cost me. I spun and discovered that the trio tailing me had caught up. Out of habit, the fingers of my right hand drifted to the empty vial pockets along my side. The men fanned out, blocking me in. The third man hadn't been in the explosion. His fatigues weren't dirt streaked, and he didn't limp like the other two.

I backed toward the dumpster.

"Where you going, pretty girl?" the new guy asked.

Wow. Flattery. I was charmed. My fingers itched for a blow tube of Knockout Powder. He wouldn't be so confident then.

My back thumped against the dumpster with a metallic clang.

"Got you cornered." He was close enough that I could see his overlapping front teeth when he smiled.

Yeah? "Marigold, dried and chopped." I pressed my lips together. So much for the witty comeback. On the plus side, my head felt better.

"What'd she say?" one of the others asked, and all three laughed.

Jerks. Maybe Knockout Powder was too humane for these losers. How about—

Something brushed by my hip, and I sidestepped with a gasp. An enormous dog stopped a few feet in front of me, his shaggy black hair darker than the shadows around us. He looked like a cross between a rottweiler and an Irish wolfhound, but bigger. Built for speed, but loaded in muscle.

Monster Dog growled, and every hair on my body stood on end. No hound I'd ever met made a sound like that. The three men backed away. A strange green glow now lit the alley, making their horrified expressions visible. Definitely not a natural dog.

I stepped away until my back pressed against the dumpster again. The giant canine snarled, and as one, the thugs let out a scream and ran. For an instant, only the dog and I remained. A soft growl—I swear it sounded almost like a chuckle—and then the hound gave chase.

Strangely, I couldn't hear the dog's tread, though I could see his toenails scraping the pavement. The thunder of fleeing boots I heard *fine.* I sagged against the dumpster, alone now. But what if the dog came back?

I squeezed between the dumpster and the wall. My small size proved advantageous for once. No way that dog could fit in here.

I huddled against that grimy wall, holding my robes out of the pungent filth, and waited. I couldn't hear the men or their monstrous pursuer. Did I dare squeeze out the other side? Running footsteps in the alley put a halt to that plan, and I sank lower in the shadows.

"Hello?" a voice called.

I leaned to the side. A young man stood a few yards from the dumpster. He bent over to grip his thighs, taking several deep breaths. I must have made some noise because he looked up and saw me. He smiled and straightened.

"Are you okay? I saw those guys harassing you." He waved a hand toward the street beyond the dumpster. Perhaps he'd seen them from the other side, but couldn't squeeze through the gap. He must have circled around.

He stepped over a thick puddle to stop outside my hiding place. I wanted to ask if that'd been his dog, but didn't want to shatter his illusion of my sanity by speaking.

He offered me a hand. "Do you need some help?" I followed his arm upward and met his green eyes.

CHAPTER 2

"Addie?"

James leaned close, wearing the same worried expression he'd worn then. I lay on my bed in the little room over the gun shop. James sat beside me.

"Did it work?" he asked.

"Sort of." I sat up and massaged my temples. My head ached.

"Sort of?" James got to his feet.

"It returned my memories to just before the Alchemica was destroyed, but nothing earlier."

"So, you know what happened to the Alchemica?"

"I'm not sure. There were guys in black fatigues who tried to abduct me, and—" I looked up, remembering those gray robes. "The Elements were there."

"You're certain?"

"I saw one of them, when everything was on fire. The Flame Lord stood just feet away from me. I recognized the robes."

"But the paper said an explosion in the lab destroyed the Alchemica." James stared at me as if I'd just suggested that the sun really did revolve around the earth.

"Maybe, maybe not." I rose to my feet and walked over to my workbench to disassemble the crude apparatus I'd constructed to brew my potion.

James joined me. "What now?"

The Final Formula

I kept my hands busy while I thought about it. I still had no idea who'd given me the memory mangling potion or why. Today's potion had probably taken me back to the moment the other took effect. If that was the case, then my memory loss and the destruction of the Alchemica weren't connected. Unless I'd learned something I shouldn't—like the Element's plans. But the Elements didn't have access to a potion like that. Hell, they'd probably see its use as beneath them.

I rubbed both hands over my face. I'd created more questions than I'd answered. How were those men in fatigues involved? Did they work for the Elements? Another alchemist? If so, I was in trouble. As far as I knew, all the Alchemica alchemists were dead.

"I want to visit the Alchemica," I said.

"It's condemned."

"I need to see it. I now know these bands are real, and it's the only place in the world I know I've been to before. It might stir some more memories." I hoped so. I didn't know any other memory-restoring potions.

"I don't think it's safe for you to go back there."

"It burned three months ago. No one is sitting around waiting for the residents to return." I didn't have a car; I had to talk James into taking me.

"You really think it'll help?"

He was coming around, but I resisted the urge to smile. "It's all I have. Please?"

His shoulders fell, and I moved in for the kill.

"Supper's on me."

"You want to go now?"

"Could we?"

He shook his head, though a smile threatened. "For the record, I still think it's a bad idea."

I snatched up my jacket and followed him out of my

workshop and back down the stairs. I stopped beside the alley door while he selected a coat from the rack.

"We can drive through Mickey Ds," I said.

"You sure you can afford it?" He grinned openly now, well aware of how much he ate.

I didn't get a chance to comment. Two forms in camo charged down the hall and slammed into James. I jumped out of the way, my hand going for a vial tucked in my front pocket, as they shoved James against the wall opposite the door. I hesitated. It was Brian and Henry—two of James's three brothers.

"Outside. Now." Henry pulled James off the wall and slammed his hands against James's chest, shoving him into the door to the alley. The doorway I stood in.

I had time to gasp, and then James slammed into me. My back collided with the door, but it offered little resistance. I windmilled my arms, trying to regain my balance as I teetered on the top step.

James turned and caught me.

"Move." Henry gave James another shove.

Overbalanced, we tumbled down the steps and landed hard on the lumpy cobbles of the alley, not far from the car with the Hamilton County plates.

"Addie! Are you okay?" James pushed himself up on an elbow to stare down at me. His legs were tangled with mine, but he'd managed not to fall on me. Barely.

"Maybe?" His brothers had ambushed us so fast that my brain still hadn't caught up.

"Now that's more like it, James." Brian joined us in the alley. "That's what you do with a woman."

James sprang to his feet, fists clenched at his sides.

I climbed to my feet in a slower, more pained motion and gave his brothers a frown. A family resemblance existed between the three of them, though the brothers were broader in build with lighter hair—Henry bordering on blond. Appearances aside, I hadn't been around them long before I wondered if James was adopted.

"What the hell are you doing?" James glared at one brother and then the other. "You could have hurt Addie."

"George said to keep you out of the shop," Brian said.

"And now you are," Henry added.

"The collected wit here is staggering." I brushed the dust from my backside.

"And this from our Addled Alchemist?" Henry gave me a sneer.

I crossed my arms. When James first brought me home, I couldn't speak. Each time I tried, it came out as alchemical nonsense. His brothers had dubbed me the Addled Alchemist—Addie for short. Since I couldn't remember my name, the new moniker stuck.

James took a step toward his brothers, but I caught his arm.

"Let it go," I said.

James hesitated, glancing from them to me.

"Wow, baby brother, she has you trained." Brian nudged Henry.

"You know why he takes those alchemy classes?" Henry asked. "It's so he can understand her pillow talk."

James launched himself at Henry before I could even think of moving. He caught his larger brother by the front of the shirt and threw him against the brick wall across the alley—a good ten feet away. Henry smacked bricks with so much force that I expected to see cracks radiate through the mortar joints around him.

"James!" Brian stepped between his brothers and caught James by the upper arms. Henry slid down the wall to sit at its base, his stunned expression mirroring my own.

Damn. That took some serious strength. How had James managed that?

Henry shook his head and pushed himself to this feet using the wall for support. "Freak." He glared at James as he spoke then turned away and almost ran into me. "Move." His teeth were gritted so tight it sounded like, "Murve."

I couldn't resist. "That's the fastest ass-kicking I've ever seen."

"Yeah?" Henry clenched his fists and took a step toward me. He stood so close, I could smell the onion rings he had for lunch. Brian wrapped a restraining arm around James.

I pulled a vial from my pocket and held it up to display the lime green liquid inside. "You should thank James. What I'd do isn't so pleasant."

"Enough," a new voice barked from the back door.

All four of us jumped like guilty children and turned to find George glaring from the top step. The eldest of the Huntsman brothers, he'd inherited the gun shop from their parents and ran it like a drill sergeant.

"You two," he frowned at Henry and Brian, "were suppose to take him to the house and keep him there." He pointed to the mouth of the alley and the two-story house across the street.

"And you." He focused on me. "Inside. I've got a customer waiting on those new bullets."

"What's going on?" James asked.

"They'll explain." George met James's eye and made a shooing gesture.

James didn't comment. A glance at me, and he turned and left with Brian and Henry.

George's attention shifted back to me. "Move your ass, alchemist."

I bit back a retort, deciding that spending less time with

him was preferable to a witty comeback. Next time, I promised myself.

I RETURNED TO THE ATTIC workshop, annoyed with the delay. Fortunately, I'd finished the bullets George wanted; I just had to pack them in their cardboard ammo boxes. George had splurged on professional printing. I loved how the boxes smelled of fresh ink—like a new magazine. With red letters on a glossy black background, they weren't fancy, but better than me penning the letters on a plain white box. Packing the bullets shouldn't take more than fifteen minutes. Though it would have gone quicker if James were here.

My mind drifted back to the alley, and I remembered how easily James had flung Henry against the wall. Maybe James deserved the wary glances his brothers gave him. And if they knew how strong he was, why didn't that earn James more respect? They usually treated him like crap—when they acknowledged him at all. I'd been here three months, and I still hadn't puzzled out this family dynamic.

Twelve boxes later, I was no closer to a solution.

The door banged open and George stormed into the room.

I jumped and dropped half the bullets I'd been holding. They clattered on the plastic table, one rolling off the far side.

"Where are they?" he demanded.

"They'd be in the box if some jerk hadn't startled me."

George smirked. My least favorite of the Huntsman brothers, he took particular pleasure in tormenting me. Worse, he actually had half a brain and sometimes he used it.

I gathered the loose bullets and began to place them in the ammo box I'd been filling.

"Hand me that one?" I pointed to the bullet that lay near George's left foot.

He crossed his large arms and leaned against the wall beside the door. Asshole. No way James could be related to this loser.

I retrieved the bullet myself and finished filling the box. "There you go." I stacked the last box on the plastic tray with the others, my task complete.

"Bring them." He turned and started down the stairs. "He wants to meet you."

"What?"

He didn't answer. No surprise.

I struggled to lift the tray with its twelve boxes of ammo and stumbled after him. He never introduced me to the buyers. I suspected he feared I'd be enticed away.

I managed the stairs without hurting myself or dropping any boxes. When we entered the shop, the man at the back counter looked up and a wave of unease swept over me. He didn't wear camo or Carhartts like most of the shop's regulars; he wore a suit.

His eyes met mine and my feet tangled with the rug. I would have fallen if George hadn't stepped forward at the last moment to catch the tray. He glared at me for the near miss, but replaced it with a smile when he turned to face the customer.

"And our special bullets. The ones you called about." George thumped the tray on the counter, causing the bullets to clink within their boxes.

The man lifted a box and turned the label toward him. "Heart Seekers?"

"It's a play on heat seeker," George needlessly explained. "Like the missile, but without all the clunky technology. And on a much smaller scale, of course."

The man opened the box and withdrew one of the bullets. His fingers looked rough, the nails yellowed and cuticles peeling.

"Ten seconds?" he asked George.

George tapped the small print on the back of the box. "Dead

in ten seconds or less, no matter where the shot hits." He pulled out a bag and began stacking the bullets inside.

"Sounds...dangerous."

"It's designed for animals," I spoke up. "Human blood won't trigger the magic."

The man's eyes rose to mine. "I assume you're the alchemist."

I took in his clothing and remembered the car in the alley. He'd traveled over two hours to see my special bullets. "And you're from the PIA." I offered my hand, refusing to let him intimidate me. "I'm Addie."

He took my hand, smiling now. The dry skin of his palm rubbed against mine before his chilled fingers enveloped my own. "Agent Lawson."

I returned the smile and hoped it didn't look like a grimace. PIA: Paranormal Investigation Agency—or as practitioners of the arcane liked to call them, Pain In the Ass. Once a branch of Homeland Security, they had become an agency in their own right in the last decade. Specifically, an agency to police the magical community. My memory might be full of holes, but I knew the PIA could make life difficult.

George's good mood baffled me. This couldn't be an investigation—on him or me. He might be personally pleased to see me arrested, but he'd be pissed to lose my financial input to the shop's coffers.

"These bullets are impressive," Lawson said. "Where were you trained?"

"I last attended Master Boris's Alchemical Academy on Ninth Street." I saw no reason to lie—no reason to tell the truth either.

"Boris Tuppins is no master. Before he decided to try his hand at alchemy, he taught chemistry at a Kentucky high school. He's never set foot inside the Alchemica."

It seemed Lawson had done his homework. "Master or not, that's where I last attended an alchemy class."

"That surprises me. While we were registering this shop's bullets, analysis suggested they might be the work of a Master."

And now his presence, and George's creepy smiles, made sense. Purveyors of magical items had to register their wares with the PIA. If the PIA gave their stamp of approval, you could advertise as such. In other words, the PIA agreed that the magic was safe and did as you claimed—and prices tended to adjust accordingly. George could probably double his profits.

"The formula is mine," I said.

Lawson frowned. "But you're not old enough."

"Old enough? Were you expecting an Alchemica Master?" I smiled, trying to make it a joke. "I thought they were all dead."

"There were no records on the numbers attending the Alchemica, so it is possible a few survived." Lawson drew a card from the inside of his coat and offered it to me. "I'd like to learn the name of the man who taught you alchemy."

Man? Was he looking for a male alchemist? I took the rectangle of crisp white cardstock. It contained only a name, Robert A. Lawson, and phone number in black ink. The number had a Cincinnati area code.

The front door of the shop opened with an electronic chime. "Addie?" James saw Lawson and started toward us.

"Shit," Lawson muttered and in one smooth move, drew his gun.

Shocked, I could only watch as he trained it on James.

"Whoa!" George threw up his hands and to my total astonishment, stepped between Agent Lawson and James.

I hurried around the counter and caught Lawson's arm. "Wait!"

He glanced over, his pupils huge, and I pulled my hand away. Crap. The man was a Sensitive. I'd heard rumors that the PIA hired them to sniff out those who failed to register their magic. But why point a gun at…

I connected the dots. James was magical. The confrontation in the alley took on a whole new light. I needed to think fast, or James was going to get some unwanted attention. Though Lawson's reaction seemed a little over the top.

"I guess my Hunter's Prowess potion is a success." I created the title on the fly then lowered my voice. "Especially if a Sensitive is picking up on it at this distance."

Lawson stiffened then lowered the gun. It looked like his sensitivity was a secret. His eyes swung in my direction, and I offered an innocent smile.

"What do you think, Agent Lawson?"

"I think I'd like you to come in for an interview, Miss Addie." His voice dropped. "You appear to be a talented young lady."

"And underappreciated."

"Hmm." He studied James for a moment longer before he tucked the gun away. "You can do that," he nudged his chin in James's direction, "with a potion?"

"I can do a lot of things with a potion." I met his gaze and held it. That's right buddy, focus right here. Ignore the boy.

"The potion will need to be registered."

"When it's perfected, it will be. Just as we registered the bullets." I waved a hand toward the counter where George had bagged up his order.

He continued to look me over as he picked up his purchases. "I'll be expecting your call." He turned toward the door.

That was it? No interrogation? No preliminary formula? He really hadn't come looking for me.

"Mr. Huntsman." Lawson nodded at George. James took a step back to let him pass, but held his stare without flinching.

Lawson pushed open the front door, the chime interrupting the silence in the shop. A silence that didn't return once the door closed.

"What the hell are you doing?" George turned on James. "Didn't you listen to Henry?"

"A PIA agent came looking for Addie and you didn't tell me?" James closed the distance with angry strides.

"You were supposed to stay in the house." George jabbed a finger toward the front door. I still couldn't believe he'd put himself in harm's way for James.

"I covered it," I spoke up. "Agent Lawson thinks I used a potion on him."

"How'd you know?" George turned on his brother and grabbed him by the shirt. "Did you tell her?"

"No one told me anything. Come on, I'm an alchemist. I bottle magic for a living."

"You made that agent focus on you." James glanced at me then dropped his gaze to the floor. "What if he'd taken you in?"

"Why would he?" George released James with a small shove. "You're the one he wants."

I ignored George and kept my attention on James. He frowned, but wouldn't meet my eyes. I didn't expect him to be so shy about this magical ability of his.

"But what about the interview?" James asked the floor. When I didn't immediately respond, he looked up.

I shrugged and hoped it didn't look as stiff as it felt. I had no intention of going for a little tête-à-tête with Agent Lawson, but I didn't want to discuss that in front of George.

"I don't trust him," James said.

"Nor should you," I said. "He's PIA."

"And that means what?" George demanded. "You got a problem with authority?"

It took me a moment to gather my wits. "You make and sell *magic* bullets, and you're defending the PIA? Do you want them to regulate every move you make?"

"We are fully sanctioned by the PIA." George took a step

toward me. "I don't want to hear anything out of that smart mouth of yours. If I do, you'll be out on your counterfeit ass."

"The ass is legit."

George fisted his hands, and the cords in his neck stood out in stark relief. Not overly tall, but packed with muscle, George made an imposing figure. I doubted he had any qualms about striking a woman. I should probably shut up.

"As for the PIA," I began.

"Addie's not going to discuss them in this household." James stepped between George and me. Taller than his brother, James had the lean, athletic build typical of his eighteen years. George made him look like a malnourished child. "Isn't that right?" James asked me.

Whatever James's magical talents, I knew he wouldn't stand up to George as he had Henry. I couldn't let my sidekick get pummeled for my inability to shut up. "Yeah, sure." I clamped my jaw closed to prevent further elaboration on the subject.

"She better not." George glared at me.

I managed to stop an eyeroll. I needed to get out of here. "You want to go for that drive?" I asked James.

"Sure. Let's go."

"You love birds got a hot date?" George snorted and eyed James. "Where do you take an alchemist?"

"The cemetery," I answered before James could. I grinned at George's scowl and patted James on the shoulder. "You pack the shovel?"

"And I remembered the crowbar this time."

I might be a bad influence.

CHAPTER

3

James parked in the municipal lot across the street from the Alchemica and shut off the engine. Neither of us spoke as we stared through the windshield at my former home. Night had fallen, but several streetlights and a nearly full moon provided enough illumination. Surrounded by a chain-link fence and Do Not Enter signs, the Alchemica looked like a construction site. Only the crumbling shell of the three-story building remained. I stared at the rubble, looking for something I remembered. Maybe it was the destruction, but I didn't recognize a thing.

"You okay?" James asked.

I picked up one of the flashlights he'd brought and put it in my jacket pocket. "Let's take a closer look." I opened the door and stepped out into the dimly lit lot.

We hadn't talked much on the two-hour drive from Portsmouth to Cincinnati. The agent's reaction to James had clearly bothered him. He'd spent the trip twiddling with the radio, rather than talking with me. I didn't mind. Preoccupied with our destination, I'd watched the Ohio farmland slide past my window, lost in my own concerns. Would the ruins of my former home awaken any new memories, or would this prove to be a wasted trip?

With James at my side, I started across the street. Behind a clump of bushes, we found a gap under the chain-link. James slid beneath the fence with ease, and I hurried to follow. Small stones ground into my stomach, and the fence snagged my jacket, but I managed to wiggle through. Between the moon and the streetlights, I didn't need to pull out my flashlight.

"I don't think it's safe," James said.

"What? Exploring a burned-out building in the dark? Where's your sense of adventure?"

"A little caution is a good thing."

I blew him a raspberry before picking my way through the ruin of a fallen wall.

"Looks like the explosion was on this side of the building," James said.

I agreed. On the other end of the building, the stone outer walls still stood. Here, that wasn't the case. With cleanup already begun, I couldn't be certain, but it looked like the walls had been blown outward. Had the Elements been inside? Odd. If I were going to burn down the place, I'd do it from outside. It'd be easier to avoid falling chunks of roof and smoke inhalation.

I climbed down into the debris field that had once been an auditorium or gym. In places, I could see sections of hardwood floor. Careful of my footing in the low light, I threaded my way around man-sized chunks of cement and twisted I-beams.

"I'm no expert," I said, hopping across a foot-deep pothole, "but this seems like a bad location to take out the building." I gestured toward the rest of the structure. "It didn't take down very much."

James cleared the pothole in one long stride. "Maybe the building wasn't the target. A room like this would be a good place for gatherings."

"Good point." I remembered nothing, of course. At the time, I'd been in my bed waiting for my head to explode. Had there been an assembly that evening? Had the Elements heard about it and decided to take us all out? Why? We'd co-existed for over a decade and a half. What had changed?

We reached an archway that might have supported double doors, and stepped through to a concrete floor. The fire had destroyed everything that would burn, leaving a cavernous space open to the night sky above.

I crossed my arms and followed James through the blackened rubble. Ash rose in a cloud around our feet, occasionally drifting high enough to tickle my nose. I searched for something familiar, but found nothing I recognized. Nothing. If I hadn't retrieved those few memories, I would believe the tattoos on my arms were fakes.

"Look. There's a basement." James turned right and picked his way to a square hole and a set of cement steps that disappeared into darkness. Without further comment, he pulled out his flashlight and started down. For someone who'd been hesitant about coming in here, he had overcome his reservations. Give him a leather coat and a fedora, and he'd be all set.

I pulled out my flashlight and followed.

The basement had survived the blaze better than the upper floors, possibly because of the block walls. A door-lined hallway stretched before me, and for the first time, my memory stirred. I stopped to analyze the feeling.

"Addie?" James halted a few feet away, his voice pitched low.

"The labs were down here," I whispered.

"You remember something?"

"Maybe."

Heat had warped the metal doors lining the hall. Most hung askew, hinges broken and painted metal surfaces gorged by prying tools. We weren't the first to find this place.

I chose a room at random and walked inside. Three rows of black graphite benches occupied the space. I ran a hand over the pitted surface. I could almost smell the reagents and hear the excited chatter of the apprentices. Shelves lined the walls, most empty or piled with worthless clutter. Nothing of value remained, but that didn't upset me. I'd been right; I'd been here before. I hurried out to try another room.

I was close, so close. Terrified the sensation would slip away, I ran from room to room searching for something I knew. Had one of these labs been mine? Would I know it if I saw it? I searched quickly, my anxiety driving me.

"Addie, slow down," James called.

I ignored him and sprinted toward the last room I'd yet to explore: the one at the end of the hall. I pushed on the door, but found it jammed. I took a step back and threw my weight against it. The door resisted, then broke free without warning. I tripped and fell forward, landing hard on my hands and knees. The force knocked the flashlight from my hand, and it rolled to a stop a foot away. A shower of dust fell through the beam of light.

"Addie! Move!"

A deafening pop sounded overhead. I snatched up my flashlight and swung it toward the ceiling. Dust fell from above, and I lifted a hand to shield my eyes. Through my fingers, I watched a wide support beam bow toward me, cracks radiating across the plaster ceiling.

I tried to regain my feet, but the marble-sized debris beneath my shoes sent me back to the floor. I skidded a few feet on my knees and bumped into James, having almost slid between his spread legs. He grunted and metal screeched overhead. I looked up and forgot to breathe.

James had caught the beam. He held it suspended over his head, the cords in his neck bulging with the effort.

Chunks of ceiling fell around us, but all I could do was stare.

"Go," he growled—literally growled. The sound rumbled deep in his throat and the hair on the back of my neck stood on end. I shoved myself to my feet once more and stumbled past him. Somehow I dodged the large chunks of cement falling around me, and reached the door.

I looked back in time to see James hurl the beam back into the room. He ran for the door and had almost reached me when a hunk of rebar-spiked concrete crashed into his shoulder with a crunch and a splatter of blood.

"James!" Only a foot away, I reached for him, but he shoved me back with a snarl. The force knocked me out into the hall where I landed hard on my butt and slid halfway to the stairs.

I swung my flashlight back toward the room. Dust billowed out, shrouding the hallway in a gritty haze, but I could see well enough to know that James hadn't made it out. I scrambled to my feet, ready to go back for him when he stumbled through the doorway. He staggered a couple of steps before dropping to a knee. His jacket gaped open revealing a crimson stain on his white T-shirt.

I swallowed, trying to force my heart out of my throat and hurried back to him. "You're bleeding." I started to kneel beside him.

"Stay back!" He snapped the words, and I hesitated. When he raised his head to glare at me, I froze. His eyes glowed like green lamps in the darkness. "Did you get any blood on you?"

I swallowed. "N-no, just a few bruises."

"Not your blood, mine." The fury in his voice made me take a step back. "Did I get any on you?"

"I, I don't think so."

"Check. Now." He started to rise, but caught himself and dropped back to his knee. "You're not checking."

"Your eyes. They're glowing."

He closed his eyes and took a deep breath. When he opened them again, the glow had dimmed. "Check, Addie. Please hurry."

"Why?"

He rubbed a shaking hand over his face. "I'm cursed. My blood is cursed."

I had to strain to hear his soft words. "Cursed?"

"It's poisonous." He looked up. "It's been long enough. If I'd gotten any on you, you'd be dead."

"That fast?" I couldn't believe that. No poison worked that fast. Not on absorption.

"Yes, that fast." He took another breath and it shook. He wasn't mad; he was scared. "Go upstairs where the light is better and check your clothes. There's a duffle bag in the car if you need to change. Take what you need and bring me the bag."

"You're still bleeding."

"Please go check. I'll take care of this."

"I could probably find some rubber gloves. I'm used to dealing with toxic substances."

"No. Please go."

He looked so miserable that I gave in and started for the stairs.

ONCE OUTSIDE THE CHAIN-LINK, I walked a short distance along the fence and stopped beneath a streetlight to examine my clothes. All clean. Well, not clean, just not blood splattered. Dust and soot covered nearly every inch of me. I leaned over to brush my thigh and caught a glimpse of the back of my hand. Four drops of crimson lay drying on my dirty skin.

I stilled, half-expecting… What? It was just blood. James had exaggerated. It wasn't as lethal as he thought. I squatted and rubbed the back of my hand in the grass. No need to upset him.

I retrieved the duffle bag from the car and jogged back toward the gap in the fence. Maybe I should have stayed with him. What if he didn't get the bleeding stopped? If he passed out, I'd never get him out of that basement. I couldn't even call for help. Neither of us had a cell phone.

Movement drew my attention, and I looked back. A man sat on his haunches beneath the streetlight I'd stopped beside earlier. I'd almost reached the gap under the fence, but I slowed my pace to watch. What was he doing? He braced his hands wide and leaned over to press his face to the ground. His tongue snaked out and licked the grass—in the same place I'd cleaned my hand.

"What did you find, my love?" An older woman stepped around the large tree to my right, nearly colliding with me. We gasped in unison.

"Oh, you startled me." She pressed a hand to her chest, her wide eyes on me.

I stared, unable to help myself. I'd never seen eyes like hers. The irises were so pale, they appeared white.

The man stood, his movements slow and awkward, and turned to face us. I expected him to greet us until his filmed-over eyes met mine. I failed to bite back the scream that bubbled up. Undignified as hell, but to my knowledge, I'd never come face-to-face with a zombie.

I dropped the duffle bag and stumbled back. A tube of Knockout Powder rested against my palm though I didn't remember pulling it from my sleeve. The zombie took an uncoordinated step toward me and then another. Through a section of missing jaw, his tongue worked the blood he'd licked from the grass.

"Are you out for a stroll, too?" the woman asked. "Lovely evening for it."

I glanced over in time to catch her wide smile. I'd guess necromancer. And something about that spaced-out twinkle in her odd eyes told me she might not be the brains of the operation. Wonderful. I had all the luck.

"You want to call off your, um, man?" I asked.

She looked confused until I gestured at the man in question. "Oh, sorry." She turned toward the advancing zombie. "Come here, Ethan, and leave the nice lady alone."

Ethan didn't listen.

"That's odd," the woman said. She scratched her head through her short graying-blonde hair, her expression puzzled.

"What's that?" I suspected her definition of odd varied a bit from my own.

"He's bound. He shouldn't ignore me."

"Are you saying you've lost control of your zombie?"

She pressed her thin lips together as she considered him. "Ethan, stop!"

He didn't. Only ten yards away, his opaque eyes remained fixed on me. I took a step back, my shoulder brushing the woman's, and mentally ran through my inventory of potions and powders. Nothing short of fire or decapitation would stop a zombie. Though what actually animated him stood beside me.

I turned and blew the Knockout Powder into the necromancer's face. She collapsed at my feet without a sound.

Unlike her zombie. He continued to shuffle toward me. What the hell? He shouldn't still be moving.

With a scream, I whirled away and slammed into the fence, smashing my nose. My eyes watered and my vision blurred. I laced my fingers through the cold chain-link, searching with my feet for the gap. It should be close. If I could put the fence between me and the zombie—

On the other side of the fence, a dark shape ran straight at me. I gasped and ducked as it vaulted eight-foot of chain-link with ease. With a huff of breath and no other sound, an enormous black dog landed beside me. The same dog that had come to my rescue the night the Alchemica burned. His head rose, and I met his eyes. His glowing green eyes.

A throaty groan and we both turned to find Ethan the zombie only feet away. A squeak escaped me, the chain-link rattling before I realized I'd pressed my back against it.

With a snarl, the dog sprang. He slammed into the zombie and the pair crashed to the ground, rolling on impact. Something flew off and landed in the grass at my feet. Ethan had lost a finger.

I worked my way down the fence, away from the pair. The dog caught an arm and with a twist of his head, ripped it off. I closed my eyes and tried not to lose the Big Mac I'd had for supper. It helped a little, but I couldn't escape the sounds: the wet tearing, the snap of bone, the gurgling of a torn throat. Worse were the muffled snarls and the snapping of canine jaws. Oh please, don't let him be eating the zombie.

When everything went silent, I drew a deep breath and regretted it. The stench of rot overwhelmed me, but when I looked, the sight proved worse than the smell. The dog stood a few feet away, black fur covered in—were those intestines? I dropped to my knees and lost the Big Mac. When I looked up, both the duffle bag and the dog were gone.

I took a shallow breath—just enough to allow me to speak. "James?"

"Be right there." His voice came from the other side of the tree, followed by the sound of a zipper. "You okay?"

I drew another breath. I could do this. "I'm fine." I wasn't going to freak out. I rubbed a hand over my face and took a few minutes to get control of myself. My best friend was a dog. Cool. I liked dogs.

Even giant black ones with glowing green eyes.

I pushed to my feet, determined to take this in stride.

James stepped around the tree, tugging a sweatshirt in place over a clean pair of jeans. His feet were bare, but aside from the tousled hair, he didn't look any different. Most importantly, he wasn't covered in zombie gore.

He stopped beside the woman, eyes narrowing as he studied her. The way his lip curled made me suddenly uneasy. "Necro." He spat the word.

"What gave it away?" I walked over to him.

He looked up, clearly surprised that I'd joined him. He probably expected a different reaction.

"I hit her with Knockout Powder," I continued, needing to say something. "Talk about a nut job."

"I hear it's part of the job description."

I smiled at his attempt at humor. "Hanging with the dead probably isn't conducive to good mental health."

He grunted, his eyes still on the unconscious woman.

"I wonder what she's doing here," I said.

"This is Cincinnati. A lot of necros live here. She probably took her pet for a walk."

"Oh."

We both fell silent. Now what? Should I say something or let him bring it up? Or would we both ignore the elephant—er, black dog—in the room?

"Shall we go?" I asked. "If a cop drives by, I don't want to be standing here with an unconscious woman and Ethan bits."

"Ethan?"

"Her buddy." I hooked a thumb in the direction of the zombie remains. My skin crawled as I thought about what lay in the grass. "He can't—"

"He's done." James shouldered the duffle bag. "You'd better drive." He started for the car and I fell in beside him.

"Is something wrong?"

"Blood loss. I'll need to sleep soon."

"Your shoulder?"

"I'm fine." His tone made it clear that he didn't want to talk about it.

"Oh. Good." I had so many questions, but his silence was contagious. I dug out a piece of gum from my jacket pocket and popped it in my mouth. Spearmint washed away the unpleasant impression Ethan had left.

We reached the car, and I slid in behind the wheel, taking a moment to adjust the seat and mirrors. James slumped in the passenger seat, his head on the headrest and eyes closed. I decided not to bother him. He'd tell me when he was ready. Meanwhile, I could try to get my mind around it. James was a shapeshifter. It wasn't a common ability. Could he heal himself when he changed? His shoulder didn't seem to bother him, and there was no blood on his shirt.

My mind ran in circles, but fortunately my driving didn't. I found the interstate without trouble and wondered if a subconscious part of my brain recognized my surroundings. After all, this had been my home. I wished it were more familiar.

"You look sad," James said.

I glanced over and found him watching me. "I'm lamenting how little I learned from this expedition."

"Like that it wasn't an explosion in the lab that blew up the Alchemica?"

True. The labs were intact. "What if the Elements did it? The Flame Lord was there."

"Why would the Flame Lord destroy the Alchemica?"

"I don't know. Professional envy?" I gripped the wheel and glared at the road through the windshield. Why else would the Flame Lord have been there? A new thought occurred. "I could ask him."

"You can't be serious."

Yes, someone who witnessed the destruction. Even if he

didn't do it, the Flame Lord could shed some light on what happened that night. If he wasn't innocent...

"You are serious." James interrupted my thoughts.

"I could do it. I know a few potions that'll make any guy talk." I'd need to pick up some ingredients. And it'd take a day to prepare.

"You going to slip it in his drink or what?"

James had a point. The delivery system might prove tricky. But first I'd have to get in to see the Flame Lord. "Don't they hear petitions?"

"How do you know your potion would even work? You know how unpredictable they can be with the magical."

"I could experiment." I kept my eyes on the road. "On you, if you'd let me. Unless there's something about your magic that's different."

"It's a curse." His low voice just reached me. "Centuries ago an ancestor made a deal."

"With the devil?" I joked.

"The details have been lost, but I do know that he bartered away not only his own life, but those of his descendants."

"Your brothers?"

"It doesn't work like that. Only one of us has to pay the price."

"The price?"

He fell silent, and I looked over to find him watching the dark landscape flashing past his window. Wow. Old Magic. Rare and wondrous, and not following any of the modern laws. Well, none of the New Magic laws. Magic, being a product of the mind, was molded by the user's beliefs. When magic returned almost two decades ago, it found a modern world rooted in science, and those beliefs colored the way New Magic manifested.

Old Magic was different. It had always been around, hiding in the dark and forgotten places, pretending not to exist. Quietly passed down through the generations to a distant descendant... like James.

I made an effort to rein in my enthusiasm. Why did he call it a curse? That sounded like a clichéd B movie.

"Werewolf?"

"No." He squinted in the glare of a passing car. "I'm a grim."

I searched my memory. "If I knew what that was, I no longer do."

"Shuck, devil dog, hellhound."

"Hellhound? Your eyes aren't red, they're green."

He grunted and leaned back in his seat again.

"I'm kidding. Come on, a hellhound?"

He didn't respond. Why didn't he want to talk about this? It wasn't like he was evil. He'd come to my rescue tonight, and it wasn't the first time.

"The night the Alchemica burned. You ran those guys off."

"Yeah."

I waited, but he didn't offer anything else. When I glanced over again, his eyes were closed. "James?"

A soft snore answered me.

CHAPTER

4

I HAD NO TROUBLE GETTING AN audience with the Lord of Flames. All it took was a phone call. As leaders of the magical community, the Elements led in a manner similar to any organization in the modern world: they maintained central offices that required an appointment. When the magical had a problem, the Elemental Offices helped them find a solution. I didn't qualify as magical, but I figured having a problem *with* the magical was close enough.

James dropped another bullet into a cardboard ammo box. "How'd you get in so soon?" We had the workshop to ourselves. He loaded bullets while I ground some dried datura flowers. The sweet aroma filled the room, masking the faint turpentine odor from an earlier experiment.

"I said I was being harassed by the PIA." It wasn't a lie. Agent Lawson had called, but I'd been visiting the Alchemica at the time. "I guess the Elements don't care for their arbitrary rules or regulations either." The Elements' receptionist wanted to schedule my audience the same day, but I had potions to brew and powders to mix. I moved it back a couple of days.

James snorted. "And the rest of it?"

"I told the truth."

"You said you were an alchemist?"

"No." Setting aside my pestle, I picked up a small glass vial and poured a quarter-teaspoon of pale green powder into my palm. "I said I could use magic. Care for a demonstration?"

He eyed the powder and his nostrils flared. "It smells like grass."

Impressive. I couldn't smell anything except datura flowers. "That's the knotweed." I rolled my hand and the fine powder coated my palm. "It's Perfect Assistant Dust. One whiff and you will obey any command given to you."

His brows rose.

"I'm going to make you do the Chicken Dance."

"Addie."

"I'm teasing. I'll save that for the Flame Lord."

"You need to take this seriously. Even if this works on me, it doesn't mean it will work on him."

"Since I know even less about your magic than I do his, I'll have to go on my instincts."

"What's to stop it from affecting you?" he asked, skirting my probe. He refused to go into detail about his magic.

"I've keyed it to me. It won't affect me, and those hit by it will only obey commands from me."

"You can do that?"

"Yep. Master alchemist, remember?" I raised my palm toward my mouth hoping he wouldn't question me further. "Ready?"

"Wait."

I lowered my hand. Crap. He wasn't going to let me off that easily.

"How did you key it to you? Any physical ingredient, like a lock of hair would need to be ashed, but I don't smell any charring."

I'd been concerned about his quick mind, but apparently I should have worried about his nose. He watched me, his expression open and curious. I couldn't lie to him.

"I used a drop of my blood."

His expression closed down, moving toward a frown. "But that's...blood alchemy."

"I guess, but it's my blood. I didn't kill to get it. I didn't torture anyone."

"What? Why would you torture someone?"

"You know, to give the blood certain...attributes." My words tumbled to a stop. I didn't have a clue where that knowledge had come from.

"You can do that?"

"Personally? Of course not." I smiled to reassure him, though my tight cheeks made it difficult. Using my own blood had been the natural, logical thing to do. Why did I feel guilty?

"No. I didn't mean—"

"So I know a little blood alchemy. Master alchemist, remember?" I repeated. I brought my hand to my mouth again. "Ready?"

He gave me a stiff nod. "Hit me."

"Thanks." I realized I was thanking him for more than letting me experiment on him. "I won't betray your trust." I blew the powder in his face.

He coughed and stumbled back, his eyes went on full glow, his pupils shrinking down to pin-pricks as he stared at me.

"You okay?" I asked.

He blinked a couple of times and the glow faded away. "Yes. For a moment I..."

"Yes?"

He shook his head. "Nothing." He flashed me a smile that looked forced. "Your command?"

"Sit."

He abruptly folded his legs and dropped to sit cross-legged on the floor. He stared at me with wide eyes.

"A success?" I asked.

"Absolutely."

I grinned. "Do as you will."

He slowly got to his feet. "How are you going to get the Flame Lord to inhale it?"

"I have a couple of approaches. If I brew the potion as a liquid, I could break in and spike all his glassware."

"Sounds risky."

I shrugged. "Once he's mine to command, I'll make him drink a truth serum."

"Can't you command him not to lie?"

"Yes, but a truth serum leaves no doubt. It compels you to tell the truth. The potion I just hit you with lacks that compulsion. Care for a demonstration?"

His brow wrinkled. "Maybe?"

"Tell me, James, what's a grim? Don't lie."

He blinked and then straightened. "Someone with hellhound blood in them." He bit his lip as if to stop the words.

"Do you see how much control you still have? If I'd used a truth serum, you'd feel compelled to tell me everything."

"I…"

"It's okay. Tell me when you're ready."

He looked away. "It's just…"

"James?"

He turned to face me, his brow wrinkling as he met my eyes.

"Do the Chicken Dance."

"Addie!" He began to flap his arms.

THE FOLLOWING EVENING FOUND ME sitting beside James beneath a large rhododendron bush. I squirmed, chilled and stiff from several hours spent watching the sprawling Victorian house that served as the Elements' Cincinnati office. We'd chosen this shrub for the cover of its glossy leaves and the clear view of the kitchen door and adjacent parking area.

It turned out to be a busy place. Delivery trucks had come and gone. A news van from a local TV station had stopped to film the building's exterior. And later, a school bus had loaded up a group of noisy children who must have been on a field trip. But now that darkness had fallen, things seemed to be winding down.

"Anyone else?" I whispered. Moments ago, we'd watched the kitchen staff leave.

James's eyes glowed faintly as he studied the house. He claimed he could hear the people inside. I'd asked him why his eyes glowed when he listened, but he wouldn't give me an answer.

"Three others, but no one near the kitchen," he said. The dim light in the kitchen barely escaped the curtained windows, and only one light shone through an upstairs window.

"Housekeeping?"

"Probably."

The Elements were long gone. A limo had pulled around front and a short time later, driven off. I assumed that had been their ride. Over the next hour, several servants in black livery had left as well. The new gods of the modern world lived a life of ease.

I shrugged off my coat and the branches rustled with the movement. "Look good?" I held out my arms to display my homemade camo.

James cleared his throat. "With or without the Shadow Dust?"

I caught a flash of teeth in the dimness and punched his arm. I'd dusted my black bodysuit with a special powder that enabled it to blend better with the shadows. It wasn't invisibility—that took a lot longer to brew—but it would conceal me well enough, as long as there were shadows.

James pulled off his shoes and wiggled his bare toes. "Wait

by those bushes by the door." He slipped off his jacket. "I'll let you in in a moment."

"How exactly are you going to get inside? That last guy to leave locked the door behind him."

He hesitated with his hands on the hem of his sweatshirt. "Leave me a few secrets, Addie."

I sighed. "Fine. I'll go be curious by the door."

He chuckled as I crept out of our thicket. I stuck to the shadows and squeezed in behind a pine shrub. The coarse needles poked through my bodysuit. I squirmed to get comfortable, stirring up musty pine scent from the old needles beneath my feet. Suddenly the back door swung open and I froze.

"Well?" James whispered from within.

I barely heard the soft word over my thundering pulse. I got to my feet and discovered him leaning around the open door. Holy crap. "How did you—"

"Just get inside." He ducked back behind the door.

I hurried inside, and when I turned to face James, a giant black hellhound stood wagging at me. Wow. I didn't realize he could shift that fast. But how had he gotten inside? More questions for later.

He sat down and his tongue rolled out in a doggy grin. I knew what he wanted, but I didn't need him to stay and watch over me.

"No, we've been over this." I held open the door. "Get dressed and bring the car around."

He gave me a low growl.

I rubbed my arms to dispel the goosebumps. "As disturbing as that is, forget it. Stick to the plan. I can handle the cleaning staff if it comes to that." I patted the slim black fanny pack strapped around my waist. "Go on, Fido."

He snorted, amused with the nickname, and a moment later, trotted outside. I closed the door, careful not to let it slam.

Taking a deep breath, I waited for my nerves to settle. A few secrets? The boy seemed to be nothing but. I shook my head. That mystery would have to wait. Right now, I needed to find the Flame Lord's glassware. I'd developed a concentrated liquid version of my Perfect Assistant Dust. A drop or two from the vial in my pouch and tomorrow's audience would go much more to my liking.

A single light shone over the commercial-grade range, leaving most of the room in shadow. A curtained doorway stood opposite the stove, and I checked it first, hoping to find the table service closet.

The closet turned out to be a food pantry. I hurried out and began a closer inspection of the dozens of cabinets scattered around the room. I found three separate sets of tableware, as well as a wide assortment of linens and two different collections of silver cutlery. Did four people really need all this? I hadn't expected a scavenger hunt. Maybe I should have told James to give me twenty minutes instead of fifteen.

A cabinet beside the sink finally yielded what I sought: several glasses with either a stylized wave or flame, a swirling gust of wind, or a trio of mountains. Water, fire, air, and earth. How cute. I began pulling the flame patterned glasses from the cabinet and set them on the counter. I reached for another and the latch on the interior door clicked open. I dived under the island opposite the sink, unable to get to the pantry quick enough.

A light flicked on across the room, and I sank back into the shadows. At least it wasn't the fluorescent bulbs overhead.

A man walked into the room, and I got a glimpse of his dark gray slacks and black loafers. He moved to the far end of the counter, and I noted the untucked shirt and rumpled brown hair. Apparently, the servants didn't bother with livery after hours.

His back to my hiding place, he set a tray on the counter and gathered the dirty dishes in his hands. He started to step away and hesitated. Crap. He'd seen the glasses.

He moved closer, limiting my view to his legs once more. The dishes clattered as he set them in the sink. "Hello?" I didn't expect such a deep voice. "I know you're in here."

He turned to face the island and stopped in front of my hiding place. His black loafers had a gold band adorning the strap that ran across the tongue. I could just make out the stylized flame engraved on it. Wow, the Elements didn't skimp on the details.

He took another step, moving on down the counter away from me. I began to release a silent breath when he spun and squatted right in front of me. Laughing gray eyes met mine, and I gasped, jerking back so quickly I smacked my head on the counter above me.

"Get lost from the tour?" he asked and held out a hand. His smile crinkled a few faint laugh lines at the corner of each eye. "Come on," he said, still holding out a hand. "I won't bite."

He thought I was a child. Well, he wouldn't think that for long. Now what? Trapped beneath the counter, I didn't have a clear shot for the Knockout Powder, not to mention, it wouldn't be the best of strategies to leave an unconscious man lying on the kitchen floor. But I didn't want to end up in jail either. I needed to think. I took his hand and let him help me up.

I watched his face and caught his surprised expression. "Not who you expected?" I had to crane my neck as he straightened. He topped six feet by several inches—a good foot taller than me. If it came down to the Knockout Powder, it'd be a challenge to get a full dose in his face.

He eyed my cat burglar suit. "I think I would have remembered you." The corner of his mouth twitched as if he tried not to smile. "What are you doing in here?"

Not the reaction I expected. Shouldn't he be threatening

to call the cops? Sneaking around in the dark and dressed like this, I must have looked like a thief—or an inept girl in black spandex. That would explain his smile. I got an idea. If I could convince him this was a prank, maybe he would let me go. No unconscious servant, no cops. Of course, I'd have to revise my plan for tomorrow, but I could do that.

I took a step closer and lowered my voice. "Promise not to tell?"

"That depends on your answer."

I chewed my lower lip in what I hoped looked like indecision and then continued in my best conspiratorial whisper. "I was dared."

"Dared?" He lifted a dark brow, but his smile encouraged me to continue.

"To break in and steal one of the Flame Lord's glasses."

He glanced over at the cluttered counter. "Ah." His attention returned to me. "This is a rather significant risk for a dare." His eyes narrowed, watching me.

Apparently, I didn't do inept very well. I'd have to try harder.

"I guess I failed." I looked up and gave him a tentative smile. "Unless you let me take one." I raised my brows in question. Come on buddy, cut me some slack.

"Well…"

Yes. I flashed him a grin and moved closer to the counter.

"I haven't said yes yet."

I turned to face him. "Yet?"

"This exchange seems a bit one-sided." He crossed his arms and leaned against the island.

Now what? I didn't have anything on me of value. "You can have a glass, too. I don't mind."

He pursed his lips. "No, I'm sure you don't." He still looked like he wanted to laugh. I didn't get what was so funny.

"What?" I asked.

"You really are a little dense."

A little dense! "Excuse me?" I flexed my wrist, adjusting the tube of Knockout Powder.

He straightened and closed the distance between us. "It's simple. Offer me a kiss for the glass."

I blinked. "You want me to kiss you?"

"Don't give me that. You've been flirting with me since I pulled you out from beneath that island."

I might have flunked inept, but this guy did clueless with style.

A protest rose to my lips, but I hesitated. Here was a way out. I glanced at the clock on the microwave. If I didn't meet James as we'd planned, he'd come looking for me. And he'd probably be furry. I doubted that the man would mention tricking a kiss out of an intruder, but he'd definitely tell his master about meeting a hellhound in the kitchen.

I looked up at my current obstacle. Damn, his height had me at a disadvantage. If this scenario failed, I'd need that Knockout Powder. I hopped up on the counter beside the glasses. "If we're going to see eye-to-eye on this, I want to be eye-to-eye."

Speaking of eyes, his were interesting. Pale gray near the pupils shaded to a rich charcoal around the perimeter. They once more twinkled with amusement.

"Wouldn't want you uncomfortable." He leaned over and picked up a glass, turning it so I could see the etched flame. "Do we have an agreement?" He rolled the glass between his fingers, and the crystal bent the low light into rainbows.

"It's just a glass." My voice came out in a shaky whisper, and I became aware of a quiver in my joints. Strange. I hadn't been remotely nervous until now. I gripped the edge of the cool granite counter in an effort to steady myself.

"A rather fancy glass," his eyes dipped to the crystal, "with the flame and all."

"Pretentious as hell." I caught my lip between my teeth, but it was too late to call back the words. Damn, I blew it.

"You think?" The laugh lines made another appearance.

"You don't?"

He turned the glass and studied it. "Maybe a bit." He met my eyes, waiting for my answer.

"Okay." I gave him an exaggerated sigh. "For the glass." I leaned up and pressed my lips to his. I squeezed my eyes shut, aware of his warm mouth moving against mine. What a bizarre turn of events—almost as weird as meeting the necromancer outside the Alchemica. Who knew I'd end my day kissing a complete stranger in the Elements' kitchen? At least he smelled better than the zombie.

"Mmm, not bad," he said when I leaned back. "But this isn't an ordinary glass. For sheer pretentiousness alone, I'm going to have to ask for more."

"You said a kiss. As in one." I held up a finger for emphasis.

"That barely qualified."

Oh for heaven's sake. I didn't have time for this. "Fine." I looped my arms around his shoulders and gave him an encore. I took my time, exploring his mouth as he explored mine. He braced his hands on the counter to either side of my hips and leaned into me. I had to admit, the man could kiss. Should I be noticing that? And how did I know? Did I have a boyfriend? A lover? Oh God, what if I was married?

I pulled away with a gasp.

He leaned back. "What is it?"

I didn't have an answer. My heart pounded and I had to get out of here. "Do I get the glass?"

He smirked. "And if I said no?"

"Then I'll leave without it."

He studied my face, trying to gauge my truthfulness, and then straightened with a sigh. He held out the glass. I wrapped my hand around it, but he didn't let go. "What's your name?"

Good question. I couldn't answer that either. "Addie." He couldn't trace that name to the Alchemica. But then, why would he even think to? Lord, he had me rattled.

"Addie?" He paused, waiting for me to offer more. "That's it?"

"That's it."

He released the glass and stepped back, allowing me to slide from the counter. "And you are?" I had no plans for the information, but I'd be foolish not to get his name.

He watched me intently, and I began to wonder if he'd answer. "Rowan."

"That's it?"

He smiled. "That's it, unless you'd like to meet again sometime. Perhaps we could haggle over a dinner plate or a piece of cutlery."

The heat rose in my cheeks. "I figured you'd suggest a whole place setting."

He leaned against the counter eying me. "I'd like that."

I was pretty sure I would, too. Not the dinnerware, the haggling. This scheme had taken a turn I hadn't anticipated. Time to go. "It was nice meeting you, Rowan."

I turned away, expecting him to say something, but the only noise in the kitchen was the sound of my footsteps. I stopped with my hand on the doorknob and glanced over my shoulder. He still stood where I'd left him, watching me.

"If you change your mind, you know where to find me." He left the room without a backward glance. Cocky bastard. Guess being the personal servant of the most feared guy in the Midwest made him think he was something special.

I looked at the glasses still on the counter and considered finishing what I'd started. No. I'd better not press my luck. Time for plan B.

CHAPTER 5

"This is completely insane," James whispered as soon as we were alone. We stood in a small, but expensively furnished waiting room just off the foyer in the Elemental Offices. Morning sunlight shone through sheer, floor-length curtains and gave the room a warm, soft glow. I eyed the half-dozen leather chairs arranged in pairs around the room, but made no move to sit in one. In minutes, my audience with the Flame Lord would begin.

"Explain to me why you chose to wear that." James gestured, not at my cloak, but at what I wore underneath: the black, slit-sleeved robes of an Alchemica Master. The same robes he'd found me in—except they smelled of fabric softener now instead of smoke.

"We've been over this." And over it, but he couldn't dissuade me. I wanted the Flame Lord to know how easily I could get to him. Last night's slip-up had become an opportunity. "The interrogation loses its punch otherwise."

"This isn't an interrogation." James leaned closer. "Come on, this is the Lord of Flames."

"Is the fancy title supposed to impress me? His Grace, Archbishop of Radiant Matter and Lord of Flames." I rolled my eyes. "Some newsman came up with the archbishop thing as a

joke. He thought radiant matter sounded like a religious term."
I snorted.

"Radiant matter?"

"The original name for the plasma phenomena."

James frowned at me. "You have no respect for the powerful."

His comment sent of bolt of fury right through me. "Because I'm a magicless human?"

"That's not what I meant. Don't put words in my mouth." He ran a hand over his face. "The point is the guy can ignite anything—you included. If he's responsible for the Alchemica's destruction, he's not going to be pleased to see you."

"I've got it covered." Through the door, I caught a glimpse of a man in black livery moving our way. "Trust me." I gripped his forearm and gave it a squeeze.

James didn't look convinced, but he'd run out of time to argue. The servant stepped into the room and gestured for us to follow. I stood straighter, my pulse accelerating in anticipation of the coming confrontation. Alchemist versus Element. Maybe I did lack the sense to respect power. We'd see.

The servant led us down a long corridor decorated in gray banners. Each banner bore its corresponding symbol in red, blue, yellow, and green—like the designs on the glasses. Tacky. The oak-paneled walls and stone-tiled floors needed no further embellishment to declare the Elements a class above the rest of us.

The servant opened a set of double doors and stepped inside. Double doors? I glanced up at James and rolled my eyes. It wasn't like the Flame Lord couldn't fit through a regular door. I knew that much about the man. Though, that's where my knowledge ended. The guy went around cloaked in those robes, hood up and face in shadow. Photographers always swarmed whenever he made an appearance, hoping for a shot of his face. But two could play that game. My hood hid my features. A subtle jab at

His Grace, but also a precaution against running into Rowan, his friendly servant from the night before.

"Your Grace?" The servant stopped a few paces inside the door. "The last petitioners of the morning." He gestured at James and me.

I stopped beside the servant, my eyes riveted on familiar gray robes hemmed in black triangles. I didn't hear the Flame Lord answer the man. I lay in the smoldering ruins of the Alchemica again, watching those robes in the flickering light of my burning home.

The doors closed with a click, and I realized the Flame Lord had dismissed his servant. I pulled myself back from the night I lost everything and focused on the man who might be responsible.

He stood before one of several bookcases in the room, an open book in his hands. The room looked more like a library than an office. I'd expected a massive desk, but found an oblong table instead. Several high-backed chairs were arranged around the polished expanse of oak. The Flame Lord stopped beside the chair at the head of the table and laid his book beside it.

"What can I do for you?" He gestured at the other chairs, inviting us to sit.

I took a deep breath. Time to see if I could play with the big boys. "I have a few questions." I closed the distance between us. "And a gesture of good will." I could almost hear James groaning behind me. I'd told him about the servant and the glass. Well, not all the details, but enough.

I hadn't been able to spike the Flame Lord's glasses the night before, but I now had evidence that I could get close to him. He'd have to respect that.

"A gesture?" The Flame Lord's voice sounded from the depths of his hood. "That's not necessary." My nearness didn't seem to upset him. Over-confident bastard.

I didn't answer. Instead, I pulled the glass from my pocket and held it up for his inspection, rotating it so he could see the stylized flame before I set it on the table beside his book. I took a step closer, an alchemically-altered bang snap between the thumb and middle finger of my opposite hand. I held the novelty firework gently. It had been an adventure to get the correct ratio of explosive silver fulminate, but this delivery system provided better accuracy than blowing an alchemic powder in his face. Good thing I'd taken the trouble; the man stood a good foot taller than me.

"Addie?"

I looked up into this hood. "Oh, shit," I muttered as I understood.

He chuckled and pushed my hood back. "Decided to return it?"

"Rowan?"

He pushed his own hood off his head revealing the man I'd met in the kitchen the night before, except in this brighter light his hair wasn't brown, but a dark shade of auburn.

Oh, hell. I resisted the urge to start gagging like a cat with a hairball.

He grinned at me.

"Addie?" James sounded confused.

I remembered my purpose, and before Rowan could do more than glance in James's direction, I raised my hand and snapped my fingers. The paper-wrapped firework exploded and my Perfect Assistant Dust puffed up into Rowan's face. I held my ground, watching his expression. The Dust had worked fine when I tested it on James, but not every magical person reacted in same way.

Rowan coughed and stepped back. Confusion lit his gray eyes, but not only confusion. An orange ring sprang to light around each pupil and began to spread through the iris. He'd called on his elemental power of fire.

Before I could give my first command, James leapt forward and caught Rowan by the front of his gray robes. The momentum carried them backward, and they slammed into a bookcase, books thumping to the floor around their feet.

"James!" Apparently, he didn't respect the powerful either.

For a heartbeat, the pair stood toe to toe. I couldn't see James's face, but I could see Rowan's. He didn't look angry, so when he attacked, he took both of us by surprise.

A couple of rapid jabs knocked James back and a sweeping kick took the boy's legs from under him. James landed on his butt at my feet.

"Stop!" I shouted.

Rowan froze and his eyes shifted to me.

"No magic." My voice echoed in the sudden silence.

Rowan's eyes widened and the orange faded away. It seemed that my Perfect Assistant Dust worked on an Element as well as it worked on a grim.

James sprang to his feet, but I stepped in front of him and passed him my cloak before he could do anything else. I expected a servant or two to come running, but none did.

I crossed my arms and the movement drew Rowan's attention. It also caused my split sleeves to part and reveal the tattoos encircling my upper arms.

"Shit," Rowan muttered.

"See? A gesture of good faith." I waved a hand at the glass sitting innocently on the table beside me. "Have a seat, Your Grace. This won't take long."

The cords in his neck stood out, but he pulled a chair from beside the table, the legs scraping across the floor. "What did you give me?" He settled into the chair.

"Do you want the formula?" I asked. He answered with a

glare so I continued. "It's just a little something to encourage your cooperation. I didn't think you'd be willing to chat with me otherwise."

"Aren't you a brilliant girl."

"Well, brilliant is stretching it." I gave him a smile. "But I can see where a one-trick pony like you might think that." I pulled a slim vial from my bodice and unscrewed the lid. A floral scent rose from the viscous liquid. "Drink this." I offered the vial to him.

A muscle ticked in his jaw, but he took the vial. "What—" He didn't get to finish as he tipped back his head and drank the dark blue liquid.

"Truth serum," I said. The unique properties of my formula opened options not available with other brews. A basic truth serum left the subject able to respond only to direct questions. Otherwise, they couldn't speak. That wasn't the case with mine. Rowan could question me, make statements, or cuss me until blue in the face. That freedom would allow for a more interesting exchange.

He dropped the vial and it shattered on the floor. "I won't betray my brethren, alchemist." He gripped the arms of his chair and a flicker of orange appeared in his eyes once more.

James stepped forward, but I caught his arm. "Would you quit?"

He stopped and turned his frown from Rowan to me.

"What have you done to him?" Rowan demanded. "He's magical." The orange had faded again.

I glanced up at James. His look of surprise shifted back to a frown. "She's given me nothing," he said, his voice just this side of a growl. "I'm hers of my own will."

Weird way to put it. "I didn't come here to chat about who my friends are," I said.

"Why are you here?" Rowan's knuckles whitened as he tightened his grip on his chair.

"To ask a question. Why you were at the Alchemica the night it burned?"

"I received an invitation from your…," he glanced at my arms, "Grand Master."

"What?" He couldn't lie to me, but his answer made no sense. "The Grand Master invited *you* to the Alchemica?"

"He invited all four of us. Shall I summon the others to vouch for me? They all saw the invitation. White linen embossed in gold. Talk about pretentious."

I frowned. "I don't need verification. At the moment, your word is enough." I tried for a confident tone, but his revelation put a dent in my armor. "You're certain the invitation came from the Grand Master?"

"You mean Aemilius Archimedes?" Rowan snorted. "You know, if you alchemists insist on hiding behind a false name, you might want to consider a more plausible one."

False names? I didn't remember that.

"Though he did scrawl Emil across the bottom of the invitation," Rowan said.

If he said anything after that, I missed it. Emil. The name echoed in my head, and I pictured the sleeveless white robes and graying-blond hair. Thick fingers with neatly trimmed nails. A kind wrinkled face and an expressive mouth.

"Addie?"

I discovered James's hand on my shoulder. "I'm okay," I whispered. The ricochet of memories settled.

"Too many potions over the years?" Rowan asked.

I gave him a glare. "What happened to the Alchemica?" No need to drag this out.

"The papers said an explosion in the lab took down the building."

"I've been there. The labs are intact. The explosion took place in the auditorium." I suddenly realized he'd diverted the question without lying. Impressive under a truth serum. The Flame Lord was strong willed and no idiot. I wished I had more time to argue with him. "You didn't answer my question."

"No, I didn't burn down your Alchemica. If not for my brother Element throwing up a wall of earth, we would have been among the injured."

"Injured? There were no injured. They all died!"

"You didn't."

I clenched my fists. "I saw you there when I lay in the rubble. What happened?" I hated the pleading note in my voice, but those images of Emil had hit me hard. I now had someone to mourn.

"All I know is that there was an explosion." His eyes met mine, and I prayed he couldn't see the depth of my despair. He didn't know anything. This effort had been for nothing.

I turned to James. "Let's go."

"That's it?" Rowan sounded surprised.

I faced him again. "Would you prefer I stay and question you some more?"

"Until this potion wears off? Yes." He smiled and I resisted the urge to step back. Clearly, he found it amusing that he could turn me to ash with a thought.

I refused to let him intimidate me. "That's not the only potion on my person."

His eyes slid down over my black robes, lingering on the snug bodice. Heat rose in my cheeks as I remembered the night before.

"I may be a one-trick pony, but it's a doozy of a trick. Are you certain you wouldn't like to stay?" His lips curved into a smug smile.

Why hadn't I recognized what that cocky attitude meant

last night? The man hadn't been remotely concerned about my presence in his kitchen.

"Tempting, but no thank you, Your Grace." I turned away and James dropped the cloak around my shoulders.

"You thought I burned the Alchemica," Rowan said.

I glanced over my shoulder as I hooked my cloak.

"And if you'd been right?"

I turned to meet his stare. "I would have avenged them."

"By killing me." He looked more amused than concerned. Bastard.

"You don't think I would?"

He studied me a moment. "I think you'd try."

"Ah, you don't think I could." I smiled. "Tell me Rowan, are you immortal?"

He gripped the arms of his chair. "Yes." The cords in his neck stood out again. He hadn't wanted to reveal that.

I blinked. Whoa. How could that be? "Magic hasn't been back long enough for you to know that."

He glared at me, and the orange ring ignited around his pupils. A muscle in his jaw ticked and then the light winked out. I still had him under my control, but with the strength of his will, he'd probably break free before the potion wore off.

I gave him a smirk of my own. "Thank you for your time, Your Grace." I didn't bother to curtsy before I led James to the double doors. Hand on the knob, I looked back, "Don't move, and don't call for help."

"This isn't over, alchemist." He glared at me from his seat.

"Sure it is." I smiled. "Nice to see you again, Rowan." I pulled the door open and left the room.

"That was completely insane," James muttered as we started down the hall.

"You mentioned that earlier." I lengthened my stride to keep up with him. "And who are you to criticize?"

"You weren't quick enough. He drew power."

"So you grabbed him?"

We walked into the foyer and I gave the receptionist a smile and a wave. She returned my smile, unaware that I'd left her lord and master immobile in his posh office. James held the door for me, and we stepped out onto the porch.

"For someone whose blood is toxic, you jump into a fight awfully quick." I glanced over and caught his frown. "What if someone scratched you?"

"I don't bleed that easily."

A cool October breeze tugged at my hair, and I pulled my cloak closer. I followed James down the front stairs, our shoes clomping on the wooden steps. He slowed to let me catch up when we reached the front walk. I expected him to speak, but he didn't.

"And?" I prompted.

He pulled his keys from his front pocket, and they jingled before he closed his fist around them. "There needs to be iron present."

"Iron? As in cold iron?" I smiled, but he kept his eyes on the sidewalk. "You don't look like a fairy."

"Not like that." His frown deepened, but he didn't elaborate.

Damn, why did he clam up anytime the conversation touched on his magical abilities? I didn't get it, and I never would if he wouldn't talk.

We started across the small paved lot heading for the car. "Will you tell me more?" Waiting for him to talk to me wasn't working. I decided to try honesty. "Old Magic fascinates me."

The keys jiggled and he gripped them again. "My blood has an affinity for iron. If it pierces my skin, my blood is drawn to it and will follow it back through the opening."

"Only iron? What if something else pierces your skin? Say, a finger nail?"

"I don't bleed."

"No way." I stopped by the passenger door. "Are you serious?"

James grunted and bent to unlock my door.

"You're so tight-lipped about this. Why?"

He opened my door and held it. His fingers tapping the window in what might be annoyance. "I'm not human. That makes some people...uneasy."

"Not me."

"Because you're too curious to know better."

"Are you implying that I lack sense?"

He finally smiled. "Enough questions. Get in. We need to get out of here."

"How can you not bleed unless cut by iron?" Talk about some handy magic. "Will you show me?"

"Later." He gestured at the passenger seat. "We need to go before the alarm is raised. A servant could walk into his office at any moment."

True. I got in and leaned over to unlock his door.

"How'd His Grace know you were magical?" I asked when James slid in behind the wheel. "Did you let your eyes glow?" I hadn't been able to see from where I stood.

He fired up the car and began to back out of our parking space. "My strength, I guess."

I hadn't considered that. "And speaking of strength." I hesitated not wanting to insult him. "Was he stronger than you?"

"He appears to know some martial arts or something."

"You don't know?"

He concentrated on his driving and didn't look over. "He won't get the drop on me again."

I smiled and leaned over to pat his knee. "I'm sure he won't. And I'll quit pestering you about your magic."

"Uh-huh." He wasn't buying that either.

"It was still a foolish risk. What if he'd incinerated you?"

"Hellhounds don't burn."

"Seriously? How—"

"Didn't you say you weren't going to pester me?" The corner of his mouth twitched upward.

I leaned back in my seat and crossed my arms. "Fine."

We drove half a block in silence.

"The Flame Lord didn't destroy the Alchemica," he said. "Now what?"

Good question. "I'll think of something."

"I don't doubt that." He chuckled and reached for the radio dial.

I propped my elbow on the armrest and watched the Elemental Offices shrink in the side view mirror. Now what?

CHAPTER 6

THE WALL CLOCK IN MY attic workshop read 1:00 p.m., and I had little to show for five hours of work aside from a clean room. The smell of bleach still hung in the air, and for the first time in months, the tables were uncluttered. Vials of purified ingredients sat in racks, labeled and alphabetized. Clean glassware rested in neat rows on the plastic shelves I'd picked up at the discount store. Even my prized fractionating column sparkled with cleanliness, ready for its next application. If only I knew what that was.

I straightened and rubbed my lower back. I'd only finished half my bullet quota for the day, having procrastinated with the cleaning. I needed to get busy, but I just wasn't with it. James and I had gotten in late yesterday afternoon, and though I'd gone to bed early, I'd managed only a few fitful hours of sleep. I'd skipped lunch, remaining in my room rather than braving the kitchen. Hunger I could handle; James's brothers I preferred to avoid. I knew they'd have something suggestive to say about our two-day absence.

In truth, avoiding the Huntsman boys wasn't the only reason I hid in my workshop. All my leads had run dry, and I had no idea how to recover my lost memories. My future held nothing beyond filling bullets destined to take the lives of innocent animals. I braced my hands on the table and bowed my head.

I must have missed something. Some clue. Some formula. Something.

"Addie!" A thump on the door accompanied George's voice.

I growled under my breath. Why wouldn't he leave me alone? "I'm busy!" I picked up the syringe and selected a bullet.

The door opened, but I didn't look up. I clenched my teeth and sunk the needle into the soft plastic of the modified Nosler tip. "If you want these finished by four, you'd better leave me alone." I depressed the syringe, careful not to overfill the tiny reservoir.

"Which is why you're going to keep this meeting short."

Meeting? I looked up.

"Hello, Addie." Rowan, Lord of Flames and Arrogance, gave me a smile and stepped past George. "So nice to see you again."

With an undignified squeak, I dropped the bullet and syringe, and took a hasty step back. My butt bumped the wall, leaving me trapped. Rowan stopped on the opposite side of the table, a predatory gleam in his gray eyes. He wore a dark sweater and slacks, but the casual clothing didn't make him any less intimidating.

"This guy claims to know you and *insisted*," George waved a one-hundred-dollar bill, "that I bring him to you. Do you really think I'd interrupt otherwise? Gotta get what work I can out of your scrawny ass before you run off with James again."

I gave George a look that expressed my feelings about him and his reasons for the interruption.

"Considering your vindictive nature," Rowan spoke up, "I'm wondering how this guy is still alive." He jerked a thumb in George's direction.

"I need the job. Ingredients for truth serum don't come cheap."

George sneered and hooked his thumbs in the front belt loops of his camos. "Don't let her fool you. She likes to pretend to be an alchemist, but she keeps getting kicked out of the academy."

"Academy?" Rowan eyed me.

"Master Boris over on Ninth." George waved a hand in that direction. "I paid him off to take her back once. He flat refused the second time."

The corners of Rowan's mouth curled upward.

I crossed my arms. "He didn't have a muffle furnace. I had to make my own; it wasn't very stable."

"A muffle furnace?" Rowan leaned a hip against the table, and his eyes slid over me. Sizing me up or seeing what it'd take to incinerate me?

I kept my arms crossed to hide my shaking hands. "It reaches very high temperatures. Might be something you'd understand."

He grinned. "Perhaps." The jerk clearly enjoyed this. A little game of cat and mouse. Unfortunately for this mouse, the cat had brought a flamethrower.

"Don't fall for that crap," George said. "She probably looked it up in some book. She's all talk."

Rowan studied me. "Is she?" He lunged across the table and caught me by the upper arms before I could even think of moving. His hands gripped my biceps, and I could feel their warmth through my shirt. I caught a whiff of smoke, and then he jerked my sleeves down my arms. They tore away from the shirt with surprising ease. He'd vaporized the stitching and left the fabric in both the body and sleeves intact—without any singe marks. Holy crap. I had no idea he could wield fire with that kind of finesse.

"What the hell?" George stared at the tattoos on my upper arms. "Are those real?" Observant as always.

"Yes." Rowan held my shirt sleeves around my forearms, looking very pleased with himself.

"You bastard," I whispered. Fantastic. George knew I was legit. He'd probably lock me in the basement.

George stepped closer, wide eyes on my arms. "She can't be the real thing. She's too incompetent."

"Incompetent?" I tried to pull free, but Rowan wouldn't let me go. "I put your little shop on the map, dumbass."

Rowan chuckled. "She's an alchemist, all right." He released my right wrist, but held on to the left. "Come along." He started to pull me around the end of the table.

"I'm not going anywhere." I dug in my heels.

"What are you doing?" George fisted his large hands and took a step toward Rowan. Anyone else, and I'd be touched by his defense of me. But George wasn't the altruistic sort. "She's mine. Get your ass out of here."

"Excuse me?" Rowan released me and turned to face George.

"Something wrong with your hearing, pal?" George gripped Rowan's arm above the elbow. "I said it's time for you to leave." He gestured at the open door to the stairs.

George might be half-a-head shorter than Rowan, but I suspected he outweighed him. As much as I disliked the guy, I had to give George credit for his dedication to the gym. I couldn't decide if he wore those black tanks because he liked to show off his arms or because his biceps wouldn't fit in regular shirt sleeves.

Rowan glanced at the hand on his arm before meeting George's glare. I got the impression that Rowan wasn't remotely intimidated. It occurred to me that if these two got into it, my little lab might not survive.

"Hey, Georgie." I held out my arms in front of me, displaying the sleeves gathered around my wrists.

He glared at me, but didn't let go of Rowan. "I'm not in the mood for your smartass shit right now."

Oh, the fun I could have with that line. Instead, I let the

sleeves dangle from my hands. "Gee, where did the stitching go? It's almost as if it vaporized."

Rowan watched me, a slight quirk at the corner of his mouth.

"Think...about...it," I said to George, drawing out each word.

George shifted his attention back to Rowan. I suspected the constipated look meant he was thinking, but I could be wrong.

"George, have I introduced you to the Flame Lord?"

Rowan's half smile became a frown that shifted to me.

"This pretty boy?" George asked. "Bullshit."

The heavy black watch encircling George's wrist vanished in a flash of light. George jerked his hand from Rowan's arm and gripped his bare wrist.

"Pretty boy?" Rowan asked.

George backed away from him, eyes narrowing. "What do you want with my alchemist?"

"As I told you: a word."

George glanced from Rowan to me, and back again. "See that that's all you do." A final glare and he turned and left the room.

I'd never accuse George of being a genius, but I wouldn't call him a coward either.

Rowan turned to face me, and his dark brows descended over glowing orange eyes. "I wish you hadn't done that."

I snatched a vial off the table and held it aloft. It contained chicory root extract, a useful ingredient in several of my formulas, but not much use against a pissed-off Fire Element.

"Back off," I said.

He took a cautious step to the side, trying to circle the table. "I'm no longer under your spell."

I assumed he referred to the formula I'd hit him with the day before. "It wasn't a spell." I stepped in the opposite direction. "It was a special formula designed to alter your brain chemistry. It left you open to suggestion. Something like chemical hypnosis with full cognizance."

"I'd accuse you of being a scientist before the magic came back, but you're not old enough." He took another step, and I did the same. At the far end of the table sat my newest Knockout Powder application: a small gas grenade.

"How did you find me?" If I could distract him until I got to the end of the table…

"Caller ID. You called from this shop to make your appointment." He gave up trying to circle the table and started down the opposite side, across from me. "You're not happy to see me?" His eyes never left mine.

"Not particularly."

He placed a hand over his heart. "Ouch." The fitted black sweater looked expensive and so did the tailored pants. He might have put the robes aside, but he would still stand out in a crowd—at least around here.

"I have no intention of telling anyone about yesterday."

"And yet you blow my cover to the first man I meet."

"Your cover?"

"Do you think I wear those robes for the fun of it? I wouldn't be able to leave my house if the world knew my face."

"If your identity is so secret, why give George the evidence and ash his watch?"

"He pissed me off." His odd calm did nothing for my nerves.

I lunged for the end of the table. My hand had just closed around the grenade when the pair of windows on the opposite wall exploded. Two dark forms dropped into the room with the clink of falling glass.

Rowan vaulted the table and caught me around the waist. Apparently his slow stalk had been for fun—or the vial of chicory extract really had deterred him. It wasn't deterring him now, so I tucked it in the front pocket of my jeans.

Two men dressed in black rose from the glass-strewn floor, and a second pair crawled through the shattered windows. I recognized their clothing and gasped. My kidnappers from the night the Alchemica burned had worn the same black fatigues. If not for Rowan's grip on my waist, I would have bolted for the stairs.

Rowan pulled me against him, my back to his chest. "They here for you?"

I drew a breath, trying to get a handle on my fear. I certainly didn't want Rowan to see it. "I don't—"

"We found the alchemist." The man on the far right raised a hand to his ear, and spoke into a hands-free radio.

My breath caught. They *were* the same men from the Alchemica.

"Guess I'm not the only one you pissed off," Rowan said, his breath warm against my temple.

A crash sounded from the stairwell followed by raised voices. Oh no, please don't let them be trashing the shop. I didn't like James's brothers, but that'd be a hell of a way to repay them for giving me this job.

All four men were armed, their guns trained on us.

"Hand over the alchemist," the man with the radio said.

Rowan's grip tightened on my waist. "No. The alchemist belongs to me."

I opened my mouth to voice my annoyance when the men's eyes widened.

"What the hell?" Radio Man muttered.

I suspected that Rowan had done his eye-glow trick.

A faint pop and the radio headset went flying from the spokesman's head. He cried out and spun away from us, clearing my line of sight to the window. James crouched on the broken seal with a gun of his own. He fired and clipped the man's gun, knocking it from his hand.

The three remaining men whirled to face him, guns coming up as they turned. I gasped, but James didn't even blink. He shot three times, the pop from his silenced pistol almost a single report, disarming each man as he had the first. I swear the boy hadn't even aimed.

"I have five bullets left," James said. "I only need four."

I didn't wait to see what they would do. I armed my grenade and tossed it. It exploded in a white puff of powder before it hit the ground. The men scrambled away from the window as the cloud grew, obscuring my view.

Crap. "I knew it needed greater range," I muttered. "If I increase the ratio of propellant—"

"Addie, move!" James waved me toward him.

The cloud was drifting our way, gradually filling the entire room.

Rowan shoved me toward James, but I didn't need encouragement. My backpack, still loaded from my trip to Cincinnati, lay on a chair near the window. I snatched it up on my way past. Rowan took the pack from me and then hoisted me up onto the sill beside James. I didn't get to comment on the unnecessary manhandling before James picked me up and leaped from the second-story window.

The alley rushed up to meet us and I cried out, wrapping my arms around his neck. James's shoes smacked the asphalt with an impact I could feel and hear. Our momentum dropped him into a crouch. A pause and he straightened and set me on my feet.

"Are you o—" James started to ask when a thump sounded behind us. We turned to find Rowan rising from a crouch as unfazed as James.

James pulled the gun from behind his waistband and trained it on Rowan. "Leave."

Suddenly James no longer held a gun, but a ball of white-hot flame. An instant later, he fisted his empty hand. Rowan had vaporized the gun.

"I said, leave," James repeated, his voice low and devoid of emotion. A glow kindled in his green eyes.

"We don't have time for this." Rowan waved a hand at the windows above us, his gaze settling on me. "That looked like a PIA SWAT team. What have you done?"

I glanced up and noticed the ropes dangling from the roof. "They can't be PIA." Lawson would have taken me in if the PIA wanted me. "I think they're the same ones who tried to abduct me the night the Alchemica burned."

"There!" a voice shouted, and I whipped around to see three more men in black fatigues enter the alley from the street. They skirted the metal trashcans lining the brick wall and started toward us. All three carried submachine guns—MP5s if my gun knowledge could be trusted.

"We found her," the man in the middle called over his shoulder. When he turned back, he gave me a smile exposing his crooked front teeth.

"It's the same guys," I whispered.

Rowan stepped forward. "By whose authorization—"

"Mine." Crooked Teeth raised his gun and fired.

Rowan dove to the side, bullets kicking up chunks of asphalt where he stood.

"Move!" Rowan sprang to his feet beside me and pushed me toward the trashcans. More bullets whined down the alley as we squeezed in between the cans and the steps to the side door.

James didn't follow us.

I pushed at Rowan, trying to see back into the alley. "James!" I screamed over the gunfire.

"Stay down." Rowan's warm hands gripped my upper arms and pushed me back against the wall. Bullets riddled the trashcans, setting the empty ones dancing and sending one lid rattling down the alley.

"Don't...move." Rowan let go of my arms and braced his hands against the wall to either side of my head.

Heat engulfed us. I gasped and hot air seared my lungs. The air grew hotter still, shimmering around us; little bursts of light exploded in the heat waves. It took me a moment to realize they were bullets.

Stunned, I looked up into Rowan's face. He'd squeezed his eyes shut; a look of intense concentration laced with anger constricted his features. Several bullets smacked into the bricks to my right and he grunted.

"Stop! What are you doing?" a voice shouted from the alley. The gunfire tapered off. "He wants her alive. If you kill her—"

A snarl drowned out the voice, the sound not of this world. James had changed form. Someone screamed and then the scream cut out with an abruptness that turned my blood cold. Oh God, had James—

Machine gun fire cut through the sudden silence, but it wasn't directed at us this time.

"James!" I lunged and almost got free. Rowan caught me around the waist with one arm, pulling me back down behind the trashcans. I gripped his forearm and he growled this time. My hand came away slick with blood. The wall hadn't caught all the stray bullets.

"Hold still," he commanded through gritted teeth. His arm tightened, pressing my back to his chest.

"Let me go!" I continued to struggle.

"Why? So you can get yourself shot?"

"There might be something I can do."

"What could you possibly do?"

The pompous ass. I pulled the lid off the nearest trashcan

and swung it back over my shoulder, trying to brain him. Unfortunately, I only clipped his upper arm.

"Pull out!" a voice shouted from beyond our trashcan barrier.

"Retreat!" someone else called from the opposite direction. God, they'd surrounded us. A vehicle door slammed, followed by the screech of tires.

"Did they—" I didn't get to finish the question as Rowan released me and rose to his feet. I hurried to follow. The alley was deserted except for three downed men.

James wasn't one of them.

"Addie?" James's low voice carried easily in the silence.

I whirled to face him. He dropped to his knees, thumping the cobbles. Naked, he slumped forward, hands braced wide and head hanging.

I hurried over and knelt beside him. "James?" I tentatively touched his shoulder. The coolness of his skin surprised me.

"You okay, son?" Rowan asked.

"Yeah," James answered, his voice soft.

"Wait here." Rowan eyed me before he swung my pack over his shoulder and started down the alley. I frowned after him and then turned to James.

A sheen of sweat covered his pale skin, but he gave me a weak smile. "I think we're being rescued by the Lord of Flames."

"Or kidnapped." The bastard had taken my pack with my robes and potions. I wasn't going anywhere without them. Then too, James looked too ill to run. "You sure you're all right?"

He glanced at the downed men. "I don't know," he whispered.

Oh God, were they dead? He hadn't dismembered them as he had the zombie. From where I knelt, I couldn't see any blood, but he wouldn't look so stricken if he'd only knocked them out.

The rumble of an engine made my heart leap. A sleek black Camaro with orange and yellow flames across the hood and front quarter panels swung into the alley. I glanced at the front tag. *Etna.* Wasn't that a volcano in the Mediterranean? I snorted as Rowan climbed out of the driver's seat. And he accused me of breaking his cover.

James cleared his throat, but before he could speak, an explosion rocked the alley. He sprang into motion, tackling me so quickly, I barely had time to gasp. He pinned me to the asphalt, his body shielding mine. Over his shoulder, I watched the upper story of the shop blow apart. Huge flaming sections of wall spun outward and slammed into the taller building across the alley. Then gravity took over.

I pressed my face into James's shoulder and squeezed my eyes closed, bracing for impact. No way those chunks of wall could miss us. The breath froze in my lungs as I waited…and waited.

"Come on, let's go," Rowan said from above us.

James pulled back and I opened my eyes. Small particles of soot floated to the ground around us. I sat up and found the alley unchanged. No debris. No flames.

"You ashed it," I said, stunned.

"Yes." Rowan held my gaze, eyes once more gray. The color of ash.

I'd grossly underestimated the man's power. Perhaps it was naiveté or, more likely, hubris. I guess they called him the most powerful magic user in the country for good reason.

I got to my feet and looked up. Fire engulfed the top floor of the shop. A plume of black smoke rose skyward, and what structure remained fueled the flames. I stared at what had been my workshop. Three months I'd struggled to pull together a place I could call my own and in a single blast, I lost it all. Again.

"Can you stand?" Rowan offered James a hand.

"Yeah." James let Rowan help him up, struggling to cover himself in the process.

Rowan helped him to the car and opened the passenger door. "There's a gym bag on the back floor. Help yourself."

James muttered his thanks and climbed inside.

Rowan turned to face me, his body between me and the passenger seat. "The vial." He held out a hand. "In your pocket."

His request confused me until I remembered the vial I'd threatened him with in the shop. I pulled it from my front pocket and placed it in his hand.

"It's chicory root extract."

"Any more?" he asked.

"No, that's all." It was my only vial of chicory extract.

"Any other *potions*?"

I looked up, surprised that he'd caught my subterfuge.

A slim orange ring encircled his pupils. "Shall I check?"

"You could?" I asked, more intrigued than afraid.

The corner of his mouth twitched. "Your call."

I pulled a couple of tubes of Knockout Powder from my back pocket and handed them to him. "That's it. Had I known you were coming, I would have been better prepared."

"Next time, I'll call ahead." He stepped aside. "Get in. We need to go." He hit a button on his key fob and the trunk popped open.

I watched him set my pack inside. "Cocky son of a—" I muttered as I slid into the passenger seat.

"Addie." James leaned forward to grip my arm. "I'm whipped and it's not safe here. Whatever his intentions, I don't think he'll hurt you."

I wasn't concerned—not about me. As for James, the magical tended to take care of their own. I glanced back at him. He'd donned a black Under Armor shirt and a pair of sweats. The fit and color emphasized how thin and pale he was.

He stared out the windshield, his eyes on the flames.

"Your brothers," I whispered. Had they been inside when the building went up? We'd have to go check—

"They're all safe." His eyes glowed faintly, just as they had when he'd surveyed the Element's office the night we broke in. The time he'd been able to tell me how many people were inside.

"You don't hear them; you see them."

Rowan closed the trunk with a thump. Sirens wailed in the distance.

James glanced at me and then dropped his eyes. "Later."

Rowan slid in behind the wheel. "Buckle up."

"Are you a bad driver?" I asked.

He revved the engine and dropped it into reverse without warning. The force threw me forward against the dash until he squealed to a stop. Jerk. He glanced over with that smug smile curling to his lips. Without comment, he shoved the stick shift into first gear and raised a brow.

I reached for my seatbelt and snapped it on. "Out of the frying pan and into the fire," I muttered.

Rowan chuckled and hit the accelerator.

CHAPTER 7

I TAPPED MY FINGERS ON THE armrest as Rowan dialed another number on his cell phone. We were already half an hour west of town. I began to fear we'd arrive in Cincinnati before the man got off the phone.

He'd made several calls, though I learned little from them. Most of the time, he listened rather than spoke. When he did speak, he gave a few terse commands and then moved on to the next call.

"I ran into some trouble," Rowan began his newest conversation. "I'm going to be late."

I resisted the urge to glance over. Instead, I quieted my breathing, trying to hear the other side of the conversation.

"No, no, it's fine. Don't reschedule," Rowan said. "I'll be there."

I caught the rumble of a deep male voice, but I couldn't make out the words.

"Late tonight," Rowan answered. "Well enough," he added. "Do me a favor. Call Waylon and find out if he had anything going in Portsmouth today."

I did glance over on that one. Rowan frowned at the slow-moving logging truck ahead of us, but I suspected the truck wasn't the reason for the frown.

"No," he said. "I have the alchemist." He gave me a quick glance. "And she's listening to everything I say."

I crossed my arms. What was I supposed to do? Plug my ears and hum? If he wanted to conduct sensitive phone calls, he shouldn't do it with me in the car.

Rowan suddenly laughed. "You have no idea."

I frowned, certain his laughter had been at my expense. He didn't look at me, but continued to smile while he listened.

"Yes," he said. "You know the drill." His smile faded. "And one more thing, I want to see Marian."

A pause.

"Yes, yes. She can predict my death all she likes, but I need her opinion."

My brows rose, but he kept his attention on the road.

He chuckled. "That's why you're the man, my friend. Make it happen." He took the phone from his ear and hit end.

"Someone threatening you?" I asked. Who'd be crazy enough to do that—aside from me?

He glanced over. "No, not like that. Marian is a seer. Ever met one?"

Maybe? "No," I said aloud.

"They love to tell you when you're going to die."

"So, when will I be rid of you?"

The corner of his mouth quirked. "I'm supposed to meet death this fall."

"Ah. Well, before you keel over, you mind telling me why you drove all the way to Portsmouth to kidnap us?"

"It was not my intention to abduct you—unless you couldn't be reasoned with." He looked back over his left shoulder before changing lanes. "It seemed in your best interest to get out of town."

"How thoughtful of you to rescue us."

He ignored my comment. "And men dressed in the same fashion tried to take you from the Alchemica?"

"Yes."

"Why?" He glanced over, our eyes meeting for a moment before he turned back to the road.

"I don't know." I wished I did.

"I can't help you if you don't tell me."

"I don't need your help."

"So, you'll let them hunt you down and destroy your next lab?"

I hadn't stopped to think about it, but he did have a point. My instincts to lie low after the Alchemica's destruction had been accurate. I had to assume they'd come after me again. But why did they want me?

"I'm not lying to you," I said. "I don't know why they want me. But I can take care of myself. Take us back to Portsmouth—"

"I can't do that. You know too much about me."

"So you're immortal. Big deal."

"You also know my name and face."

And how he kissed. But I sure as hell wasn't going to mention that.

"Plus there's the boy," he continued. "I need to make certain you're not controlling him as you did me."

"You hear that, James?" I turned to look in the back seat. James slumped in one corner, his long legs stretched across the leather seat, his eyes closed. He still looked unnaturally pale.

"James?" When he didn't respond, I unhooked my belt and climbed into the back seat. It wasn't easy in the tight confines of the sports car, but I managed. Being small is sometimes a good thing.

I touched my fingers to his cheek and found his skin chilled. A blue tinge colored the nails of the hand resting on his stomach. But his chest rose and fell in a slow, regular rhythm.

"He's freezing," I told Rowan. "Turn up the heat."

"I'd rather not."

I met his eyes in the rear view mirror. "You're an ass."

"When the situation warrants." He slowed the car and pulled off onto a narrow side road. A few winding turns later, he stopped the Camaro in a wide gravel berm.

"What are you doing?" I gripped James's cool hand, wishing he'd wake up.

"You said the boy was cold." Rowan set the parking brake and opened the door. "Is his magic new to him?"

"How is that pertinent?"

"Sometimes there's an adjustment period. How old is he?"

I wanted to tell him none of his business, but that would be foolish. This guy knew magic like I never could. "Eighteen."

Rowan grunted. "A little old for it to be new. Magic often manifests at puberty. If it's going to kill you, it'll do it then. Your friend has been living with this for several years—if he wasn't born with it."

Before I could question him, he was out of the car and rummaging through the trunk.

The car idled, a soft rumble beneath my feet. I eyed the empty driver's seat and glanced behind me through the back glass. The trunk lid obscured my view, but the soft thumps indicated that Rowan was still rooting around back there.

I sprang forward, squeezing between the front seats, and dropped into the driver's seat. I didn't have time to adjust the seat. Sliding up until my butt rested on the edge, I gripped the wheel and shoved in the clutch. I had to extend my leg until the tip of my toe depressed the petal. Clinging to the wheel, I pushed the gearshift into first and released the parking break.

Gravel flew as I hit the gas. My opposite foot slipped off the clutch and the car lunged forward. I wrapped my arms around the wheel to keep the momentum from slinging me back into the seat. Somehow I managed not to kill the engine.

The car fishtailed a little on the loose gravel, but I kept my foot on the gas, angling for the road at the far end of the berm.

Suddenly, the back end dropped on the left side, the undercarriage dragging the ground. Had I hit a pothole? The car continued to spin out, slinging me to the side. My foot slipped off the gas, and it was all I could do to cling to the wheel.

The car rolled to a stop, and I scooted forward, reaching for the gas as the engine sputtered and died. For a moment, the only sound was my rapid breathing, then the driver's door flew open.

"Out!" Rowan commanded.

I released the wheel and slid back. Damn. I'd almost made it. Perhaps I should have taken a moment to adjust the seat then I wouldn't have lost control.

Rowan stepped back as I climbed out. A muscle ticked in his jaw and fire burned in his eyes, literally.

"What the hell do you think you're doing?" He enunciated each word, the tension keeping the words short and clipped.

I raised my chin, refusing to back down. "Did you think I'd sit back and let you kidnap us?"

"I'm not kidnapping you."

"I'm not a willing passenger on this road trip. How would you describe it?"

He stepped forward, keeping me backed against the side of the car. "I—"

A thump sounded on the far side of the car and the passenger door opened.

Rowan shifted to the side, keeping both me and the door in view.

James rose to his feet. "Addie? What's wrong?"

I released a breath, relieved that he was better, but didn't immediately answer.

He circled around the back of the car. "Oh." His attention focused at my feet, and I looked down. The back wheel was missing—or the tire was. The rim was buried several inches in the gravel, a long rut trailing behind it.

I looked up at Rowan. "You ashed the tire?"

"Would you have preferred the gas?" Rowan leaned in the driver's side and pulled out the keys. "You'd better hope the spare has air in it."

"What happened?" James asked.

"She tried to steal my car."

"Borrow." After all, I hadn't intended to keep it.

"Seriously?" James asked.

A final glare from Rowan and he went to dig out the spare.

James watched him go before turning to me. "You stole his car?" He slumped against the fender, his complexion still too pale.

"Are you all right?" I asked. "You were so cold earlier that your nails were blue."

James glanced toward the trunk and the racket Rowan was making. He pushed off the side of the car. "I just need some air." He didn't wait for a response before walking off into the trees.

"James?" I called after him, but he didn't answer.

Rowan dropped the jack in the gravel by the back wheel. "Is he okay?"

After the anger, his concern surprised me. "I don't know. He didn't look so good. What if he's sick?"

"Of course he's sick. Taking life is never easy, even in self defense." He squatted beside the wheel and began wiggling the jack into position. "I wish I'd realized his intent. I would have stopped him."

I almost asked how and caught myself. Rowan didn't know what James was, and it wasn't my place to reveal it. I took another approach. "Is that why you didn't kill those men?"

"Burning is a terrible way to die."

Something in his tone suggested a story, but I didn't know him well enough to ask.

"Usually, the threat is enough. Often my title restores order before a confrontation is necessary." The arrogance had crept back into his tone. "Unfortunately, that option wasn't open to me."

I rolled my eyes. "I didn't peg you as a pacifist."

He didn't look up, but I caught his frown. "I'm far from a pacifist."

"Right. You did track me halfway across the state. Did I shame you that much?"

"No, alchemist. You're a pain in the ass, but at least you have the courage to face me rather than go after…" He stopped. "Nevermind."

"What happened? Did somebody hurt someone you care about?" I didn't think he had any children, but I wasn't certain.

"It's none of your concern. Why don't you stop prying and go check on the boy. This won't take long."

Prying? What an asshole. I gritted my teeth and bit back what I really wanted to say. Instead I spun on my heel and marched away.

I found James down by a small creek a short walk from the Camaro. Or rather, he found me. I jumped when he stepped out of the trees to my right.

"Sorry," he said. "Does Rowan need help?"

"Nah. I'm sure he can just command the spare to jump on the car." I walked over and plopped down on a log beside the stream. "Self-absorbed jerk."

James walked over, but didn't sit beside me. Instead, he sat on the ground at my feet. "You really don't like the guy." He braced an elbow on the log and looked up at me.

"I *really* don't like the guy," I agreed.

James frowned.

"But that doesn't mean you have to dislike him." It wouldn't please me, but it wasn't my place to pick his friends. "After all, you're magical, and he leads the magical community."

His brow wrinkled, but not in anger. He pulled his elbow from the log and leaned back beside my knees. "He doesn't know what I am, just that I can…take life if I choose."

I could tell his thoughts had returned to the alley behind the shop. "They were shooting at us. You acted in self-defense."

"Very little can harm me, and Rowan had you. I knew that and still…"

I leaned forward and gripped his shoulder. "It's okay." I gave him a squeeze.

"No, it's not. I ripped their souls from their bodies."

"What?" Did he mean that literally? I remembered the bodies. No blood. No obvious injury.

"I tore out their souls and took them to hell," he whispered.

A chill slid up my spine, but I forced myself to keep my hand on his shoulder. "Actual hell? Fire, brimstone, and all that?"

He pulled away from my hand and spun to face me, his movement so fast that my hand hung in space before I could pull it back. "I'm a hellhound, remember?" A faint glow backlit his green eyes.

I gripped my hands, but held his gaze. If he was testing me, I wasn't going to fail. His revelation might be terrifying, but he would never be. Not to me.

"You're also my friend," I said. "My best friend."

He dropped his eyes, and I could see how much it cost him to confess this. Time to swallow my shock and roll with another of his revelations. Though, maybe I should have seen this one coming. I leaned forward to grip his shoulder once more. "You probably saved my life—again. How many times does that make?"

"Rowan saved you this time."

I blew a raspberry. "No way in *hell* will I ever concede that."

He'd bowed his head, but I still caught a glimpse of a smile. Good.

"Who's to say you didn't save me *and* Rowan? What if you hadn't drawn off their fire and scared them away? Rowan couldn't catch every bullet."

He didn't respond.

"James?"

"It was so easy," he whispered. "And it…"

"Don't do this to yourself. Please? You're a good person. If you weren't, this wouldn't bother you."

He didn't say anything.

"I'm right, you know. I'm always right."

He snorted. "Except when you're wrong."

I mussed his hair. "Watch it, Fido." He didn't deserve this. "Why couldn't one of your worthless brothers end up with this curse?"

He looked up. "Maybe because they wouldn't view it as a curse."

"Yeah, punish you for being the conscientious one."

"Nice guys finish last."

"You could apprentice yourself to Rowan. He does jerk with such class."

James smiled and without warning, rose up on his knees and wrapped me in a hug. "Thanks," he whispered close to my ear. "You ground me."

Before I could return the hug, he released me and got to his feet. "I'll go help Rowan with the tire." He started to turn away, then stopped. "It'd be best if we don't tell him what I am."

"Why?"

"I'm Old Magic."

"So?"

James glanced toward the road before looking back at me. "Nineteen years ago, a grim killed the European Elements."

I rose to my feet. "Seriously?" The Elements were the top of the magical food chain and nineteen years ago magic had just returned. "I didn't realize that any of the Elemental families had organized then."

"They organized, but remained hidden until the...problem was destroyed."

"The grim." I studied him. "But how do you know all this?"

"Family history."

"Okay." I could tell by the way he wouldn't meet my eyes that there was more to this. "Go on."

"I'm not registered, and that wouldn't go over well."

"It'll piss Rowan off?"

James closed the distance between us. "I possess one of the few magics lethal to an Element. *You* took me into their offices."

He was protecting me.

"Please, Addie. Don't tell Rowan what I am. It wouldn't end well."

I held his gaze, annoyed that he was trying to protect me, but worried for him all the same. I didn't want the Elements coming after him.

"Okay."

He nodded then turned and walked away.

As I watched him go, I suddenly remembered one of Rowan's many phone calls. He had requested a consultation with his seer. Could she tell Rowan what James was?

I started for the road. Time to cooperate with His Grace—and get away from him as quickly as possible.

CHAPTER 8

"**W**HY ARE YOU TAKING US to the Alchemica?" I asked when Rowan took the exit to my former home.

"It was on the way." He drove the Camaro through the same streets James and I had traveled a few days ago. He seemed to know the route well. In minutes, he pulled the Camaro to a stop outside the locked gate and shut off the engine.

I stared at the ruin through the windshield, noting how different it looked in the afternoon sunlight. Different, but not familiar.

"I want you to show me what you observed," Rowan said. "If it truly wasn't the labs, then we might have been set up."

"You think the Alchemica was destroyed to get to you?" Did the man's ego know no bounds?

"It does seem an elaborate plan, but I won't know until you show me what you found." He pulled the keys from the ignition and climbed out of the car.

"Can you believe this guy?" I asked James.

My buddy grunted and pushed the driver's seat forward so he could climb out. Given no alternative, I followed.

The broken shell of the Alchemica still stood within its chainlink enclosure. A bulldozer had been parked inside the gate, but it didn't look like it'd been put to use yet.

From up the street, the shouts of children at play drew my attention. Nestled in the wooded lot opposite the Alchemica, a park was visible. Several people strolled along the sidewalk bordering the street.

"You know, it might be best if I waited in the car," I said. "James can show you around."

Rowan turned to face me. "Why?"

I patted my bare left arm. "The alterations you made to my wardrobe are a bit conspicuous."

"Any clothes in your pack?"

"Just my robes." And potions.

He grunted and turned back to the car. "Come here."

Curious, I followed him to the trunk. It turned out that my backpack wasn't the only piece of luggage. He unzipped a compact carry-on and riffled through the neatly folded clothing.

"Prepared for every contingency?" I asked.

"I was supposed to fly to California this morning," he answered without looking up.

"Business or pleasure?"

He pulled a white button-up shirt from the stack and handed it to me. "Best I can do."

I accepted the shirt and let it fall open. "Thanks." It was way too big, but I pulled it on anyway. "If you weren't so paranoid, you wouldn't have had to cancel your trip."

He ignored my comment and reached for the zipper on the suitcase. That's when I noticed the bloodstain on his sweater sleeve. I'd forgotten about that bullet clipping him in the alley.

"How's the arm? I have some hydrogen peroxide in my pack."

"It's nothing."

"Nothing doesn't typically leave such a large bloodstain."

He studied me for one long moment and then pulled up his sleeve. Some dried blood matted the hair on his arm, but there was no other evidence of an injury.

"What—"

"One of the perks of being an Element."

Being an Element or being immortal? Or perhaps the terms were synonymous. Of course, he didn't like me knowing about either.

He snapped the truck closed. "Come along, alchemist. Give me the tour."

I glared at his back, but followed him to the gate. Maybe I'd pop a button or two off his expensive shirt.

James raised a brow in question, but I didn't respond. Busy cuffing my sleeves, I jumped in surprise as the chain and heavy lock slid to the ground with a thunk. Rowan had vaporized a link of the chain. Without comment, he pushed open the gate and walked inside.

I glanced over at James, but he just shrugged. I guess I shouldn't be too concerned. Since the building's destruction had been deemed a laboratory accident and not arson, the site wasn't off-limits for legal reasons. It was locked up for safety reasons—or to protect the earth-moving equipment from vandalism. Besides, Rowan was the Lord of Flames. He could probably do as he pleased.

We gave Rowan a quick tour, stepping carefully through the debris. Broken masonry shifted underfoot, stirring up the scent of damp cinders. We showed him the basement location of the labs with respect to the far more damaged auditorium. He showed us where he and the other Elements had been standing. They'd been close. Very close.

"We were set up," Rowan said. "It was a bomb." He stood frowning at the hole in the auditorium floor. I hadn't noticed it during our last visit, but in the bright sunlight, it did appear to be the epicenter of an explosion. The walls closest to the hole had been blown outward. No basement lay beneath this side of the building, only a crawl space. A good place to plant a bomb.

"You're sure?" I asked.

"It wasn't the lab and it wasn't me. What do you think?"

I stared at the blackened hole in the scattered remains of the hardwood floor. My Grand Master had invited the Elements.

"It couldn't have been Emil. This place was his dream."

"It does seem unlikely that he would destroy it," Rowan said. "It's also possible that the invitation I received wasn't from your Grand Master. Someone else wanted to take out both problems with one bomb."

"The ones who tried to kidnap you," James said to me.

"But they were caught in the explosion, too." I hadn't really thought about that. "Did they forget to synchronize their watches or is there even more going on here?" I rubbed my forehead before looking up at Rowan. "You're sure it was a bomb?"

"I have experience with what things look like after an explosion."

"So does Addie." James flashed me a grin.

I rolled my eyes, though deep down, I was relieved to hear him joking—even if the joke was at my expense.

"I'm sure that's true," Rowan said, "but I referred to my doctorate in volcanology. I spent several years in the field before magic returned."

I couldn't imagine him stumbling through sulfur fumes and ash on some volcanic mountainside. I tried not to laugh and failed.

"You find that amusing?"

"Please. You'd smudge your loafers."

Rowan gave me a dark look and walked around to the other side of the crater. His interest in volcanology wasn't a surprise. It was a common phenomenon for the magical to have had an occupation or hobby similar to their talent prior to magic's return. Then there were people like James who had some forgotten magic awaken and take a bite out of them.

Rowan continued to study the blast site, and I felt a twinge of guilt for laughing at him. "So, what do you do with that degree now?"

"I used to teach. Now it's just the occasional guest lecture."

"Seriously?" I glanced back at his car and the *Etna* license plate. "The Camaro. It's a pun on your profession, not your talent."

"Technically, it's both." His attention returned to the crater. "I want a sample."

"What?" James asked.

"A soil sample. I have a friend who can analyze it for me and determine the type of bomb."

"Good idea, but that was three months ago," I said. "It's hopelessly contaminated now."

"I'd like to try." Rowan turned to James. "The water bottle on—"

"I have sterile vials in my pack," I said.

Rowan pulled out his keys and tossed them to James. Without comment, James turned and jogged back the way we'd come, circling the bulldozer to reach the open gate. Once at the Camaro, he opened the trunk and ducked under the lid. I guess James had no qualms about taking orders from the Flame Lord. He hadn't even glanced at me.

"You bossing around my buddy now?" I asked.

Rowan smiled. "Did I undermine your authority?"

"You implying that I like to boss him around? He's my friend."

"He's magical."

"So?"

The chain-link rattled, and we glanced over to watch James take a shortcut and vault the fence. Show off. No need to hide what he was from us. He jogged up and handed Rowan the vial, and then gave me a frown. "What?"

"She's offended that I gave you an order and you obeyed." Rowan ripped open the packaging.

"I am not." I cringed at how childish that sounded.

Rowan gave me a smirk and squatted beside the crater.

"I thought it was a good idea to learn more about the bomb," James said to me. "Plus, I don't want you wandering around by yourself after what happened last time."

"What happened last time?" Rowan capped the vial and stood.

"Addie was attacked by a necro and her slave."

"Here? In Cincinnati?" Rowan's look of surprise shifted to me. "So much for the ordinance prohibiting zombies within city limits." He looked annoyed.

"Perhaps you should keep better tabs on your people," I said.

"The necros aren't mine."

"Because they're old magic?"

"Because they're sick bastards."

I laughed. "Good reason, Your Grace." I glanced over at James, but he was studying his toes.

Rowan tucked the vial in his pocket. "Let's go." He pulled out his cell phone, typing what appeared to be a text.

"You'll take us home now?"

Rowan started walking toward the gate. "You're not going back to Portsmouth. You're the key to this, alchemist, so I'm keeping you close until I figure out what this threat is. Consider it protective custody."

I hurried after him. "An Element protecting an alchemist?" Uttering the sentence made me want to laugh.

Rowan grunted. "If I didn't know better, I'd think you put something in my water."

"Trust me; if I had, it wouldn't be in an effort to spend more time with you."

He glanced over. "I'm crushed. I thought I'd made a better first impression." His lips curled into a knowing smile.

I remembered our first meeting and my cheeks heated. "Whatever," I muttered, praying he wouldn't notice my blush.

He chuckled. "Not much of a comeback."

I stopped, but he didn't. "If you think I'll be your meek little captive, you're in for a surprise."

He took a few more strides before he turned to face me. "I doubt I'll be surprised. Annoyed, possibly pissed, but not surprised."

I gritted my teeth and marched past him toward the car.

"Addie?" Rowan called.

I stopped and looked back. Would he apologize? Make some excuse that this wasn't captivity? Relent and take us home?

"You're cute when you blush," he said.

James actually put a hand over his mouth in an effort not to laugh. The traitor. Thank God he didn't know the true reason for the blush. I spun on my heel and headed for the car.

I CLIMBED OUT OF ROWAN's Camaro and looked up at the small farmhouse. I wasn't sure what I expected, but it wasn't this. I tugged at my over-sized shirt, wishing I didn't look like a refugee. Rowan had told us that the scientist who'd be analyzing the soil sample lived here. I wanted to make a good impression on a potential colleague. Who knew when I might need a lab.

James and I followed Rowan along the front walk and up onto the wrap-around front porch.

We didn't need to knock. A woman opened the door and invited us inside before we'd stepped on the welcome mat. Something about her face seemed wrong, but it wasn't until she smiled, or attempted to, that I understood. Her face had that uneven look of someone who'd undergone reconstructive surgery, but whether from a birth defect or injury, I wasn't certain.

"Please, come in." She waved us inside. The place smelled of freshly baked cookies.

"I'm sorry about the short notice," Rowan said.

"It's no problem." Her eyes shifted to me, then James.

"Lydia, allow me to introduce Addie and James."

She offered us another lopsided smile. "Now which of you is the alchemist and which is magical?"

"Alchemist." I raised my hand.

"And that must make you magical by default," she said to James.

"Yes, ma'am."

"And so polite." She patted his arm and then turned to Rowan.

I frowned at her back. I guess I'd been dismissed. No need to give the non-magical more attention than she deserved.

"Gerald brought the little one over," Lydia said. "They're waiting for you in the den. Shall we?" When Rowan agreed, she led us through a narrow hall and into a modest book-lined room that I loved immediately.

"Roe!" A young girl of about seven or eight years came running, her blonde ponytails flying out behind her.

Rowan dropped to a knee and caught her in a hug. She threw her arms around his neck and planted a kiss on his cheek before leaning back to grin at him.

"I told Gerald you'd be on time," the girl said. She waved a hand at the room's other occupant: a mousy-looking man in thick glasses.

Rowan rose to his feet, taking the girl with him, and propped her on one hip. "Thank you for playing chauffeur."

"It wasn't any trouble, Your Grace." Gerald tugged at his sweater vest. "It's never any trouble."

"You want me to meet someone," the girl said to Rowan. It wasn't a question.

"Yes." Rowan turned to us. "Marian, meet Addie and James."

My breath caught in my throat. Marian. Wasn't that the name of Rowan's seer?

The little girl's bright blue eyes shifted from me to James and back to Rowan. "Ha," she gave him another big grin. "I told you you'd meet death this fall."

CHAPTER 9

"**W**HAT DOES THAT MEAN?" Rowan's tone held a calm that made the fine hairs on the back of my neck stand up. I expected to see fire in his eyes, but for the moment, they remained gray.

"She doesn't mean you're going to die," James said. "She means you'll meet the personification of death."

"He's a grim." Marian gave James a big smile.

Lydia gasped and stepped forward to take Marian from Rowan's arms.

"Where are we going?" Marian asked as Lydia whisked her from the room.

I started to comment when Rowan's eyes, which had never left James, went completely orange.

"James!" I stepped between them, not sure what I could do.

"No!" Gerald sprang forward and grabbed me by the front of my shirt. Did he think I'd given James some sort of command?

A wave of vertigo hit me, distorting my vision. An instant later, something slammed into my back, or perhaps I slammed into something. My head spun and the sunlight hurt my eyes. Sunlight?

I squinted at the blue sky and finally made sense of my surroundings. I was outside, on my back in the grass. Somehow

Gerald had teleported me outside. And he had his hands around my throat.

"I won't let you kill him," he whispered. He straddled my body, both hands squeezing my throat. "Send your pet back to hell!" He pulled me off the ground and slammed me back down again. My head collided with the earth and sparkling stars swam across my vision.

I gripped his wrists, trying in vain to pull away his hands. Darkness haloed my vision and I dug my nails into Gerald's wrists. Panicking, I twisted and thrashed, trying to find some leverage, anything to get him off me.

Suddenly, his hands left my throat and his weight no longer pinned me to the ground. I sat up, coughing. An animal snarled and gooseflesh pebbled every inch of my body. Gerald screamed. I twisted around and found him lying several yards away, pinned beneath a massive black dog. Or more accurately, a hellhound.

I'd seen James furry before, but never in the bright light of day. His shaggy coat was a slash of darkness that, like his growl, didn't belong in a world of sunlight and bright fall foliage. But more disturbing than the wrongness of his presence was his size. This form had to outweigh his human body. Gerald wasn't a big man, but James came close to making two of him. He flexed his paws, unsheathing ebony claws like a cat. They sank into Gerald's shoulders, and he screamed again.

"James! Don't!" Rowan ran around the side of Lydia's house. Gerald had put me down in her backyard.

Rowan picked up a wooden Adirondack chair and without slowing, slung it into James. It hit him broadside, and I cringed. The impact knocked him off Gerald, rolling him several feet. Concerned, I cleared my throat in an effort to call out to him, but I needn't have worried. James rolled to his feet, his claws digging into the turf to stop himself.

Gerald got to his knees before James turned back to him

with another hair-raising snarl. Gerald's scream cut out in mid-crescendo. He was no longer there.

James whirled to face the house and darkness swallowed him. I didn't know how else to describe it. For an instant, less than an instant, he wasn't the hellhound and he wasn't the boy I knew. He was something in between. He stood on two legs, but that's where the semblance to humanity ended. Covered in black fur, he still had the muzzle and pointed ears of the hellhound. His clawed hands held open a rip in the darkness, and beyond him, I caught a glimpse of other eyes. And then he and the darkness were gone. If I'd blinked, I would have missed it. Like Gerald, it seemed that he'd simply vanished.

"Shit, he slipped planes," Rowan muttered. "Where—"

A scream came from the front of the house.

Rowan ran toward the sound, and I scrambled to my feet. Dizzy from the choking and the adrenaline, I staggered for the first few strides, but managed to keep my feet under me. I followed Rowan around the side of the house to the front, the snarls growing louder as I ran.

James had Gerald backed up against the side of a Honda Civic in the driveway.

"James," I called, my voice a hoarse croak. I didn't feel too generous toward Gerald right now, but I didn't want James to kill him.

Gerald circled the car putting it between him and James. I tried calling to James again, but he didn't even glance in my direction.

Gerald staggered away from the car, keeping James in sight. He backed up the walk and caught his heel on the bottom step. Off balance, he fell across the steps, grunting in pain. "Oh God," he whispered, his wide eyes still on the driveway.

I turned my head in time to watch James step out of the side of the Civic. He'd simply walked right through it, as if it wasn't there. Or he wasn't. Grim. Ghost dog. I now understood how he'd gotten into the Elemental Offices the night we'd broken in. He could walk through walls.

"James!" I tried again and produced a little more volume.

He didn't glance over, his eyes intent on his target. His large paws fell on the walk, claws gouging the cement without sound.

Suddenly, a white-hot fireball engulfed James, and I screamed.

I couldn't believe it. "You bastard!" I whirled and slammed both hands against Rowan's chest. He took a step back, but his hands shot out, catching my wrists.

James leapt from the flames, and the next instant they vanished. Only bare earth remained where the slab of the sidewalk had been. Rowan had incinerated it, not James.

"Let me go," I twisted in his hold, but couldn't break his grip.

James stopped advancing on Gerald and turned his head to look at us. His glowing green eyes focused on Rowan.

"Stay back." Rowan pulled me behind him. I pushed at his back and tried to step around him, but he held out an arm, blocking my path.

"You're protecting her?" James asked.

Startled, I glanced around Rowan and found the boy I knew, sans clothes, kneeling in the grass before us.

"From me?" James added. His eyes still glowed and his dark hair looked a little wild, but otherwise he appeared himself.

"Until you regain control, yes."

I realized that Rowan had grabbed me to draw James's attention away from Gerald. That was no small risk.

James leaned forward, hands braced on the ground, and bowed his head. "He shouldn't have run."

Movement drew my attention to the porch. Lydia helped

Gerald up and herded him into the house, stepping past Marian who stood in the doorway, her wide eyes on us.

I began unbuttoning my shirt and pushed past Rowan, but he was already handing James his coat. I stopped, uncertain.

"Gerald didn't exactly run." My voice still sounded a bit rough, and it hurt to swallow, but it didn't seem Gerald had broken anything.

"He can bend space-time and travel between the two points," Rowan said.

I turned to stare at him. "He can create wormholes? No freaking way. Let me guess. He's a physicist."

"Actually, he owns a video rental store in Batavia, but I understand he's a big science fiction fan."

I snorted and glanced over at James. He was on his feet, one hand holding Rowan's jacket around his hips. The glow had left his eyes.

The two men studied each other for one long moment.

"You should have told me you were a grim," Rowan said.

"Should have told you?" I said. "You freaked out and tried to incinerate him the moment you found out."

James's hand settled on my shoulder and pulled me back. "It's okay, Ad."

"Okay? How is that okay?"

Footfalls thumped on the wooden porch steps, and I looked over to find Marian approaching us. She walked up to James and tugged on his arm.

James's brows rose in question.

"Come here." She crooked a finger at him.

James glanced at Rowan and then me before he squatted down beside her.

She leaned over and whispered in his ear, cupping her hand around her mouth like any child sharing a secret.

James suddenly pulled back, his eyes widening. "What do you mean?"

"I thought you'd know. You don't?"

James shook his head.

She studied him. "You really can turn into a dog."

"Yeah."

"Cool." She gave him a grin. She might know what he was, but she didn't understand.

"Come, child," Lydia called from the porch.

Marian glanced in her direction before she turned back to James. "I have to go. Will you let me know if you figure it out?"

"Sure."

She flashed him another grin then leaned over and kissed his cheek.

James blinked in surprise. "Thanks," he whispered.

Marian turned and ran back to Lydia, leaping across the missing chunk of sidewalk on the way. Her laughter carried back to us before the older woman took her hand and led her inside.

James rose to his feet beside me. I arched a brow and a bit of color bloomed in his cheeks. What had Marian told him?

Rowan sighed and ran a hand over his face, stopping to pinch the bridge of his nose. Did he have a headache?

"I was born in this country," James said. "I've never even been to Europe."

Rowan dropped his hand. "I didn't think it was you."

His easy admission threw me. "Then why did you try to incinerate him?"

"I didn't." He looked annoyed that I'd even suggest it. "Grims are said to be the only thing impervious to the power of an Element. I was curious. It turned out to be true. I couldn't see in him."

"See *in* him?"

He studied me a moment. "You don't understand how my power works?"

"Elements manipulate their element as it exists around them. Though, it's not technically an element, but a state of matter: solid, liquid, gas, and plasma. I think of it as a matter-specific form of telekinesis."

"Not a bad analogy."

I thought about that. "And to manipulate your state of matter, you must see *in* it?" Whoa. "You see the atoms?"

"I don't know about that, and it's more feel than sight." Rowan shrugged. For a man who was always so decisive, the shrug made me smile.

"What?" he asked.

This time I shrugged. "So what do *you* do? Where does the fire come from?"

"Fire is different." Rowan dug his keys out of his pocket and tossed them to James. "You know where the clothes are."

"Yes. Thanks." He gripped the keys in his fist. "Sorry." He frowned at the grass at his feet.

"I can teach you control," Rowan said.

James looked up, surprise evident on his features—and something else. Hope.

"But I'm not…like you."

"Anyone can lose control. You don't even have to be magical."

James frowned faintly then nodded. "Thanks." He turned and walked off toward the car.

"Yes, thank you," I said once James was out of earshot.

Rowan's attention shifted to me. "I wish you'd told me."

"Not my secret to tell."

Rowan studied me a moment then nodded. "I need to go speak to Gerald."

"Are you going to kick his ass?"

"He thought he was defending me."

"By attacking me? I'm not the grim."

Rowan's brow wrinkled and his eyes dropped to my neck. "I'm sorry."

Wow. He *could* apologize for something. Before I could comment, he touched the tender skin of my throat. His warm fingers slid upward to my jaw, lifting my chin slightly while he leaned down for a closer look.

I took a hasty step back.

Rowan frowned, though it wasn't in anger. "Gerald must have thought you were controlling James. The grim is supposed to be a product of alchemy."

"What?"

"You didn't know that? I thought..." He glanced back at the car.

"You thought what? That I was using him? Experimenting on him?" I remembered my Perfect Assistant Dust and hurried on. "He's my friend. He rescued me from those SWAT guys—twice now. He was there for me when no one else was. Hell, you were at the Alchemica. Did you even bother to look for survivors?"

"I—"

"No, you didn't. I saw you. I was lying not fifteen feet from you. You were busy instructing your servant to bring the car around."

"Where my phone was—which I used to call the squad."

I crossed my arms. "How magnanimous."

"You're very quick to judge—and apparently require no facts to make such an assessment."

I wanted to tell him to bite me or something equally crude, but James returned. He'd donned a pair of gray sweatpants, but still held the T-shirt. He hadn't bothered with shoes.

"Addie—" James began.

"I'd appreciate it if the two of you would stay out here."

Without waiting for a response, Rowan turned and walked into the house.

"He'd appreciate it." I rolled my eyes.

"Addie." James's brow furrowed in concern.

I flopped down on the bottom step to the porch. He pulled on the plain white T-shirt, and sat down beside me, though not very close. He gripped his hands in his lap.

"You okay?" I asked. He didn't look as pale as he had after the attack on the shop, but then, he hadn't ripped any souls here.

"I scared you," he whispered.

"I think you scared everyone. You're one terrifying pooch, Fido."

"I'm sorry. When Gerald did his wormhole thing, I couldn't feel you, and I sort of lost it."

"Feel me?"

"On the mortal plane."

"And you left it, too. When you became…something else."

He looked up, eyes wide. "You saw that? You shouldn't have seen that."

"I admit, it was disturbing, but I—"

"No, I mean you shouldn't have been able to see it. Those bound to the mortal plane can't see any other."

I cocked my head, studying him. "How do you know all this?"

He lifted one shoulder and let it fall. As always, he went silent when I asked too much about his magic. I thought about what Rowan had said.

"Rowan said there's a connection between grims and alchemy."

He looked up, surprise absent in his expression.

"That's why you study alchemy. You're looking for a cure."

He gave me a bitter smile. "There is no cure."

"Tell me what you know. I may be able to—"

He pushed up to his feet. "I don't think even you can fix this." He turned toward the drive.

Gravel crunched. A teal blue BMW rounded the corner and pulled to a stop beside Rowan's Camaro.

I sat up straighter, but didn't get to my feet. Now what?

A pair of women climbed out of the car and started for the house. The driver, her brunette hair neatly coiffed, wore a dark blue pant suit. She looked every inch the hard-nosed executive as she studied us with cool blue eyes. The girl that followed was anything but. Blonde and dressed in a rainbow of bright colors, she didn't look much older than James.

The brunette continued toward us, her heels clacking on the walk until she reached the section Rowan had destroyed. "What happened here?"

"A misunderstanding." I didn't bother to get up.

Her eyes narrowed. "You're the alchemist."

"My cover is blown."

"Where is he?"

"If you mean Rowan, he's inside." I hooked a thumb toward the house.

"You shouldn't use his name. You don't know who I am."

"Since you haven't bothered to introduce yourself, yeah, you nailed another one."

She gave me a glare and climbed the steps beside me. "Come along," she said to the girl.

The blonde tore her gaze away from James. "He's cute," she said—and not all that softly.

A blush colored James's cheeks, and I snorted. I couldn't help it.

"I smell cookies," the blonde continued, unfazed by the reaction her comment had gotten. "Can I have one?"

The slamming of the screen door blocked out the brunette's answer as the pair disappeared inside.

"I think she liked you," I told James.

"Addie."

"The brunette's a bitch, though."

He dropped to a seat beside me. "You weren't exactly friendly."

"She started it."

"She could be someone important."

"And that matters why?"

He sighed, but didn't respond.

I fumed in silence. Someone important, which in the Elements' world meant someone with magic. The way she'd sneered when she called me an alchemist made that clear.

My eyes settled on Rowan's Camaro. Of course, I didn't have to be without my magic. I stood and looked back over my shoulder at the house.

"What is it?" James rose to his feet beside me.

"Anyone coming?"

He glanced back at the house. "No."

I flashed him a grin and then hurried down the walk toward the driveway.

"What are you doing?" James asked when I stopped beside the Camaro.

"I'm tired of being defenseless." I opened the driver's door. "Let me know when you hear someone coming."

James released a sigh, but did as I asked.

I squatted beside the car and examined the floor around the driver's seat looking for a trunk release. Rowan had taken the keys, so that option was out. The black interior made it hard to see, so I leaned in for a closer look. It didn't help that evening approached, taking the sunlight with it.

Leaning too far, I caught myself on the driver's door, my fingers slipping into a pocket along the door's base. A pair of smooth cylindrical objects clinked together with the familiar sound of glass on glass. Curious, I reached in the pocket and found what I suspected: a pair of empty vials.

"What's that?" James asked.

"I think His Grace is cheating on me."

A small label clung to each vial. I turned one on its side and squinted at the tiny words. *Take by mouth, once an hour, as needed.* Unscrewing the lid, I sniffed the contents. Nothing. I pressed my index finger over the opening and inverted the vial. A pale blue droplet now rested on my fingertip. I brought it to my mouth and lightly touched it to my tongue.

Bleh! The bitter taste lingered. Not the work of an alchemist. Magic brews had a certain bite I'd come to recognize. Only medicine would taste that nasty. Now, what did Rowan need medicine for? He looked fit. Very fit.

A faint cry rang out and I came to my feet.

"What was that?" I asked.

James turned toward the house, his eyes glowing faintly. "This way." He took off at a jog around the side of the house.

I pushed the door closed and hurried after him, hoping Gerald wasn't assaulting someone else.

CHAPTER 10

We swung wide around a flowerbed and came upon a small side porch. I could hear sobbing through the screen door. James hesitated, his eyes still glowing faintly.

"What do you see when you do that?" I stepped in front of him and gripped the door handle.

"Souls." He met my gaze and the glow faded from his eyes.

"Oh." I guess that made sense. He had to see what he took. I couldn't decide if I was amazed or disturbed.

I pulled open the door and found myself in Lydia's kitchen. Sobbing echoed through the room, but it took me a moment to locate the source. The blonde girl sat on the floor before an open oven. A cookie sheet lay nearby, globs of dough scattered around it.

"Hey, are you okay?" I hurried over to her. Heat radiated out of the oven, and I leaned over to close the door.

She clutched her right forearm and looked up with a tear-streaked face. "He'll be so mad. I'm not supposed to use the oven."

Okay. I knelt beside her. "Did you burn yourself? Let me see."

"Lydia had a tray ready to go in the oven, so I thought I'd help. That'd be nice, right?"

"Yes, very nice." I took her forearm and pulled away her opposite hand. An angry red welt marred her arm. A nasty burn, but nothing for a girl her age to get that excited about. James had stopped inside the door. He frowned at the girl, clearly as puzzled by her erratic comments as I was.

"You're pretty," she said.

I returned my attention to the girl. "Thanks." I met her amber eyes, wondering where that had come from.

She gave me a big smile. "Do I know your name? Sometimes I forget." She touched her temple beneath her short, spiky blonde hair.

"We haven't been introduced." I began to suspect she might have a mental problem. "I'm Addie."

"I'm Era. Will you make some more cookies?"

"Um, how about I make a salve for your arm first?"

She gripped my arm so tightly it hurt. "You won't tell him, will you? I'm not allowed to use the oven."

Yes, there was something wrong with the poor girl. "Let's run some water on your arm while I make the salve."

"Thanks!" She threw her arms around my neck, almost strangling me—for the second time today.

I assisted her to her feet while James walked to the sink and turned on the faucet. "Let me help you," he said.

Era turned with a gasp.

"I'm James."

I escorted Era to the sink, and she stood in silence, letting James hold her arm under the running water. I fought back a laugh watching her stare at him. I left him to sooth her, and went in search of the ingredients I'd need for my salve.

I never started a major project in the lab without a jar of burn salve. I made it so often, I could whip up a batch in my sleep. Fortunately, the ingredients were rather mundane, and I found everything I needed in Lydia's kitchen and the small bathroom down the hall. Granted, this would be a stripped down version of my standard salve, but Era's minor burn would respond well to it.

I cleaned up her mess in front of the oven while the salve simmered on the stovetop. When finished, I poured the heavy, dark green liquid into a mason jar I'd found in the pantry. It smelled like Lydia's botanical blend shampoo, the ingredient I substituted for my usual comfrey extract. Era moved to my side to examine the contents of the jar.

"What are you doing?" The brunette stood in the doorway. "Step away from her." The woman started toward us, her heels clacking on the linoleum.

"Did you find her?" Rowan walked into the room. When he saw us, he stopped so suddenly that Lydia, who was following him into the kitchen, almost ran into him. "What's going on here?"

"I'm mixing some burn salve."

Rowan frowned. "Why do you need burn salve?"

Era let out a startled squeak and ducked under the island.

"Excuse me." I sat the jar down and squatted beside her.

"You said you wouldn't tell him." Era's whisper wasn't all that soft.

"You were talking about Rowan?"

"What didn't you tell me?" Rowan squatted on the other side of the island.

Era threw her arms around me, knocking me back into one of the island legs, and pressed her face into my shoulder.

"Era?" Rowan didn't look angry; he looked worried and perhaps a little sad. "Tell me what happened." His eyes rose to mine, questioning.

It's okay, I mouthed the words, and then tipped my head to the side to better see Era. "You need to tell him, honey."

"But..."

"When you do wrong, you have to own up to it." I met Rowan's eyes again as I spoke, hoping he wouldn't go off on her. I could feel the poor girl shaking.

He held my gaze and for several heartbeats neither of us looked away.

Era sat up and rubbed a hand across her eyes. "I used the oven, Roe."

He closed his eyes and then opened them again. I could see him struggle for control. No doubt he wanted to yell at her for her foolishness. "And you hurt yourself?"

"I burnt my arm."

"Stand up. Let me see."

We all climbed out from under the island. Era held her arm out to Rowan. He took her hand and gently turned her arm beneath the light.

"Damn it, Era," the brunette said. "How many times have we—"

"Cora." Rowan cut her off.

Lydia moved to Era's other side and wrapped an arm around her shoulders. "You know why we told you not to mess with the oven, right?"

I wordlessly scooted my jar of salve into the center of the island. Rowan glanced at it and then me.

"You're not seriously considering that," Cora said. "She's an alchemist."

"Which pretty much sums up my qualifications," I said.

"Exactly," Cora responded.

I gritted my teeth. "Afraid this mundane human can do things you can't?"

Cora crossed her arms and gave me a cool stare.

"Try to keep up." I turned and pressed my hand to the still hot burner on the stove. Heat seared my palm and I jerked my hand back, with a gasp. Damn, that hurt.

"Addie!" Surprisingly, Rowan reacted first. He rounded the island and caught my wrist, rotating my hand to reveal the red stripes across my palm.

"Even better," Cora said. "She's crazy."

I pulled my hand away from Rowan. "Give it a rest." I squeezed my undamaged hand through the wide mouth of the Mason jar and dipped my fingertips in the warm salve. James leaned over to hold the jar for me as I withdrew my hand. He gave me a grin; he'd seen what my salve could do.

I rubbed the salve over my burnt palm and then held it up for the others to watch. The pain faded in seconds, and I knew the redness did the same.

Once again, Rowan caught my wrist. Cupping the back of my hand, he lightly ran his fingers over my unblemished palm.

My breath caught at the light brush of his fingers. Surprised, I pulled my hand away. "Well?" I rubbed my hand on my pant leg, hoping he didn't notice my reaction.

"Do it," he said.

"Rowan," Cora protested.

I ignored her and once more dipped my fingers into the salve. I moved over to where Lydia still held Era, and gently rubbed it into the red welt across her forearm. Her burn, being older and deeper, took a little longer to fade. Thirty seconds instead of five.

"Oh my," Lydia whispered. "You should bottle that stuff."

"It loses potency after twenty-four hours."

"Then give the formula to the medical profession," Rowan said, his tone soft. "The burn-unit patients would certainly benefit from it."

"I'd be glad to give them the formula, but it takes an alchemist to mix it. I know you think I'm only a hopped up chemist, but there is a skill to this."

"I don't think that." His subdued tone surprised me. What happened to my mouthy Flame Lord?

"Give it up, Your Grace. I'm just a human playing at magic."

"Are you nuts?" Era stared at her arm. "This is magic. Way more cool than kicking up a breeze."

I smiled at the girl, touched in spite of myself. I glanced at Rowan. "Your Element of Air."

Rowan sighed, which was all the answer I needed.

"Come along, Era," Cora said, interrupting my feel-good moment. "We need to go."

"Let me walk you out," Lydia said.

"Did you see that?" Era followed the two women into the hall. "My burn disappeared."

"I hope that salve doesn't give you a rash, dear." Cora's voice carried back to us. We stood in silence listening to Era's cheerful banter before the closing of a door cut off the sound.

I turned to Rowan. "Cora's charming. And she is?"

"Water."

I grunted. "Lucky you."

I picked up my saucepan and took it to the sink where I'd left a spoon and a measuring cup. It didn't take long to wash up.

James busied himself putting away the ingredients. "Where'd you get the shampoo?" he asked, holding up the bottle.

"Bathroom cabinet, up the hall."

He nodded and left the room.

Drying my hands on a blue-checkered towel, I turned to find Rowan still standing beside the island watching me.

"Yes?" I draped the towel over one side of the dish drainer.

"Thank you for taking care of Era."

After our earlier argument, I didn't expect gratitude. I leaned back against the sink. "She's the one, isn't she?" I remembered the comment he'd made while changing the tire. "The one who was hurt to get to you?"

His brow furled, but not in anger. "Yes."

I pushed off the sink and walked to the island. "Will you tell me what happened?" I placed the lid on the burn salve. "Maybe I can help."

When he didn't respond, I looked up. He still watched me with that odd intensity.

"What?"

"Are you really an Alchemica alchemist?"

"Yes." I frowned. "Why?"

"I've never met one who cared about anything except earning their final band."

I crossed my arms, wanting to argue, but what could I say? I might have been as shallow and self-absorbed as he suggested. "I'd like to help. Won't you tell me what happened?"

He rubbed his forehead and sighed. "Almost four months ago, Era was abducted." He dropped his hand and met my eyes. "I tore this city apart for four days, unable to find any sign of her. No ransom note, no indication of who had taken her. On the fifth day, she was returned."

"Returned?"

"I found her that morning on the front porch of the Offices, unconscious. Physically, she hadn't been…touched, but mentally," he hesitated. "She should have started her senior year of college this fall. I had to call and—"

He fell silent, and I got the impression he'd said more than he intended. I reached over to grip his forearm. He looked down, his eyes meeting mine. Heat climbed my cheeks, and I pulled my hand away, alarmed that I'd tried to comfort him.

"She's the reason you wanted us to meet your seer." I tried to draw his attention away from my gesture of compassion.

"Yes, I needed to know if it'd be safe for the two of you to share a house with her."

"And? What did Marian tell you?"

"She told me nothing; you told me all I needed to know." He gestured at the salve.

My cheeks flushed again, but before I could comment, James returned. Then I caught what else Rowan said. "Share a house with you?"

"Don't you want to find out what happened to the Alchemica?"

I opened my mouth and closed it. "What?"

"The Alchemica. The PIA declared it an accident, and it clearly wasn't. I want to know why. Don't you?"

"Yes." Next to my memories, I wanted that more than anything.

"Well then, shall we?" He gestured toward the door.

I met his questioning gaze. The Flame Lord was offering to help me, an alchemist. Why? Should I be concerned?

I glanced at James and he shrugged. I remembered his eagerness when Rowan offered to teach him control.

I took a breath and released it. "Okay, we're in."

It took a good thirty minutes to drive from Lydia's home to Rowan's. I learned on the ride over that he shared a house with his brother and sister Elements. No spouses, no children—just the four of them. I managed not to groan when he told us. Era wasn't a factor, but Rowan annoyed me, and Cora pissed me off. I didn't have high hopes for Earth's temperament.

I'd originally thought it a good idea to give James the front seat and take the more cramped back seat. After fifteen minutes of winding country road, I began to regret the decision. Rowan finally slowed and drove through the open gate of a long, paved drive.

Unhooking my seat belt, I scooted up between the front seats to get a better view of the Elements' house—if such a structure could be called a house. Words such as "mansion" and "estate" came to mind. I guess I should have expected it after seeing the Elemental Offices. Vines obscured the weathered stone exterior in places while the upper story had the exposed timber look I equated with a Tudor style. Overall, it looked like a quaint English cottage—on steroids.

Rowan parked near a side entrance not far from an attached garage that could house a family of four all on its own. I followed James from the car, and we joined Rowan on the cobbled area between the garage and side entrance.

"Nice place," I said.

"It serves our needs." Rowan started toward the house.

"My pack—"

"Will remain in my possession," Rowan said over his shoulder.

"But I passed your test."

"And you understand why I gave it."

I opened my mouth, but didn't get to speak as a large man opened the door. Rowan stepped past him into the house, but I slowed my pace. The man saw my hesitation and gave me a smile.

"Please come in," he said, his voice deep, but cheerful.

James stepped in front of me and went through the doorway first. The man dwarfed him. My buddy might be lean, but at six-two, I wouldn't call him small.

I followed James inside and the big guy closed the door behind me. The interior of the house maintained the rustic cottage vibe with its stone floor and rough plastered walls above dark wainscoting. It gave the impression of age, but didn't disguise the wealth.

Rowan gestured at the big man who still stood beside us. "Addie, James, allow me to introduce Donovan."

"Nice to meet you." Donovan gave each of us a smile, then

exchanged a handshake with James, who stood closer. The gold highlights in his brown hair and deep tan spoke of a man who spent a lot of time outdoors. Though, the full beard and flannel shirt pushed him toward the Grizzly Adams category of outdoorsman.

"And the little alchemist." He turned to me with a smile.

"I doubt there are many people you can't call little." My hand disappeared into his.

His hazel eyes twinkled. "Not many."

"Earth Element, right?"

His grin broadened, but before he could speak, the outer door opened. Cora walked in, Era following in her wake. I suppressed a groan. Both women pulled up short when they saw us.

Cora rounded on Rowan. "What are *they* doing here?"

"I'll go get my camera," Era announced. She didn't wait for a response before darting off down the hallway leading deeper into the house. I wasn't sure what to make of her comment, but didn't get to ask.

"Donovan, would you show our guests to their rooms?" Rowan asked.

"Guests?" Cora demanded. "No. You will not bring an alchemist and a grim into our home."

"Cora."

"Our *home*, Rowan."

"They're already here." He turned toward the hall Era had disappeared into. "Join me."

"I will not stand for this. Isn't it enough that you let her rub some poison into Era's arm?"

"Poison?" I demanded. "That was—"

She whirled to face me. "You are not a part of this conversation, alchemist."

"You're talking about me. Technically, I *am* the conversation."

Cora caught a handful of the over-sized button-up shirt I still wore. She gave it a faint frown then pulled me in her face. "Do not test me." Her eyes shifted from cornflower blue to black indigo.

James appeared beside me and caught her wrist. "Let her go."

"James, don't. It's okay." I didn't want him sullying his reputation on my behalf. Of course, being a grim might have covered that.

"Addie means you no harm, and neither do I." He released her, but didn't step away.

Cora let go of my shirt. "I'm going to hold you to that, grim." She spoke to him, but her eyes never left mine.

"His name is James." I held her gaze, refusing to be the first to look away.

"Cora, join me," Rowan repeated. He didn't wait for a response, but turned and walked off down the hall.

Cora gave me a final glare and started after him, her heels clacking on the floor.

"Have you eaten?" Donovan asked.

"Um, no." I studied the big guy, trying to gage his reaction to our houseguest status. He looked more amused than angry.

"Let me show you to your rooms, then we'll take care of that." He started up the stairs that ran along one wall.

I glanced at James. "Well, this should be fun."

He didn't look so certain.

"Come on." I patted his shoulder. "It can't be any worse than your brothers."

He grunted, but followed me up the stairs.

SOMEONE KNOCKED AT MY DOOR, and I sat up so fast I tumbled off the bed. I landed on my butt and sat there. This wasn't my workshop. I ran my fingers through my loose hair as the events of the day before returned to me. I looked up at the clock on the nightstand. 7:39 a.m. The lateness of the hour surprised me. I didn't usually sleep so soundly.

Another knock got me on my feet, and I tugged Rowan's white button-up shirt into place. I'd used it as a nightgown since I had nothing else with me. The shirt hung to mid-thigh, longer than some mini-skirts I'd seen.

I pulled the door open. "Yeah?" I expected James; I didn't expect *him*.

Rowan cocked a brow. "Good morning to you, too."

I resisted the urge to give my makeshift nightgown another tug. "Forgive me," I said. "I figured the social niceties were beyond you. You left us last night without so much as a good night."

"My apologies. I didn't realize my actions would cause you such distress."

I laughed. "Hardly. What do you want?"

"Not a morning person, I take it."

"Not when I have to deal with you first thing."

"Again with the insults... and when I come bearing gifts." He held out one of two white shopping bags.

"What's this?" I eyed the bag, but didn't take it.

"Clothing, although," he looked me over, "I do enjoy seeing you in only my shirt."

I snatched the bag from his hand, hoping my blush wasn't visible.

The door across the hall opened and James stepped out. He wore the sweatpants and nothing else. "Addie?" He rubbed one eye with the heel of his hand, his dark hair sticking out at odd angles.

Rowan handed James the other bag, describing its contents.

I opened my bag and glanced inside to find a pair of jeans,

a black shirt, a pack of socks and a pack of undies. Everything still had the tags.

"Breakfast will be served in the sunroom at eight o'clock," Rowan said.

"The sunroom?"

"Back of the house. You'll know it when you see it."

"You're giving us twenty minutes to get ready?"

Rowan glanced at this wristwatch. "Nineteen minutes."

He turned and headed back down the hall. "Hustle up."

With a growl, I stepped back into my room and slammed the door.

Rowan's gift didn't improve my humor. Oh, the clothes fit well. Disturbingly well. I even approved of the black three-quarter-sleeve shirt. My problem lay with the red block letters emblazoned across the front that read "Flammable."

After a bit of exploring, I found the sunroom Rowan had mentioned. The man sat in a wicker chair reading a newspaper, the sun shining through the floor-to-ceiling windows that lined most of the back wall. Another wall displayed a series of black and white photos that looked like something from a museum gallery, but I didn't stop to look. I marched across the room and stopped before him.

"I suppose you think this is funny," I said.

He turned the page, but didn't look up. "What's that?" Sunlight caught on his hair, setting the dark red strands aglow.

I crossed my arms. He knew exactly what I meant.

After a moment of silence, he sighed and lowered his paper. I gestured at my shirt. "This."

His eyes dipped to the bold red letters across my chest and his lips quirked. "I find it more refreshing than funny."

"Hey, what's up?" James asked, walking up behind me. I jumped in surprise. I hadn't heard him enter.

"I'm complimenting His Grace on his charming fashion sense." I turned to face him.

James glanced at my shirt and immediately rubbed his lower face. He wasn't fooling me. He thought it funny, too. Apparently, Rowan didn't pick on his magical guests. James wore jeans and a retro bowling shirt in dark green and black.

The paper rattled and Rowan got to his feet. He looked more casual today in a beige pullover, though he still wore the dark slacks. I suspected Rowan wasn't a jeans kind of guy.

"Before this is over, I'm buying you a shirt," I said.

"What will it say?"

A man in the now familiar black livery entered the room pushing a cart. He stopped beside a round table close to the glass wall and began unloading it. James moved closer to inspect the platters of sausage and eggs.

"Well?" Rowan looked at me expectantly.

"You're a pompous ass."

"I've been called worse." Rowan started for the table. "While you're thinking of a slogan, let me share what I learned from the PIA."

"What?" I hurried after him.

"I spoke to Director Waylon at the regional office downtown. He had no raids in Portsmouth yesterday—nor any the night the Alchemica burned."

"Damn." Another dead end. I dropped into a seat while Rowan pulled out the chair beside mine.

"I also asked who oversaw the Alchemica investigation, and Waylon thought him competent."

I looked up. "What did he say?"

Rowan picked up the plate of sausages and selected a few.

"It's a man who's been with the agency nearly a decade. Waylon has high confidence in him."

"Did you get his name?" I didn't expect to know him, but maybe we could look the guy up, get his take on the investigation.

Rowan passed the plate to James. "It's an agent by the name of Robert Lawson."

"Lawson?" I hadn't expected that.

James looked up, his gaze meeting mine. He clearly remembered the name.

"You know him?" Rowan asked.

"He visited the shop a few days before the raid. He claimed to be registering my bullets. He's also a Sensitive and nearly wet himself when he saw James."

James snorted.

Rowan glanced between us. "What happened?"

"Addie told him she used a potion on me," James answered. "She made him focus on her."

"He was there to see me anyway."

"And he bought it?" Rowan asked.

"I threw in a little blackmail. I let him know that I knew he was a Sensitive."

"And a few days, later the gun shop was raided."

"Are you implying the raid was my fault—because I learned his secret?"

"They *were* there for you," Rowan reminded me. "But I don't think it's because you learned his secret."

"Then why?"

"That is the question, isn't it?" He pulled his phone from his pants pocket. "Waylon needs to know about this agent's involvement in both cases."

I leaned over and caught his wrist. "Wait."

Rowan looked up, his brows raised in question.

"You blow the whistle, and we might lose him."

"Lose him? The PIA will have him."

"And I won't." I released his wrist.

"Ah." The corner of his mouth twisted. James was already grinning.

"He gave me his card," I continued. "He wanted me to come in for an interview. I think it's time I obliged him—but I won't be the one talking."

"I think I see where this is going," Rowan said.

"Yeah. I hope he doesn't track me across the state and force me to come live with him."

James pressed a hand to his mouth, trying not to laugh.

"It's only until we straighten this out." Rowan turned his attention to his breakfast. "You're entirely too much trouble for an extended stay."

CHAPTER 11

I pressed the phone to my ear and drummed my fingers on Rowan's desk, waiting for Agent Lawson to answer. Unlike Rowan's office downtown, his office here at the manor contained a large mahogany desk. My pack lay on the polished surface between us, the front pocket open where I'd dug out Lawson's card.

"Lawson," a male voice said in my ear.

I jerked my attention back to the phone. "Addie."

A moment's silence. "The little alchemist from Portsmouth."

I bit back a retort. "You wanted me to call," I reminded him. "To set up an interview?"

"Yes, I do, but I'm no longer in Portsmouth. I'm in Cincinnati. Can I—"

"You're in Cincinnati?" I glanced at Rowan. He straightened and leaned forward to brace his elbows on his desk. James stood beside me, listening as intently. "What a coincidence, so am I."

"You are?" Agent Lawson sounded surprised.

"Yep. I'm available today if you'd like to meet somewhere."

"Today." He seemed to think on it. "Would you hold a moment?"

I could hear muffled movement in the background, and then silence.

"Sounds like he left the room," James said.

I placed a hand over the receiver. "You can hear that?"

He shrugged.

"A shame you passed out after the shop blew. I didn't have much luck eavesdropping on the two-dozen calls His Grace made on the way out of Portsmouth."

Rowan leaned back in his chair. "Hardly two dozen." A corner of his mouth quirked.

"You do know it's dangerous to talk on the phone and drive? Or is that not a concern you have?"

A rattle on the phone and Lawson came back on the line. "I'm really tied up with a stakeout, but maybe we could meet before—"

"Stakeout?" I cut in. "Cool. Will you be sitting in a car, drinking bad coffee, and watching some nefarious alchemist roam the shadows?"

He chuckled. "You watch too many movies. It's a nightclub."

I grunted. "Not an alchemist then."

"Actually." He stopped.

"Don't leave me hanging, Agent Lawson. Anyone I know?"

"That depends. You want to level with me?"

"Level?"

"Those bullets you make are the work of a master."

"I keep one chained in the basement."

"Now, Addie."

I bit my lip. I wanted in on this. If he tailed an alchemist, it might be someone I knew. Someone who could help shine some light on what happened to the Alchemica, and by extension, what happened to me. Maybe I wasn't the only one to survive. My heart beat harder considering it. And if my growing suspicions were right, Lawson might be the guy to lead me to him.

"Here's the deal," I said. "Let me tag along, and I'll level with you."

"Tag along?"

"If I'm who you think I am, I might be able to ID this guy."

Silence. I could almost hear the wheels turning.

"Being a Sensitive isn't going to help you get close to an alchemist." A little blackmail never hurts.

"All right," Lawson said. "We'll meet early, before he gets there. We can have a little chat first."

"Sounds good. Where and when?"

"I could pick you up."

"This isn't a date. Where and when?"

He sighed and then rattled off the details. I wrote down the address and ended the call.

"Well?" Rowan took the phone from me and returned it to the charging cradle.

"Lawson is in town tailing an alchemist. That's all I know. I'm going to meet him at a nightclub tonight."

Rowan propped an elbow on the arm of his chair and rubbed his chin. "Did he say why he's so interested in you?"

"He knows that those bullets were made by a master. *How* is one of several questions I want answered."

"And are you going to level with him? If he insists on seeing your arms?"

I'd already considered that. "I intend for him to see my arms, but he won't see my tattoos." I gestured at my pack where it lay on the desk between us. "Shall I show you?"

"The cream?" James asked. He turned to Rowan. "It's the coolest thing."

Rowan considered us both and then nodded.

I turned and grinned at James. Finally, we were back in the chase to find some answers. "Want to take me dancing?"

James returned my grin. "Sounds like fun."

My night out wasn't going to be as much fun as I thought—

not that I really thought it would be. I'm not a social butterfly; I'm an alchemist. Give me a beaker, a hot plate, and a few random ingredients, and I'm happy. Make me spend the evening at a nightclub, and well, a root canal is suddenly looking like a great alternative. But my social apathy wasn't the problem tonight. It was the company I was forced to keep.

We stopped across the street from the neon monstrosity that was our destination and observed a moment of silence.

I cleared my throat. "An alchemist, an Element, and a grim walk into a bar..."

"It's a club," James said.

"Why do you get top billing?" Rowan asked.

"It's my joke," I said.

"What's the punch line?"

"Why do we need you again?"

"That's not all that funny."

I sighed and started across the street. Rowan, Lord of Flames and Wit. At least they give you Novocain with a root canal.

"Quit fidgeting," Rowan said as we stepped up on the curb.

"I don't understand why you wouldn't let me have my vials."

"You don't need them when you're with me."

The egotistical— I took a deep breath and forced myself to hold my tongue.

"Besides, where would you put them?" he continued.

I released the breath I'd just taken. "I hate this. I feel naked."

"Without your potions or in that outfit?"

I glared at him and kept walking. I wasn't comfortable in these clothes, but Era had insisted. With Rowan's help, she had found me suitable clothing for this outing. I'd suggested something sleeveless, but the open back and short skirt had been her idea. As we drew near the line outside the club, I could see that she was right. The young women, most with bare arms crossed against the chill, wore as little as I did.

"You look good." Rowan's warm breath brushed against my ear. I jumped in surprise at his nearness. I'd been so intent on our surroundings that I hadn't seen him lean down.

He straightened. "Follow me."

He took the lead, and I frowned at his back. I couldn't even exchange an eye roll with James; he was busy studying the crowd. Era had settled on the bad boy look for my sidekick. The distressed jeans and fitted black T-shirt suited him. More than one girl elbowed her neighbor as we passed. Well, the girls who weren't watching Rowan. He wore black slacks and a black button-up shirt of some silky material. He'd rolled up the sleeves and left the buttons open at his throat, but even that attempt at casualness didn't take away from his presence. The man moved through the crowd like he owned it, and no one challenged him. It wasn't the clothing, and without the gray robes, no one knew his identity as Flame Lord. He commanded respect on attitude alone.

Rowan led us straight to the front of the line. A mumbled word and a handshake with the bouncer, and we were through the doors and into the dark, bass-pumping atmosphere. I'd pointed out before we arrived that neither James nor I had any identification on us. I guess Rowan had been right about it not being a problem.

He didn't hesitate, but led us to the upper level in the back, overlooking the rest of the club. Lawson said he'd meet me here, but he wasn't at any of the tables.

"Have you been here before?" I asked Rowan.

"No." He pulled out a high-backed stool from the nearest table and held it for me. I let him help me into the chair. "I'll send you a drink. What'll you have?" He and James would be waiting at the bar while I met with Lawson.

As always, the personal question threw me. What did I like to drink? Did I drink?

"Addie?" Rowan prompted.

"Surprise me."

He nodded and then he and James headed for the bar.

I turned my attention to the crowd, looking for Lawson or his mystery alchemist. Fearing I'd give too much away, I hadn't asked Lawson if he sought an Alchemica alchemist. If he did, I had no clue why he'd look in a place like this. Assuming my fellow alchemists were like me, this would be the last place they'd want to spend an evening.

A waitress stopped at my table to deliver a drink in a long-stemmed glass. I took a tentative sip and smiled to myself. Not bad. I guess Rowan was better at selecting my drinks than my T-shirts.

Low voices drew my attention to the next table, and the trio of young men gathered around it.

"Seriously, man, it's amazing," a guy in a loud paisley shirt told his friend. He sat something down in front of him and I stared in surprise. A vial.

"It'll ramp you up," Paisley said.

His friend eyed the vial and licked his thin lips.

"Brady tried it," Paisley said, waving a hand toward the third young man. "Last weekend."

"Yeah, man," Brady said. "It was a trip. Next pay day, I'm going to up the dosage."

"You felt the magic?" Thin Lips asked.

Magic? I doubted that.

"It was such a rush," Brady agreed.

Thin Lips picked up the vial, glancing around them. He caught me watching and got to his feet. A gesture, and he led his companions away.

I sighed and turned back to my drink. Nice. It seemed magic had even made its way into the recreational drugs. Or at least it was advertised as such. It probably wasn't legitimate. No wonder alchemists had such a bad name. Anyone could mix some crap, call it a potion, and claim to be an alchemist.

I went back to scanning the crowd and noticed a few other vials trading hands in the darkness. This must have been what led Lawson to this place. I'd have to ask him...if he ever made an appearance.

The skin crawled between my shoulder blades, and I twisted around to check behind me. The dim lighting left the cluster of couches along the back wall in shadow. I couldn't pick out any particular person watching me, but between the darkness and the crowd, I couldn't tell.

Shaking off the sensation, I turned back to my drink. Lawson must be running late.

I hadn't worn a watch, so I didn't know how long I sat there by myself. I'd eaten most of the peanuts in the bowl on the table and my third drink stood half empty when James returned. He sat his beer on the table and took a seat beside me.

I glanced at his beverage, but decided not to tease him about being underage. "I think I've been stood up," I said instead.

"His loss. That's a great look."

It took me a moment to realize he referred to my clothes. I threw a peanut at him. He snapped it out of the air and popped it in his mouth.

"Yeah, I can go work the corner when we're through here."

"It's not that bad. Hot, but tasteful."

"Thanks, but I'm a jeans and T-shirt gal."

"Or black robes. That concealing cream is awesome. You can't see your tattoos at all."

I glanced down at my upper arms. The absence of my tattoos left me feeling even more naked—if that was possible.

"Where'd Rowan go?" I wanted to tell him about my observations and see if he'd heard of any recreational drugs in the form of potions. Plus, I'd had about enough of this place. "I hope we're leaving."

"It's not a bad place."

Maybe to an eighteen year old. "Too noisy." I nodded toward the dance floor. "And sweaty."

James laughed. "You sound like an old woman."

I chucked another peanut, which he caught and ate. "You could scoot closer to the bowl. You needn't insult me to get some peanuts."

He smiled and leaned over to grab a handful. "What? You're always telling me you're older than me."

"Not old enough to be your mother." I glanced toward the bar. "Oh, joy. Look who's about to *grace* us with his presence."

James snorted and ate a few more peanuts as Rowan approached the table.

"What's with the frown?" Rowan took the third stool, a tumbler full of an amber liquid in hand. "Club not to your liking?"

"Do you like it?"

"It's a bit loud." He took a sip from his glass.

James laughed. "See?"

"What?" Rowan asked.

"He's accusing us of being old."

"I prefer mature."

"That's it?" I asked. "No argument? Or do you not have the same aging concerns as the rest of us?"

He gave me a smirk and took another sip from his glass.

"How old are you?" I asked.

"How old are you?"

"I asked first."

He set his glass on the table and leaned forward to fold his arms beside it. "I was thirty-seven when the magic came back."

I did the math and blinked. "You're fifty-six?"

"I will be next month."

Holy crap. "You don't even look thirty-seven."

He grinned, and I noticed those faint laugh lines in the corners of his eyes again. "Thank you." He lifted his glass in salute and leaned back in his chair once more. "Now that we've discovered how little I belong here, we can finish these drinks and—"

"Excuse me," a voice said beside me. A pretty blonde stood between James and me. "Would you like to dance?" she asked James.

I had to fight the urge to giggle at his surprised expression.

"Um, we were—" he began.

"Go on," I cut in. "Don't let us old farts hold you back."

He and the girl both gave me a frown, though for different reasons I suspected.

"Addie," James tried again.

"My brother's a little shy," I told the girl. "Go on, James. It took a lot of courage for…" I arched a questioning brow at the girl.

"Tasha." She smiled.

"For Tasha to ask," I finished.

James shook his head, but got to his feet. "Thank you," he said to the girl. "You old folks enjoy yourselves." He led the girl toward the dance floor.

I propped my chin on my hand and watched them walk away.

"You look pleased with yourself," Rowan said.

"I've been trying for months to get him to acknowledge the interest girls show in him."

"He's a grim."

"So? He's adorable." James had made it to the dance floor. "And damn, the boy can move." I guess I shouldn't be surprised, what with the animal grace and all.

"Boy? You've got what, a couple of months on him?" Rowan returned to the prior topic of my age.

I took a sip from my glass.

"I've been wondering how someone barely out of high school could rack up nine bands." He glanced at my upper arms where my tattoos should be. "I understood it took decades."

"I'm a prodigy?"

"You sound uncertain."

"No, that would be annoyed."

He leaned up and braced his elbows on the table once more. "And why is that?"

"You already know too much about me," I turned his previous words back on him.

He caught my jest and that smirk appeared. "I don't know how you dance."

"Excuse me?"

"Dance with me."

"I..."

"No respect for the courage it took me to ask?"

"Please. You do not lack the courage."

"Then shall we show the children that we're not the fuddy-duddies you claim?"

Hearing Rowan use such a term made me laugh. I couldn't help it, though I suspected the three drinks had something to do with it.

He grinned and got to his feet. "Come on, alchemist, or do you lack the courage to try something new?"

"How do you know this is new?" I didn't know that.

"Just a guess."

I frowned, annoyed that he'd think me so unworldly—even if I was.

"Is this all part of your master plan? Take my vials, get me drunk, and have me make a fool of myself. Vengeance is yours."

"If I wanted to get you back, it wouldn't be like that."

"Yeah. Way too complicated for you."

"Wow, you must really be afraid if you have to resort to insults."

"I'm not afraid."

He held out a hand. "Prove it."

"Fine." I took his hand. He'd intentionally goaded me into this. I knew it, and I'd given in anyway. Bizarre. He pulled me to my feet and my head spun.

"Careful," Rowan said and put a hand on my hip to steady me. "Maybe you should have stopped at two."

"You've had at least as many, and I suspect yours were stronger." I had no idea why I argued that point.

"I'm a lot bigger than you." He probably thought he could get the better of me now that I was a little tipsy. His hand moved to the small of my back and steered me toward the dance floor.

All right, no more alcohol. I'd been denied my alchemical protection; I couldn't let my mental abilities be impaired as well.

Lost in my musings, I didn't notice that we'd reached the dance floor until Rowan stopped. "Oh God. I'm going to need another drink."

Rowan chuckled, took my hand and pulled me out among the gyrating bodies.

This couldn't be happening. Me, dancing at a nightclub with an Element. The Flame Lord, no less. Maybe this was all a bizarre dream. Or maybe I still lay in the ashes of the Alchemica, my mind turned to mush.

It wasn't hard to feel the music. The thumping techno beat vibrated the floor beneath my feet, and all I had to do was move with it. I might have been premature in praising James's dancing skill. In his own way, Rowan moved just as well. Bastard. I had yet to discover something he couldn't do.

The crowd parted and suddenly James joined us with Tasha

tow. He grinned at me, and I gave him a wink. "Having fun?" he leaned over to ask.

"Can't you tell?"

James laughed at the obvious sarcasm and danced beside me. Tasha stared at him in wide-eyed wonder. Normally, I would have been more critical of the skimpy outfit she wore, but I was firmly ensconced in my house of glass, so I kept my opinion to myself.

A crowd of Tasha's friends joined us, and before long, I found myself dancing with people I didn't even know. Strange men danced close, light touches and smiles among the heat and moving bodies. I looked around, trying to find James, but my height put me at a disadvantage.

Hands settled on my hips and a male body pressed against my back. Laughing, I glanced over my shoulder and met familiar gray eyes rather than the green I expected. Rowan grinned at my surprise, but I refused to let him intimidate me. Instead, I leaned back and continued to dance, my movements now in sync with his. I expected a few beats of dirty dancing. I didn't expect his hands to slide down over my lower stomach and press me tight against him.

"Rowan!" I forced a laugh and stepped away before turning to face him. He grinned and continued to dance. Amused, I shook my head and joined him. Yep, the Flame Lord had an ornery streak.

Rowan closed the distance between us and pulled me into something like a waltz. I laughed at how ridiculous we must look.

"You're showing your age," I told him.

"Am I?" He pulled me closer like the couples around us. "Is this better?"

How to answer that? Pressed so close, I couldn't help but notice the muscle beneath the black silk, or the way his warm hands slid over the bare skin of my back. I glanced up and found him watching me. His gray eyes were hooded, but I still caught a glimpse of burning orange around his pupils. Was the room so warm from the press of dancing bodies or something a little more Elemental?

He leaned down. "You're thinking again." His lips brushed my ear as he spoke, and hot as I was, chill bumps rose. "What about?"

I needed a reprieve. Distance. Time. Something. "I'm thirsty," I blurted.

"I can fix that." He slid an arm behind my back and guided me through the press to the bar. I guess I wasn't going to get the distance. Maybe I should have said I needed to use the restroom.

We worked our way through the crowd, and I slipped into a slim gap at one end of the bar. Rowan stood behind me with his hands on my shoulders. It wasn't like I blocked his view—he could almost rest his chin on the top of my head if he wished.

The barmaid standing closest to us looked up from the drink she was mixing and gave Rowan a smile. "Back again? What'll it be?"

While he ordered, I caught the dark looks from several patrons who'd been waiting longer. Oddly, no one said anything. Curious, I turned to look at Rowan.

"What?" he asked. Dark brows rose over those unusual gray eyes. What was it about this man that commanded such instant respect from everyone? Well, everyone but me.

"How do you do that?" I asked.

"Do what?"

"Get your way all the time. No waiting in line outside. No waiting at the bar."

"I tip well."

I frowned. "No."

He propped a foot on the rail beside my ankles. "Yes." His

hand found my waist again, his warm palm sliding around to the bare skin of my back. "How do you get your skin so soft? An alchemical secret?"

The question threw me. "Are you coming on to me?"

"You just noticed?"

Whoa. "I'm an alchemist, remember?" I lowered my voice. "Your sworn enemy."

"I don't believe I swore anything of the sort."

"You drunk?"

"Buzzing pleasantly." His hand rose to my cheek. "You?"

Warmth crept up my neck, though the brush of his fingers made me want to shiver. "The same."

"I remember kissing you in the kitchen. I liked it." He watched my mouth as he spoke.

"Are you going to kiss me again?"

His eyes rose to mine. "Will you expect another glass if I do?"

"I'm never going to live that down, am I?"

He chuckled and I could feel the rumble beneath the hand I'd placed on his chest—whether to push him away or not, I hadn't decided.

"You're not afraid of me at all, are you?" he asked.

"Nope."

He leaned over to my ear. "I've been known to lose my temper and ignite things I shouldn't."

Ah, a little insight into his burn phobia. "I'm not afraid of you," I whispered.

He moved back enough so I could focus on his face. Orange encircled his pupils again, but it was such a slim line, I doubted it was visible to those around us. I wondered why he kept doing that. I considered asking, but before I could, he leaned in and covered my mouth with his.

My hands fisted in his shirt, but I didn't push him away.

Instead, I kissed him back, parting my lips to let him in. The faint scent of his cologne took me back to our first meeting, and I discovered that I remembered the particulars very well. Unfortunately, my mind hadn't exaggerated his skill.

I pulled back and he did the same. "Your eyes are glowing," I whispered.

"I'm hot."

I snorted. "You have a high opinion of yourself."

He grinned and his eyelids lowered over his blazing eyes. His full lips were damp and flushed from our kiss, and I wanted to kiss him again.

What was wrong with me? I pushed him back, but he caught my wrist.

"Addie?"

"I need to visit the ladies' room."

He frowned. "No, you're running."

"I've had too much to drink. Let me go."

He studied me a moment longer and then released my wrist. I hurried away and didn't look back.

I SPENT MORE TIME THAN necessary in the restroom trying to regain my composure, or at least sober up. No more alcohol. Dear God, I'd kissed Rowan—again. He might be attractive, but shouldn't I at least like the guy before sticking my tongue in his mouth?

I remembered those glowing eyes and shivered. Apparently, they didn't only glow when he lit fires—unless you counted the one he lit in me. Damn it. I hadn't even told him about the vials I'd seen around the club. I'd come here for a reason, and making out with Rowan wasn't it. I needed to go find James. His common sense would straighten me out.

My goal in mind, I left my refuge and walked out into the

dimly lit hall. The ladies' room and men's room lay at opposite ends of a corridor that was bisected by an opening back to the club. An exit sign glowed over a door across from the opening, casting a red haze over the area. I'd nearly reached the entrance to the club when a man stepped into the hall, but he didn't head toward the men's room. Glancing over his shoulder, he hit the release bar on the exit door and stepped outside. Light spilled across his face for a moment, catching on his blond hair.

I stopped where I stood and watched the door begin to swing closed. At the last instant, I hurried forward and followed the man outside. I'd recognized him, and for a girl with no memory, a familiar face was not something to be ignored.

A well-lit parking lot greeted me. The man hurried away along the back wall of the club, but glanced over his shoulder when the door slammed shut. He stumbled when he saw me. Memories surged, but the young man before me didn't match the image of the sixty-year-old man from my memories.

"Emil?" My voice was little more than a whisper, but he stopped and stared. He slipped a hand behind his back and I tensed. "Grand Master, it's me," I said a little louder. I hoped he knew who I was—that'd make one of us.

"It can't be," he said.

My doubts vanished. That wonderfully familiar voice set off a volley of images ricocheting through my skull. The lab and years of experiments with one familiar figure running through them all. An older man with graying blond hair.

"Emil," I whispered, lost in the memories.

Hands gripped my shoulders. I blinked and looked up into his familiar face. Or was it? How was it possible that we looked the same age? His shocked expression matched my own, and then his brow wrinkled in what looked like apprehension.

I gripped his wrists while he held my shoulders. "Tell me you know me. Or did they get you, too?"

"Get me?"

"I remember nothing before the night the Alchemica burned. Nothing except alchemy."

The youthful face of my mentor frowned. "Nothing?"

I shook my head. "What happened? I thought you were dead." Tears slid down my cheeks, but I ignored them. "Please tell me you know me."

A familiar smile—minus the lines at the corners—curled his lips. "Of course, I know you." His hands rose to cup my face. "I thought *you* were dead."

"Not dead, lost." I cried in earnest now. "So lost."

He opened his mouth to answer when a crash sounded behind us. I spun and instinctively reached behind my waistband for the potions that weren't there. Damn it, Rowan.

Smoke suddenly billowed around me, and I dropped into a crouch. Fingers brushed my shoulder before slipping away. I opened my mouth to call out to Emil and pulled in a lung full of smoke. It wasn't smoke; it was Knockout Gas. And thanks to Rowan, I didn't have the antidote on me. Had Emil thrown the grenade in our defense? If so, he'd gotten the ratio of powder to propellant just right. I smiled and my world went dark.

CHAPTER 12

I WOKE CHOKING ON AMMONIA FUMES. My eyes flew open and focused on a hand holding a slim vial inches from my face. Smelling salts. I jerked back and smacked my head on the wall behind me.

The man with the salts squatted beside the cot I lay on, but rose to his feet as I sat up.

"Who are you?" I rubbed the back of my head, squinting up at him in the low light.

He didn't answer. Instead, he capped the vial and set it on the table beside my narrow bed before moving toward the door on the far wall.

I lowered my arm and caught a glimpse of the black bands encircling my biceps. I'd been out at least three hours if the concealing cream had worn off. James and Rowan had lost me.

The man reached the door and flipped the light switch. Bright florescent light replaced the dim emergency glow. Squinting, I glanced around the small windowless room. It was little more than a closet with nondescript beige walls and matching commercial-grade carpet. A second cot sat against the opposite wall, the small table between. I hadn't a clue where I was.

"It really is you," the man said, drawing my attention back to him.

Something about his voice stirred my memory, but it didn't set off the disorienting ricochet that seeing Emil had. I looked him over, trying to link the familiar voice with the man before me. Gray colored his brown hair at the temples and a slight paunch beneath the open sport coat marked him as middle-aged. An average looking guy of average height. I wouldn't have looked twice if we'd passed on the street.

"You know me?" I got to my feet.

Dark brows descended over brown eyes, and he closed the distance between us. "Did you think I wouldn't?"

I stepped back, uncertain of his intentions. "You don't understand."

"Oh, I understand." His eyes dropped to the tattoos encircling my arms and he frowned. "You insult me, Amelia."

I started to respond and stopped. "Who?"

"Me. You insult me. Why—"

"No, I meant, what name did you call me?"

He crossed his arms and pursed his lips as he seemed to contemplate whether to answer.

"Amelia was it?" The name didn't trigger any memories. "I think you have the wrong person."

He barked a short laugh. "Do you really think I'd fall for that? I've known you since you were twenty-three."

Twenty-three? I didn't look much older than that now, but even a short-term acquaintance wasn't something I could ignore. I took a step closer before I thought better of it. "Who am I?"

His eyes narrowed. "Testing me, I see. Okay, I'll play along. You're Amelia Daulton, master alchemist and according to Emil, his most promising protégé." He spoke the last words in an accurate mimic of Emil's voice. So accurate that I had to grip the table as the déjà vu made my head spin.

When I blinked my eyes back into focus, he was frowning at me.

"Who *are* you?" I asked.

He studied me for one long moment, his countenance no longer amused. "Why the—"

"Who are you?" I repeated with more force.

"Neil Dunstan."

Neil. Another wave of déjà vu washed over me, but oddly, no memories surfaced.

"Amelia?" He gripped my shoulders.

"I don't remember," I admitted.

"Don't remember what?"

"You. Me. Anything. Nothing before the night the Alchemica burned. Nothing except alchemy."

"Are you serious?" Neil straightened, his arms falling to his sides.

"Very. So you can stop acting all pissy because I don't remember you."

The door opened, and we both turned to face the newcomer.

"What's taking so long? You were supposed to revive her and bring her to me." Agent Lawson stepped into the room.

"You." I fisted my hands as his gaze settled on me. He'd set me up, used me to try to catch Emil. It occurred to me that when he'd come to the gun shop, he'd been looking for a man. It'd been Emil all along. I didn't know what part Neil had played, but I wasn't about to stand around and find out.

I snatched up the vial of smelling salts and pulled off the cap in the same motion. An irritant, the weak solution of ammonium carbonate wouldn't do much…unless it connected with something sensitive. I slung the contents in Lawson's face and bolted for the door. Neil didn't try to stop me.

The same shade of beige colored the hall outside my room, but the worn commercial-grade carpet was a few shades darker. Definitely an office building of some sort, and judging by the elevator at one end, a multi-story building. Perhaps downtown?

I didn't stop to figure it out, but sprinted down the corridor—or tried to in my heeled boots and tight skirt. I didn't have time to wait on an elevator. I needed the stairs.

The smell of coffee wafted out of a small break room on my right. A man and a woman stood before a vending machine and looked up as I ran past.

Footsteps thumped on the carpeted hall behind me, but I didn't turn to see who it was. Perhaps Neil had decided to come after me, or maybe it was the man or woman from the break room. It wouldn't be Lawson. An ammonia solution to the face should take him out for a bit.

The elevator dinged and slid open. I skidded to a halt and gasped as James stepped off the car, followed by a pair of robed Elements: Rowan and Donovan.

"Addie!" James leapt across the space separating us and pulled me into a painfully tight embrace.

"Freeze," a voice said from behind us.

I looked back and my jaw dropped open. Lawson stood only feet away. Liquid coated his cheeks, but he didn't even blink as he trained the gun on me. I must have missed his eyes.

James's unnatural snarl coated my skin in gooseflesh.

"James, wait," Rowan said.

Without warning, James released me and sprang forward.

I reached for him. "Don't—"

The report of the gun deafened me in the enclosed space.

"James!"

He rocked back with the impact, but didn't go down.

"Shit!" Lawson scrambled back, raising his gun once more.

Gray robes filled my peripheral vision to either side.

"The gun," Rowan said.

"I got it," Donovan answered. Neither sounded that excited.

Lawson pulled the trigger and the gun clinked. He tried

again and again, backing away when James took an unsteady step toward him, then another.

"James." A note of admonishment entered Rowan's tone.

Without warning, James sprang and caught Lawson by the throat, slamming him against the wall. With one arm, James held him off the floor.

"She was in your line of fire." His words were a barely intelligible snarl.

Lawson choked, unable to respond. His gun clattered to the floor as he used both hands to cling to James's wrist.

The people from the break room charged forward, guns leveled on James. More agents? Suddenly their weapons went up in a white-hot blaze of light.

"Enough!" Rowan shouted. "James, release him."

I belatedly realized that James still held Lawson. I couldn't let him strangle the guy. I stepped forward and gripped James by the forearm. "It's okay. Let him go."

James didn't respond, though he'd quit snarling. His breath wheezed in and out, but he didn't seem to notice.

"James, please." I tugged at his arm.

He finally relented, and Lawson slid to the floor at our feet. I pushed James back a few paces to give Lawson some air. James continued to glare at the downed agent, eyes at full glow, but he wrapped an arm around his ribs. A hole marred his shirt on the lower left side of his chest. Through the rent in the fabric, I could see the wound the bullet had left in his flesh. The lack of blood unsettled me. If someone opened fire on a wax manikin, I imagined it would look the same.

"What's the meaning of this, Your Grace?" An older man in a gray suit had joined us, several more men and women following.

"Director." Rowan dipped his hooded head in the man's direction, confirming my suspicions that these were the PIA offices. "I came to collect what was taken from me." To my surprise, his hand came to rest on my shoulder. "She was under my protection. My personal protection."

"But she's an alchemist. She's human." The director's agents gathered behind him, but no one pulled a weapon—or spoke.

"She's mine." Rowan's tone left no room for argument. His statement grated, but I didn't want to argue while we had a PIA audience. I'd save it for later.

The director glanced between us. "I didn't know," he finally said.

Nice. It seemed that the director of the PIA, the man who kept order among the magical, caved to Rowan's will as quickly as the next man.

"Bill me for the guns." Rowan turned away.

"And the burns?" Waylon asked.

"There aren't any." Rowan turned back toward the elevator and Donovan joined him. James and I hurried to follow. I remembered the time Rowan had incinerated a gun James held. It hadn't burned him, but I credited that to James's natural immunity to fire. I guess that wasn't the case. I'd have to ask how that worked sometime.

"Wait," Director Waylon stopped us. "There's still the matter of the formula—"

I turned to face him. "What formula?"

"The Final Formula."

"What?"

"We believe your Grand Master may have found the Final Formula."

I remembered Emil's youthful face and a wave of despair washed over me. I braced a hand against the elevator doorframe. He'd beaten me to it. Emil had found the Final Formula first. My life's work. The culmination of—

"No," I whispered. The sound of my own voice brought me

back. I shook my head trying to dispel the foreign emotion. Where had that come from?

"Addie?" Rowan stepped up behind me.

The surge of disappointment faded, the emotion so distant it seemed to belong to someone else. Goosebumps rose on my arms. Had I connected to the person I once was? Rowan claimed that all Alchemica alchemists were obsessed with finding the Final Formula. Maybe he was right.

"Your Grand Master didn't discover the Final Formula?" the director asked.

"I—"

A thump sounded, and I looked back to find James slumped in the corner of the elevator.

"I've got to go."

"Miss Daulton," the director said.

"Your agent shot my friend. He needs medical attention." I stepped back onto the elevator. "You know where to find me."

The director frowned, but didn't argue. The elevator door slid closed between us.

I moved to James's side.

"Hey." I gripped his arm. "How bad is it?"

"I'll be okay," he breathed.

"Your Grand Master?" Rowan leaned against the wall beside the control panel, his face in shadow beneath his hood.

"He's alive." I turned to smile up at James. "Emil's alive. I saw him outside the club. The PIA gassed us, but he got away."

"He abandoned you?" Rowan asked.

I rounded on him. "He probably expected me to have the Knockout Gas antidote—like any alchemist would—but some asshole took my vials and left me defenseless."

The elevator stopped and the doors slid open. Without a word, Rowan exited. I followed, still fuming.

"Amelia?" Neil waited not far away. He must have run down

the stairs to catch us. He walked over and offered me a manila folder. "Your file. Or as much as they'd share with me."

I studied it a moment before plucking it from Neil's hand. "Why give me this?"

He leaned closer to whisper, "It might help you remember—and then you'll know why."

"That's cryptic as hell."

He smiled and handed me a business card. "Should you need to reach me." He nodded to the others. "Gentlemen." Without another word, he stepped onto the elevator and the doors slid closed.

"Amelia?" Rowan prompted.

"That's who they think I am." I held up the folder.

He hesitated, then turned toward the lobby doors. "You can explain in the car."

It was then that I noticed the silence in the lobby. At least a dozen people were standing around the large room. All were staring at us.

Donovan held the door and we followed Rowan outside. A flash of light exploded in my face, then another. It took me a second to realize that it was a camera. More flashes followed us down the steps to the waiting limo.

"Your Grace!"

"Your Grace!"

A couple of reporters clamored for Rowan's attention, then they saw me. With my bare arms in clear view, it didn't take long before the words Alchemica alchemist were on their lips. Rowan didn't slow until he reached the car. He stood to the side while we entered, and climbed in last. He never did answer the reporters.

"Must be a slow news day," I muttered.

"It's always like this when we show up at the PIA offices in the limo and robes," Donovan said. "I suspect the doorman tips off the media."

I sat beside James, and Rowan and Donovan took the seat across from us. The white leather seats and gray carpet gave the small space an expansive feel.

"Do you need to go to the hospital?" I asked James.

"I need to change," he answered in an airy whisper.

"Can you do it here?"

"Not enough room."

"We'll be at the office in ten minutes," Rowan said. He leaned his head back, but didn't bother to lower the hood. The sunlight filtering through the tinted windows illuminated his unshaven lower face. His lips pressed together in a thin line before he spoke. "I'm very disappointed in you, James. You might have damaged my relationship with the PIA." He sounded more tired than angry.

James didn't immediately respond. When I opened my mouth to argue his case, James gripped my arm. "Addie was between us." James's words came out soft and pained. "When he drew his weapon—"

"No," Rowan cut him off. "I asked you to wait and you didn't. You frightened him, and he recognized you for the predator you are. The fault wasn't his." Rowan leaned up and the hood slid back off his head. He looked like a man who'd been up all night. His pale skin emphasized the dark circles under his eyes. "You make the rest of us look bad."

"But I'm not yours. I'm…Old Magic."

Rowan leaned his head back and closed his eyes. "You're mine."

James bowed his head. "Thank you. I'm sorry."

Rowan didn't respond.

"Rowan, are you okay?" I asked.

"Headache," he muttered.

I met Donovan's eyes and saw worry reflected there.

We arrived at the Elemental Offices nine minutes later. It had been a silent trip. James curled in on himself, his breathing shallow. Rowan appeared to have fallen asleep. When the limo stopped, Donovan touched his knee. He straightened without comment and both men pulled up their hoods before climbing out.

Donovan hung back to help James from the car. James managed without help, but walked doubled-over up the sidewalk to the big Victorian house. I knew bullet wounds weren't fatal to him, but it really bothered me to see him in pain. Once inside, Donovan quickly ushered him from the room. Rowan exchanged a few words with the receptionist, who'd come to her feet when we entered, then he showed me to the library.

I recognized the room from my first and only visit to the Elemental Offices. The time I hit Rowan with my truth serum. I hoped he wasn't remembering the same thing.

Rowan closed the door and pushed back his hood. "So what did that agent give you?" He led me to the large oval table that took up one side of the room. Morning sunlight shown through the opaque drapes providing plenty of natural light.

"I don't think he's an agent. He claimed to know me."

"You didn't know him?"

I laid the folder on the table, but didn't open it. Time to tell him everything—as much as I hated to. "I have amnesia. The burning of the Alchemica is my earliest memory. Beyond that, all I remember is alchemy."

"Amnesia doesn't work like that." He studied me with shadowed eyes. "Unless it was a potion. Was it?"

"How would I know?"

He grunted. "Why didn't you tell me?"

"It didn't seem pertinent."

"And now it does? Why?"

I didn't answer. Instead I opened the folder. The first page was a standard database form. The column headers across the top of the page were: name, age, date of birth, and other personal information. Most of fields below them were empty.

Rowan leaned forward, reading the form along with me. "Amelia Daulton, age forty-two. This is who the PIA thinks you are?"

I pointed to a line further down the page. "I suspect this is why. She's the only female master." Though that couldn't be right. I was a master alchemist, but I'd never heard of Amelia Daulton.

I turned the page and found myself staring at a photo of four people: me, Emil, and two young men. One was Neil.

The caption beneath the photo stated that it had been taken eighteen years ago—one year after magic returned—at the founding of the Alchemica. I looked heavier, but not any older than I did now. Emil looked like a man well into middle age. Nothing like the man I'd met last night. And Neil looked barely out of his teens.

With a shaking hand, I turned another page. The next picture was taken last spring in front of the still-standing Alchemica. A white-haired Emil stood beside a pudgy, middle-aged woman I knew intimately.

"Dear God, is that you?" Rowan asked.

I flipped the folder closed and backed away from the table.

"I don't know," I whispered.

"Addie?" James stepped up beside me and I jumped. As usual, I hadn't heard him enter. Though it surprised me to see Donovan with him. The big guy could move quietly as well.

"What's wrong?" James asked.

I gestured at the folder, unable to speak. The PIA agents had been right. I was Amelia Daulton. A forty-two-year-old master alchemist. I ran my hand through my loose hair. Why didn't the name stir any memories? I'd had varying degrees of déjà vu upon hearing both Emil's and Neil's names. Yet my own name stirred nothing inside me.

James studied the contents of the folder, flipping through the pages. "Dear God," he whispered, just as Rowan had earlier. I bit my lip to keep the hysterical laughter at bay. Kind of funny to hear a hellhound swear like that.

James raised wide eyes to mine. "You're forty-two?"

I took a deep breath, trying to calm myself. "Maybe?"

He stared at me.

"Told you I was older than you." I tried to smile, but the joke fell flat.

"Twenty-two maybe." He gave his head a shake and turned his attention back to the folder.

"I need to find Emil." I looked at Rowan. "I saw him last night at the club. He didn't look much over twenty-two either."

Everyone took a moment to absorb that. "What do you think happened?" Rowan asked.

"I think Emil found the Final Formula." Just as the director suspected.

"The what?" Donovan asked.

"The Elixir of Life." Rowan's voice softened. "It's what every alchemist throughout time has searched for. It grants eternal life and youth."

All three men looked at me.

"I think that's what Neil, the guy who gave me the folder, concluded when he saw me. He's in the first picture." I gestured toward the table.

"You're immortal?" James asked.

I shrugged, unwilling to consider that. I hadn't come to terms with Emil finding the Formula yet, let alone what it meant if I had taken it.

Rowan turned and left the room. Was he angry? Sick? I could see it in his eyes that his headache was hitting him hard.

I dropped into the nearest chair while James told Donovan about my amnesia. He flipped through my file, but there weren't any other pictures and very little information aside from a list of eight formulas that had been registered in my name. As I'd noticed in my prior searches for information, Alchemica alchemists tended to be very secretive.

Rowan walked back into the room, a white envelope clutched in one hand. "The Grand Master's invitation," he said.

I rose from my chair to accept it. With an unsteady hand, I pulled the invitation from the envelope, noting the expensive cardstock, gold foil, and Emil's elaborate signature at the bottom. "We hope you'll join us to witness magic's evolution," I read aloud.

"He was going to announce that he'd found the Final Formula?" James asked.

I didn't know what else it could be. I studied the invitation and tried to get my mind around it.

"That's why the Alchemica was bombed," Donovan said. "Someone wanted to destroy this formula."

That made sense. And suddenly the list of suspects grew. "No member of the magical community would want us to have that knowledge."

"Nor any of the human extremists," James added.

"Well, at least they weren't targeting the Elements." I passed the invitation back to Rowan.

"Yes, there's that," Rowan whispered. He took the card back, and I noticed how his hand shook.

"Rowan?" I looked up in time to see a drop of crimson fall from his upper lip. It landed on the chest of his gray robes beside another drop. He swayed on his feet, and I reached for him. James reflexes were better. He caught him before he hit the floor.

CHAPTER 13

"**Y**ou're killing him," Cora said.

I looked up and found her standing in the library doorway, her blue eyes on me, not James who sat in the chair to my left. I hadn't seen her since she and Era arrived. They'd been upstairs with Rowan. I learned that he was prone to nasty headaches from time to time, though for such a common ailment, his fellow Elements seemed pretty worked up about it.

"Excuse me?" I asked.

"All this stress you've given him."

She blamed me for his headache? "I don't—"

"First the gun shop and now this." She waved a hand at the folder that still lay on the table. "How often has he used fire in your presence?"

I sat up a little straighter. "Many times. I haven't kept count."

Cora huffed, turned on her heel and left.

I caught James's eye. "There's more to this."

"I think so, yes."

"You up for some research?"

"What do you have in mind?"

I sent him to talk to Era. Maybe it was unethical to send the pretty boy to scoop the mentally challenged girl, but I was getting concerned.

James returned half an hour later, the expression on his face somber. He pulled the door closed and crossed to his chair. "According to my source, it's not good. But how reliable she is—"

"What did Era say?"

"Rowan's dying."

I straightened in my chair. "What? Now? From a headache? I thought he was immortal."

"Elements don't age, but they can die. It's not just a headache; it's a cumulative condition. Since the magic came back, he's been living on borrowed time."

"Because he's an Element?"

"A Fire Element. Apparently, they don't live long. Rowan's survived the longest. Remember the Japanese Fire Element that died a few years ago? He came in second. He lasted fifteen years."

"Oh God." I leaned back, gripping my hands in my lap. Rowan pissed me off more often than not, but I didn't want him to die. "Why don't they survive?"

"Something about the fire they create. The other Elements don't have any trouble. None of them have died the world over—well, except the European Elements." He grimaced.

I thought about the other Elements. Earth, water, and air. Solid, liquid, and gas. The three states of matter until science added a fourth: plasma. It took something special to reach that state. Since meeting Rowan, I'd watched him use his gift many times—and most of that had been because of me. My stomach clenched. Cora was right. I'd brought this on him. I had to fix it. I got to my feet.

"Where are you going?" James asked.

"To see Rowan. Maybe talk to Donovan—I know Cora won't listen. I might be able to find a solution."

"A potion."

"Of course."

He studied me with those intense green eyes and then gave me an odd little smile. "If this can be fixed, I bet you'll find a way."

My heart swelled at the praise. I could never understand why he had such faith in me. "Thanks, Fido." I hurried from the room.

THE DOOR TO THE ROOM where Rowan rested stood open a few inches. I brushed the varnished surface with my fingertips and the door swung inward without a sound. Pausing a few steps past the threshold, I let my eyes adjust to the dimly lit room. The heavy drapes had been drawn, blocking most of the morning sunshine.

"I wondered how long it'd be before you snuck in."

I whirled to face the shadows near the door, smothering a scream. Donovan sat in an oversized chair a few yards away. He rose to his feet and towered over me. "I'm glad you're here," he continued. "You can sit with him for a few. I need another cup of coffee."

I glanced across the room at the daybed shoved against the far wall. Rowan lay atop the covers, a shadowed shape in the low light. I hurried after Donovan and caught up to him in the hall. "Donovan?"

The big guy stopped and turned to face me.

"Era told us what's wrong. Is he…" I swallowed. "Is he going to die?"

Donovan sobered. "No. Not yet. But it's the worst I've seen him in a long time."

"This happens often?"

"The headaches, but they rarely incapacitate him."

"It's because he's had to use his gift so much lately."

Donovan's big hand came to rest on my shoulder, and I

jumped in spite of myself. "It's not your fault. It's his nature to help people." A hint of that fun-loving smile surfaced. "You've needed more help than most."

"I'll fix this, Donovan."

His smile softened. "Don't torture yourself. You're not to blame."

"You don't think I can? Look at me." I spread my arms. "I'm forty-two years old. This is the power of alchemy. I can do this."

He studied me, his hazel eyes glinting in the sunlight streaming through a window to my right. "If it's possible, I believe you will."

"Impossible is not in my vocabulary."

A final smile, and he turned and continued toward the stairs.

Not sure what to make of the big guy, I returned to the darkened room. The heavy drapes on the window closest to the bed let in a thin band of light that fell across the foot rail. Rowan lay on his side, facing me. He'd removed his robe and shoes, and I could see that, like James and me, he wore the same clothes he'd worn to the club. His face looked peaceful in sleep, but even in the dim light, his pallor showed. A day's worth of stubble covered his cheeks, and I couldn't help but smile. I'd never seen His Grace look anything less than immaculate.

I carefully sat down on the edge of the bed. When he didn't stir, I laid a hand on his forehead. The warmth of his skin surprised me. A basin of water sat on the nightstand, a damp washcloth draped over the side. I wet it and wrung out the excess before touching it to Rowan's forehead and temples.

"Cor?" Rowan rasped. His voice startled me.

"No."

He rolled back and turned his face toward me. My breath caught as I glimpsed the faint orange ring around his pupils. His eyes weren't the lamps James's were in the dimness, but they did give off a faint glow.

"Addie?"

"You sound like you could use a drink." I returned the washcloth to the bowl, picked up the empty glass, and walked to the bathroom to get cold water from the tap.

While I stood at the sink filling the glass, I glanced down and noticed the tissues in the wastebasket. Judging by the shape of the bloodstains, I'd guess them the remnants of his earlier nosebleed. An idea forming, I took one of the tissues and tucked it into my pocket before I carried the glass back into the bedroom.

Rowan had left the bed for a nearby chair. He'd tried to pull on his shoes, and currently had one on and one off. At the moment, his head rested against the back of the chair and his eyes were closed. Foolish man. I walked over and he opened his eyes. I sighed in relief that the orange glow had vanished.

"Here you go." I handed him the glass. He drained it in nearly one swallow.

"You didn't need to get up." I took back the glass and returned it to the nightstand.

"Cora will be back shortly with my medicine and then we'll be going."

"The blue stuff in the vial?"

Rowan frowned and I hurried on. "I was…trying to find the trunk release and came across them. Apothecary?"

He sighed. "Yes."

"Give me the info, and I'll blow his skills out of the water."

He chuckled and amusement finally won out over the pain in his eyes. "You have got to be the cockiest—"

"Me? Have you looked in a mirror lately?"

Head resting against the back of his chair, he smirked up at me, but the pain was returning to his eyes. Before I realized what I was doing, I reached out to touch those faint laugh lines. His expression sobered, and I forced myself not to jerk my hand away. I'd rather he didn't know how much my own reaction had unsettled me.

"You don't trust me to help you?" I asked.

"It has nothing to do with my trust in you."

I moved my fingers to his temple and began to gently massage. When he closed his eyes, my other hand moved to the opposite temple. "Then what is it?"

"Any knowledge I give you could be forcibly taken from you."

I worked my fingers back into his soft auburn hair and carefully massaged his scalp. He tipped his head forward, letting me work my way up over his crown. I stood between his knees now, my fingers having worked their way to the base of his skull.

"I won't betray you," I said.

"If it was only me, I wouldn't hesitate." He leaned forward and rested his forehead against my stomach. For an instant, I froze. It was an oddly vulnerable position on his part. Maybe he did trust me. My skin warmed at the thought.

I massaged my way down the back of his neck and slid my hands inside the open collar of his shirt to work on his shoulders. I bit my lip. He had great shoulders.

"Harder," he muttered and then groaned when I complied. The sound tightened the muscles below my navel, and I bit my lip harder. It's just a massage, I reminded myself. He's hurting and I'm relieving the pain. It makes him feel better. Donovan could be doing this and he'd still groan.

I revised my opinion when Rowan's arms came around me. His over-warm hands found the bare skin of my back. With a sigh, he pressed his cheek to my stomach. "Don't stop," he whispered when I hesitated.

"A soak in a hot bath might help."

"Want to join me?"

"Rowan."

"To continue the massage, of course."

The mental image almost stilled my hands. "Of course." I hoped I sounded more annoyed than intrigued.

"Rowan?" Cora asked from the doorway.

I jerked my hands out from beneath his shirt.

"What are you doing?" Her heels tapped out a staccato beat on the hardwood floor as she crossed the space between us.

"Did you get it?" Rowan released me and leaned back in his chair.

Cora glared at me, but she handed Rowan the familiar vial of blue liquid. He drank it without hesitation.

"I can do better," I said. "You don't have to tell me anything. I can tweak the apothecary's mixture. Let me try?"

"What?" Cora snapped. "No way in hell will I let you—"

"Cora." Donovan's deep voice carried from the door and I jumped in surprise. I hadn't noticed him, but I had been a bit distracted.

I ignored Cora and met Rowan's eyes. "Let me try?" I repeated.

He studied me for one long moment. "Drive her to the clinic, Donovan."

"Rowan!" Cora protested.

He ignored her and pulled on his other shoe. A deep breath and he pushed himself up out of his chair.

"Damn it, Rowan." This time Cora's tone was one of alarm. She pressed her hands to his chest to steady him, but he just smiled and cupped her cheek.

"It's okay, sis," he told her, his tone soft and understanding. "Help me with my robes?"

Donovan came forward, Rowan's robes in his hands. "Right here, my brother."

I left them to get ready and went to collect James. I found

him in the library with Era. Of all the crazy things, she had a camera, and at the moment, he was her subject.

James looked up. "Era's a photographer, Ad. Those photos in the sun room are hers."

"Really? Cool." I gave her a smile. "We're leaving. You two ready?"

Era grabbed James by the hand and pulled him toward the door. "It's so great that you guys get to spend the night again. We can watch movies." She looked up at James. "Do you like horror movies?"

"Sure." He gave me a grin. "But I bet Addie will be afraid."

"You can sit by me," Era told me solemnly. "We can have popcorn."

I thanked her and then herded them out into the hall in time to meet the other three Elements.

"Roe!" Era threw her arms around Rowan's waist and hugged him fiercely. "You're okay," she whispered against his robes.

"Yes." He ran a hand over her short blonde hair. "Pull up your hood, honey. We're going home."

Like Rowan, they all wore the same dark gray robes. Only the black symbols stitched around the hem varied. I found it amusing that they'd chosen alchemical symbols to represent their elements.

Era hurried to comply, and the six of us headed down the hall toward the lobby. We'd almost reached it when I heard the sound of voices.

"I don't care if he's in or not, I'm here to see her," a male voice said.

I knew that voice. I ran the rest of the way to the lobby. Emil stood at the receptionist's desk, scowling at the woman, but he looked up when I ran into the room. The frown became a wide smile. "Amelia!"

I didn't slow; instead I launched myself at him and threw my arms around his neck. "Emil!" I hugged him tight, so relieved to see him. "How did you find me?"

"The news. The footage of you leaving the PIA offices is on every channel. Turns out that a live Alchemica alchemist is big news."

I leaned back to look up at him. "Oh. That can't be good."

"Sure it is. It helped me find you." He grinned and then leaned down to cover my mouth with his.

CHAPTER

14

I FROZE, TOO STUNNED TO RESPOND when Emil pressed his lips to mine. My vague memories of him didn't include anything like this. Though, it could be nothing more than a chaste kiss of greeting. I decided not to make a scene—then his wet tongue slid between my lips.

I pulled away. "Nice to see you, too." I tried to keep my tone light, but my smile failed.

Emil caught my face between his hands, a puzzled frown creasing his brow. His look of puzzlement shifted to understanding. "You really have forgotten."

My heart beat faster at the implications. "Forgotten what?" I met his blue eyes. They were the only feature that still resembled the man I thought I remembered. "Please tell me we're not married," I whispered.

"Would that disappoint you?" He caressed one cheek with his thumb while he kept my face trapped between his palms.

"I—"

He laughed. "Fear not." He leaned closer, his mouth to my ear. "We're lovers."

"Oh." I didn't know what else to say.

"Release her," Rowan said from behind us.

Emil whirled to face him, a hand slipping behind his back. Before I could stop him, he shattered a glass vial against the floor at Rowan's feet. A cloud of yellow gas filled the air at an alarming rate.

James snarled and grabbed Era by the arm, pulling her back into the hallway before the gas obscured my view.

Suddenly the very air ignited in a roar of heat and flames—and in the next instant, vanished completely. Rowan had burned away the gas. His eyes blazed orange within the shadow of his hood, and like the flames, abruptly winked out. Donovan caught him as he collapsed.

A choking noise drew my attention back to Emil. He'd doubled over and had a white-knuckled grip on his knees.

"Are you aware that the human body is mostly water?" Cora asked, stopping in front of him. "Next time you try something that stupid, I'll rip every liquid from your body. Do you understand?"

Emil made another choking noise, but Cora wasn't listening. She watched over her shoulder as Donovan grunted beneath Rowan's weight, pulling him back toward the hall. James stepped forward and with a soft word to Donovan, lifted Rowan in his arms. Bizarre that the lean teenager could lift what the much larger man had struggled with.

Once Rowan was gone, Cora must have released Emil because he gasped and stumbled back to drop into one of the high-backed leather chairs arranged in pairs around the room.

I rounded on Emil. "What were you thinking?" I clutched my hands to keep from smacking him upside the head. It had been a minor fire of short duration, but Rowan shouldn't be lighting a match right now.

"I couldn't let them have you." Emil's eyes flicked to Cora and back to me.

"Have me? I'm not their prisoner. The Elements have been helping me figure out what happened to the Alchemica."

Cora rolled her eyes, then moved over to speak to Donovan who'd just returned to the room.

Emil gripped the arms of his chair, but lowered his voice before he continued. "Have you stopped to consider that perhaps *they* happened to the Alchemica?"

"Yes, I did consider it—until I hit His Grace with a truth serum."

"How did you manage that?" Emil scanned the room then frowned, no doubt wondering where Rowan had gone. "A truth serum must be ingested. I couldn't even get a gas—"

"What was that?" I asked, curious about the potion Emil had thrown. Besides, I didn't want to go into detail about how I'd gotten the better of Rowan.

"It's one of my staple formulas. I'm surprised you've forgotten that. You helped me name it: Identity Crisis."

The hairs on my arms stood up, but it was a gut-level reaction. I didn't recall what the formula did.

"The subject forgets who they are for a time," Emil said. "A good defense against the magical."

Because if they forgot who they were, they'd possibly forget how to use their magic. I shivered again. Even if short-lived, the idea of losing your identity was a concept I was a little too familiar with.

"You need to leave." Cora returned to us. Donovan stopped behind her, his large arms crossed over his wide chest. Of the two hooded Elements, he looked the most imposing, but I now wondered if that were true. Water had seemed the most limited of the foursome, but I'd failed to consider the liquids in the body.

"It was a misunderstanding," I said. "He thought—"

"I don't care what he thought or didn't think. He leaves. Now."

"Okay, I'm going." Emil pushed himself up out of the chair. "Are you coming, Amelia?"

I glanced at Donovan, though I couldn't see his face, before turning back to Emil. "There's something I need to do. Give me your number. I'll call when I finish."

"When you finish? What could you possibly need to finish?"

I ignored his question and stepped over to the receptionist's desk. The woman had backed her chair against the wall and sat watching us with wide eyes. When I asked for something to write on, she shoved a pen and notepad toward me.

"Number?" I asked Emil.

He sighed, but gave it to me.

"Let me walk you out," I said after writing down the number. I half expected Cora to protest, but she turned and walked off down the hall, no doubt going to check on Rowan.

I led Emil to the front door and reached for the knob. The sun shone through the sidelights making me squint in the brightness as I looked out on the front lawn.

"What the hell?" I stared at the news vans lining the street. Apparently, no one was brave enough to risk the Elements ire by camping on the front lawn, but at least three cameramen stood on the sidewalk, cameras trained on the house.

"As I said," Emil followed my gaze, "a living Alchemica alchemist is big news."

"I can't go out there." I glanced up at my mentor. "And I'm not certain you should either."

"No one will recognize me."

I continued to stare at him, noting his youthful, wrinkle-free complexion, the lack of white in his blond hair.

"You found it, didn't you? You found the Final Formula."

He studied me a moment. "Yes, I did."

I turned away and led Emil into the small room where James

The Final Formula

and I had waited for our first visit with Rowan. "You gave it to me?"

"You insisted." A smile colored Emil's words.

Even hearing him say it, I had trouble believing it. I fought back the despair. I really had failed to find it first. "I saw the invitation you sent the Elements. Were you going to reveal that you'd found the Formula?"

"Yes."

"Did anyone else know?"

"Dmitri."

I gripped the back of the nearest chair as a wave of déjà vu rolled over me.

"What is it?" Emil moved closer.

"I know that name."

"Of course you do. He's a fellow master. Been with us since I founded the Alchemica."

I remembered the first picture in the file Neil had given me. The other young man was Dmitri. Tall and slender, he'd preferred the solitude of the lab to interacting with others.

"Are you okay?" Emil asked.

"I get a bit of déjà vu from time to time. I'm fine." I rubbed a hand over my face and turned to face him.

"You really can't remember anything before the night the Alchemica burned?"

"I remember the alchemy. Formulas, techniques—all of it."

"Every formula?" He folded his hands behind his back. For a moment, I thought he reached for a potion. What a silly thought.

The low growl registered at the same moment a weight settled against my hip.

"What the hell?" Emil stumbled back, staring at the enormous black dog that leaned against my side.

"Fido," I chided, laying my hand on his shoulder. The softness of his fur surprised me. "This is hardly necessary."

"He walked through the wall," Emil said.

With my back to the wall, I'd missed James's entrance.

Emil's eyes widened. "Is that a grim?"

His accurate assessment surprised and annoyed me. Was I the only one who'd never heard of a grim?

"What's he doing here? With the Elements?" Emil asked.

"Technically, he's with me."

Emil considered this a moment, and then a smile spread over his face. "And now it all comes clear."

"What does?"

"Your working relationship with the Elements." He shook his head. "You've always been a resourceful woman. I really shouldn't be surprised, but I do wonder how you found him."

He thought I was using James to influence the Elements. "Emil—"

James growled, circling around me and forcing me to take a step to the side—toward the door. Had Rowan gotten worse? I twined my fingers in James's fur.

"I need to get back. I'll call you."

Emil took a step toward me, but stopped when James snarled. "Soon, Amelia." He didn't wait for a response before he turned and headed for the front door.

Sunlight caught in his blond hair, reminding me of the way it'd caught the light in the parking lot last night.

"Emil?"

My mentor stopped and looked back at me.

"Why were you at that club?"

"You don't believe I was there for the atmosphere?" A smile tugged at the corners of his mouth.

"I saw vials changing hands. You were selling potions." I didn't phrase it as a question.

"You don't miss much. You never have."

"What potion?"

"Something new. The subject temporarily believes he can wield magic."

Whoa. "Can he?"

"The power of the mind, Amelia." He tapped his temple and grinned. "Brain chemistry is such a delicate balance." He gave me a wink then pulled open the front door and walked out.

James growled.

"Unethical, yes, but brilliant all the same."

James bumped his shoulder against my ribs.

"Okay, okay. I'm coming."

We found the Elements in the library, or rather, James led me to them. I was relieved to see Rowan sitting up—almost. He shared a small couch with Cora and Era, his head on Cora's shoulder and one hand clasped in both of Era's. Donovan had been at the window, watching Emil leave, I assumed.

"What's the meaning of this?" Cora frowned at James. "Are you trying to threaten us?"

I sighed. "No. Fido thought it'd be fun to mess with Emil."

Era patted her leg and to my amusement, James walked over and sat down beside the couch. He placed his head on her knees, letting her rub his ears.

"Emil thought you'd abducted me," I told Rowan. "He thought I needed rescue."

"What kind of potion was that?" Rowan asked.

"It temporarily confuses the target. Makes them forget who they are and what they're capable of."

"It would cut us off from our element," Cora said.

"Not technically. It'd just make you forget you have one." I met Rowan's eye. "Though in your case, that may not be a bad thing."

"No, thank you," he muttered. His eyes slid closed once more.

A knock sounded before I could comment further. Donovan

walked to the door and opened it. I expected the receptionist; I didn't expect Gerald.

"I got your call. I—" Gerald's eyes widened behind his glasses as they settled on James. Donovan gripped his shoulder; otherwise I suspected he would have bolted.

"Thank you for coming so quickly," Donovan said. "Rowan's a little under the weather. Care to give us a lift to the manor?"

"So that's how you've managed to keep the location of the manor secret." I'd wondered how they'd avoided having the media follow them home.

"Until now," Cora said.

"I'm not going to tell anyone."

She glared at me. I guess she and Rowan hadn't agreed on my stay at the manor. Though I didn't realize until now how much he'd put on the line to let us stay. Had my attention to Era meant that much or had Marian said something?

"Normally, Marlowe, our driver, can take care of anyone brazen enough to follow," Donovan explained, "but I thought it best we not walk outside right now." His eyes flicked to Rowan before returning to me. In other words, he didn't want a camera crew filming Rowan's weakness.

James rose to his feet and stepped away from the couch. I opened my mouth to tell him to behave when that dark portal shimmered open. Glowing green eyes meet mine, then he leapt through the dark tear before it winked out.

"Where'd he go?" Era asked.

"I suspect he's waiting for us at the manor," I said.

"He what?" Cora rose to her feet.

"We can discuss it later," Donovan walked to the couch. "After I take Addie to the clinic."

"Sounds good." I watched him help Rowan up. "We need to get Rowan well. It weirds me out when he doesn't argue with me."

Rowan's lips curled at the comment.

I STOOD AT THE CLINIC'S front counter between James and Donovan, waiting for the receptionist. Donovan had called ahead, but maybe they didn't get too excited when an Element came to visit.

James had been waiting for us at the manor, much to Cora's consternation, but we didn't stick around for the drama. A quick shower and change of clothes, then Donovan drove us to the clinic in his big green Suburban.

I looked around the clinic's full waiting room noting the clean, but well-worn decor. I'd estimate the faded wallpaper a good decade out of fashion and the furniture even older. "This isn't the place I imagined giving exclusive care to Elements."

"We're here to see the apothecary, not the doctor," Donovan said.

"I'm surprised a clinic like this hires an apothecary," James said. "It looks so...mundane."

By his hesitation, I suspected he meant nonmagical. "Apothecaries aren't magical," I explained. "Think of it as alternative medicine."

The receptionist arrived and gave Donovan a smile of recognition. "Ginny told me you were coming. You can head on back."

"Thank you, Angie." Donovan led us around the counter to an empty hall.

"Does she know who you are?"

"No. Just Ginny."

"Oh, okay." I made a mental note not to give away his Element status. Not that I expected it to come up in conversation. Aside from his size, Donovan was an unassuming guy without the robes.

He led us to a door at the end of the short hall. I followed him inside and stopped. I was in a lab. Not a modern lab, but one from times past. The smell of dried herbs rose from several enormous mortars and pestles on a nearby table. A variety of apparatuses occupied the bench lining the far wall, most with mixtures bubbling happily over old fashion gas burners.

"Be with you in a moment," a muffled voice called. A portly, gray-haired woman bent beside one of her set-ups, adjusting the flame beneath a porcelain dish. She wore a wispy dress of teal blue and her feet were bare. She grumbled when her adjustment caused the flame to wink out.

"Let me help you," I offered, snatching up a gas lighter. A rasp of steel on flint, a tweak of the temperamental knob, and I had a healthy blue flame. "Boil or simmer?"

"Simmer." She looked up and her hazel eyes widened. "You're the alchemist."

"Addie." I slipped the flame back into position under the dish.

"Ginny." She wiped her hand on her floral-print apron before offering it to me. "I'm honored to have you in my lab."

"I'm honored to be in a lab." I took her hand. "It looks wonderful." In truth, it looked a little strange with beaded window dressings and assorted wind chimes hanging from the florescent lights, but all the lab equipment was quality—if a little eclectic.

Ginny smiled at the praise. "Let me show you the tonic recipe you're here for. I've laid out all the ingredients."

She led me to an open notebook, and I soon lost track of the world around me.

AFTER REFINING THE BLOOD SAMPLE I'd taken from Rowan's wastebasket, I devised a pair of remedies. One, an antidote for his current symptoms, and the other geared at prevention. I doubted he'd be pleased with the effects of the prevention potion, but it might be handy to have around in an emergency.

When Donovan returned a few hours later, I handed him the antidote.

"It looks different." He held the vial of deep violet liquid up to the light.

"I tweaked Ginny's recipe a bit. Well, quite a bit, actually. I'd be glad to give you the formula—"

"I trust you, Addie. You wouldn't hurt, Rowan." His simple statement of trust surprised me. What had I done to earn that?

He lowered the vial. "This will cure him?"

I sighed. "Cure, no. That will take a lot more work—and a better understanding of how his power works. But I think I've figured out why he's different."

Donovan raised his brows, but let me continue.

"Rowan must create his own element. He produces fire by transforming various states of matter to a plasma. None of the rest of you does—or can. Cora can't turn water to ice. Era can't turn water vapor to rain. That's a phase change. Rowan's talent is nothing but a phase change, and somehow it damages him in the process."

Donovan dipped his head in agreement.

Good, I was on the right track at least. "Ginny's tonic helped with the symptoms of the damage, but not the damage itself. What you hold is a formula to accelerate healing. But I had something Ginny didn't." I hurried on before I lost my nerve. "I stole a bloody tissue from Rowan's wastebasket."

"So, this is specific to him." Donovan held up the vial.

"Yes."

He lowered the vial and his hazel eyes met mine. A brow lifted in question.

"That doesn't upset you?" I asked.

"I assume you refer to your use of blood alchemy?"

He knew the term. I wanted to grip my hands, but forced them to remain loose at my sides. "Yes."

"Since you didn't kill anyone to get the blood, I really don't have a problem with it." He tucked the vial into an inner pocket of his jacket.

I opened my mouth and closed it. I decided not to describe all the things a talented alchemist could do with a drop of blood. What *I* could do with a drop of blood. Granted, I'd done a good thing here, but the use of blood alchemy was taboo for a reason. It was a slippery slope, and I couldn't help but wonder how far I'd slid in my forgotten past.

"My goal is to get him back on his feet," I said, shifting the conversation away from blood alchemy. "Next, I'll work on prevention."

"Prevention?"

"His gift is killing him. I need to find a way around that. Prevent the damage in some manner. I've got another formula going. Would you like to see my notes?"

"I'll take your word on it." He gently patted his jacket over the vial. "We'll start with this."

"Thank you for trusting me to help."

A big hand came to rest on my shoulder. "You're a good girl, with a caring heart and a kick-ass brain."

I laughed. "I think that's the first time I've ever had any part of me described as kick-ass."

He grinned and then turned to open the door.

"Do you mind if James and I stay to finish the other formula? Ginny said she'd be here until six." And if she had the ingredients, I wanted to whip up a self-defense potion. After last night, I didn't want to be caught without a way to defend myself.

"Then I'll be back for you at six."

"Thanks, Donovan." I followed him out into the hall. "You could loan us a car and then you wouldn't have to play chauffeur."

"Rowan wouldn't want you out on your own."

"Oh. Right."

"You're a valuable commodity, little alchemist."

"Thanks. I feel the love."

He laughed, gave me a wink, and headed off down the hall. I watched him go, feeling warm inside. Who knew I'd befriend an Element?

I'D BROUGHT THE FILE NEIL had given me and decided to study it closer while waiting for my newest formula to dry. It was so surreal to look at pictures of me I didn't remember.

The first photo fascinated me. I didn't look younger than I did now—just heavier. But something in my expression betrayed a different me. I looked like a kid.

My eyes drifted to Neil. The passing of years was much more apparent with him. He looked like a teenager in the picture, so different from the middle-aged man I'd met today.

I dug out the business card he'd given me when he'd handed me the folder. Neil Dunstan, alchemist. And below that, a local phone number.

I glanced up at his picture. He'd been nice to me today, and I felt certain, back then. "What do I have to lose?"

Neil answered on the second ring. "Amelia, how are you?" he said after I'd identified myself. A smile colored his tone. "Did you get a chance to read the file?"

"I did. Thank you." I hesitated, not sure how to proceed. "You're an Alchemica alchemist?"

"I was."

"You..." I didn't want to say flunked out. "You quit?"

"Not exactly." He shifted the phone around. "I'm driving.

Could I call you back, or better yet, stop by? Your memory problems concern me. Maybe I can help?"

That was exactly what I wanted from him, but should I invite him here? James stood across the room, helping Ginny grind some herbs. Even if Neil's intentions weren't so pure, I wasn't alone.

I agreed and gave him the clinic's address. Neil must have been in the area because he arrived ten minutes later. He greeted James, smiling like he knew him well, before joining me at the bench.

"Just like old times." He eyed my setup.

"I'll take your word on that."

"Right. Sorry. What are you working on?"

I didn't think Rowan would appreciate my sharing his weakness, so I shaded the truth. "His Grace suffers from migraines." Not exactly, but close. "I thought I'd try to brew him something to help."

"Nice of you." He took a seat on a nearby stool.

"He's been good to me."

"And the boy?" Neil nodded toward James and lowered his voice. "One of his?"

Rowan *had* claimed him. "Yes." I pulled my notes closer, pretending to need to read them. "What of you? Do you work for the PIA now?"

"On a contractual basis, though it does grant me access to a lab."

"Nice."

"It pays the bills."

We drifted into an awkward silence. "So, um, you weren't at the Alchemica when it was destroyed?"

"You got me kicked out."

"What?" I looked up.

To my surprise, he laughed. "Don't worry about it. In the

grand scheme of things, you probably saved my life. I would have been at the Alchemica when it blew."

"Maybe, but... What did I do?"

"I cheated. Some of the work I was doing for you drew attention to that. The Grand Master isn't...open-minded."

"Oh. So, I didn't rat you out or anything?"

"You were too absorbed in your own work to get involved. I doubt you even noticed I was gone." He laughed to take the sting out of his words, but it didn't help.

"That doesn't paint a very nice picture."

"You were driven, Amelia. Focused. As was I." He gave me a wink and rose to his feet. "Slide me your journal, and I'll write down a couple of the memory potions I know."

"Off the top of your head?"

"I don't have your memory for formulas, but I've used these recently." He sighed. "Mother suffers from dementia."

"Oh, I'm sorry."

He gestured at my journal.

"Go ahead." I wasn't concerned about him seeing any of my notes. Like he said, I had near perfect recall. My notes left out a lot of the details.

He took my journal to the corner table and for the next fifteen minutes, busied himself filling several pages.

"What's up?" James asked, joining me.

"Neil's sharing a few memory formulas he knows." I shrugged. "Something else to try."

"Cool." He gazed at Neil, his forehead wrinkling.

"You busy?" I asked him.

James's attention returned to me. "Not at the moment."

I set a mortar and pestle in front of him—these considerably smaller than the set he'd manned for Ginny.

His dark brows rose. "I'm just a food processor to you."

"You're more than that and you know it." I patted his arm. "Now get choppin'."

James laughed and set to work. His strength would create some really fine powders. I'd have to grind for an hour to produce what he could make in minutes.

"A powder?" Neil asked, stopping beside us.

"So it can be portioned out, adjusting the dose accordingly."

"Mmm. Good idea." He handed me the journal. "I hope something here helps. Let me know?"

"You're leaving?" I tried to hide my disappointment. I'd hoped to spend more time discussing the past. He'd known me, and from the sound of things, he'd known me well.

"I got a text." He sighed. "Mother."

"I understand." I walked with him to the door. "Thanks for coming by. Maybe we can get together another time."

"That shouldn't be a problem." He gripped my shoulder. "It's good to have you back, Amelia."

"Addie. Call me Addie."

He studied me. "That might take some getting used to." He released my shoulder and with a fond smile, left.

I PLACED THE LAST OF the beakers on the drying rack and stretched to relieve the stiffness in my shoulders. I loved being back in an actual lab, but after six hours on my feet, it was time to call it a day. Rubbing my lower back, I crossed to the table where I'd left my notes.

"Need a massage?" a voice asked from behind me.

I gasped and turned toward the door. Rowan leaned against the jamb watching me.

"Oh my God," I whispered. "It worked."

He frowned and started toward me. "Don't say that with such surprise."

I could only stare. He looked good. Damn good. And the way he moved...

I gave myself a mental shake. "I meant, it worked this fast." He stopped in front of me and reached for my face. I froze, but he only pulled a pen from behind my ear and offered it to me.

"Thanks," I said.

"No, thank you." He'd shaved and changed clothes, though he still wore black. This time, a fitted mock-turtleneck with the usual tailored slacks. They fit way too well to be off-the-rack. When he lifted a brow, I realized he'd caught me looking.

The heat rose in my cheeks and I turned back to my notes. "You don't have to thank me. Just doing what I do."

"Eliminating pain and saving lives? You sure you're an alchemist?"

"That'd be the one thing I am sure of." I kept my attention on my notes.

"Right. The amnesia." Rowan leaned against the table beside me, tucking his hands in his front pockets. "What name shall I call you?"

"Addie's fine. I know who she is."

"A mouthy little alchemist?"

"See, you know her, too." I sighed and grew serious. "I haven't a clue who Amelia Daulton is." I hated admitting that, especially to him. Perhaps I did lack humility, but my intellect was a source of pride. My sole source in all honesty.

"Did Emil really discover the Final Formula?"

"That's what he said."

"Was he telling the truth?"

I stopped fiddling with my notes and looked up at him. "You think he's lying?"

"I don't know what to think. That's why I asked you."

"You don't like him because he's an alchemist."

"That's not why I don't like him."

I hadn't expected Rowan to admit his dislike. "Then why?"

"I can't answer that. It's intuitive."

Okay. Not an answer I thought I'd hear from the ever decisive and always opinionated Flame Lord.

"Have you considered that perhaps it was you who found the Formula?" Rowan asked.

I smiled at his flattery, but the feeling faded quickly. "Alchemy is the one thing I do remember. I don't know the Final Formula." I shook my head and dropped my eyes to my notes. "Guess I'll have to find another obsession."

Rowan took a moment to respond. "I'm sorry, Addie."

His sincerity surprised me. "I'll survive."

"Of course you will; otherwise, my life would be too easy."

I smiled. I couldn't help myself.

"So." He hesitated. "You and your Grand Master?"

"That's what he tells me."

Rowan snorted. "Yeah, that's what I'd tell you, too."

I looked up, not sure how to take that. He raised a brow daring me to ask—

A scream rang out and we both jumped in surprise. Running footsteps echoed in the hall. An instant later the door banged open. Ginny stood on the threshold, her gray hair a mess and the lower part of her dress streaked in dirt.

"Three men in camo," she gasped. "In the parking lot, with crossbows. They called James by name."

I gripped Rowan's arm. "The idiot brothers."

"And then they shot him." Ginny pressed her shaking hands to her wet cheeks. "I...I think he's dead."

CHAPTER 15

I pushed past Ginny and ran out into the hall, sprinting toward the clinic's back door and the employee parking lot beyond. Ginny must be mistaken. James's brothers would never kill him.

I hit the back door at a run and cringed as it clanged against the rear wall of the clinic. The sound rang through the small parking lot, and I skidded to a halt. The sun had set, leaving a deep red smudge on the western horizon. A single streetlight stood near the center of the parking area, its flickering light unable to reach the hedge-lined edges of the lot, but it was bright enough to illuminate James's prone form. He lay on his side, back toward me, a few feet away from what I presumed was Ginny's car. The trunk stood open, a crate lay tumbled on the asphalt.

I didn't notice much else, my attention focused on James. He wasn't moving.

Arms wrapped around me from behind, and I had an instant to realize it was Rowan before he dropped us both to the ground.

"Are you insane?" Rowan demanded, his mouth near my ear. He raised his head to survey the shadows, his eyes already aglow. He pulled me up so we were both crouching and eased us back toward the door, his flaming eyes sweeping the parking lot.

"You can't use fire right now," I whispered. "I don't know how well that healing formula worked."

"Get inside," he said, ignoring my warning.

Why was I not surprised that he didn't listen? I slipped a finger beneath the sweatband I'd shoved up around my biceps, hidden under my shirtsleeve. Rowan would never forgive me for this, but he wasn't going to kill himself over me. I pulled out a slim straw—a stir stick I'd taken from the clinic break room—and blew the powder I'd packed inside into his face.

"You're not going to kill yourself on my watch," I said. He doubled over with a gasp and I shoved him back through the open door. He stumbled, colliding with the interior wall and dropped to a knee. I slammed the door closed.

A quarrel clanged into the metal door right in front of my face, and I bit back a cry. The Huntsman boys didn't miss; the shot had been a warning. I whirled to face the parking lot. George leaned against the side of Ginny's car, a crossbow hanging casually from one hand.

"Stupid move, Addie." George pulled another quarrel from his quiver and flashed me a grin. The whiteness of his teeth stood out against the patches of black face paint he'd applied in a camo pattern. He continued to smile as he loaded his bow.

"You're not going to shoot me," I started toward James.

"You sound pretty confident."

"You would have shot me already." I hesitated when he raised his bow.

He studied me across the sights a moment then started to laugh before lowering his weapon. With one booted foot, he nudged James over onto his back.

I covered my mouth with one hand. A quarrel was embedded in James chest, directly over his heart.

I ran the last few steps and dropped to my knees beside him. I heard my knees smack the asphalt rather than felt it. I'd gone numb. I stared at his chest noting the lack of blood—and movement.

"He's not breathing!" It came out as a startled gasp rather than the accusation I'd intended. I pressed my fingers to his throat and jerked my hand back in surprise. His skin was cold. How could he be that cold when he'd only been shot moments ago? I touched him again, searching for a pulse and found nothing.

I raised my eyes to George, trying to blink my blurring vision into focus. "You killed him?" My voice broke on the last word. I swallowed and tried again. "You killed your own brother?"

George began to laugh, and I came off my knees, going for the bastard's throat. Not the smartest of moves, but damn it, I wanted the satisfaction of strangling him with my bare hands.

I should have gone for a potion. My outstretched hands didn't even make contact. He backhanded me and sent me sprawling, face down, not far from James's still form. I sucked in a breath of tar-scented asphalt and pushed myself up on my hands and knees. I paused, considering the potions on my person.

Aside from the potions I'd designed for Rowan, I hadn't accomplished much in my few hours in the lab, but I did have a blow tube of alchemically enhanced pepper dust. Before I could reach for it, a hand gripped me by the collar and pulled me to my feet.

"Idiot," Henry said, his hot breath against my temple.

I tried to pull away, but he pressed something cold and sharp against my throat. I'd guess his favorite bowie knife.

"He never told you, did he?" George gestured at James's body.

"That he's a grim, yes." I swallowed. That he *was* a grim. Oh God. I couldn't stop the hot tears that spilled down my cheeks. How could he be gone? The one person who'd been there for me when I had no one. My partner in crime. My sidekick. My best friend.

"Brian!" Henry's shout caused me to jump, and his knife bit into my throat. "You find it?" If Brian heard, he didn't answer.

"Why do this?" I asked.

George studied me, looking far too amused for a man who'd just killed his brother.

"Did you really think we'd let you take him?" Henry asked. "He is ours. Our family treasure."

"If you treasure him, why did you kill him?"

Henry and George laughed.

Brian walked around the far end of the building, something clanking in his hand. As he drew closer, I saw that it was a collar. A rusted, metal collar. He dropped to a knee beside James and began to fasten it around his throat, snapping a padlock in place when finished. Why, I hadn't a clue. Some sick joke on James's other form?

George braced a foot on James's shoulder and leaned over to grip the quarrel shaft. His large biceps flexed and he pulled it free with a wet sound. James gasped and his eyes flew open. Blood immediately bloomed around the hole in his gray T-shirt.

"James?" I couldn't believe what I was seeing. I'd been so certain he was dead.

"Addie?" James turned his head and saw me. "Let her go!" He struggled to rise.

"Lie still." George leaned an elbow on his knee, his foot still braced on James's shoulder. "You're bleeding. You wouldn't want to get any of that on her. She's not one of us." George lifted his eyes to mine then licked the bloody arrowhead. His hazel eyes took on a faint green glow.

"To share the power of his blood, you must be genetically like him—as only full brothers can be," Henry said. His grip tightened on my shoulder. "You won't be able to do anything with him, alchemist—except die."

"Get that knife away from her throat, Henry." James tried

to rise again, the padlock clanking against the iron encircling his throat. Was this their plan? Collar him and treat him like an actual dog?

"I'm not going to let you do this," I said to George.

"Really? And how will you stop me?" George turned to Brian. "Bring the truck around."

Brian gave me a grin before he ran off to do George's bidding. I clinched my fists.

"You have nothing," George continued. "The one man who might have stood a chance against us, you took out of the picture." He gestured toward the back door of the clinic. "What did you blow in his face anyway?"

I didn't answer, but it did alarm me that Rowan hadn't tried to come after me. Had my newly designed Extinguishing Dust had a side effect I hadn't anticipated, or was he that pissed at me for knocking out his power? Maybe it was a dumb move on my part, but if Rowan killed himself because of me, I didn't think I could live with that. I'd take my chances with the idiot brothers.

"It doesn't matter," George continued when I remained silent.

"Let her go," James said. "I'll come willingly."

George grinned, leaning heavily on his knee and forcing a grunt from James. "You won't put up much of a fight with that iron collar around your throat." George looked up at me. "Besides, she is a bit of an asset to the business. A real Alchemica alchemist." He looked down at James again. "She's the one who invited you to the Alchemica three months ago, isn't she? No wonder you ran off so quick. Did she mention on the phone that she was a necrophile?"

"What—" I didn't get to finish my question.

James snarled and lunged at George, managing enough force to dislodge George's boot and send him stumbling back a few paces. James came up on his knees, but made it no further. He doubled over, a hand to his chest.

George tsked and walked back over to him. He gripped a handful of James's black hair and jerked his head back. "Careful or I might lock you in the vault."

The vault? The one in the gun shop basement? Had it survived the blaze? The building had once been a bank and the old steel vault remained. I swallowed. Steel contained iron.

George looked up with a frown. "Where the hell is Brian with the truck?"

"Here," a familiar voice said. Rowan stepped around the side of the building, a knife to Brian's throat. I recognized the over-sized hunting knife Brian always favored. Rowan forced him toward us, using Brian's body as a shield against George's crossbow.

"Well, him, not the truck," Rowan amended.

I released a silent breath. No nasty side effect from my formula then. Rowan had been biding his time, waiting for such an opportunity.

"No fire, Your Grace?" George asked. "Did you blow your wad on my shop last Saturday?"

What a dumbass. "Did you miss the guys in the black fatigues?" I asked. "*They* blew up the workshop."

Something thumped on the other side of Ginny's car and a moment later, I heard a groan. A similar sound rose from the shadows across the parking lot, quickly followed by another.

"Oh God," Henry gasped and shoved me so hard I fell to my knees a few paces away. He turned his back to me, his bowie knife glinting in the dim light. Beyond him, a form shuffled our way.

"What the hell?" George turned to face a half-dozen other forms staggering toward us.

I recognized the uneven tread and my skin crawled. "Zombies." I hurried to my feet.

"George, release me," James said. "I'll take care of them."

George answered by releasing a crossbow bolt into the nearest dead guy. The man staggered, the bolt through his chest, but he didn't go down. He regained his balance and started to shuffle forward once more.

"You have to decapitate them to stop them," I said.

"Or incinerate them," Rowan added. I didn't miss the frown he gave me. He pushed Brian away.

Brian bent and drew a knife from his boot top, but he didn't turn on Rowan. Instead, he turned outward as well. We stood in a rough circle, backs to one another, as eight zombies encircled us.

George tossed aside his crossbow and drew a hunting knife with a ten-inch blade. I suppressed a shiver. He'd have to get close to use that. He gave Rowan a quick glance. "Well?"

I sighed. "He can't. I hit him with a neurological inhibitor specifically designed for those brain cells which have been shown to be active during—"

"In English," George cut in.

"No fire." I watched the zombies move closer. "It'll wear off in a couple of hours."

"That was fucking brilliant. Why the hell did you do that?"

"He's as fond of James as I am. I was doing you a favor," I lied.

"He's fucking him, too?"

"Watch it," James said. He'd climbed to his feet, though he still held a hand over the hole in his chest.

Suddenly, the zombies stopped advancing. They stood within the circle of light cast by the streetlight, and I noticed that they looked much…fresher than the zombie James and I had faced outside the Alchemica. The male zombies wore suits and the females wore dresses. They stood in odd contrast to one that was naked. I could clearly see the y-incision on his torso. Were they fresh from some funeral home? Maybe I didn't imagine that faint odor of formaldehyde. I was definitely going with cremation when my time came.

James stepped closer and gripped George's arm. "They're being controlled. Necros," he whispered, tone urgent. "You need to—"

George bashed his forearm into James face and he staggered back. I hated seeing my normally unstoppable sidekick so weak. I crossed my arms, a finger slipping beneath my sleeve to the hidden blow tube of pepper dust.

"The truck," Brian muttered. He turned and ran toward the street. Did he plan to use the truck to run down the undead, or just escape?

To my surprise, two of the male zombies broke formation and took off after him. Now the Huntsman boys are fast, but apparently, the dead are faster. After watching them shuffle around, I would have never believed they could move like that, but they caught Brian before he was even halfway to the street and took him to the ground. Brian screamed.

George whipped a knife from his boot top and, with a flick of the wrist, sent it glinting through the dim light toward the tangle of bodies. The knife thunked into the side of one zombie's throat, and an instant later, Henry repeated the same move on the other zombie. Lethal blows both, but neither zombie seemed to notice.

"That'll do," a female voice said.

I gasped and turned to find a brown-robed figure a few feet beyond the motionless zombies encircling us. The two attacking Brian immediately stopped and climbed to their feet.

"Bring him here," she said, and the pair pulled Brian to his feet and dragged him over to us. They dropped him, bloodied and wide-eyed at her feet, but she was no longer interested. She stepped around him to stop before James.

"What have you done to my grim?" she asked.

James growled, low in his throat, but took a step back and then another.

"Your grim?" George asked. "Look lady—"

"You don't belong here, Clarissa." Rowan stepped forward.

The woman pushed back her hood, and I stared in surprise. It was the crazy necro I'd met outside the Alchemica. Gray threaded her short-cropped hair and deep lines etched her face, but it was her eyes I remembered. The irises were so faded they looked white in the dim light.

"Hello, Rowan." Her gaze slid over him. "Looking good as always—but then, you never change."

"How about you fuck off?" George closed the distance between them, but hesitated when one of her zombies stepped into his path.

"Perhaps I'll kill you and make you mine." Clarissa eyed George as if giving this serious thought. He stepped back so fast it was comical.

Clarissa didn't watch him go, her attention shifted to James. "Come here." She waved him closer and to my shock, he obeyed, though a muscle ticked in his jaw.

"Oh, my poor baby. Someone's made a mess of you," Clarissa purred the words. She reached out to touch his bloodied shirt, but seemed to think better of it. Instead, she brushed her fingers across his cheekbone. "So beautiful—and warm." She whispered the last with a sense of awe.

James growled, but made no other move.

No one was paying any attention to me, so I slipped the pepper dust out of my sleeve. I closed my fist around it and took a step toward Clarissa. To my annoyance, Rowan caught my upper arm.

Clarissa looked up at the movement and her pale eyes shifted to me. "The alchemist."

"She's none of your concern," Rowan said, tightening his grip on my arm. "The grim is mine."

Clarissa's smile displayed a lot of teeth. "This is Old Magic, Flame Lord. My magic. You have no jurisdiction over the dead."

"Neither of you has anything," George spoke up. "He's my brother." Henry and Brian had shifted over behind him, forming a united front. It would be a touching show of brotherly love if I didn't know the true reason behind it.

"Hunters." Clarissa made the word a sneer. "You have no comprehension of the gift you've been given. You would lock him away as your ancestors did." She reached up and touched James's face again. "He should be kept close and enjoyed."

I couldn't take any more of this. "He's a person, not a possession." I jerked my arm free of Rowan's grip. "He should be respected for the unique soul he is."

Clarissa threw back her head and laughed while James studied his toes.

"You poor inept human." She gave me a sad smile. "He has no soul."

It was my turn to snort. "Oh, please."

"It's true, Ad," James whispered, his eyes still on the ground.

"How else could I control him?" Clarissa asked. "I give him a bit of my soul to fill the void where his should be." She reached up and threaded her fingers through his dark hair. "He likes it; he feels complete." Her eyes glinted as she watched him. "Kiss me, my love."

If I'd had any doubts, they vanished when James leaned down and kissed her. She controlled him like one of her zombies. I wasn't prepared to take that realization through to the obvious conclusion. Right now, I just wanted to get James away from this crazy woman. I took a step toward her, but the zombies shifted closer, dead eyes on me.

Clarissa finally pulled away. She smiled up at James, her pale lips flushed from their kiss. Abruptly she frowned and poked at the collar he wore. She turned her head to glare at George. "Remove this."

"What do I fucking look like? One of your fucked up dead guys?"

Thank goodness for the f-word or poor George wouldn't be able to communicate.

Clarissa didn't appear as grateful. "Convince him." She waved a hand and three of the zombies started toward George.

George had time to raise his hunting knife, and then they were upon him.

"George!" Henry sprang forward to help while Brian hung back. Perhaps it was his lack of weapons, or maybe he remembered his own experience beneath impossible strength and gnashing teeth.

George cried out and I flinched. James snarled and started toward his brother.

"Heel, my love," Clarissa said, and James returned to her side.

"Clarissa, stop this," Rowan said.

She gave him an annoyed look. "Very well, but only because it distresses him so." She patted James's shoulder. "You see his soul is still intact, my sweet. He merely bleeds."

Several of the stationary zombies groaned, and a couple shuffled a little closer to George.

"Now, now." Clarissa smiled at them and they stilled at once. "I'll feed you later." She returned her attention to George. "The collar?"

George knelt on the ground, bleeding from multiple bites. "Brian," he said through gritted teeth.

Looking like he wanted to be anywhere except nearer Clarissa, Brian slunk closer, pulling a set of keys from his pocket. He removed the collar, keeping an eye on Clarissa the whole time, and then he hurried back to George.

"Better?" Clarissa asked James.

He didn't answer.

She clasped her hands and grinned. "This is going to be such fun. Change!"

A familiar flash of darkness and James the hellhound stood before her. Stunned, I could do nothing but watch.

Clarissa clapped her hands in delight. "Oh, what a rush. That's positively orgasmic. How you enjoy that!"

James snarled, the sound unnerving as it always was when he was in this form.

"I bet you'll love the next part." Her pale eyes lifted to Rowan. "It's said that a grim extracts the soul so perfectly that nothing about the body is disturbed. Even the magic remains."

"No," I whispered.

James whined.

"The necromancer who commanded that grim in Europe had a full Elemental contingent for awhile," Clarissa said.

"Until he was hunted down and killed," Rowan said.

Clarissa smiled. "What necromancer fears death?"

"I believe that's the one thing all necros fear." Rowan didn't step away and his cool gray eyes remained unchanged.

Clarissa's eyes flicked in my direction and she smiled. "You neutered him very well."

How long had she been standing in the shadows listening to us? I considered using George's favorite word, but refrained. "Don't do this." The straw dug into my palm.

Clarissa gave me a smile and stroked the fur of James's head. Abruptly, she lifted her hand, and jabbed an index finger at Rowan. "Rip out his soul!"

CHAPTER 16

James's glowing green eyes focused on Rowan. I gripped the blow tube of pepper dust, judging the distance between Clarissa and me. No way I could get to her before James got to Rowan.

"James, don't," I pleaded, hoping the strength of our friendship could break through whatever compulsion Clarissa had on him. For a second, he hesitated and hope surged in my heart—until he sunk low on his haunches, the muscles beneath his shaggy black fur quivering.

I forgot about Clarissa and lunged for James. He sprang forward, and I caught a fleeting grip of fur. He stumbled, but didn't fall. Still, the misstep gave Rowan time to dive out of his path.

James's claws bit into the asphalt, sending up sparks as he pulled himself to a halt. Rowan meanwhile regained his feet and backed away.

"Please don't do this," I tried again.

James's lip curled, exposing wicked-sharp teeth, but he didn't snarl or growl. It looked more like a cringe. Somehow it seemed worse that he knew what he was being forced to do, but could still do nothing to stop it.

"I'm waiting." Clarissa crossed her arms and tapped her foot.

I fisted my hands and wished I had something stronger than pepper dust to hit the bitch with.

James snarled and leapt forward. Rowan dove to the side, rolling out of James's path and coming up on his knees. James anticipated the move this time. Claws digging in, he altered his course with that unnatural agility and launched himself at Rowan.

Darkness rose up behind Rowan, the hell portal opening where James would land. From where he knelt, Rowan could do nothing except watch James soar through the air like a great black arrow aimed at his soul.

"No!" I leapt forward at the last moment. My hip slammed into Rowan's shoulder, knocking him aside.

James's eyes widened in surprise and horror, and then he collided with me. Or he should have. At the last moment, he must have gone ghost because he didn't slam against me; he jumped through me. No, he jumped *into* me.

Ice punctured my heart and radiated outward, racing to my fingers and toes in less than a heartbeat. Did it beat still? Or had he taken my soul?

I fell backward into darkness, but an arm caught me before I hit the ground. The arm tightened, pulling me close. My face pressed against fur. Warmth replaced the cold, and I drew a deep breath to prove that I still needed to. I recognized the musky scent I'd always associated with James's cologne. He held me. I hugged him back, aware that the body I embraced was neither canine nor human, but something in between—and much larger than the James I knew. I lifted my face from his chest, not certain I wanted to see, but unable to deny my curiosity.

We stood within the threshold of that black portal, though it seemed less dark now and considerably warmer. Sweat beaded along my spine while my eyes adjusted to the dim glow that surrounded us. James had his back to the parking lot we'd just left, with one clawed hand braced against what would be a jamb if it were an actual doorway. He couldn't pull us back into the parking lot or Clarissa would have him again, but if he let go, would I be trapped here?

He flexed his other hand against my shoulder and his claws pricked my flesh through the fabric of my T-shirt. I suspected he tried to soothe me, but his physical limitations hindered him.

"James?" I whispered, unable to reconcile the face before me with the boy I knew. Like the rest of him, it was a mesh between the canine and human, and far more terrifying than any Hollywood werewolf. But the eyes were familiar, and when they met mine, my throat tightened. I couldn't imagine a less worthy recipient of this curse.

A growl sounded behind me, very close behind me, and James's eyes snapped up, focusing over my head.

What have you brought us, Little Brother? The pure malevolence of the voice stood my hair on end.

James's hand slid up to the back of my head, and he pressed my face into his furry chest once more. *She's not for you.* James's tone was as dark and sinister. And something else: neither had spoken aloud. Both spoke directly into my mind.

Though I knew James would never willingly harm me, panic rose, dumping adrenaline into my blood stream. Against all logic, I struggled to pull away from his suffocating closeness.

James stroked a hand over my hair, trying to calm me, but one of his claws snagged my pony-tail holder and must have severed it. My hair fell free, dropping around my shoulders. Against the light-stealing blackness of his fur, my dark hair appeared several shades lighter.

"Here." A hand touched my back, and I whipped my head around with a gasp. Rowan stood beside James. Had he ducked beneath James's arm to step into the portal with us? He could do that? I looked up into his cool gray eyes and bit back a sob. I'd worry about what an immortal Fire Element could and couldn't do later. For now, his presence was enough. James released me, and I fell into Rowan's arms, grateful for a human embrace in a world where I didn't belong.

The growl sounded behind me once more, and Rowan raised his eyes. He didn't flinch or look away. Maybe it wasn't as bad as it sounded.

Take her and go. James's voice set off another inexplicable panic inside me. Rowan's arms tightened, and I wondered if he felt the same.

We slipped past James to return to the clinic's parking lot. The cool autumn air blew across my sweat-dampened skin, chilling me. Nothing had changed. No one had even moved. Brian and Henry knelt beside George. The two of them busy binding George's wounds while his narrowed eyes were focused on the portal. Clarissa watched as well, her expression awed.

I turned my head and James released the portal, allowing the darkness to swallow him. In that instant, I glimpsed the creature that had stood behind me. Within the darkness, it appeared a shadow against shadows. But the shape was familiar: a grim, like James, only larger. Its eyes were still on me, bright with rabid interest. Eyes that glowed red, not green. Light from our world glinted on one claw and then another as it flexed a hand—then the portal vanished.

"Oh God," I whispered and pressed my face into Rowan's chest once more. His arms tightened around me, but he didn't speak. I knew that thing would haunt my nightmares for a long time. Worse, we'd left James alone with it.

"So, it's true," Clarissa said. Distracted by the other grim, I'd almost forgotten about her. "This formula of hers does give her power over death."

"What?" I turned my head, not yet willing to release Rowan.

"You can journey to the realm of the dead and return with

your soul intact." She stepped closer, eyes wide in wonder. "Only the most powerful necromancer can do that." She now watched me the way she'd watched James earlier. It seemed she'd forgotten all about him. "A formula did this?"

"You know about the Final Formula?" I released Rowan and turned fully to face her. "How?"

Clarissa started to speak and stopped. "I know a lot of things." Her chin came up, her body language reminding me of a spoiled child.

A zombie shuffled closer, and I took an involuntary step back, bumping against Rowan. Out of the corner of my eye, I could see Brian and Henry helping George to his feet. I probably only had seconds before they did something stupid.

"Yes, it was a formula," I told Clarissa. "I can do a lot of interesting things with potions. Would you like to see another?" I did my best to ignore the zombie and took a step closer.

"What does it do?" She clasped her hands and grinned, her unsettling white eyes focused on me.

"Careful," Rowan muttered from behind me.

"It's really cool," I told Clarissa. I shifted the straw in my fingers and took another step toward her. She was a tall woman, but it wouldn't take much of this particular formula to get the desired effect. I took another step.

"Here let me show you." I brought the straw to my lips and puffed the powder in her face.

Clarissa screamed and began batting at the air as if attacked by bees.

The zombie made a grab for me. I jumped back, narrowly avoiding the reaching hands. Rowan stepped up beside me and landed a solid kick to the zombie's mid-section. The thing stumbled back several yards, but immediately straightened and started toward us once more.

Clarissa screamed again, digging at her eyes before she

turned and ran. I didn't get to watch her progress because the same zombie was on us once more.

With a throaty moan, it came right at me. I didn't think it bright enough to recognize me as the threat. Had Clarissa given a nonverbal command? Could she?

I twisted away and Rowan charged forward. With some momentum behind his kick this time, he knocked the zombie to the ground.

"What the hell was that?" George demanded. He and his brothers shifted toward us.

"Something like pepper spray," I answered

"And the point?"

"To make her lose control of the zombies."

George limped back a step as the zombies advanced. "That worked really well."

Tires squealed beyond the hedge and I looked up in surprise. Clarissa's vision would be too impaired for her to be driving. She had an accomplice. The car sped away, yet the zombies continued to move.

"Why are they still…animated?"

"They've been fed," Rowan answered. "A necromancer can use her own blood to animate the dead."

"How long does it last?"

"Depends on the power of the necromancer." Rowan turned, surveying the zombies that had once more encircled us. "Clarissa is the current Deacon's sister."

"The Deacon?" I watched George bend to retrieve a crossbow.

"Leader of the local necros and the most powerful among them." Rowan's arm brushed my shoulder. "If we live through this, I'm going to strangle you."

The nearest zombie broke into a run and Brian screamed.

CHAPTER 17

ROWAN SPRINTED FORWARD TO MEET the zombie.

The thing made a grab for him and I gasped, but Rowan dropped into a crouch, avoiding the outstretched hands. Rolling to the side, he kicked out with one leg, knocking the zombie to the asphalt.

Henry sprang forward, landing with a knee in the zombie's gut and burying his hunting knife in its chest.

"Not the body, the neck," Rowan shouted. "We need to remove the head."

"With a fucking knife?" Henry snarled the words and jerked the knife free. He whirled the blade in his hand before hacking into the zombie's throat.

Rowan didn't answer, already rising to meet the next zombie.

I tore my eyes from the scene and turned around, looking for something to use as a weapon. My eyes settled on Ginny's car. Though only ten feet away, I could just make out the contents of the trunk in the dim light. An idea forming, I ran to the vehicle.

"Addie!" Rowan shouted.

I turned toward him.

"What are you—" He didn't get to finish before a zombie closed in on him.

I bit back a scream, but Rowan ducked just in time. A

crossbow quarrel thunked into the zombie's left eye. The thing staggered back with the impact, but didn't fall.

"I'm out of quarrels," George shouted.

Standing here watching wasn't helping anyone. I pushed up the lid and took a quick inventory. A laundry basket filled with towels and aprons sat to one side. The opposite side held everything the well-prepared motorist could need: a gallon of gas, jumper cables, tire chains, and even a small, short-handled shovel.

I picked up the shovel and the tire chains, overturning a box of assorted tools and highway flares in the process.

"Rowan!" I took several steps in his direction and when he looked up, I tossed him the shovel and chains.

He snatched each out of the air and, in the same motion, slammed the shovel into the nearest zombie's face.

I hurried back to Ginny's trunk. I couldn't let the fight distract me. I lifted the box of laundry detergent out of the basket and grabbed the red plastic gas container.

I squatted beside the crate of lab supplies James had been helping her carry inside. Broken glass tinkled as I righted it. Inside I found a wide-mouthed, 2-liter beaker still intact. I also found a Teflon stir-stick among the glass shards. Perfect. I reached for it and jerked my hand back with a gasp. A slim shard of glass protruded from my middle finger. I gritted my teeth and pulled it out. Blood immediately welled along the minor wound. I wiped it on my pants, hoping it'd be too insignificant for the zombies to notice.

A loud clank rang out and I looked up.

Rowan stood poised with his shovel; one of the well-dressed zombies had gotten too close. The zombie staggered back several paces. He wobbled to a stop and immediately started back toward Rowan.

"Shit." I turned my attention back to my beaker, dumping in

several scoops of detergent. I kept my head down, ignoring the occasional clang of the shovel. I needed to get the viscosity of my mixture right. Once there, I pulled a vial from my pocket: the refined essence of Rowan's blood. I up-ended the vial, sprinkling the last of the orange powder over the thin paste in my beaker. Now I needed an ignition source. I remembered the flares that had rolled across the trunk when I overturned Ginny's toolbox. I could—

A groan made me look up, and I found one of the female zombies only a few yards away. She appeared the stereotypical grandma with her helmet of perfect gray curls, flower print dress, and two-inch high heels.

I grabbed up the detergent scoop and my beaker, and climbed to my feet. Wrapping my left arm around the unwieldy container, I cradled it against my body and scooped out a cup of incendiary solution.

Grandma shuffled closer, dead eyes fixed on me. It took me a moment to realize that the soft mewing sound I kept hearing came from my own throat. I prided myself in keeping a level head in times of crisis, but dear God, the dead creeped me out.

I stiffened my resolve and let her shuffle closer before I emptied my scoop across the front of her dress. The adhesive properties of the mixture worked as I'd hoped, and the paste clung to the fabric. I spun away and, in three strides, returned to Ginny's trunk. Setting the beaker on the carpeted floor, I reached behind the laundry basket, frantically searching for a flare.

The scuff of a high heel shoe was my only warning before a hand settled on my shoulder. Thin fingers dug into my flesh with a strength that pulled a cry from my throat.

I gripped the lip of the trunk to keep her from pulling me away while my other hand continued to fumble for a flare. A moan sounded close to my ear at the same time my fingers slid along a smooth cylindrical surface. I gripped the flare then screamed as teeth sunk into my shoulder.

I let go of the car to tug the cap off the end of the flare. The flare lit much like a match with the abrasive striking surface on the end of the cap. My hands shook so much, I almost dropped it. Tightening my grip on both components, I struck the two surfaces together.

Nothing happened. Did flares expire? What if the thing had been lying in Ginny's trunk for years?

Grandma pulled me back a step, teeth still clamped on my shoulder. Something warm rolled down my back. I hoped it was blood and not something…from her. She adjusted her oral grip, working her teeth closer together. Tears blurred my vision, but I didn't dare pull away. She wasn't letting go. A struggle on my part would only rip a chunk of flesh from my shoulder. Though she might manage that on her own.

I slid the cap across the end of the flare again. Harder this time. A whiff of sulfur and the flare sprang to light, sputtering weakly.

Grandma had turned me around, our backs to the trunk now. If this flare fizzled, I had no chance of finding another—unless I managed to get free after she took her bite.

Another sputter and the flare caught, burning a bright red. Relief surged through me, but I couldn't indulge in it. I twisted my arm behind my back and pressed the flare against Grandma's stomach. I had a second to wonder if I'd made contact with the paste when a mighty whoosh slammed me face-first into the asphalt and sent Grandma flying in the opposite direction. She landed with a metallic thump that told me she'd collided with the car. I guess I should have used a little less essence of Flame Lord.

"Addie!" Rowan shouted and the clang of his shovel followed.

I raised my head and saw him swatting zombies out of his path. He worked his way down the side of the car, moving toward me.

I sat up and discovered that Grandma, her dress in flames, had landed in the trunk of the car. With my beaker.

"No!" I pushed myself to my feet and ran. I slammed into Rowan, the impact taking us both to the ground, only yards away from the driver's door.

"Down!" I screamed at the Huntsman boys.

I didn't see if they reacted before the whole back end of Ginny's car exploded.

Now I blow things up on a regular basis, but this was far and away my most stunning accomplishment to date. I turned my head to watch the fireball roar a good twenty feet in the air and hurl Ginny's car across the lot and through the hedges. Good thing Rowan and I were beside the car and not in front of it. Glass and other bits of shrapnel still pelted us. The crumpled trunk lid slammed down only a few feet away.

"What the hell was that?" Rowan asked. A bleeding gash marred one cheek below his left eye.

I untangled myself from him and sat up. The concussion had thrown the other zombies to the ground, but they were already starting to rise. George and Brian were also on the ground, but they were moving. Where was Henry?

Smoke drifted across the parking lot from the burning ruin of Ginny's car and the smoldering hedges. Through the haze, four of the five remaining zombies had regained their feet and were shuffling toward us.

Rowan turned to face them, tire chains jangling in one fist while he gripped the shovel with the other. The wind shifted, blowing more black smoke across the parking lot. For a moment, we were immersed in an acrid fog. We both coughed and I rubbed my eyes to clear them.

A moan sounded, and I whirled to find a zombie creeping up behind us. My bleeding shoulder must have drawn him. Crap.

"We're surrounded," I said.

The zombie stumbled closer and I stepped back, grunting when my injured shoulder bumped against Rowan's back. It was the naked zombie. Some time during the fight his incision had come undone. His body cavity gaped open revealing the emptiness inside.

A whimper rose in my throat, and I pressed against Rowan harder, the pain now a welcome distraction.

"Addie?"

"His guts are missing." I tried to explain my reaction. Rowan must think me the biggest weenie on the planet. "I can see his spine—from the front." Not only his spine, but his rib cage, too. Red muscle interspersed with white bone. Along the edges, the skin had rolled back reveling the neatness of the cut. No ragged edges. No bleeding. Like meat from the butcher—minus the freezer paper.

Naked Man raised his arms, compressing the y-shaped hole in his torso as he reached for me. I screamed and stumbled back against Rowan once more.

Tires squealed, and I looked up in time to see George's big 4X4 slide into the lot, Henry behind the wheel.

The truck came right at me. I cried out and gave Rowan another shove. We avoided being run down, but Naked Man wasn't so fortunate. The impact sent him flying, and he tumbled head over naked ass into the hedge bordering the lot.

Henry whipped the truck around, taking down three more zombies in the process before skidding to a halt beside his brothers. Brian clambered over the side of the bed while George pulled open the passenger door.

"This isn't over," George told us. "We will have our brother back."

He climbed in and the truck was moving before he even slammed the door. Tires squealed once more, and with a flash of brake lights, they were gone.

"Inside." Rowan pushed me back toward the clinic. The zombies were still climbing to their feet, giving us time to run for the door. In moments, I was blinking in the bright florescent light of the clinic's back hall.

Ginny stood nearby, cell phone in hand. "Should I call the PIA...or 911?"

Rowan sprinted off down the hall.

"No. Wait—" I jumped at the sound of shattering glass. An instant later, Rowan returned with a large, red-handled fireman's ax.

I opened my mouth, but didn't get to comment before he hit the release on the back door and shoved it open.

"Rowan!" I started after him.

He whirled to face me and I stumbled to a stop.

"Stay." He jabbed a finger at the hall behind me. "You've done enough." He disappeared outside and the door slammed in my face.

Stay, my ass. Taking inspiration from him, I pulled the nearest fire extinguisher from the wall and followed him outside.

Rowan was finishing a sweeping kick that took the legs out from under the nearest zombie. It landed on its back, but didn't get a chance to rise before Rowan spun and brought the ax down on its neck. It took two strikes before the head rolled free.

I swallowed the knot in my throat and hoped I wouldn't vomit.

Rowan tugged at the ax handle, trying to free it from the asphalt. A second zombie stepped up behind him, hands outstretched.

"Rowan, behind you!"

He spun, dropping into a crouch, and I unloaded a blast

of monoammonium phosphate into the zombie's face. I didn't expect much. The dead don't feel pain, nor do they need to breathe. Yet the blast disoriented the creature long enough for Rowan to jerk his ax free. Another kick and chop made short work of the threat.

Working as a team, we took down the rest of the zombies in a similar fashion. When the last zombie fell, we stood in silence, surveying the corpse-strewn parking lot.

I set down my fire extinguisher and eyed his gore-covered fireman's ax. "We could moonlight for the local fire department."

Rowan gave me a dark look. "I think you've extinguished enough." He turned and started for the clinic.

Rowan wouldn't speak to me on the ride home. I tried to start a conversation a couple of times, but his answers consisted of monosyllabic grunts. The only time he spoke was during his short call to the Deacon, demanding the man come clean up his sister's mess. When I asked about the Deacon's response after the call, Rowan turned up the radio—just in time to catch a news story about the reappearance of an Alchemica alchemist. When the DJ suggested that this alchemist was working with the Flame Lord, Rowan changed the station.

I was actually relieved when the manor came into view, but that relief faded when we found Cora waiting in the foyer.

"Rowan." She hurried to him. "You're still well? You're—" Her eyes roamed over him, taking in the dirt, cuts, and bruises.

"It's superficial. I'm fine," he snapped, pushing away the hand she'd raised toward his face.

"What happened? How—"

"James's brothers, a necromancer, and the alchemist." Rowan waved a hand in my direction.

"The name's Addie, and if I'd had my vials, I—"

"What?" He rounded on me, and it took everything I had not to step back. "How in the hell could that accomplish anything except make matters worse? You have access to a lab for one day." He raised a single finger for emphasis. "One freaking day. And you take advantage of me again."

"Take advantage? I'm trying to save your life, you egotistical ass!"

"Thanks, but no thanks." He turned on his heel to head deeper into the house.

"Then get me my things and I'm out of here. Now."

He spun and in two long strides was in my face. "Aren't you paying attention? You're all over the local news. The PIA wants you. Those men who attacked the gun shop want you. And it seems even the necromancers are aware of you. There'll be no peace until we learn more about this formula you may or may not know."

"What? You think I know the Final Formula? You think I'm holding out on you?"

"Wouldn't be the first time."

I fisted my hands and somehow managed not to punch him. "I'm entitled to my secrets. Especially those that aren't pertinent."

"Aren't pertinent? Your amnesia is a direct result of someone trying to get that formula from you. The reason you kept it secret was because you were embarrassed that your brilliant mind had been compromised."

"That's not true."

"It's completely true. Even now, after you learned your name, you refuse to use it because you don't know if you're living up to the master you were."

"I'm every bit the master I was. You don't know shit."

"Then why are you so defensive, *Amelia*?"

I was going to hit him. I was going to punch him right in that smart mouth. Or maybe knee him in the—

"That's enough, Rowan," Cora said. We both turned to stare. Had she defended me?

"You can continue this argument in the morning," she went on. "Right now you both need to go to your rooms and cool down."

"I'm as cool as I've been in nineteen years!" he answered.

"Rowan. Go."

The pair stared each other down for another long minute, and then, to my surprise, Rowan turned and walked away. I still hadn't recovered when Cora turned to face me. "What did you do?"

I saw no reason to sugar coat it. "I designed a formula that cuts him off from his element."

Cora blinked. "And you used it because…"

"He had just recovered. He may not have intended to incinerate James's brothers, but he was going to do something."

Cora sighed. "How long does it last?"

"Couple of hours. Probably less for him."

She glanced in the direction he'd gone. "Then he'll be himself soon."

"How many more times can he wield fire before it kills him?"

Eyes of multi-hued blue returned to mine. "Perhaps dozens. Or maybe only once." She continued to watch me. "You did the right thing."

I was fairly certain my jaw rested on the floor.

"And if you admit to him that I said that, I'll pull every liquid from your body between one breath and the next."

"Sounds uncomfortable."

Her lips curled upward. "Go to bed, Addie. Rowan will be himself come morning."

"Oh, yea," I muttered and started for the stairs. It wasn't until I reached my room that I realized she'd called me Addie.

CHAPTER 18

I ran through darkness, trying to find my way back to the portal. Claws scraped the ground behind me, the rhythm matching my own rapid footfalls. I didn't turn. I knew what I'd see if I did. Terrified of what followed me, I didn't see what stood before me until I ran into him.

"Addie?" James caught me by the shoulders and the footfalls behind me vanished. He was the boy I knew and not the werewolf-looking thing from the portal. Laughing, I looked up...and met his red eyes.

I screamed myself awake, bolting upright in the process.

"Addie!" Hands caught me by the shoulders, and I bit back another scream. James sat on the side of my bed, his pale face inches from my own. I jerked back so fast, I slipped his grip and cracked my skull against the headboard.

He immediately rose to his feet holding his palms toward me as he backed away. "I'm sorry. I'll go."

I shook my head, trying to rid myself of the nightmare. I sat on top of my rumpled bed spread, still dressed in my clothes from the night before. I hadn't wanted to go to sleep without knowing what had happened to...

"James!" I bounced off the bed and ran after him.

He turned, his expression uncertain, but I didn't give him

a chance to question. I threw my arms around his waist and hugged him tight.

"Thank God you're okay," I said against his dark T-shirt. "I was so worried. We shouldn't have left you there, alone with that...thing."

"My predecessor."

I pushed back to look up at him. "The grim before you? The one that killed the European Elements?" A new thought occurred to me. "It saw Rowan. What if it comes after him?"

"*He* can't leave that plane," James emphasized the pronoun. "He has no body to return to. Even if he could, I don't think he'd hunt Elements. He was under necromantic control."

I remembered Clarissa saying something about that.

"Like me," James whispered. He turned his face aside. "I was almost forced to commit the same crime."

"James." I fell silent, not sure what to say.

He stood still a moment, perhaps waiting for me to say more. When I didn't, his shoulders slumped. "I should have told you everything the night we explored the Alchemica, but..."

"It wouldn't make a difference. I—"

"Wouldn't make a difference?" He turned his head to look at me. His eyes weren't glowing, but they were the most intense I'd ever seen them. "I'm dead," he whispered.

"That makes no sense. Your skin is warm. Your mind is agile. You're not a zombie."

"I'm not alive; I'm animated. My soul left my body before my birth. I have no heartbeat." He caught my hand and pressed it against his chest, left of his sternum. We stood unmoving until my burning lungs reminded me that I wasn't breathing. Nothing stirred beneath my palm.

"That's not possible," I whispered.

"The hellhound blood keeps this body...alive. As long as the blood remains within it, I am bound to it."

I kept my hand pressed to his chest, emphasizing that I wasn't repulsed by his explanation.

"Is that why you can shape-shift into the hound?"

He nodded. "The blood's original form."

I didn't want to ask, but I needed to know. "In the portal?"

He lowered his eyes. "My true form: human and hellhound merged into one."

"Oh." I let my hand fall to my side.

"Don't worry," he said, immediately. "I can't assume that shape here."

"I'm not worried."

"You were terrified." He reached out as if to touch my shoulder, but let his hand drop instead. "I felt you shaking."

I rubbed both hands over my face, groaning in frustration. "I couldn't help it. That place, the other guy, everything—it freaked me out. Something inside me kept screaming that I should run."

"I understand."

I gripped his forearms. "Damn it, James. I'm not afraid of you."

"I believe you." He wouldn't make eye contact.

"I don't think you do."

He took a deep breath, eyes focused on the far wall. "I should go. I'm a threat here. To you, Rowan, everyone. If another necro—"

"No!" I gripped his arms tighter.

"It's for the best. If I return to my brothers, they'd have no reason to bother—"

"Oh, hell no. You aren't going anywhere near those losers."

He smiled for the first time. A sad smile, but it still reminded me of the boy I knew.

"I'm serious." I reached up and caught his face between my palms, forcing him to look at me. "You're not leaving me."

"Ad."

A knock sounded on my door, and I gave it a frown before turning back to him. "I love you. I'm not going to let you throw your life away." I held his eyes, willing him to hear me. To believe in me. "I'll find a solution, and meanwhile, we'll avoid necromancers."

The knock sounded again, louder this time, and I released him.

"A solution?" he whispered. "There's not—"

"Hey, where's that unfailing faith you've always had in me?" I grinned back over my shoulder as I headed for the door. He ducked his head, but I still caught the blush. I pulled open the door—and almost slammed it closed when I saw who stood on the threshold.

"We have a guest," Rowan said with no effort at civility. He gave my crumpled clothes a frown. "I expect you to make yourself presentable and—"

"Presentable?" I balked, eying his silver-gray sweater and dark slacks. What the hell did that mean? "Who's here?"

"Lydia. She delivered the results from the soil analysis."

Soil analysis? Oh, the sample he'd taken from the Alchemica. I had completely forgotten about that.

"Their analyst is back in town?" James asked, stepping up beside me.

I gave him a frown. Where was I when this information was being shared? For that matter, Rowan didn't look surprised to see James back. Had James visited him first? Why did that feel like betrayal?

"She got in yesterday," Rowan answered before his gray eyes drifted back to me. "The sunroom in half an hour." He turned and walked away.

I resisted the urge to make a gesture at his back.

James slipped past me to step out into the hall. "I'd better let you get ready."

I caught his arm. "You're staying, right?"

"You asked me not to leave. I won't."

I smiled. "Thanks." I let go of his arm. "Now I'd better do as His Grace commands." I caught a glimpse of James's grin as I closed the door.

FORTY-FIVE MINUTES LATER, I WALKED into the sunroom. Rowan stood with Lydia near the wall of photos. They leaned close, talking in low voices, but fell silent as soon as I walked in. If I were a paranoid person, that might bother me.

"About time you could join us." Rowan frowned at my bare feet.

I dug my toes into the plush carpet. "You said presentable. I didn't want to disappoint."

My shower had been thorough, and then I'd made a point to dry my hair completely. I'd brushed and flossed my teeth, filed my nails, and then got distracted examining the bite in my shoulder, or what was left of it. Only a pair of pink lines marked the skin, the scabs having fallen away during my lengthy shower. Grandma must not have bitten as deeply as I'd thought. Perhaps it was the terror that made it seem worse.

Lydia glanced between us. It was difficult to tell on her uneven features, but she might have been amused. She stepped forward and offered a hand. The gesture surprised me. The last time we'd met, her buddy Gerald had tried to strangle me. Hesitant, I took her hand.

A quick squeeze and she released me. "Good morning." She gave me a smile, though on her damaged face, it looked more like a grimace. "Forgive me, I've forgotten your name."

I guess Rowan didn't call me by name to his friends. "I'm the Addled Alchemist, but you can call me Addie."

She frowned, obviously not certain what to make of that.

I ignored her confusion and moved on. "I didn't realize you were the one doing the soil analysis."

"Not me. I'm a geneticist, but I have colleagues who specialize in other areas. One is skilled at picking up residual magic."

"Residual…" I frowned at Rowan. "I thought you sent the sample off for a chemical analysis. Why check for magic?"

"I wanted to cover every contingency."

"And we did do a chemical composition on it," Lydia added. "Though it wasn't as conclusive as the magical."

"You found magic where the bomb exploded?" I asked. Rowan and Donovan had been standing close to the scene, but I knew it hadn't been Rowan. Did it have something to do with the magical defense Donovan had used?

"It appears to be alchemical," Rowan said.

I scoffed. "In other words, you found evidence of alchemy at the Alchemica. I'm astonished."

Rowan didn't look amused.

"Within the matrix of the actual soil," Lydia explained. "Magic had been done to the soil itself."

"If a potion had been spilled…"

"Beneath the floor of the auditorium?" Rowan asked.

"It could have seeped through the floor or through the surrounding soil."

"A possibility," Lydia cut in, "but the magnitude of the residual left behind suggests otherwise."

"But how do you know it was alchemical? What if it were from someone magical? Say, His Grace decided to torch the place?"

Rowan's lips crooked upward.

"It's dependent on the gift," Lydia said, "and how said gift alters the environment. With Rowan, there's nothing left to check."

I grunted. Wasn't that convenient?

"Also, through the chemical analysis, we picked up evidence of what we believe is the potion." She turned to the briefcase sitting open on the table and passed me a sheet of paper. "Granted, it could be contamination or any number of things, but you can see that we found several substances that shouldn't be there."

I skimmed down the list, noting the percentages and identifying possible contaminates. Nothing obvious jumped out at me, yet I could see possibilities. If purified and combined in a certain order, several of the ingredients...

"Your conclusion?" Rowan's voice in the silence startled me.

I lowered the paper. "Lydia's right; it's inconclusive." I continued to go over possible combinations in my mind. One formula in particular. It'd be a good one for this purpose. It could even be detonated remotely or triggered to explode under certain conditions.

It occurred to me that no one was talking. Rowan watched me, a faint frown marring his brow.

"Yes?" I prompted.

He turned to Lydia. "Thank you for bringing this over. I appreciate you sticking around to answer Addie's questions. I hope we haven't made you late."

I gritted my teeth. Sure, blame me.

Lydia glanced at her watch. "I've still got time, but I need to leave now."

"Let me walk you out," Rowan said.

Lydia nodded and once more offered me her hand. "If you need anything else, let me know? I'd love to have you stop by our institute one day."

"Institute?"

"For magical research. I could show you my lab."

"I'd like that, but biochemistry wasn't my strength, it was… Emil's." I fell silent. Where had that knowledge come from? Another memory that meeting my mentor had unlocked? One that hadn't had reason to surface until now?

Lydia gave me another grimace-smile. "Even so. I think you understand magic in ways we've never considered."

"I'm only human."

"We all were. Once." She gave me one last smile and let Rowan lead her from the room.

"I never was," James said.

I jumped and turned to find him standing just inside the door. "You love doing that, don't you?" I turned my attention back to the analysis report.

"It's not intentional. You tend to become oblivious to your surroundings when you're engrossed in something. Like now." He stopped beside me. "You see something?"

"Possibilities."

He walked away, moving to stand before the floor-to-ceiling windows lining the back wall.

I skimmed over the list again. Yes, there was definitely a formula here. Damn it. Lydia was right. The bomb had been alchemical.

"Ad?" James asked.

"Mmm?" A bit disturbing that I knew the formula, but I knew a lot of disturbing formulas.

"Something you said upstairs…"

"Afraid he's right."

"What? Who?"

"Rowan. An alchemist blew up the Alchemica."

"Okay." He raked a hand back through his dark hair.

The door opened and Donovan stuck his head in. "Here you are." His hazel eyes settled on James. "You ready to go?"

"Go? Go where?" I asked.

"I need to speak to my brothers," James said.

"We discussed this. You're not going back to them."

"They'll keep hunting me if I don't go see them, and I don't want them ending up here." He gestured at our surroundings.

"James."

"We're only going to talk."

"I'll keep an eye on him," Donovan said.

"You know they only miss if they want to."

"They won't get a shot off around me." His hazel eyes twinkled, and he gave me a wink. I remembered how Lawson's gun had jammed at the PIA offices. Of course, he'd already shot James by then.

Rowan stepped around Donovan and walked into the room. "You're leaving now?" he asked Donovan.

"I don't like this," I said.

"No need to worry about us, little alchemist." Donovan gave me a smile and clapped James on the shoulder. My sidekick gave me a final glance and followed Donovan out the door.

"I'm going to hold you to that, dirt boy," I called after them.

Donovan's booming laugh carried back to us.

I frowned up at Rowan. "I really don't like this."

"He needs to call off his brothers. We have enough to worry about." He gestured at the soil analysis sheet I still held. "What do you see?"

"What makes you think I saw anything?"

"Your expression."

I frowned. Was I that easy to read? I returned the sheet to the table.

"By your refusal to answer, I'm going to assume that you've come to the same conclusion as Lydia: the bomb was alchemical."

"Oh, really. That's my conclusion?"

"If you'd found something to disprove it, I'd hear about it."

I crossed my arms. I hated it when he was right. "Fine. I can see a formula there. It is possible that the bomb was alchemical."

"Possible? Don't you mean probable?"

"If I'd meant probable, I would have said probable." I raised my hand to silence him. "And before you say it, no, it wasn't Emil who bombed the Alchemica."

"Why not?"

"The Alchemica was his life's work. He wouldn't destroy that." Of that I felt certain. The Alchemica was Emil's dream.

"How do you know? If you couldn't remember your own name—"

"You're an ass."

"Damn it, that's not a criticism." He stepped closer. "There are things you don't remember. Someone like Emil can use that to his advantage."

"Whatever."

He pinched the bridge of his nose, a gesture I'd come to recognize as frustration. A long exhale, and he focused on me once more. "Is Addie really short for Addled?"

I suppressed a groan. I wasn't in the mood for this. "When James found me, I couldn't speak. All that came out were garbled ingredient lists and random action steps. His brothers nicknamed me the Addled Alchemist. I shortened it to Addie."

"It's derogatory."

"It's who I am, Rowan." It wasn't until the words were out of my mouth that I realized it was true.

"Emil calls you Amelia and since you think so much of him—"

"Would you give it a rest?" I threw my hands in the air. "I didn't ask for your opinion or your help."

"You can't solve this on your own." He gestured at the analysis sheet, taking credit for it, no doubt.

"Yeah? Watch me." I started to turn, but he caught me by the shoulders, preventing the movement.

"You need me." He leaned down until his eyes were almost level with mine.

"You keep telling yourself that." I refused to back down.

"Where does this infernal pride come from?"

My chin came up. "I'm an alchemist. I create magic from intellect and skill."

"You create trouble."

"I do not—"

He laid a finger across my mouth, silencing me. "Trouble follows you." He drew his finger down my lips and cupped my chin in his palm. His thumb slid beneath my lower lip, tracing it. "You need to listen to me, Addie."

"I'll take your words under advisement," I whispered.

He traced my lip again. "Good." His gaze dropped to my mouth.

"Rowan?"

His eyes returned to mine.

"I'm sorry about last night."

He sighed. "Me, too."

Wow. That surprised me. Another brush of his thumb and I longed to tip my face up and let him kiss me. If I just kept quiet...

"I won't hesitate to do it again," I said.

He dropped his hand and stepped back. "You put us both at risk."

"We were at risk because you took my vials."

"Enough!" A ring of orange ignited around his pupils.

"Would you stop!" I shoved both hands against his chest—or tried to. He caught my wrists and, in one smooth move, pinned my hands behind my back, trapping me in the circle of his arms.

"Damn it. I'm trying to help you." Only an inch or two separated my chest from his.

"Your methods suck."

"Screw you."

He hesitated and then the corners of his mouth curled upward. "Okay."

I arched a brow and his smile grew. Cocky bastard.

"Rowan, your eyes are still glowing."

He sighed and released me. "It only hurts me if I use it."

"You're not just saying that?"

"No." He studied me a moment then smiled.

"What?"

"You care about me."

I was so not going there. "Can I use your phone? I want to call Emil."

The orange light died and he studied me with cool gray eyes. "Why?"

"I want to tell him what we found out."

"I don't see the wisdom in that."

I didn't bother to answer, I just held out my hand. After a moment, he sighed and passed me his cell phone. I punched in the number Emil had given me the day before. The call went straight to voice mail. From my vague recollections of the man, I didn't think him the type to forget to turn on his phone. I left him a short message, promising to call again when I could.

The door opened and Era walked in.

"Hey, Addie, Roe." She gave us a big grin. "Have you seem James?"

"He and Donovan had to run an errand," Rowan answered. "What do you need, honey?"

"Oh." Her smile vanished. "He was going to let me take some pictures."

"He shouldn't be gone long."

Era bounced back—literally. She rocked up and down on the balls of her feet. "Thanks, Roe." She bounded out of the room.

Rowan stood frowning at the open door.

"It's only a crush. You know James would never—"

"I know."

I studied the man before me. "You really are okay with this."

He turned his frown on me. "Trust me. I am not okay with this."

"But you said—"

"She's twenty-three years old. She should be dragging him off to her bed, not blushing over a little hand-holding."

I blinked. "You want her to bag James?"

"No." He rubbed a hand over his face. "I mean, she should be acting like a college senior, not a seventh-grade girl."

"Oh." I passed him back his phone. "Still, you treat her like a daughter. That's not a very fatherly attitude."

He hit a series of buttons on his phone. "She's an Element."

"Meaning?"

"The usual concerns aren't valid."

"The usual concerns?"

"Disease." He kept his eyes on his phone, scrolling through his contacts. "Pregnancy."

I stared at him. "Are you saying that because she's an Element, she can't—"

He looked up from his phone, those unusual gray eyes holding mine. "There's a price for immortality."

I held his gaze, wondering if he referred to my supposed immortality. Come to think of it, I hadn't had so much as a cold in the last three months. As for the rest of it...

Rowan's phone buzzed, and he returned his eyes to the screen. I waited while he read the text.

"What's making you frown?" I asked.

"The Deacon paid for last night's damages."

"That makes you angry?"

Rowan looked up. "He doesn't know where his sister is or why she attacked us."

"Is he telling the truth?"

"It's possible."

"I want to meet him."

Rowan studied me for a moment then shocked me by nodding.

"Really? You'll take me to meet him?"

"On one condition." He held up a finger. "No truth serum. It'll piss him off."

"Speaking from experience, Your Grace?"

"I tracked you halfway across the state, remember?"

"Um, good point. Having a necromancer do the same wouldn't be nearly as much fun."

The corner of Rowan's mouth curled upward. "Get your shoes, alchemist. Let's see if you give Old Magic as much trouble as you give New."

CHAPTER 19

"I'M SURPRISED YOU TOOK THE Camaro," I said once we were on the road. "And what about your robes?"

"The robes are for the public and the paparazzi. Among the magical, I don't have the same concerns."

"Among your people, maybe, but this is Old Magic."

"It's a gentlemen's agreement. If he sells me out, I can do the same to him—and destroy his business."

"What business?"

"Xander owns nearly every funeral home in Cincinnati. Would you take your dear departed mother to a necro? What if his crazy sister takes her for a walk?"

"Oh, man." I slumped in my seat, the horror of the night before still fresh in my mind. "Those zombies were from her brother's funeral home?" I thought about my napalm and Rowan's ax. "What will he tell the families?"

"Ironically, there was a fire in a funeral home not far from the clinic last night." He glanced back over his shoulder as he changed lanes.

Whoa. "Expensive cover."

"But easier to explain then missing or mutilated corpses."

I grunted. He had a point. And the Deacon no doubt had everything insured. It probably wasn't the first time something like that had happened. I suppressed a shiver. Every funeral home in Cincinnati? That meant that nearly everyone who died in the area passed through necro hands on the way to their final resting place. Not a soothing thought.

I pulled my mind back to the matter at hand. "What are you going to say to him?"

"I want to know how Clarissa knew about you and James."

"We bumped into her that night we visited the Alchemica, or rather, I did."

Rowan glanced over. "*She* was the necro? Why didn't you mention that when you first told me?"

"I didn't know who she was until last night. And you weren't all that interested in talking after our confrontation with her at the clinic."

He frowned out the windshield. "You should have made me listen."

Yeah, right. I decided not to go down that road. "She didn't see James that night. I knocked her out before he arrived and ripped up her zombie." I wondered where she'd gotten the dead man. Had her brother had to cover for that mishap as well?

"She must have seen him earlier or something."

"What I want to know is how she knows that I took the Final Formula. Only the PIA knew about that."

"Emil knows."

"I doubt Emil is colluding with a crazy necromancer."

It was Rowan's turn to grunt.

"The next question," I continued, "is whether she's working alone or not. Do you want to go in there demanding to know why the Deacon is trying to take your grim? If the Deacon isn't aware of James, I'd prefer to keep it that way."

"Clarissa had an accomplice who drove her away."

"You noticed that, too?"

"Yes."

"The Deacon?"

"Driving the getaway car isn't his style." Rowan took the next exit and followed the off ramp into a nice-looking neighborhood.

I watched the scenery slip past noting the jack-o-lanterns and Halloween decorations on a lot of porches. Appropriate I supposed, since we were going to meet a necromancer. *The* necromancer, it seemed.

A large brick colonial sat on a rise overlooking the street. It stood three stories tall and took up most of the block. The columned entryway rose to the roofline, reminding me of a governor's mansion. On the front lawn, a marquee among the manicured shrubs declared it Nelson Funeral Parlor.

Rowan parked at the curb and pulled the keys from the ignition. "How do you recommend we handle this?"

The request surprised me, but I tried not to let it show. "Let him do most of the talking. Demand to know why Clarissa was there and see if he says anything about grims or formulas."

He nodded once and opened his door. "Let's do this."

I hurried to follow, pleased that he trusted me enough to set up this meeting, and that he valued my opinion enough to ask it. Maybe he'd finally come to respect my abilities—even if they weren't magical.

"Let me do the talking," Rowan said as we started up the steps.

And maybe I'd been too generous with my praise. "No fire," I reminded him.

"The Deacon and I don't see eye-to-eye on a lot of things, but our relationship isn't that rocky."

I studied the front door of the funeral home. "I bet he has a whole basement full of corpses."

"Yes." Rowan pulled open the front door and held it for me.

"Maybe we should have brought the ax."

Rowan chuckled and followed me inside.

The interior looked like a typical funeral home. The

hardwood floors and paneling had darkened with age, giving the atmosphere an elegant, but somber feel. The high-ceiling foyer opened onto a pair of sitting rooms to either side, while a wide-open doorway led into the parlor before us. The scent of fresh flowers filled the air. Dozens of bouquets decorated the room, most gathered around an empty space along the far wall. The sliding doors behind the space stood open, revealing a wide hallway.

A clatter echoed from the opening, and a moment later, a pair of young men entered carrying folding chairs. Both wore suits and ties, though they'd doffed their coats and loosened their ties for the task. Were they both necromancers or just the hired help? They must have noticed us, but didn't stop what they were doing, intent on adding their chairs to the rows already set up in the room.

Rowan started toward them and I followed. "Is Xander in?"

The two young men eyed each other before one stepped forward to answer. "He was expecting someone. Red hair. New Magic." He eyed Rowan with a mixture of curiosity and disdain.

"Yes," Rowan agreed.

The youth waited, but when it became clear that Rowan wasn't going to give him anything, his attention shifted to me. "He didn't say anything about a girl."

"He wants to meet her." Rowan gestured toward the sliding doors. "Is he in his office?"

"No, downstairs."

Downstairs? I glanced at Rowan, but he didn't appear concerned.

"You've been here before?" The young man frowned.

"Several times. Do you need to call him or shall we head down?"

"I'll tell him," the other young man offered and hurried from the room.

The first guy continued to watch us. "So, what can you do?" he asked Rowan. His smug expression made it clear that he didn't expect much.

"I possess the ability to adjust the thermodynamic state of substance up to the point of ionization." Rowan shrugged. "That's all. I've been called a one-trick pony."

I snorted at his reference to a comment I'd once made. The confused look the kid was giving him didn't make biting back my laughter any easier. Rowan had just admitted to being a Fire Element, but that bit of information had flown right over the kid's head.

My snort drew the boy's attention, and he turned his frown on me. "What about you?"

"I suffer no such limitations." I glanced up at Rowan and caught the tension around his mouth and the slight crinkling at the corners of his eyes. He was trying not to smile.

I returned my attention to the frowning youth. "I'm an alchemist."

The kid blew out a breath that became a raspberry. "You're not even magical."

"Like I said: no limitations."

Rowan cleared his throat and rubbed a hand over his lower face.

I didn't get to comment as the thumping of footsteps announced the other young man's return. He paused on the threshold to catch his breath, and then hurried to us. "He'll see you now. The girl, too."

"Thank you," Rowan told him. "I know the way." He didn't wait for permission, but started toward the open sliding door before either of them could give it.

I followed Rowan from the room and then fell in beside him when he turned down a wide back hall. A freight elevator stood open on one end. At least a dozen folded chairs leaned against the wall.

At the end of the hall, Rowan pushed open an *Employees Only* door exposing a stairwell.

"We're meeting him down there?"

Rowan hesitated, glancing back at me. "I'm sorry, but it seems he's chosen today to mess with me."

"What do you mean?"

"His magic is not something he can call to hand without other conditions being met."

"Conditions being dead people. So it's a display of power."

"Or a test." Rowan looked up as the two young men returned to the elevator to gather more chairs. Not wanting them to see my hesitation, I stepped into the stairwell and Rowan followed.

"A test?" I didn't like the way that sounded.

"Of our fortitude."

"He's preparing a body for burial."

"More than likely." Rowan started down the stairs and I hurried after him, wondering if anything fazed him. I'd seen him face down men with guns, zombies, and James's red-eyed predecessor. Perhaps his day-to-day dealings with the magical made such excitement common place.

The basement was a stripped down version of the hall above us. An unadorned cement floor stretched between block walls broken by the occasional door. Most stood open. A glance within one revealed a larger room with several caskets. A man stood near one, arranging the satin liner—unless he was the casket's occupant and he was adjusting his sheets.

I shivered and picked up my pace. Rowan didn't bother to glance in the rooms, but walked straight toward an open door at the end of the hall. Muffled voices grew louder as we drew closer. My pace slowed of its own accord.

Three yards from the door, Rowan stopped and looked back

at me. I increased my stride to catch up, lifting an inquiring brow when I stopped beside him. Perhaps he thought I'd fallen behind due to my sightseeing.

"He will test you," Rowan said, his voice soft, though not quite a whisper. "Are you okay with this?"

I lifted my chin and met his gaze with what I hoped looked like confidence. "Of course."

He studied me for one long moment and then the corner of his mouth twitched. "No explosions."

I crossed my arms. "Shouldn't I be telling you that?"

"I don't blow things up."

"No, you're too controlled for that. You get excited and ionize things."

"Usually just vaporize."

"Oh. Right." I glanced toward the open door. Not even swapping barbs with Rowan could make me forget what waited for us in there. "Can you really create a plasma?"

"Yes."

"Damn," I whispered. That was like surface-of-the-sun hot. I took a deep breath. Distraction wasn't working. Time to suck it up and face my fears. "Okay, Hot Stuff, let's go." I took a step toward the door.

"Hot Stuff?" Rowan fell in beside me. "Did you finally think of a slogan for my T-shirt?"

"Hmm. It does express your opinion of yourself."

"My opinion or yours?"

"Don't flatter yourself." We'd reached the door. Rowan's hand settled on the small of my back and we walked through.

"Ah, here you are." A big man stepped forward to greet us. Like the young men upstairs, he wore a suit, but had doffed the coat. An apron covered his linen shirt and tie, giving him the appearance of an old-world baker rather than a mortician.

Although, with the blond hair, blue eyes, and broad shoulders, the helm of a Viking ship might be more appropriate.

He stripped off one latex glove and extended a hand to Rowan. He wasn't Donovan's size, but he had no trouble looking Rowan in the eye. "You're early," he said. "I'm afraid you caught me working." He gestured at the scene behind him, taking in the second man and the body on the table. I didn't look too closely at the room's horizontal occupant.

"My apologies." Rowan took the offered hand. "Traffic wasn't what I expected."

"Well, that's a good thing, right?" the big man asked. Eyes the color of faded denim shifted to me and back again.

"Usually." Rowan released his hand. "Good to see you well, Xander."

"Good to be well." Xander chuckled. "Wouldn't want to fall over dead around this lot."

The man's levity surprised me. This was the Deacon? I'd expected someone a little more...vile.

Xander turned to include the man standing at the table in the conversation. "You remember my son Douglas?"

"Of course." Rowan and the younger man, who strongly resembled his father in appearance, exchanged greetings before Rowan turned to me. "Allow me to introduce Addie...Daulton." He fumbled a bit on the last name.

"I caught the clip on the news." Xander offered his hand. "A surviving Alchemica alchemist." He smiled as he said it, but something in his tone made it clear that he didn't approve.

"Disappointed the explosion missed one?" I took his hand, noting that it was dry and not clammy. He hadn't been wearing the gloves long. Perhaps he'd just pulled them on for our entrance.

"No, of course not." He released my hand. "I have the utmost respect for alchemy. You know our disciplines have a long history together."

"I've heard that," I said, but it surprised me that he knew.

"Some of us still practice it," Douglas said.

I glanced toward the younger man and then wished that I hadn't. He lifted a glossy gray-pink...something out of the body cavity of the naked man on the table. My stomach rolled over, and I quickly averted my eyes.

"He refers to my nephew," Xander explained.

I swallowed. "Oh, okay." Come on, Addie, focus.

"Clarissa's son?" Rowan asked.

"Yes." Xander sighed. "He's not your typical necromancer, but then his mother is insane."

"Is that your defense for her actions last night?" Rowan asked.

A muscle ticked in Xander's jaw. "*My* defense?" His cheerful demeanor slipped. "I lost eight corpses and one of my nicer homes. Trust me, if I could find her this morning, I'd happily give her to you for kindling."

"That's not why I'm here."

"I paid the damages." Xander turned toward his son. "You delivered the check this morning, right?"

"I personally handed it to his secretary." Douglas dropped the wet organ into the stainless-steel tray on the cart beside the table. It landed with a splat.

I gritted my teeth against another wave of nausea. Rowan had nailed it. They were definitely testing us—and I was failing.

"I appreciate your attention to the matter," Rowan said, his composure unbroken. "But I want to know why she did it."

Xander barked a short laugh. "I doubt she knows why. Since Ethan died last year, she's been worse than ever."

Goosebumps rose on my arms. "Ethan?" That's what she called the zombie she was with at the Alchemica.

Xander turned to me. "Her husband."

"Oh." Had the zombie been her deceased husband? I could feel Rowan watching me and suppressed a shiver.

A thump sounded from Douglas's direction, and I glanced over before I could think better of it. The body on the table sat up on its own accord, its open torso not as empty as that of the zombie I'd met the night before.

Douglas looked up, his eyes meeting mine. His irises had faded to white, reminding me of Clarissa. Were white eyes a reflection of a necro using his gift? He shoved a gloved hand into the gaping hole in the man's torso and began tugging out ropes of blue-gray intestines. He dropped them into the tray where they wiggled like snakes, unwilling to stay put. My stomach lurched and I jerked my eyes away. Cheeks warming, a knot rose in my throat. I had to get out of here.

"Oh, crap," I said, drawing both Xander and Rowan's attention. "I completely forgot. I need to make a call." I turned to Rowan. "Can I use your phone?"

His brow wrinkled while he held my gaze, and then, to my shock, he wordlessly handed me his phone.

With fingers not exactly steady, I turned on the screen. "Damn, no signal," I mumbled, not even seeing the screen. "Be right back."

No one tried to stop me as I left the room, making my escape into the empty hall. The air seemed fresher here—and cooler. My entire body had broken out into a cold sweat. I stumbled away from the room and back up the hall. I'd find the stairwell and go back outside. Maybe sit on the curb beside Rowan's car. I hated to appear weak in front of him, but better that than to pass out at the Deacon's feet.

I reached the end of the hall and opened the door only to discover that it wasn't the stairwell. In my confusion, I'd opened the door on the left rather than the right, but thoughts of stairs and curbs had left my mind. The room before me was a lab. An alchemy lab.

CHAPTER

20

Mesmerized, I walked into the lab. It wasn't a large setup, but the equipment was quality. The alembic and retort, standard tools of the trade, looked brand new. Volumetric flasks, graduated cylinders, and stoppered test tubes sat in neat rows on the shelves over the polished stainless-steel bench top. None of the glassware appeared chipped or cracked. I ran a hand over a rack of digital pipetters. What I wouldn't give for a lab like this. Did it belong to the Deacon's nephew, or were there others who studied the art? Either way, it showed an acceptance of alchemy I hadn't expected.

Rowan's phone buzzed in my hand, and I jumped, nearly dropping it. The screen lit up and a bar across the top showed the first line of an incoming text.

Brothers gone further afield than expected. We—

I resisted the urge to touch the bar and read the rest. It appeared to be from Donovan. Perhaps reporting on his and James's progress with the Huntsman boys. What were they going to do?

I pulled my eyes from the screen and once more took in my surroundings. What was *I* going to do? The situation presented a unique opportunity to nose around. If Clarissa's son used this lab, I might be able to learn something.

Shoving Rowan's phone in my back pocket, I began a closer

inspection of the lab. Nothing was brewing at the moment, but I might stumble upon some notes or a journal. I moved quickly, glancing toward the door often and listening for the sound of Rowan's departure. I didn't want to get caught in here. Claiming I'd picked up a cell signal in the basement room probably wouldn't fly. I closed the drawer I'd opened and hurried on.

The lab was tidy and devoid of any scrawled notes or a notebook of formulas. It clearly wasn't my place. I was about to give up when I noticed a desktop computer against the far wall. Unfortunately, it wasn't on, but that didn't stop me from going through the desk. In the wide center drawer, I found a legal pad covered with dense notes. I pulled out the pad and studied the notes written in a neat hand. A wave of déjà vu washed over me, and I had to grip the edge of the desk to steady myself. Wh—

A thump in the hall, and I whirled to face the open door. No one stood there, nor the hall beyond, but something heavy rolled across the floor nearby. I remembered the man in the room with the caskets. Was he wheeling one around? I needed to get moving.

My eyes drifted back to the legal pad. I wanted to study it more closely, but didn't think I should take it with me. I glanced at the printer/scanner attached to the computer. If only—

Rowan's phone!

I pulled it from my pocket and hit the power button. There, in the bottom right-hand corner: a camera icon. I touched the screen and it became a viewfinder.

Feeling like a secret agent in some spy movie, I began to snap pictures. I worked quickly, not bothering to read the notes that covered the next few pages. That could wait until later. I turned the page and hesitated. The notes stopped halfway down the sheet. Below them, written at a sideways slant, was an address. The writing was hurried and less tidy than the meticulous notes above, but clearly in the same hand.

Careful to get everything in the frame, I snapped a picture and turned the page. It was blank, as were the ones that followed. I flicked back to the front and began to replace the pad in the drawer. A manila folder caught my eye.

I glanced toward the door. The casket rolling had quieted, but the silence did nothing for my nerves. I slid out the folder and opened it. Emil stared up at me from a glossy photo. Startled, I gasped and fumbled the folder. Fortunately, the photo was paper-clipped to the inside cover. Hands shaking, I laid the folder on the desk and removed the paper clip. Two other photos lay behind the first. All three were candid shots. Two were taken from an elevated position behind the club were I'd met Emil. The third showed Emil climbing a set of steps along the outside of a brick building I didn't recognize.

I turned to the rest of the folder's contents and, this time, found my own image. A newspaper clipping from the day before showed James and me leaving the PIA offices. Unnerved, I flipped through the rest of the folder. All were newspaper clipping or printouts from Internet news sites. Stories about the Alchemica's destruction or news of what had become of the alchemists. I longed to read the stories, but limited myself to a few quick shots of the more interesting headlines. I might be able to look them up later.

A door slammed with a heavy metallic clang, and I dropped into a crouch. Belatedly, I realized it was the freight elevator upstairs. Heart hammering, I closed the folder and shoved it and the pad back in the drawer. I'd been in here too long.

I peeked out into the hall and discovered a casket between me and the stairwell door. A quick glance in both directions and I stepped out. The freight elevator on my immediate right was closed, but the thrum of its motor indicated that it was on the move. I began to circle the casket, moving toward the stairs.

"I'll call you when we find her." Xander's voice preceded him into the hall.

I ducked behind the casket and immediately regretted the action. I should have started toward him, pretending to be returning from my call—or lost. I couldn't very well stand up now. He'd see me cowering—or worse, wonder what I'd been doing.

"I want to question her," Rowan said, joining him. Their footfalls echoed off the unadorned walls as they approached.

"Do what you will." Anger colored Xander's tone. "I don't care what you do. I'm tired of cleaning up her messes."

I assumed he spoke of his sister. Charming people, necromancers.

A heavy latch released and the thick door to the freight elevator began to open behind me. Not wanting Xander, or Rowan, to find me cowering there, I lifted the drape encircling the base of the casket. A simple aluminum frame held the coffin, leaving a space beneath. I stepped over a support bar and let the drape fall behind me—just as the elevator clanked open.

I froze, waiting for the person on the elevator to notice the movement of the drape. Fortunately, the heavy fabric stopped moving almost immediately. Once settled, it cleared the floor by millimeters so my feet weren't visible.

"Good morning, sir." The man's voice echoed within the elevator.

I didn't get a chance to savor my near-miss as the casket began to move. Gripping the rail to either side, I shuffled along with the coffin. I had to bend so far over, I was in danger of kneeing myself in the nose. The wheels grated first over concrete and then the metal surface of the elevator floor. Oh, crap. Where was he taking me?

The door closed with a reverberating clank and the elevator shuddered into motion. I suspected I'd hitched a ride with the evening's guest of honor in the parlor upstairs. I hoped I could make my escape before visitation started.

The elevator stopped, and a moment later, the doors banged open. The casket started forward, and I moved with it. The slow progress made me nervous. No doubt, Rowan had left the building by now. And he would probably come looking if he didn't find me outside.

I stumbled as the casket moved from tile to carpet, but my grip on the support rails kept me from falling. I assumed we'd arrived in the viewing parlor.

"Wait," a youthful voice called. It sounded like one of the boys we'd met upon our arrival. "Don't come any further. That's the cart with the gimpy wheel. Xander will be pissed if you rip the carpet."

A door slammed nearby and footsteps approached. "Problem?" a new voice asked. The tone was authoritative, but I didn't think it was Xander. Maybe Douglas?

"The stand has a bad wheel," the young man explained. "It'll damage the carpet."

"So bring up another one and shift the casket onto it."

"Yes, sir," answered the man who'd been pushing the casket. The elevator thumped closed and a low hum announced its descent. I had to get out of here before he returned with the new cart.

"So, you guys hanging out with New Magic now?" the young man asked.

"No."

Silence followed the statement, and I imagined the young man was waiting for Douglas to elaborate. He didn't.

"Come on, Doug, spill," the young man tried a more direct approach. "Who was that guy? He walked around here like he owned the place."

"Aunt Clar set eight dead on him last night. He wasn't happy."

"Sweet. I wish I had—"

Footsteps approached. "Gentlemen, is there a problem?" Xander.

The young man launched into another recitation of the gimpy-wheeled casket cart.

"Why don't you run down and help Hank select the right one?" Xander suggested.

"Yes, sir." A door slammed a moment later. The stairwell, I assumed. Now there were only two people I needed to get rid of.

Go on. I silently encouraged them. *No need to trouble yourself with this minor task.*

"He gone?" Doug asked. For a moment, I thought he referred to the young man, then realized he meant Rowan.

"Yes."

"So, he bought it?"

Bought what? I stopped pleading with them to move on and listened closer. Maybe they had been aware of Clarissa's actions.

"Don't underestimate him," Xander said.

Doug grunted. "Sounds like Aunt Clar did."

"Perhaps, but I believe the alchemist had a lot to do with it."

"The alchemist? Come on. She nearly puked downstairs. She wouldn't stand a chance against Clar." Doug laughed.

Bastard. I made a finger gesture in his direction. Rowan's phone buzzed in my back pocket, and I just managed not to thump my head against the bottom of the casket. Good thing the phone was set on vibrate. Trying not to move the drape, I pulled the phone from my pocket.

You there? the text read. Donovan again? Unless Rowan had found another phone.

"I want you to go find your cousin," Xander continued. "I'm sure he had a hand in this."

I raised my head and frowned at the curtain. Was he talking about Clarissa's son? Maybe the Deacon wasn't involved.

"Give me a break," Doug complained.

The elevator doors clanked below us. I'd run out of time. An idea forming, I pulled Rowan's phone closer and began to scroll through his contacts. He'd have to excuse this invasion of privacy. There. Xander Nelson. I hit call then cringed as the faint sound of the ring came from the speaker. Would they hear—

A phone rang from somewhere nearby, but it didn't drown out the hum of the elevator.

"Don't argue with me," Xander said, his voice moving away. "I want to know what they're up to."

"Making us look bad," Doug muttered. He walked away—much to my relief.

The hum changed pitch and abruptly cut off with a thump. I took a breath and climbed from beneath the casket. It rested half in and half out of the visitation parlor. Staying low, I backed away. I could see the back of Doug's blond head as he walked off down the hall.

My elbow clipped an easel displaying a large floral wreath and it leaned precariously to one side. I caught the easel leg and rose to my feet in time to catch the wreath. The upper curve pressed against my face, the fresh flowers rubbing cool petals over my cheeks. The elevator doors banged open, and I shifted the wreath back onto its stand. A few petals fell to the carpet, but I left them to dart deeper into the visitation parlor. Multiple rows of chairs now filled the room, but thankfully it was otherwise empty.

Voices carried from the direction of the elevator. I turned and ran across the room, stopping right before the foyer entrance. When I saw no one; I hurried toward the front door.

"Hey!"

I jumped and spun to find Doug walking out of the sitting room to my left. I guess the back hall must tie into it.

"Hey," I replied in an attempt to sound casual. I hoped my leaping pulse wasn't visible in my throat.

"What are you still doing here?" he asked, closing the distance between us. His eyes were blue again.

I gripped Rowan's phone, but my fictitious call would seem a weak excuse after all this time. "Restroom," I answered. They had to have a public bathroom. I just hoped my current location supported the excuse. I didn't actually know where the restrooms were.

Doug eyed me a moment, and I began to fear my excuse had fallen flat.

"You nearly jumped out of your shoes there." He gave me a smug smile, a dimple forming in one cheek. He might have been handsome if he wasn't such a jerk.

"You startled me."

"I think we make you uneasy." He raised his pale brows in question, but he didn't look concerned. "You seemed… uncomfortable downstairs."

Rowan's phone buzzed and I jumped again. Damn it. I needed to get out of here. I glanced at the screen. *Nelson Funeral Parlor.* Crap. Xander had read his caller ID and was returning the call.

"You're an ass," I told Doug and turned toward the front door. I almost collided with Rowan.

"Is my phone ringing?" he asked me, ignoring Doug completely.

"Yes." I slipped past him and out the front door.

Rowan followed me outside, the front door slamming behind him. "Are you going to let me answer it?"

I handed him the still buzzing phone. "It's Xander. Tell him I accidentally butt-dialed him."

"You what?"

"Hit a wrong button and called him." I started down the front steps.

Rowan answered his phone. He didn't use the term *butt-dial*, but he did give Xander my excuse. While he tied up that loose end, I hurried around to my side of the car and got in. I leaned my head back and closed my eyes.

Rowan's door opened and the car shifted as he sat down. "Any particular reason why you're pranking the Deacon and cussing his son?"

I opened my eyes and leaned forward. Rowan wasn't smiling, but the glint in his eyes suggested amusement.

"I might have found us a lead."

He pulled his door closed. "Go on."

I told him of the alchemy lab and directed him to the pictures I'd taken. He shuffled through the photos while I told my tale.

"Do you think it's Clarissa's son?" I asked.

"This is the clinic's address."

"What?" I leaned over to see the last page of notes on Rowan's screen. He'd zoomed in on the scrawled address.

"Whoever this alchemist is, he's connected to Clarissa," Rowan said.

"And he's searching for Emil. May I try to call again?"

Rowan passed me his phone without comment. My call went straight to voice mail.

"He might have turned off his phone," Rowan suggested when I told him.

"Or they already have him."

"What do you suggest?"

I considered that. How could I locate Emil in a city the size of Cincinnati? An idea forming, I met Rowan's gaze. "I'm going to need a lab."

"Why am I not surprised?"

"Do you want the Deacon to end up with the Final Formula?" I knew that would get Rowan's attention more quickly than helping Emil.

He slid his key in the ignition. "I didn't think just anyone could brew a formula like that."

I scrolled back to the notes I'd photographed. "I think Xander already has someone who can brew it."

"His nephew's a master alchemist?"

"Possibly." I frowned at the screen, trying to puzzle out what the man had been working on. If it was a formula, it wasn't one I recognized. And that never happened.

"Very well." Rowan started the car. "On the way over, you can tell me why you needed to butt-dial the Deacon."

CHAPTER 21

"WHAT DO YOU THINK?" ROWAN stepped aside so I could look into the fondue pot he'd been stirring. Not my choice of lab equipment, but this was Ginny's lab. Rowan had taken me back to the clinic.

I picked up a clean spatula and ran it across the thin layer of viscous liquid in the bottom of the pot. "Perfect."

"The potion or my technique?" He removed the pot from the water bath and set it on a folded hand towel.

I bit my lip to keep my smile from escaping. "The potion, of course. I wouldn't dare compliment you. If that head gets any bigger, it won't fit in your hot little sports car."

"Ah, so you admit, the car *is* hot." He twitched an eyebrow, his expression smug.

I rolled my eyes and went back to gathering up the dirty glassware. Elemental distraction aside, I'd had a very productive afternoon. And to be truthful, Rowan's presence in the lab turned out to be an asset rather than the hindrance I'd expected. I guess I shouldn't be surprised. The man had been a scientist before the magic returned.

The real shocker was how well we worked together. I didn't expect a control freak like him to take instruction well, but he didn't question a single request. Well, he did balk at the apron I insisted he wear. Though to be fair, I wanted to balk myself. Ginny's frilly floral-print aprons were not what I'd call appropriate lab wear, but I had been kind enough to give Rowan the jewel tones instead of the pastel.

Rowan stepped up to the sink beside me. "Let me do those. You go finish your fire hazard concoction."

I handed him the beaker brush. "Ooo, I like the name. Can I use it?"

"You and your goofy potion names."

"Goofy? I happen to think they're witty."

"Ah." He leaned over and turned on the water. "That explains it."

Now who was being the witty one? "Have I mentioned how cute you look in your apron?"

"It does bring out the color in my eyes." He glanced over and his eyes flashed orange.

"Yeah. Look for the positive."

He gave me a wink and returned to his washing.

I let myself smile on the way back to the bench. When he wasn't being an ass, Rowan could be a lot of fun. This morning's adventure with the Deacon seemed to have left him in better spirits. It'd taken most of the drive to pry the full story from me, but I'd never seen the man laugh so hard.

"You'll give me a heads-up if I need to duck?" he asked over his shoulder. "It makes me a little nervous turning my back on you."

"Ha ha." I gave the black smudge on the ceiling a guilty glance. "Thanks for the blood, by the way."

When I'd explained how I'd used the essence of his blood to blow up Ginny's car, he'd actually offered a sample. Perhaps he wasn't aware that blood alchemy was frowned on in some circles—okay, most circles.

He shrugged one shoulder, but didn't look back. "Just remember I opened a vein for you."

"You pricked your finger and these little beauties will come in handy the next time we're cornered by zombies." I selected one of my new Fire Hazard potions, rotating the glass vial in my fingers. Flecks of gold within the thick orange liquid caught the light, reminding me of Rowan's eyes when they were on full glow. I'd designed this potion to ignite on impact. It wasn't always easy to find an ignition source—as I'd learned firsthand.

"You are gifted with explosives." He set a clean beaker on the drying rack, clinking it against its neighbor.

"You say the sweetest things, Your Grace."

He glanced over, but didn't get to fire off a comeback before Ginny walked into the room, followed by James and Donovan. She'd gone to open the back door and let them in.

"Your Grace. Let me do that." Ginny hurried to his side.

"Now, now." I carried a few more beakers to the sink. "He volunteered to be my assistant. I'd hate to deny him the full experience." I nudged him with my shoulder, careful not to knock the beaker he held out of his hands.

He didn't comment, but I did catch the curl of his lips. Ginny stared at me.

"But thank you," Rowan said to her. He turned his attention to James and Donovan. "Did you get everything?"

"What are you wearing?" Donovan asked, his booming laugh following.

James put a hand over his mouth, but mirth still gleamed in his eyes.

Rowan gave them both a dark look, but continued scrubbing the beaker he held.

"Don't pick on my assistant, Don. He's rather handy at the bench. I'm thinking of apprenticing him."

James snorted, and this time, I got Rowan's annoyed look. "What? Look at that glassware. It's spotless."

The corner of Rowan's mouth crooked, but he didn't answer me. "Well?" he asked Donovan.

"One compass and the invitation to the Alchemica." Donovan placed both items on the bench before me. "Now what are you two up to? Rowan is perfectly aware that he doesn't need a compass with me around."

"Is that a survivalist thing or an Earth Element thing?" I asked.

"Both." Donovan raised his bushy brows at Rowan, but it was James who answered.

"Addie's trying to locate…Emil?"

"Very good." I picked up the invitation and handed it to him. "All I need is the signature."

James nodded. "Powder or liquid?"

"Powder. Rowan spent a lot of time getting the viscosity of the foundation just right."

James grunted and then got to work without further questions. Rowan had done well, but it was nice to have a trained apprentice at my side. Though still a beginner, James had the potential to be a skilled alchemist someday.

"Why are you searching for Emil?" Donovan asked. "Didn't you get his number?"

I glanced at Rowan, surprised he hadn't told them more in the texts they'd exchanged. "He's not answering his phone. I fear he may have been abducted." I spent the next ten minutes explaining what I'd found in the lab at the funeral home. I skimmed over my misadventure beneath the casket, highlighting instead the photos of Emil.

"What did Xander say?" Donovan asked Rowan when I finished my tale. "Do you think he's involved?"

"No," I answered for Rowan. "I overheard him speaking to his son. He wanted to know what Clarissa and her son were up to."

James coughed. "Do I want to know how you managed all this snooping and spying?"

"It's an amusing tale," Rowan said.

"How's the signature coming?" I asked James, attempting to cut off that story.

A grin tugged at the corners of his mouth, but he turned his attention back to the crucible that held the well-charred scrap of paper. "Almost done."

Rowan cleared his throat.

"Don't you have some dishes to wash?" I reminded him.

He met my gaze, a glint in his gray eyes, and to my complete surprise, wordlessly returned to the sink.

"You run a tight ship, little alchemist." Donovan smiled, deep laugh lines creasing the corners of his eyes. "No dawdling for the apprentices."

"That's right. No idleness in my lab." I set the compass before him. "Disassemble that for me?"

Donovan chuckled, but set right to work.

An hour later, I held the modified compass in my hand and waited for the needle to hold steady. After a moment, it did. "That way." I pointed to the south wall of Ginny's lab. The late afternoon sun glinted off the half-dozen prisms suspended by fishing twine in the window.

"I don't guess you know how far." Rowan stood at the bench beside me, eying the compass.

"No, just the direction." I set the compass on the bench top and began to replace the glass face Donovan had removed earlier. Protecting the alchemically treated needle would preserve its effectiveness and extend the life of the gadget by days. I just hoped it wouldn't take that long to find Emil.

"It's still amazing." Donovan sat on a stool beside my bench. "Could you track one of us if we went AWOL?"

"Sure." I kept my eyes on my work.

"But you'd need our signature?"

"Not necessarily. Just something uniquely yours."

"A thread from a recently worn article of clothing or a strand of your hair," James said. He picked up the ring stand and carried it to the cabinet where they'd been stored.

"You can even use an ingredient that represents the attribute you wish to embody in the potion," I added. "I might toss in a pinch of dirt if I sought an Earth Element."

"From where?" Donovan asked. "The composition of dirt can vary dramatically."

"Doesn't matter." I looked up at him. "It's part of the magic, not the chemistry. That's why I added Emil's signature last. We refer to them as quintessent or quint ingredients. Think of it as blueberries in pancake batter, chocolate chips in cookie dough."

"Remind me not to eat your cooking," Rowan muttered.

"Fascinating," Donovan said. "What about Rowan?"

I glanced at the man standing beside me. His brows rose, awaiting my answer. "A lit match."

"Of course." Donovan chuckled. "Cora?"

"A few drops of purified water."

"Why purified?"

"She doesn't strike me as a tap water kind of gal."

Donovan laughed, hands braced on his thighs. "Good point."

"Era," Rowan said, no longer smiling.

My breath caught. It was clear what he was thinking. I forced myself to continue, keeping my tone light. "A piece of fabric from a recently flown kite."

"But you used direct representations of our elements," Donovan said.

"I can't toss in a handful of air."

"A balloon?"

"The air is captive. To me, Era is a free spirit." I shrugged, not sure I could explain it. Alchemy wasn't always logical. I turned back to the compass and finished tightening the ring securing the glass cover. My hands shook a little, clinking the ring against the glass before I lined it up.

"So, you could have found her for us—before she was damaged," Rowan said.

I looked up, meeting his eyes. My chest tightened at the pain I saw reflected there. "Yes."

He released a breath. "May I see the compass?"

I laid the compass in his palm. The needle swung around wildly, never stopping in one place.

"It's keyed to you," Rowan said.

"It's my formula."

Rowan looked up, a frown shadowing his eyes. "How is that possible when you have no magic?"

"The power of the mind. Alchemists are optimists. We believe that anything is possible. My formulas do not fail." I held his gaze and put all my conviction into my words. "That's why master alchemists are rare."

"And why she drives you crazy." Donovan chuckled and rose to his feet. "Self-doubt is a concept foreign to her—much like a certain Fire Element I know."

"But the compass doesn't work now," Rowan said.

"It works fine—if you trust it to guide you." I continued to hold his gaze.

James stopped beside Rowan and plucked the compass from his hand. The needle immediately stilled, pointing south once more.

"Works fine." James gave me a grin.

The two Elements were frowning.

"Come on, guys," I said. "You're New Magic. You should get this. Magic is a belief-based phenomena."

The two men stood silent a moment, considering this.

"If it's belief-based, would another alchemist's formula work on you?" Rowan asked.

"That depends on my estimation of their skill, and my confidence in my ability to break free."

"So alchemy is all about perception?" Donovan asked.

"Yes and no. It's still bottled magic, but you can counter it a little if you have the knowledge and conviction."

"I see." Rowan took the compass back and once again balanced it on his palm. The needle's movements slowed until it steadied, pointing south once more.

I looked up into those unusual gray eyes. "You believe me."

He smiled and my knees went weak. If James and Donovan hadn't been present, I would have hugged him. Instead I just accepted the compass when he passed it back to me.

"Shall we go find your Grand Master?" he asked.

Still shocked by his faith in me, I could only nod.

CHAPTER 22

"That's it?" James asked, glancing from the pub to the compass I held. "We spent the last hour chasing a compass needle because your Grand Master wouldn't answer his phone, and we find him in a bar?"

I eyed the weathered establishment before us. "So it would seem." We'd circled the block to make sure.

"Only one way to find out." Rowan started forward, giving James and me no choice but to follow. Donovan had gone to find a place to park his big green Suburban. The narrow streets here in Covington, Kentucky made it tough to find a spot.

On the crowded sidewalk, I had to dodge a witch, a cowboy, and a guy dressed as what appeared to be a zombie. I did a double take to make certain it was a costume. Tonight being the Saturday before Halloween, it seemed everyone was getting into the holiday spirit. Little kids might dress up and go door-to-door, but here the adults liked to dress up and go pub-to-pub.

Rowan opened the front door and held it for me. I hesitated on the threshold, surprised by the crowd inside. Apparently, we'd found another destination on the pub crawl.

"Busy place," James commented and led the way inside.

James was right. Every table and stool was occupied. More people stood in clusters around the room. The compass pointed into the room, but Emil was nowhere in sight.

"There's a back room," James said.

"And a loft." Rowan nodded toward a staircase and the open balcony above.

"I'll check the loft," I said. The compass wasn't much help in a multi-story building. I turned to Rowan. "You want to do your thing and chat with the bartender?"

"My thing?"

"The part where you cut to the head of the line. I believe you referred to it as tipping well."

"Ah."

"I'll check the back room," James offered. He didn't wait for a comment, but started forward, weaving his way through the crowd.

"Wait and I'll go upstairs with you," Rowan said.

"I can manage. Go on."

He gave me a frown, but started toward the bar.

A man and woman squeezed past me, momentarily blocking my view of Rowan's progress. I gave up trying to watch and headed for the stairs. Halfway up, I glanced back. Rowan had made it to the bar and was already chatting with the barmaid. A good tipper, my ass.

Smiling, I pulled out my compass. The needle still pointed to the back wall.

The loft was larger than the room downstairs, taking up the space over it as well as the back room James had gone to investigate. A second bar lined one wall, every stool taken. A band played country music on a small stage in the back, and much like downstairs, every table was full. I scanned the crowd, looking for Emil's blond head. This wasn't a place I'd expect him to be, but my compass didn't lie.

Five minutes later, with a quick tour of the room behind me, I still didn't know where Emil was. Maybe James and Rowan had better luck.

The Final Formula

I turned back toward the stairs and caught a glimpse of blond hair. It wasn't Emil, this guy wore a pirate suit, but there was something familiar about him. He stopped to let a pair of women exit the stairs, and I got a look at his face. It was one of the young men I'd seen at the nightclub. The ones exchanging vials.

He headed down the stairs and I hurried after him. Before I reached the bottom, a group of costumed revelers started up, forcing me to squeeze against the wall to let them pass. It held me up, but I was able to see my guy slip out the front door.

By the time I reached the first floor, he was long gone. I glanced around, hoping to catch sight of Rowan or James, but couldn't see much past the crowd. Not wanting to lose my man, I stepped outside. If I'd waited a moment longer, I would have missed him as he headed down the alley beside the bar. The furtive glance he shot over his shoulder made me want to follow.

I hesitated. Rowan would be pissed if I wandered off on my own, but seeing this same young man here, where Emil was, couldn't be a coincidence. Rowan could whine about it later. Decision made, I hurried to the corner of the building and looked down the alley.

The young man was nearly to the opposite end, walking side-by-side with a second man. Something about this man was familiar, too. Another guy from the nightclub? The second fellow wore a fleece jacket and dark pants. It could be a military costume, but I couldn't pick out the details in the dim light.

The pair rounded the corner at the far end of the alley, and I sprinted after them. Running on my toes to silence my tread, I slowed when I neared the corner then carefully peeked out. The men had stopped a few feet away, both with their backs to my position. I quickly ducked out of sight to be sure I wasn't spotted. I leaned against the weathered brick. What should I do?

"There. He works in that room over the garage. Maybe even lives there." The voice was youthful. Tentative.

I leaned out enough to see the building he referred to, and blinked in surprise. It was the building in the photograph I'd found in Xander's basement. In it, Emil had been climbing that exterior staircase.

"You're certain?" the young man's companion spoke, startling me. His voice was rough, as if he hadn't spoken in awhile or had a cold. I pulled back out of sight once more.

"Yeah. I can—"

"No. Thank you. You may go."

"Go? You're not going to arrest me?" Relief crept into the young man's tone.

"As far as I'm concerned, you've done nothing wrong. You've been very helpful, Mr. Voran."

"Oh, okay. Sure. And the alchemist?"

"Unregistered formulas may not be sold to the public. We enforce those laws for your safety."

We? The guy was PIA? I peeked out to take another look.

"Um, okay. Thanks." The young man turned back toward my alley.

Stifling a gasp, I pulled back then hurried away from the corner. A darkened doorway interrupted the brick wall ten feet away. Heart thumping, I slipped into the alcove it created. Something rattled at my feet and I looked down. An empty beer can. The noise had been slight, but…

Footsteps approached, the pace rapid. I pressed my back to the wall and tried to blend with the shadows. The young man in his pirate garb hurried past, giving no indication that he'd heard me. Perhaps he was too absorbed in his own worries to notice.

I gave him time to reach the street before I left the deep shadows around the door. The rumble of a male voice drew me back to my vantage point at the corner. Who was the PIA guy talking to now?

"Affirmative," he said, and I realized he spoke into a cell phone. "Target is said to be inside, though I haven't confirmed it."

He paced as he spoke, and his path crossed the pool of light near the back door of the bar. He turned and my breathing grew shallow. Beneath the jacket, he wore black fatigues. Then too, if he really was PIA, he could be part of a SWAT team.

Another step and the light fell across his face. I stopped breathing entirely. I'd seen him before, both at the Alchemica and the gun shop. Though he wasn't smiling now, I knew that if he did, I'd see his overlapping front teeth. He was the one who'd cornered me against that dumpster where I first met James.

So, he wasn't PIA, or his actions weren't sanctioned by them. The director had claimed that the raid on the Alchemica and the gun shop weren't his. I just hoped the director had been telling the truth.

"I hardly think this warrants a full extraction team." He paced out of the light as he continued to talk. His stride carried him back to his starting point.

"That was different," he said. "She had help. Magical help."

I fisted my hands. He was talking about me.

He shoved his free hand in his jacket pocket and stopped pacing. "Whatever you think best. What's your ETA?"

I glanced up at the upper story over the garage. The blinds were drawn, but light leaked around the edges. Was Emil home? How did I warn him? Did I have time to find Rowan and James?

"Three minutes. I'll be waiting." He took the phone from his ear and ended the call.

Three minutes. It was up to me then.

An idea forming, I ducked back into the alley and retraced my steps to the alcove. The empty beer can lay were I'd kicked it earlier. I picked it up and hesitated. This could be a bad idea, but I didn't see myself having much choice. Releasing a breath, I hurled the can against the opposite wall. Within the narrow alley, it made quite a racket. Pulling out a straw of my special pepper dust, I pressed my back into the alcove and waited. If the guy was preparing to extract someone, he'd want the area clear.

I wasn't disappointed. In only a matter of seconds, he stepped into the alley. He didn't call out, but walked forward, his stride confident as he scanned the shadows.

Keeping my eyes on the man, I removed the Parafilm I'd used to seal the ends of the straw and waited.

He stopped before my alcove. He shouldn't be able to see more than my silhouette, but that didn't stop him from starting toward me. "What are you doing?"

"Waiting."

For the first time, he hesitated. "You're a girl."

"You're a genius." I stepped forward to meet him and brought the straw to my lips. I had the satisfaction of seeing his eyes widen in recognition before I blew the pepper dust in his face. I didn't need to be close. A little went a long way.

He grunted and stepped back, but I didn't stick around to see his reaction. I took off at a dead run for Emil's door. Making no effort to be quiet, I thumped up the stairs and pounded my fist against his door.

"Emil! It's Amelia. Open up!" I banged a few more times.

The door abruptly opened, and I stumbled through the doorway—right into Emil.

"Amelia? What—"

I grabbed the door and slammed it closed, then threw the deadbolt. "Why haven't you answered your phone?" I didn't wait for an answer. Gripping his arm, I pulled him away from the door.

"What's going on?"

A thump sounded against the door and I jumped.

"A team is here for you. Guys in black fatigues. They look like PIA, but I don't think they are."

Emil frowned at the door when a second thump followed. That made up his mind and he turned back into the room.

"Do you have any potions?" I eyed the apparatuses set up on folding tables around the room. Emil had cobbled together a lab reminiscent of my own, though his cash flow must have been better. His equipment reflected that.

"How many are there?" He moved around the tables, grabbing up several vials.

"I'm not sure. They must have just arrived." No way it could be Crooked Teeth. He was probably still rolling around in the alley. "Do you have a back door?"

"No." He had to raise his voice as something slammed into the door. It sounded like they were trying to break it down.

"What potions do you have?" he asked.

"Some alchemically enhanced pepper dust."

"That's it?"

Well, that and a vial of Rowan's headache remedy, but that wouldn't help much here.

"You need to get away from those Elements." Emil pocketed another vial.

"They're the reason I—"

The door crashed open, and I turned with a gasp expecting a team with a battering ram. Instead, Crooked Teeth stood on the threshold, the door dangling from one hinge.

Before I could process that, Emil stepped past me. I caught the glint of a vial as he raised his hand to throw.

Crooked Teeth's arm came up as well, a high caliber pistol gripped in his hand.

"Emil!"

A pop accompanied a flash of light from the gun barrel. Emil grunted and stumbled forward.

"No!" I reached for him, but stopped as glass shattered at his feet. He'd dropped the vial.

A dingy brown cloud filled the air around him, forcing me back. He crumpled to the ground and lay still.

"Don't move," Crooked Teeth said. The cloud did little to hamper visibility. I could see that he had the gun trained on me.

I wanted to go to Emil, but I didn't want to chance the gas cloud—or the gun.

"What kind of potion was that?" Crooked Teeth asked.

"I don't know."

"You're an alchemist."

"It was his potion, okay?"

The cloud had nearly dissipated, but I couldn't wait any longer. Keeping an eye on his gun, I started forward. When he made no move to stop me, I knelt beside Emil. A bloodstain spread over his stomach, but his chest rose and fell as it should.

"Frank, what happened?"

I gasped and looked up to find a second man in black standing in the doorway.

"He tried to throw a potion at me." Crooked Teeth—Frank—kept his gun and eyes on me. "I'll keep an eye on her. You get him."

The other man came forward, and with an ease that surprised me, lifted Emil in his arms.

"Up." Frank gestured with his gun.

I rose to my feet watching the other man carry Emil toward the door.

"What are you doing with him?"

Neither man answered me as Emil was carried out of the room. I started after him, but Frank raised his gun, stopping me.

"What a stroke of luck finding you here." Frank smiled, exposing those overlapping front teeth. It wasn't a friendly smile. "I've lost several good men hunting you."

"And that's my fault?"

He didn't answer me. Instead, he gestured toward the door with his gun. It looked like he was finally going to accomplish what he'd attempted at both the Alchemica and the gun shop. I had to get word to Rowan and James. Let them know that I'd been taken. But how—

The compass! I stuffed my hand in my pocket and closed it in my fist.

"Freeze!" Frank leveled the gun between my eyes. "What do you have there?"

"A compass?" I slowly pulled it out and showed him.

"Turn out your pockets."

I set the compass on a nearby table and proceeded to do as told. All my other pockets were empty.

"Let's go," Frank said once I'd shown him the insides of my pockets.

I left the room without a backward glance. Maybe Rowan and James would find the compass and follow it to Emil…and me.

A dark, late-model car waited at the base of the stairs, the trunk open. I was shocked to see Emil lying inside.

"The trunk?" I asked. "Is that really necessary?"

"Move." Frank made it clear that it wasn't up for discussion. When I reached the car, he stopped. "Climb in with him."

"What?"

He leveled the gun on me. "I'm to deliver you alive. The number of holes you collect is up to you."

"Deliver us to whom?"

"You'll see soon enough."

Having delayed all I could, I climbed into the trunk with Emil. It was a large car, but the fit was still close. The lid slammed closed, plunging us into complete darkness. It looked like I'd finally find out who'd been chasing me all these months.

CHAPTER
23

We didn't drive far, though it was hard to judge distance or even the passage of time while locked in a trunk with a bleeding man. I couldn't see, but I patted Emil down and found the wet place on his stomach. I wiggled around until I had my jacket off and used it as a compress. At least, I hoped that was what I was doing. The darkness was too complete to tell more, but I did find the vials he'd slipped in his pocket. I guess Frank didn't think an unconscious man a threat to throw a potion. I tucked them away, hoping to find a use for them later.

Unable to do anything else for Emil, I turned my attention to my surroundings. I couldn't find any kind of release for the trunk lid, nor were the taillights accessible from the inside. So much for alerting any following motorist to our plight.

The car came to a stop, the faint squeal of old brakes loud in what sounded like an enclosed space. Doors slammed, and a few minutes later, the trunk lid opened. I squinted against the bright light, focusing on the familiar man standing over me.

"You!" I gripped the lip of the trunk and pulled myself upright. Agent Lawson took a step back as I scrambled out, but one of the men caught me by the arm before I could close the distance between us.

"If you wanted to talk to me, all you had to do was call. Emil's been shot!"

"What's this?" Lawson returned to the trunk, his footfalls echoing off the unpainted cinder block walls. We were in a garage—a run-down, two-car garage that smelled of rust and old oil. Like the others, Lawson was dressed in black fatigues, the PIA insignia stitched in dark thread on his black jacket. I wouldn't have noticed it if not for the bright light of the bare bulb overhead.

"He was going to throw a potion at me." Frank curled his lip, exposing those overlapping front teeth. "The wound isn't mortal."

"How do you know?" I demanded. "He was shot in the stomach. Bullets ricochet, organs seep. It could—"

"I don't guess it matters," Lawson said.

"Doesn't matter?" I tried to tug my arm free, but the man holding me tightened his grip. "He needs medical attention!"

Lawson frowned at Emil's unmoving form. "Is that why he's unconscious?"

"I think his own potion knocked him out," Frank said.

"What shall I do with her?" the man who held me asked.

"Cuff her to something." Lawson tossed him a set of handcuffs.

"Hey," I protested as the man pulled me across the room. I tried to dig in my heels, but it made no difference. The guy was seriously strong. "This goes way beyond bringing me in for questioning," I shouted at Lawson.

No one bothered to answer. The man stopped near a workbench and snapped one cuff around my wrist before snapping the other to a vertical piece of conduit.

"You're sure they know this formula?" Frank asked.

"One of them does," Lawson answered. "She's forty-two and he's sixty-six."

"Wow." Frank braced his hands on the lip of the trunk, looking down at Emil. "It really works then. Eternal youth—and life." He spoke the words in a reverent tone.

"You should get back before you're missed," Lawson told the men.

"You'll keep us posted?" The man who'd cuffed me walked back to Lawson, a limp in his stride. He gripped Lawson's shoulder in an oddly sympathetic gesture as he passed.

"Of course." Lawson followed the men to the door and after a quiet exchange, closed it after them.

"So, you're the guy behind this," I said now that we were alone. "The Alchemica, the gun shop, and over in Covington tonight."

Lawson pulled out an old-model flip phone and opened it. "You're an elusive woman, Ms. Daulton." He hit a button and brought the phone to his ear.

I gritted my teeth, annoyed that he'd made no effort to deny anything. I pulled at my handcuff, but there was no give. The bracket tacking the conduit to the wall prevented me from lowering my hand below the level of my waist.

"I got them," Lawson said into the phone. "Both alchemists."

I stopped rattling the cuffs to listen.

"Shall I bring them to you or—" He fell silent, tapping a finger to the phone pressed to his ear.

"An old garage outside Covington," Lawson said. "The Grand Master has been shot."

At least he'd acknowledged it. I'd begun to wonder if he even knew that Emil was bleeding on his trunk floor.

"His color is still good, but it was a gut shot. If anything was—" He fell silent once more, and the tapping finger stilled.

"Yes, sir," he answered after a moment. "I will." He pulled the phone from his ear and ended the call.

"So, you're not running the show."

His gaze shifted to me, forehead bunching as he looked me over.

"What?"

He moved closer. "You're really not magical."

"No, I'm not."

"Then why is he registering you?"

"What? Who?"

"The Flame Lord. He started your registration with the PIA."

"He did?" When Rowan had claimed me before the director, I'd thought it was a ruse to get the PIA to let me go. It pissed me off that he hadn't told me about it, but I didn't want to react in front of Lawson.

"You didn't know? Is he holding you against your will?" Lawson seemed genuinely outraged. Perhaps he had some scruples after all.

"And this upsets you why?"

"Declaring you magical gives him jurisdiction over you." Lawson fisted his hands. "He shouldn't be allowed to get away with it."

"And yet you kidnap me and allow Emil to be shot. From where I stand," I rattled my cuff, "I'm not seeing the difference."

"No, I suppose not." He turned on his heel. Several angry strides took him across the garage before he spun around and came back to me. "The PIA was created to keep the magical in their place, and yet the agency bows and scrapes like everyone else." He smashed his fist into his palm.

"I get the sense you don't like the magical much."

He gave me a glare.

"Doesn't that make you a bit of a hypocrite, Agent Lawson?"

He leaned forward, bracing a hand to either side of my head. "I sense magic; I cannot use it. I am *not* one of them."

I itched to use a potion, but I'd still be cuffed to the wall even if it did incapacitate him. I'd have to wait until he released me.

"You lied to me about the boy." Lawson pushed off the wall, but didn't move away. "It wasn't a potion."

James.

"The Flame Lord is registering him as well," Lawson continued. "He claims the boy is a shape-shifter."

Close enough.

"He's powerful. Very powerful."

I held his gaze, refusing to give him any more information. Lawson was a magic hater. A magic hater that worked for the PIA. Not a good combination.

Lawson held my gaze for a few more seconds. "Why do you work for the Elements, Ms. Daulton?"

"Who said I did?"

Lawson gave me a look that said he believed differently.

"The question is who do you work for? Who wants the Final Formula?"

"Who doesn't?" He turned and walked away, this time he left the garage entirely, slamming the pedestrian door behind him.

"Emil?" I called out.

Silence answered me.

For the next few minutes, I gave the cuffs a thorough workout, but found no give in either the handcuffs or the conduit. Unwilling to concede defeat, I turned my attention to the workbench beside me. A rusted toolbox took up most of the lower shelf, but it was too far away to reach.

Greasy bottles of oil and cans of assorted lubricants and solvents sat closer. Most were flammable, but burning down the garage wasn't an option. There were plenty of alchemical applications for the ingredients before me, but without time or a lab, I was a bit limited. However, a simple mechanical adaptation might be practical. With my small hands and a little oil, I might be able to slip the cuff.

I stretched out as far as I could, reaching with one foot toward the shelf holding the oil. The toe of my sneaker touched one bottle. I leaned further, resting my weight on the handcuff and the other leg. I lunged, but instead of slipping my foot behind the bottle, I tapped it dead center and toppled it over backwards.

"Crap." I fell to the side, slamming my shoulder against the corner of the workbench. "Damn it." That hurt.

I regained my balance for another attempt when the pedestrian door opened. Smothering a gasp, I stumbled back against the wall as Lawson walked in. I didn't want him to see the advantages of my current position. He might move me elsewhere.

My fears proved unfounded. He had his cell phone pressed firmly to one ear and didn't even glance in my direction. Out of options, I slipped my hand into my front pocket and fisted one of Emil's vials.

"Now?" Lawson stopped beside the car and paused to listen. "Okay. Where?" He listened a moment longer then ended the call.

"Time to go," he said to me. He pulled out a keyring.

"Go where?"

Without answering, he slipped a key into the lock and removed the cuff from the pipe. Now was my chance.

I flicked the cap off the vial and flung the contents in his face. I wasn't certain what the potion was or how it would affect him, but any liquid thrown in the eyes tended to slow someone down. Or it should. I hadn't much luck with the smelling salts.

Not waiting for a reaction, I turned and ran. If I could make it outside, maybe I could lose him in the dark.

"No!" he shouted.

I'd reached the car, halfway to the pedestrian door, when he fired. Pain laced through my right calf. My leg buckled, throwing me into the front fender of the car. I thumped into the metal hard enough to leave a dent. Pushing myself upright, I turned to face him.

"Don't move," Lawson started toward me, his gun trained on my chest. "I will shoot you again."

"What about the Formula? If Emil or I know it—"

"You've both taken it." He continued toward me. "You're immortal."

"It's an anti-aging potion, not a get-out-of-death-free pass." Was that why he was so indifferent about Emil's injury?

He stopped a foot away. The potion ran down his cheeks and dripped off his chin. "What?"

"I don't age, but I can die."

"That's not what—" He frowned and shook his head before turning wide eyes on me, his pupils fully dilated. "What was in this potion?" He ran one hand over his wet cheek.

"It was Emil's. I was just hoping it was acidic."

His eyes swept over me, lingering on my hips. "What's in your pocket?" He twitched the gun at my right pocket. "I feel confusion."

Stunned, I pulled a vial of orange liquid from my pocket. Rotating it, I read the small label taped to the glass. "Identity Crisis." It was the same potion Emil had attempted to hit Rowan with at the Elemental Offices. "It causes a temporary memory lapse."

"Your left ankle holds pain. What is it?"

"A blow tube of pepper dust." Perhaps I should have made an effort to reach it.

I studied him. Was that what a Sensitive saw—not only the magic, but its purpose? Well, a powerful Sensitive anyway. Emil's potion must have elevated Lawson's skills. Impressive.

"What's—" Lawson stopped and glanced back over his shoulder. To my surprise, he turned to face the garage door.

Limping, I took a step back and then another, eying the distance to the pedestrian door. It felt like a red-hot poker had been jabbed in my calf, but it held my weight. That would have to do. I turned and ran.

I made it half the distance before he opened fire. Expecting a bullet, I dove to the side, but slipped on a patch of oil. I went down on one knee, cracking it against the concrete. The new pain momentarily masked the old.

A snarl stood my hair on end, and I twisted around to look behind me. A massive hellhound stood before the garage door. A door now pockmarked with several bullet holes. Lawson hadn't been shooting at me.

James's glowing green eyes shifted to me before returning to Lawson. He started forward, his claws clicking on the cement floor.

"Shit," Lawson whispered and pulled the trigger again. The garage door shook with the impact, the bullet passing right through James. Lawson squeezed off a couple more shots that left my ears ringing. Wood splinters rained down on James, or through him rather, scattering on the floor at his feet.

Lawson staggered back, gun trained on James. "What is he?"

"That's your shape-shifter," I answered.

"The boy?" Lawson stepped back until he stood even with me. "No, he's more. He's death."

I glanced up at the wide-eyed man beside me. Considering that he could now see magic's purpose, that was disturbing.

James continued toward us, his attention focused on Lawson.

"Stop!" Lawson cried. When his command failed to get the desired result, he grabbed me, shielding his body with mine. "I'll blow her head off." He shoved the gun barrel into the soft underside of my jaw. I gripped his forearm, but didn't have the strength to pull him away.

James hesitated. His hackles rose and black lips lifted to reveal gleaming teeth that looked far more plentiful than the typical canine's. He crouched, the muscles beneath his shaggy fur quivering.

A hot gust of air ruffled my hair as if a furnace had kicked on.

Lawson glanced over his shoulder and whimpered. His gun ground deeper into my jaw, forcing my head back.

"Dinner, little brother?" a dark voice whispered from behind us. The other grim. James had opened the portal. He intended to rip Lawson's soul. I had to stop him; I couldn't question the dead.

"James—"

The pedestrian door rattled and Lawson turned slightly, keeping both James and the door in view. The lock snicked and the door swung open. Rowan stood on the threshold, Donovan's bulk filling the space behind him. Rowan hesitated, taking in the scene, and then flames ignited in his eyes.

"It's him," Lawson whispered and swung the gun toward Rowan.

Rowan lunged forward and Lawson fired.

"Rowan!" I screamed.

James sprang, but I knew he was too late.

Fire raced across the garage, lapping up the very air as it roared toward us. I squeezed my eyes shut and heat enveloped me, so intense I feared I'd been roasted alive. And in the next instant it was gone—and so was Lawson. Released from his support, I staggered away and almost went down before arms once more embraced me.

"I've got you," Rowan said against my ear.

"Addie!" James caught my face in his palms, tipping my head

up to look in my eyes. A frown replaced his worried expression. "Damn it, Rowan, her skin is hot."

"It's just a flush. She was never in danger." His arms tightened around me.

I pressed my hands against James's bare chest and pushed him back, giving myself room to step out of Rowan's arms.

"Sorry," James muttered. He dropped his hands to cover himself and stepped out of my line of sight.

I raked my fingers through my hair. It wasn't his nudity that was the problem. Lawson was gone. Rowan had ashed him. Well, I assumed Rowan had killed him. James might have gotten his soul first—not that it mattered. My only lead was gone.

"James." Donovan tossed him a sack and then turned to close the door.

"What happened?" Rowan asked.

"I found Emil, but guys in black fatigues found him first." I limped around to the open trunk.

"Addie you're bleeding," James said.

"Lawson shot me." I leaned in the trunk and touched Emil's cheek. His skin was warm and his breathing seemed okay, but a stain darkened the carpet beneath him.

"He shot you?" Rowan stepped up beside me.

"I wish you hadn't ashed Lawson. How am I supposed to find out who he called?"

"What do you mean?"

James, clothed now, squatted beside me and ran his hands lightly along my injured calf.

"Lawson wasn't running the show. He called someone to find out where to deliver us." I gasped in surprise as James ripped open my lower pant leg. The force threw me into Rowan.

"Easy," Rowan said.

"God," James whispered.

I looked down and saw my white sock soaked in blood,

trickles running over the sides and heel of my shoe. I'd been fine up to that moment. Now a cold sweat coated my skin and the edges of my vision began to darken.

The world swung around me and then seemed to stabilize. It took me a moment to realize that Rowan had picked me up.

"Sorry," I muttered. "I don't do so well with blood. Or autopsies. Or zombies."

"That's all right." Rowan turned toward the door. "You have other skills that make up for your shortcomings." He began walking toward the open door.

"Emil." I suddenly remembered. "We have to get him to a hospital."

"We need to get you to a hospital," Rowan said.

"I got him, Ad," James called from behind us.

I looked back and watched James lift Emil from the trunk. Relieved, I let my head rest on Rowan's shoulder. I inhaled the scent of his cologne and relaxed. All the excitement was beginning to catch up with me, leaving me exhausted. My forehead came to rest against the side of his neck. His skin was very warm.

"If I should pass out, there's a vial of your headache remedy in my bra."

"Does that mean I have your permission to search for it?" Was he smiling?

I considered his question. "I think I'd prefer to be conscious for that."

"Really?"

The warmth of my skin now rivaled his. "So I can smack you, of course."

"Of course."

Yeah, he was definitely smiling.

CHAPTER 24

I opened my eyes and waited for the outdated wallpaper to swim into focus. A TV mounted high on the wall flickered through a weather broadcast without sound. Nope, not my room at the manor. I squinted at the time in the lower right-hand corner of the screen. 8:32 a.m.

James's concerned face came into view. "Addie?" My bed shifted as he settled on the edge.

"Hey, Fido." His dark hair stood in disarray like he'd just gone furry—or had been raking his hands through it. "Is everything okay?"

"It is now." He smiled. "How do you feel?"

"I'm conscious. I think."

"You seem pretty lucid to me." He pushed back my hair where it'd fallen over one cheek. "I was worried."

"Why? I got shot in the leg, not the head."

"I know, but…" His brow wrinkled. "I don't know what I'd do without you."

I smiled at his concern. "You'd still have Era," I teased.

"Era?" He looked up with a frown. "She likes me, not the other way around. I haven't the heart to chase her away. She wouldn't understand."

He was such a sweet guy. I patted his hand then pushed

myself up into a sitting position to look around. "They gave me a room?"

"Rowan insisted."

I smiled and shook my head. "So, no problems with the surgery?"

"None. The doc stitched you up and dug out the bullet."

"Not in that order, I hope."

He snorted. "Yeah, you're fine." He stood up and I pushed back the sheet. A large bandage covered my calf. I flexed my leg. It was sore, but not overly so.

"Don't get too crazy," he said. "You'll pull the stitches."

"It doesn't hurt."

"Pain killers."

"Ah." The wound must have been shallow. A powerful painkiller would have left me loopy. I felt clearheaded. "Just me and you?" I hoped I didn't sound too disappointed.

"Rowan walked downstairs to use the phone. Or were you referring to Emil?"

Guilt wormed its way through my gut. I'd forgotten. "How is Emil?"

"He came through surgery fine, but..." James turned away. "Let me find you a wheelchair. You need to see him."

"Why? What's wrong?" I swung my legs over the edge of the bed and slid off. The room wavered and I gripped the bedrail. I guess the painkillers hadn't completely worn off.

"Addie. Your leg." James stepped forward and steadied me with a hand on my elbow.

My head cleared and I glanced down. I had no trouble standing. "It's just a little tender." I tried to take a step toward the door, but he wouldn't release me.

"Let me see."

I figured it was easier to comply than argue. I sat back down and leaned over to peel back the bandage. A faint pink line about three inches long bisected my calf. I pulled the bandage off and a tangle of dark knots fell out. I realized they'd been stitches.

"Dear God," James whispered. "You're healed."

"How many stitches?" Stunned, I stared at the three-inch scar.

"I don't recall, but they had to dig deep. The bullet lodged against the back of your shin bone."

I looked up, meeting his wide eyes. "It has to be the Formula. I'm not magical."

"No, just immortal."

Rapid healing, no aging. I'd been so caught up with being the first to find the Formula, I hadn't fully understood what immortality meant. I still didn't, but I had time—lots of time—to come to terms with it.

"Help me find a robe," I said. "Then let's go see Emil." Perhaps he was healed by now as well.

DRESSED IN MY STYLISH ROBE and slippers, I walked with James through the hospital corridors. The stark white walls were broken up by a dark blue handrail and the occasional landscape picture. I guess they made up for the lack of windows.

We passed a little old lady shuffling in the opposite direction. She didn't glance up; too busy trying to coordinate her small steps with the movement of her walker. I watched her as we passed, noting the concentration on her lined face and the white-knuckled grip of her claw-like hands. Would that ever be me?

I glanced over at James, his youth such a contrast to the old woman.

"Will you age?" I kept my voice low.

He looked over, dark brows raised in question. "That came out of the blue."

"Not really. I'm wondering about immortality." I hooked a thumb in the direction of the old lady.

James glanced over his shoulder. "Ah." Green eyes shifted back to me. "But why ask about me?"

"I know the Elements don't age. I wondered if you were the same."

"I should be about done. Once we come into our full powers, Gavin says we stop aging."

"Gavin? The other grim?" I suppressed a shiver at the thought of the red-eyed fiend. "Do you converse with him often?" I didn't like the sound of that.

"From time to time. More when I was younger. It was nice to have someone who understood, though ole Gav is quite mad." He sighed. "Centuries of entombment, you know?"

"So, you could…visit that place when you were younger?"

"I've always been able to. I'm told that before I could walk, I used to shift forms and go around on all fours." He chuckled at that. "That's why I was home schooled."

I smiled, imagining James as a puppy, but my amusement faded as I considered the rest of it. "By full powers, you mean rip souls. At the gun shop, that was the first time, wasn't it?"

"Yes. That's why it wiped me out afterward." He shoved his hands in his pockets.

We walked in silence for a few strides. "You were going to soul-rip Lawson."

"Yes." He didn't seem remotely troubled by the admission.

I remember the way James had gone after Gerald. "I don't think I could have called you off."

"No."

I stopped and he turned to face me.

"He had a gun to your head."

"Yes, but—"

A faint glow backlit his eyes and a growl crept into his words. "I protect what is mine."

I smiled in spite of my misgivings. "I think Rowan is a bad influence."

James returned a hesitant smile. "If you think I'm hell on earth, you should see him when he gets pissed."

"What happened?"

"I smelled Emil's blood from the alley and then Rowan found your compass." James shook his head. "You saw what happened as soon as he saw Lawson."

"Is he all right?" I touched the front of my robe, wondering what had become of my bra. "I had another vial of his headache relief."

"He's fine." James gave me a tight-lipped smile.

"What?"

"You. You're such a good person."

I arched a brow. "Who's addled now?"

"I'm serious." He tried not to smile and failed. "Look at Rowan. You obviously can't stand the guy, yet you try to help him."

"You think I hate him?"

"Not even George can piss you off as fast as Rowan does."

I grunted. Lumping Rowan and George into the same category wasn't something I cared for.

"I bet you'd even help George if the situation warranted."

"Not to shatter your illusions, but if I found George lying in the street bleeding, I'd back up and run over him again."

James laughed and I started walking.

"So, what's this about Emil?" I asked.

"Ironically, it returns to your questions about immortality." He gestured at the next room. "We're here."

I walked in ahead of him, uneasy about what I might find. How badly had Emil been injured? And why hadn't the Final

Formula healed him as it had me? I stepped into the room and almost collided with someone walking out. He caught me by the shoulders to avoid a collision and I looked up.

"Neil?" My old Alchemica colleague gave me a surprised smile. He was the last person I expected here.

"Amelia." His eyes flicked to James and back to me, skimming downward to take in my hospital attire. "I heard you were injured. Are you okay?"

"Yes." I walked passed him, circling around the curtain. "I wouldn't expect you to visit the man who kicked you out of the Alchemica."

I turned toward the bed and got my first look at the man lying there. An incredibly familiar man: my white-haired mentor from the Alchemica. Before I could puzzle out why Emil appeared in his sixties again, a wave of déjà vu washed over me, and I fell into a memory.

Emil sat on the side of my bed, his white robes a soft glow in the dim light of my bedside lamp. He brushed back my hair, running a hand down my cheek.

"Ah, Amelia," he sighed my name. "I wish you could accompany me. I also wish he'd remove that damn hood so I could see his expression. What do you think he'll say when I show him this?" He pushed aside the sleeve of his robe, revealing the five bands encircling his right biceps. Even in the dim light, the angry flush around the newest band was clear.

"Of course, the real visual will be when I take the Formula before his eyes." He flashed me a grin and rose to his feet. "He'll have to declare me magical now." He leaned over and retrieved something from my nightstand: a syringe. He rolled it between his fingers, and I realized it was blood.

"Addie? Hey, you with me?" James's voice broke into my consciousness and the image of Emil floated away.

I blinked and focused on the face before me.

"Here." James touched a tissue to my upper lip. "Your nose is bleeding."

"Oh." I took the tissue from him and dabbed away the smear of blood.

"What happened?" Neil stood a few feet away, watching me with concerned eyes.

"Déjà vu," James said.

"That's what I call it. Sometimes I get these little flashes of memory." I sat in one of those oversized hospital chairs, though I didn't remember sitting down. Unable to see Emil from my position, I pushed myself to my feet. James moved closer, ready to catch me, but the déjà vu didn't return.

Sixty-six-year-old Emil lay sleeping beneath the sheets. An IV and several monitors flashed and beeped softly at his bedside.

"What's wrong with him?" I asked. "Did the bullet puncture something?"

"He got lucky with the gun shot. The surgery was uneventful, but he hasn't regained consciousness. And then there's his appearance." James looked at me. "Can you explain it?"

I glanced over at Neil who'd moved to the opposite side of Emil's bed.

"He didn't take the Final Formula," Neil said.

"So it would seem." I pushed up the right sleeve of Emil's hospital gown, revealing the five bands. The newest a little darker than the others, but long-since healed. "He must have tested the formula on me first."

"Why?" James asked. "He's a master alchemist. Self-doubt is not part of that equation."

Wishing I could ask Emil, I sat down on the side of his bed and laid my hand on his forehead. His temperature felt good—neither feverish nor chilled. I touched the deep lines at the corner of one eye. I felt so much closer to him. This was the man I remembered. My mentor and teacher.

"Emil," I whispered, letting my hand slide down to his wrinkled cheek. "Grand Master, can you hear me? It's Ad—" I stumbled on my name. "It's Amelia."

The curtain between us and the open door rattled open. I jerked my fingers from Emil's cheek and I looked up with a gasp—right into Rowan's angry gray eyes.

"Why aren't you in your bed?" he demanded.

"Because I don't want to be?"

His frown deepened and I sighed. No wonder James thought I hated the guy.

Rowan's frown shifted to Neil.

"I should go," Neil said, stepping back from the bed. His brown eyes met mine. "Call me if you learn something?"

"Yeah, sure," I said.

Neil nodded. "Gentlemen," he said to Rowan and James, and then left the room.

"What was he doing here?" Rowan asked.

"He heard I'd been injured."

"How?"

I realized I hadn't asked. Who had told Neil? Someone at the PIA?

"You shouldn't be walking around." Rowan's voice interrupted my thoughts.

"She heals like an Element," James said. "Nothing but a pink line where the incision was."

"The Formula?" Rowan asked.

I shrugged, uncomfortable with the way he watched me. I hoped my cheeks weren't as flushed as they felt.

"So, what happened to him?" Rowan moved to the other side of the bed.

"He never took the Final Formula. I'm guessing his youth was the product of an age potion." An extremely powerful one, which was an accomplishment almost as impressive. "I suspect that's why he didn't answer his phone. He was in the middle of metamorphosis. Age potions take time to manifest."

Rowan grunted. He studied Emil in silence while I stole a glance at him. Like James, he wore the same clothes from the night before, his face shadowed with his morning beard. I remembered how he'd carried me away from the garage, and my cheeks warmed again.

His eyes rose to mine and I quickly looked away.

"If he found the Final Formula, then why didn't he take it?" Rowan asked.

I told him about my newest memory. "He planned to take it before an audience. You. That was the purpose of the invitations he sent out."

"And then the Alchemica blew."

"We won't know until he wakes, but that's what I think, yes."

Rowan studied Emil, but whatever he was thinking, he kept to himself.

I stepped away from the bed. "I'm going to go see if I have anything to wear."

"I had some things sent over." Rowan glanced at his watch and turned to James. "Would you care to go down to the lobby and see if Donovan is here?"

"Sure," James said. "I'll get your things, Ad."

"Okay. Thanks." I turned to follow him from the room.

"Addie?" Rowan stopped me, but before he could say anything else, his phone rang.

"Who is it?"

"Waylon."

I stepped forward and gripped his wrist. "Don't answer it."

"Why not?"

"Have you told him anything?"

"I called earlier, but he was out of the office."

"Don't give him any information."

"You're still angry at him for taking you in for questioning." Rowan's phone stopped ringing.

"And when he claims to know nothing about Lawson's terrorism sideline, we're going to take him at his word?"

"Do we have reason to believe he's lying?"

I glanced over, gauging the seriousness of Rowan's expression. He raised his brows in question. He seemed to want to know what I thought.

I rubbed my forehead. "Maybe. I don't know. I guess it doesn't matter."

A final glance at Emil, and I headed back to my room. Rowan walked beside me, but to my surprise, didn't say anything the entire length of the hall.

"What's wrong?" Rowan asked when we reached my room.

I circled the curtain divider, disappointed that James hadn't returned with my things. "I had a lead; you ashed him."

"He'd shoved a gun under your jaw." A hint of anger laced his tone.

"So?" I turned to face him. "I've seen you ash guns before."

He crossed his arms, pulling his sweater tight across his shoulders. "It's not that simple."

"You were close enough. Hell, you were able to distinguish between him and me." I still remembered that terrifying instant the heat enveloped me.

"Drop it. I did what I had to. What the hell were you doing outside the bar anyway? You were supposed to check the loft."

"I saw one of Emil's customers from the club and followed him."

"You followed a drug addict into a dark alley."

"He took potions, not drugs. I caught him meeting with one of the SWAT guys from the raid on the Alchemica."

Rowan pinched the bridge of his nose and squeezed his eyes shut in obvious frustration. "Give me strength," he muttered. He dropped his hand and frowned at me. "Why didn't you get James or me?"

"I didn't have time. He called for back up. I had to warn Emil."

"And *you* were taken as well."

"If I had my potions—"

"Enough!"

I jumped at his outburst.

He closed the distance between us and clamped a hand on the back of my neck, his fingers threading through my loose hair. "You drive me crazy, you know that?" His voice dropped, and he continued in a harsh whisper. "Half the time I can't decide if I want to strangle you or kiss you."

I blinked.

A knock sounded on the door beyond the curtain. "Addie?" James called.

Rowan held my gaze for one long moment before he released me and stepped back. Did he say things like that to keep me unbalanced or was he truly attracted to me?

"Yeah. Come in," I called.

Donovan followed James into the room. He carried a small suitcase that looked even tinier in his large hands, and placed it on the bed.

"Thanks for bringing that over."

"No problem." He abruptly wrapped me in a hug. "I'm glad you're okay, little alchemist."

His concern and clear relief left me blinking. I hugged him back, surprised by my own reaction.

"Donovan will give you and James a ride back to the manor," Rowan said.

I stepped out of Donovan's embrace and turned to face Rowan. "Where are you going?"

"I have things to do at the Offices."

Right. The Flame Lord was a busy man. My escapades must be seriously cutting into his limited time.

"Don't work too hard."

Rowan held my gaze. "You stay out of trouble." He turned and left the room.

A KNOCK PULLED ME FROM the nap I hadn't intended to take. I sat up and looked around, reassuring myself that I was back in my room at the manor. The trip home from the hospital made me realize that I wasn't as recovered as I thought. I'd decided to lie down for a bit; I hadn't meant to fall asleep.

I swung my legs over the side of the bed. "Yeah, come in."

I suppressed a groan when Cora stepped in the room. "Good, you're up." She crossed to the foot of my bed.

"Sort of." I rubbed a hand over my face.

"Rowan would like to see you in his office."

I dropped my hand. "He's already back?"

"You've been asleep most of the day."

"Oh."

She lifted a strap from her shoulder and set a familiar pack on the foot of my bed.

"My vials!" I sprang to my feet and reached for the pack. I started to open it and hesitated. Rowan hadn't seemed too keen on returning my vials earlier. "Does Rowan know about this?"

"It was his idea."

I stared at my pack.

"Is something wrong?" Cora asked.

"I didn't think he'd ever return my vials—at least, not while I was staying with all of you."

"It's not a choice I supported."

I looked up. Surprised and yet not surprised by her bluntness.

"Betray his trust and you'll deal with me."

I held her gaze, refusing to let her see how much she intimidated me. "I won't betray him—or you."

She studied me one long moment. "This is no small matter. Rowan doesn't trust easily. To trust is to relinquish control, and that's not who he is. Or perhaps I should say, *what* he is."

"I don't understand."

"Being an Element is more than being able to wield a certain type of magic; it is who we are. It defines us."

"Okay." I still didn't get what she was telling me.

"Fire is the most volatile of the Elements. Rowan lost control once, not long after the magic returned. His family paid the price."

"What—"

"It's not my place to say, but he vowed to never lose control again. And he hasn't."

I thought about that, remembering his reaction with Lawson. Was that what had him so upset? Had he overreacted and ashed the man when he could have ashed the gun? How close had he come to hurting me?

"I believe that is why he has lived as long as he has," Cora added.

I forced my attention back to the conversation. "And because being an Element defines more than his magic, he has to control everything."

"You are indeed a bright girl."

"Thanks for the condescension."

She placed a hand on my shoulder, an oddly warm gesture

from the woman who'd so casually threatened me. "You confound Rowan's attempts to control you."

"So, he threw in the towel and returned my vials."

"I'm not sure what he was thinking there." Without another word, she turned for the door.

"What about water?" I called after her.

She hesitated and glanced back. Cool and elegant on the surface, but I'd caught a glimpse of the dark undercurrents beneath. She gave me a knowing smile and left without a word.

I released a breath I hadn't realized I'd been holding. "Elements."

I ducked into the bathroom to splash a little water on my face and pulled my hair into a ponytail. No need to look like I'd lain in bed all afternoon. What did Rowan want?

Anxious, I hurried to his office at the back of the house. The door stood partially open, so I gave it a light knock.

James opened the door and flashed me a grin. "Come in."

I took a few steps into the room and stopped. Rowan had company. A man stood with his back to me, engaged in conversation with Rowan. I frowned, trying to puzzle out why the guy seemed familiar when Rowan looked up, catching my eye.

"Finally," he said.

The other man turned, the movement drawing my attention. I gasped as he faced me.

"Hello, Addie," Agent Lawson said.

CHAPTER

25

For a moment, I could do nothing but stare at the man before me. This made no sense. Rowan had ashed him. James even confirmed it.

Agent Lawson gave me an odd smile and I reached for my back pocket.

"Addie, don't." James caught my wrist. "It's not Lawson. It's Lydia."

"Lydia?" Rowan's friend? The one with the facial deformity? I glanced at Rowan, but he said nothing. He leaned against the front of his desk, an amused glint in his gray eyes.

"I'm sorry to startle you," Lydia/Lawson said, pulling my attention back to her/him.

"How...?" I stumbled on the question, not sure what to ask. Dear God, she looked exactly like him. Same hair, same height. Even the voice sounded the same.

"I'm a mimic," she answered. A frown creased Lawson's brow. "You didn't know that?" She looked back at Rowan.

"But it's so perfect," I said before Rowan could speak. "The voice, everything."

"I mimic at the genetic level."

"He must have driven that car in the garage," James explained. "Lydia found some DNA...or something."

She gave him a fond smile—which looked really weird on Lawson's face.

"But why look like him? What are you going to do?" I directed the question at Rowan.

"Lydia will search his office, and when we locate it, his home."

"You think the PIA *is* involved?"

"I believe Lawson's behavior warrants further investigation. That doesn't mean the agency as a whole had anything to do with it, but I prefer to remove all doubt and investigate him myself."

I smiled, pleased that he wasn't going to rely on the PIA's word, but before I could comment, Donovan walked in. He turned to James. "Are we ready?"

"Lydia?" James prompted.

"You're going?" I asked him.

"I'm going to walk in with her, pretend like I'm there to see an agent."

"I'm driving the getaway car," Donovan said. He gave me a wink, and I couldn't help but grin. The big guy had a knack for making me smile.

"I expect frequent updates," Rowan said.

"You're not going?" I asked.

"No need. James can watch her back."

I turned back to James and he smiled. It struck me then how much my sidekick had come into his own over these last few days. The Elements turned to him more and more, trusting him with Era and now Lydia.

I stepped forward and hugged him. "You'll be careful?"

He drew in a breath, perhaps surprised by my actions, but quickly regained his composure. "Always." He hugged me back. "Don't wander off again. We had a hell of a time tracking you—even with your compass."

I released him. "I'll behave."

"Yeah, right." He grinned.

"Shall we?" Lydia asked.

The others agreed and, promising to call Rowan with any news, they left the room. Donovan pulled the door shut behind him. I guess now was as good a time as any. I took a deep breath and turned to face Rowan.

"Thank you for returning my vials."

He straightened and walked around behind the desk to his chair. "I hope I haven't made a mistake."

"You think I'd use a potion against you or—"

"No." He leaned forward, bracing his elbows on the polished surface. "I fear the return of your potions will make you over-confident."

"Over-confident?"

"Your tendency to jump into situations without thought."

"I do not. I—"

"So, you thought it a good idea to take on those guys by yourself?"

"Are we back on this? Look, it wasn't—"

The cell phone lying on his desk began to buzz. "Hold that thought," he said and picked up the phone. He glanced at the screen and then brought it to his ear. "I'm listening."

His Grace could really use a catchier greeting.

He picked up a pen and pulled a notepad closer. "Go ahead."

I stepped back from his desk and sat in one of the other chairs while he wrote. I fumed in silence, annoyed that he'd take a call in the middle of our argument. Over-confident. Bullshit. My confidence was completely warranted.

"Yes, thank you." Rowan ended the call. He ripped the top sheet from his notepad and got to his feet.

"What is it?" I asked.

"My contact at the police department was able to get me the last number Lawson called."

"What?" I came to my feet. I hadn't even realized that was a possibility. "Who was it?"

Rowan glanced at his paper. "The number is registered to an Ian Mallory at 601 Beechnut Street."

"Do you know him?"

"No." He came around the side of his desk.

I stepped in front of him, blocking his path. "What are you going to do?"

"I thought I'd drive over and take a look."

"Now?" It was all I could do not to rub my hands together in anticipation. I'd finally meet the man who commanded Lawson. The man who'd been after me all these months. "I'm coming with you."

"You were just released from the hospital. You're staying here." He moved to step around me, but I caught his arm.

"You're not going without me."

Rowan frowned. "And your presence will help how?"

"I'm not without resources. I snuck into your offices."

"And I caught you."

"So?" Okay, not much of a comeback, but he wasn't going to win this argument.

"If you get caught tonight, you may not be able to kiss your way out of trouble."

I ignored the heat in my cheeks. "A little faith, Your Grace."

He studied me a moment.

"Don't leave me out of this." I gripped his arm tightly. "Please."

He held my gaze for one long moment before releasing a sigh. "Very well. Get what you need."

I tried not to grin. "You might want to change into something dark and a little less," I gestured at his expensive sweater and slacks, "GQ."

The corner of his mouth quirked. "Well, you are the breaking and entering pro."

I ignored that and hurried from the room.

ROWAN PULLED TO THE CURB and put the Camaro in neutral. The sun had set, leaving only the occasional streetlight to illuminate the tree-lined avenue. A light wind set the bare branches in motion, causing a play of shadows along the cemetery entrance across from us.

"Do you want to call your guy back and check the address?" I asked.

Rowan picked up his notepaper and held it closer to the driver's-side window, reading it in the illumination of the nearest streetlight. "We must have missed a house. Are you sure the last one was 599?"

I scooted forward, squinting through the windshield. "Check out the gate. Specifically, the arch."

He rested an arm atop the steering wheel, tipping his head to see around the rearview mirror. The light just reached the cemetery entrance. The numbers worked into the metal arch were in shadow, but still visible—601. The *house* number we were looking for.

Rowan pulled out his phone and dialed. A short conversation, and he tucked it back in his pocket. "This is the address registered to the number Lawson called."

"Maybe it was a cover." I assumed a phone could be registered to a false address.

Rowan grunted. "Possible." He shut off the car and pulled the key from the ignition. "Ever go walking through a graveyard after dark?"

"Not in the last three months." If he thought the suggestion would frighten me, he was wrong. I opened my door.

Rowan chuckled and we climbed out of the car. The headlights flashed as he locked the doors. In silence, we walked side-by-side toward the entrance. At least we wouldn't have to do any breaking and entering.

"I once took a girl to a cemetery—back in my high school days," Rowan admitted.

I grinned. "How'd that work out, Casanova?"

"She went into hysterics and I had to take her home."

I snorted. "So, not a venue you ever tried again?"

"Until now."

I gave his shoulder a shove as we stepped beneath the arch and into the cemetery. "No offense, but I'm more likely to throw a potion than jump into your arms."

"Let me know when I need to duck."

I rolled my eyes and turned my attention to our surroundings. "Wow." The cemetery spread before us, taking up several city blocks. Streetlights dotted the narrow roads that wove among the graves, but the bulk of the place lay in darkness. Large trees crowded the headstones, their bare branches casting eerie shadows in the half-light.

"Nice place," I said. We started forward, our shoes on the asphalt the only noise.

"It does have a certain ambiance."

I glanced over, amused, but he kept his attention on our surroundings. I didn't see a caretaker's building, just hundreds of headstones and a half-dozen mausoleums.

"Since we suspect necromantic involvement, should we be concerned that we've ended up in a graveyard?" I asked.

"Caskets are buried within a cement sarcophagus under six feet of soil. Even accounting for the unnatural strength of the dead, I doubt any could be raised to attack us."

Good point, but it didn't completely alleviate my unease.

"Besides, you have me," he added.

I chewed my lip and managed to stop an eye roll. "Let's hope it doesn't come to that."

We walked for perhaps half an hour, staying on the road. No need to wet our shoes in the dewy grass. It wasn't like we'd find the mystery phone hidden in a planter.

It surprised me that Rowan bothered to examine the place so thoroughly. Perhaps, like me, he hated to admit defeat. Seeming to hear my thoughts, he stopped at the next intersection.

"I suspect this is a waste of time. I think you're right about using this address as a cover." He crossed his arms and frowned back toward the lights of downtown.

I hated to see his disappointment—and that wasn't the reaction I thought I should be feeling. Shouldn't I be disappointed for myself alone? Another lead had run dry. Rowan had put a lot of effort into helping me, but learning what had happened to the Alchemica and recovering my memory was ultimately my problem.

"Maybe Lydia and James found something," I said.

"Maybe."

"Or perhaps James could look Lawson up in hell and interrogate him."

The corner of Rowan's mouth quirked.

As I was contemplating another option, a low thump interrupted. Oddly, I felt it as much as heard it—as if it came from underground.

Rowan dropped his arms to his sides, his eyes meeting mine.

"I take it you heard that," I whispered.

He looked around, eyes sweeping the shadows. I did the same, not so sure I wanted to locate the source. He'd said it'd be nearly impossible for the dead to escape their graves, but at the moment, I wasn't so sure.

"This way." He stepped into the grass. "I think."

He led me a dozen yards and stopped. Time slipped past as we stood listening, and I began to doubt what I'd heard. Sound could carry in odd ways, especially at night.

Stone grated on stone from somewhere close by. Rowan caught my arm and pulled me down behind the nearest headstone. We crouched in the damp grass, waiting. I wondered if I'd be able to hear anything over my pounding heart.

"The mausoleum," Rowan whispered. He nodded toward the large stone structure about thirty yards away.

I squinted, trying to make out the building's contours in the shadows. Something glinted in the darkness, and I leaned forward, pressing my palm against cold granite to keep my balance.

Another flicker satisfied my suspicion. "There's a light, under the door," I whispered. "Maybe a candle." The dead would have no need for a candle. Would they?

"Let's check it out." He still held my upper arm, but slid his hand down to grasp mine as we stood.

Surprised by the handholding, I followed him on a meandering course that drew us closer and closer to the building. The headstones in this part of the cemetery were worn almost smooth with age, and I noted that most had been here since the 1800s. Rowan led me over behind another headstone. No light flickered beneath the door. Everything was as quiet as…well, the grave. Which upon reflection, was how I preferred my graves.

Rowan started forward and I followed, hoping we wouldn't have to venture inside the mausoleum. I gripped his hand and got a squeeze in return, though he kept his eyes on our destination. In weathered stone above the door, the name Mallory was inscribed. I pulled up short.

"What is it?" Rowan whispered.

"The name. Over the door." I nodded at it.

"Good catch. I missed it." He gave my hand another squeeze and pulled me forward. I guess he didn't share my apprehension.

A metal door barred the entrance. A hasp with a rusted bolt through the staple appeared to be the only security measure. Where were the chains and padlocks? Didn't the family worry about vandalism? Or maybe, considering the age of most of the graves, there was no longer any family to look after the place.

Rowan plucked out the bolt and opened the hasp. He released my hand to take the door handle in both of his. The thing looked heavy.

I tensed, ready for the screech of metal on metal, but it swung open silently—and judging by Rowan's expression, easily.

I expected darkness within, but found it as well lit inside as out, thanks to a multitude of holes in the roof. Years of leaf litter lay piled against the sides of the room, leaving the center oddly clear. Sealed vaults lined the walls, but I didn't stop to read the names. My attention centered on the sarcophagus in the center of the room. Constructed of flat black stone, it seemed to be made of shadow. More disturbing was the lid leaning against its side. Was this the source of the noise we'd heard?

Rowan started forward and I followed, adjusting the fanny pack strapped around my waist. The confidence my vials lent me diminished with each step. I let Rowan move ahead of me. He clearly intended to peek inside. Myself, I could forgo that pleasure—until he looked over the side and grunted.

I stepped up beside Rowan and understood his surprise. It wasn't a sarcophagus with a body inside. It was an empty space, with a staircase leading down into some kind of cellar. A light flickered on the wall below.

The sarcophagus stood waist high, and Rowan vaulted the side with ease, dropping down onto a landing at the top of the steps. Wordlessly, he offered me a hand. I didn't want to go, but

I didn't want him to go alone. Nor did I want to remain here alone.

I took his hand and let him help me into the sarcophagus. The stairs below the first two were rough-hewn rock. Fitted stone of the same variety lined the walls. The floor might have been more of the same, but I couldn't see it for the dark red area rug.

We stopped at the bottom of the stairs and stared in awe—or at least, I did. Bookcases lined two of the walls, their shelves loaded. I couldn't be certain in the dim light, but they looked like hardbound volumes from centuries past. No cheap paperbacks or glossy dust jackets. A pair of wingback chairs sat in one corner, a table between them. The candle sat flickering next to an open volume, but whoever had been reading wasn't in the room.

I took a step forward and then another, my tread muffled by the thick carpet.

Rowan's hand settled on the small of my back, and I almost jumped out of my skin.

"Get the candle," he whispered.

I looked back and saw why. The stairs had descended along one wall, but beneath them stood an arched doorway. The candlelight reached no more than a foot into the blackness.

I did as asked, glancing at the open book on the table. It appeared to be an old medical book. Dense text covered one page while the other presented a rather graphic illustration of an amputation. Great. Like I needed to see that at this moment.

I snatched up the candle in its old-fashioned metal holder and hurried back to where Rowan waited for me at the doorway. I let him take the candle, keeping my hands free to fling a potion if necessary.

The hallway, or should I say, tunnel, pressed close. The arched ceiling cleared Rowan's head by inches and the walls brushed his shoulders in spots. Tight spaces had never bothered me before, but this did. I couldn't seem to draw a breath deep enough.

Rowan's body blocked most of the light, throwing the room we'd just left into darkness. I rested a hand on his waist, reassuring myself with his nearness, and tried not to think about my exposed back—or the fact that I'd never hear anyone approach across that thick carpet.

Rowan stopped and I bumped into him. Before I could apologize, something scraped across the stone floor behind me. I whirled and pressed my back against Rowan's, struggling to find the zipper on my fanny pack as I strained to see in the darkness behind me.

"Addie?" he whispered, half turning toward me. The light of his candle illuminated the empty corridor behind me, but it didn't reach far into the room beyond. Dim light from the mausoleum filtered down the open stairwell, revealing a room of dark shapes and shadows.

"Sorry," I whispered. "I'm being a weenie." I belied my light tone by pressing against his side.

His arm slid around my shoulders. "It's okay. This was all part of my plan, remember?"

I looked up and caught a grin in the flickering light. "Scaring me into your arms?"

The grin became a smile. "Seems to be working."

"Yes, it does."

He studied me for one long moment, his expression growing more serious. His eyes kindled, and like me, he glanced back up the hall to the other room. "I feel like we're being watched."

"Thanks. Nothing like having my fears confirmed."

"You feel it, too?"

"Yes."

He nodded and then stepped sideways, pulling me forward into another chamber. He held the candle aloft, revealing a space of similar size to the last room, but not as well decorated. Here the stone floor and walls were unadorned. The light didn't reach the far wall, but it did illuminate a table to our right.

"Oh, wow." Forgetting my fear, I moved closer. The table held an assortment of alchemical equipment. I stared in wonder at the alembic and assorted glassware. A small cauldron sat on an iron tripod with an unlit Sterno burner beneath. Archaic, but functional, though I had to wonder about a practitioner who heated chemicals in such an enclosed space.

"Alchemy?" Rowan asked.

"Yeah. Really old school. This equipment is incredible. I could be wrong, but I don't think they're reproductions."

Rowan grunted and moved on down the wall, taking the light with him. I guess he wasn't impressed.

I started to turn away and noticed a stack of paper near the far end of the table. Moving closer, I discovered notes written on the top page. I couldn't read it in the dimness, so I picked it up and stuffed it in my jacket pocket. Taking another alchemist's notes gave me a twinge of conscience, but the idea of learning more about him overrode my scruples. Who did alchemy in a hidden room beneath a mausoleum?

"Addie?" Rowan's voice pulled me from my musings. He stood by the back wall, his light illuminating a series of shelves. Most held extra glassware and jars of what appeared to be ingredients. Curious, I moved closer. You could learn a lot about an alchemist from his ingredient shelf.

"What do you make of this?" Rowan whispered. He moved the candle closer to a group of wide-mouth glass jars. Each filled with a liquid and...something else.

Not wanting to look, but knowing he expected me to, I stepped up beside him. A piece of meat floated in each jar. No, not meat. "Organs," I whispered.

"Hearts," Rowan said. "They're all hearts."

I swallowed. He was right.

"Blood alchemy?" he asked.

I looked up. "You've heard of it?"

"Yes. Why do you look surprised?"

"You gave me your blood."

"It made sense to use it in your potion. Besides, I trust you."

Warmth suffused my body, and I turned my attention back to the jars to hide my blush. "Given the lab equipment and ingredients, you might be right. This does look like blood alchemy." I didn't admit it, but I could think of a dozen applications for the ingredient before me.

Something moved within a jar. A flicker of light upon the glass? I leaned in closer. The movement came again and I jerked back with a gasp.

"It moved!" I pointed a shaking finger at the jar.

Rowan moved the candle closer and leaned in for a look. He pulled back an instant later. "Shit." He looked back at me. "This isn't blood alchemy. It's—"

A low growl filled the chamber.

I turned toward the doorway, squinting my eyes to better see in the dim glow of Rowan's candle. A dark canine shape stepped from the shadows. For a second, I thought it was James, and then I noticed the white patches. The animal stepped farther into the room, and I realized it wasn't white fur, it was bone. It looked up and its filmed-over dead eyes met mine.

"Necromancy," I finished for Rowan. I stumbled back and my butt bumped the table, causing the glassware to chime. Without warning, the zombie dog went up in a flash of flame. I closed my eyes, but it was already too late to save my night vision.

Snarls echoed around the room and Rowan shouted. I whirled in time to see two more dogs pull him down from behind. The candle hit the floor with a metallic clatter and winked out.

CHAPTER

26

Rowan cried out again, this time in pain. In total darkness, I felt for my fanny pack and dug out a foam-insulated case. My fumbling fingers found the two vials stored inside: my newly designed Fire Hazard potions. I pulled out a vial without dropping it and stopped to listen. Grunts and snarls pinpointed my target, but I hesitated. I could hit Rowan as easily as the dogs.

I turned and hurled the vial at the opposite wall. It hit with a tink of broken glass, followed by a bright flash. The thin paste splattered across the wall and ignited on contact. As it burned through the stone, it illuminated the room.

The two zombie dogs had Rowan on the floor, one with a grip on his thigh while the other went for his throat. He twisted aside and the animal caught his shoulder instead. Why hadn't he incinerated them?

I pulled out the other vial and ran toward him. The dog released his shoulder and lunged for Rowan's neck once more. He caught it by the throat, baring his own teeth with his effort to hold it back. The animal didn't notice me, and I landed a solid kick to the creature's ribs. Bone crunched like dry twigs and the thing went flying, smashing into the wall with another crunch. It must not weigh much, because I'm not that strong.

I drew back my arm to throw and stopped, stunned by what

I saw. The dog's caved-in ribcage began to rebuild itself. When the dog rolled to its stomach and prepared to stand, I threw the vial. It shattered against the wall, but enough of the paste landed on the dog to ignite it. The flesh that wasn't burning continued to mend. In a matter of seconds, the dog rose to its feet, dead eyes focused on Rowan. Neither dog had even glanced at me.

Rowan continued to struggle with the other dog. He pulled up his opposite leg, trying to kick the animal in the face. A couple of weak attempts and Rowan slumped against the floor, chest heaving. Something wasn't right.

I ran at the second dog and punted it across the room as I had the first. It smacked the wall and collapsed at its base, but like the first dog, it immediately began to regenerate.

"I'm out of fire," I shouted at Rowan. I positioned myself between him and the dog. Its flaming companion was now fully engulfed, though it managed a few more steps before it fell to pieces.

"Can you move?" I asked Rowan while I kept my eye on the remaining dog.

Something touched my shoulder.

I screamed and whirled, taking a hasty step back. Only a foot separated me from a hooded figure. He reached for me with one skeletal hand, scraps of flesh clinging to the yellowed bone.

I stumbled away and my heels caught something solid. Another cry escaped as I fell, landing hard on my butt, my legs draped over Rowan's.

"Addie?" he whispered.

He's strong, the hooded figure said. I wondered how it could speak if its lips and tongue were as decayed as its hand. Then I realized it hadn't spoken. Not aloud. Like James in his hell dimension, this thing had projected the words directly into my mind.

My hounds feed on the life force of the living. It waved a hand toward the remaining dog.

Life force? The hairs on my forearms stood up. That sounded eerily similar to what James could do, but these creatures didn't appear to be hellhounds. The remaining animal had finished rebuilding its emaciated form and rose to its feet.

I pulled my legs off Rowan and got to my knees. Rowan's gray eyes opened a moment before they slid closed again. He wasn't unconscious, just drained. It occurred to me that he hadn't tried to incinerate anything since the dogs got him. An idea forming, I bent over him to hide my actions and slid my fingers into the front pocket of my fanny pack.

Few survive a prolonged bite, the hooded figure continued. *But this is the first time they've chewed on an Element.*

Alarmed, I looked up. He knew what Rowan was. "Who are you?" I would have liked to put more force behind the words, but they came out as a broken whisper. Had the thing been watching us? Was this the presence we'd both felt?

A dry rasping sound answered me, and I realized that it was laughing. The dog paced closer, but didn't attack.

"What do you want?" I demanded, my voice stronger this time. I wormed the vial out of my pocket.

Freedom, but I'll settle for you. It moved closer, the frayed ends of its robe dragging the floor.

Rowan tried to sit up, but failed. "Lich," he whispered.

Lich King, the thing answered with another rasping laugh.

I didn't get the significance of the exchange. I knew that a lich was an animated corpse with a consciousness, but that was the extent of my knowledge.

"Drink this," I whispered to Rowan while the thing still laughed. I brought the vial to Rowan's lips and watched him swallow. It was Emil's magic enhancing potion—the same stuff

I'd used on Lawson. It had upped Lawson's magical ability. Maybe it would do the same for Rowan.

Rowan cried out and rolled onto his side, cradling his head in his hands.

Oh God. What if I'd hurt him? "Rowan!" I gripped his shoulder.

What did you do? the lich demanded. A gesture and the dog started toward us. It moved in silence. No growling, no menace, just dead eyes focused on Rowan. That was enough.

I rose to my feet, ready to intercept it, when it suddenly exploded in a flash of light. No flames, no sense of burning. It had simply vaporized. I looked back at Rowan and found him sitting up, hands braced against the floor. He stared at me with wide eyes at full glow, the gold flaring so bright it nearly masked the orange. He turned his head to where the lich stood, but it was gone.

No way the thing could have made it back across the room to the doorway. It could either move very quickly or it could turn invisible. I didn't want to consider either alternative.

Rowan closed his eyes, the cords in his neck visible in the fading light of my fire potions. I hurried back to his side.

"Get away from me," he whispered. "I can't control it." As if to illustrate, something on the table popped in a flash of light.

"You're going to have to." I knelt to get my shoulder under his arm. "We're getting out of here."

"Addie—"

"I know you're hurt, but I need you to help me. I can't carry you."

"Go without me. Call for help. I'll—"

"Less talk, more moving." I wrapped an arm around his back and tried to pull him up.

He quit arguing and started to help me. "Why don't you ever

listen?" He drew a loud breath when he tried to put weight on his injured leg.

"It's part of my charm." I took more of his weight when he came to his feet. Damn, he was heavy.

The light was fading fast. I didn't want to think about what might be in the dark with us once it went out. Instead, I put everything I had into moving him through the tight corridor—we had to turn sideways—and into the first room. Random things kept exploding in flashes of blinding light. I could have complained about the beating my eyes were taking, but I decided just to be grateful I wasn't the latest flash.

The stairs took an eternity to climb, but we finally made it to the landing at the top. We both gripped the wall of the sarcophagus, gasping for breath.

Rowan's shoulders slumped and his chin dropped to his chest.

"Hey," I gripped his upper arm.

His eyes slid closed and he dropped to a knee, one hand still gripping the lip of the sarcophagus. The dim glow from the roof holes illuminated his face—and the blood on his upper lip. His nose was bleeding.

Clutching his shoulder, I squatted beside him. "Rowan." I touched his cheek and jerked my fingers away at the flare of heat. He was burning up—maybe literally.

"Shit, shit, shit." I unzipped my jacket and reached down the front of my shirt for the vial I now kept in my bra.

Rise! the now familiar voice intoned.

I looked around, trying to see where it came from, even looking back down the stairs, but I couldn't see the lich anywhere. A rumble from within the mausoleum brought me to my feet. One of the burial vaults slid open and then another. One by one, each drawer slid out.

"Rowan?" I squeezed his shoulder. "I need you."

He didn't respond. Instead, he released the wall and began to fall. I moved to intercept him, positioning myself between him and the open stairs. I caught him, but his weight and momentum pulled me down. We teetered on the edge of the stairs before I was able to shove him back onto the landing. I collapsed against the wall with him slumped against me. Familiar moans sounded from the room above us. Zombies. Hundred-year-old zombies. The fresh ones were nasty enough. I didn't want to see what was shuffling around up there.

"Rowan," I whispered, patting his hot cheek. He mumbled something, but I couldn't understand him.

I uncapped the vial and shifted him around until I had his head tipped back. "Drink this." I poured the vial's contents into his mouth, careful to keep his head back so it'd roll down his throat. His Adam's apple bobbed and I released a breath. At least, I hadn't drowned him.

Now what, alchemist? the lich whispered.

I gasped and turned my head. It stood a few steps below us. If not for the low hood, I'd be looking it in the face. The moans and shuffles within the mausoleum surrounded us. In seconds, they'd be looking over the wall.

"Call off your buddies and let's talk." I tried for a confident tone, but wasn't so certain it won out over the terror. God, I hated zombies.

The lich seemed to consider my request. Above me, a skeletal hand gripped the top of the wall, and across from it another.

Hold, the lich said. Silence took the place of the moans and shuffles.

"You're a necromancer. Or you were."

Very good, Amelia.

Goosebumps rose on my arms.

I hope you don't mind if I call you Amelia.

"Call me what you will, Ian."

The rasping laugh escaped his hood.

"So, you are the guy Lawson called."

Called what?

He wasn't going to make this easy. I tried another approach. "You said you wanted me. Why?"

You could very well be the greatest alchemist of your time. Maybe all time.

"Flattering me isn't necessary. You already have the advantage."

Another breathy laugh followed. It occurred to me that he must be using some magical means to speak, but the laugh was produced from whatever was left of his body. I shivered.

"What do you want from me?" I repeated.

The immortality that resides in your blood. He raised his hand offering an empty vial pinched between the bare bones of his forefinger and thumb.

No one else was using the mausoleum as a secret lab. The lich was the alchemist—and not just any alchemist. A blood alchemist with a necromancer's power.

"You created dogs that can feed on a person's soul?"

Not the soul. He made a sound that might have been a sigh. *An alchemist of your caliber and yet you know so little of your past.*

Another chill stood my hair on end. "M-my past? What could you possibly know of my past?"

Not your personal past. Your history. Our history. The history of alchemy. His tone was scolding. *But we digress.* He tapped his finger bone against the vial with a tink. *I believe we were about to come to an arrangement.*

Rowan mumbled something and shifted against me before going still again.

"What's the...arrangement?" I asked.

Your blood for your freedom.

"And his."

A dry chuckle followed. *Yes, of course. Your mastery of the elements is quite impressive, but then, is that not the goal of every alchemist?*

"You're rather witty for a dead guy."

I'm glad you appreciate it. My cousins don't find me all that amusing. He waved a fleshless hand toward the mausoleum. *But they do have their uses.* He tapped the vial again, and I took it from him, careful not to touch him in the process.

Was this all he wanted from me? My blood? Lawson had made it sound like he wanted the Final Formula. I was missing something here, but what?

Well? he prompted as I hesitated. *My cousins aren't a patient lot.*

The hand on the wall above me began to move. Oh, please, I thought, don't let the zombie look over the wall. I hurried to dig my Swiss Army knife from my fanny pack. I pricked my finger and squeezed a few drops into his vial.

"That's all you get," I said, holding up the vial. "If you're really an alchemist, that's all you'll need."

He took the vial from my fingers. Rowan stirred against me, and I almost fumbled the exchange.

Blood freely given, the lich whispered. *We'll meet again.*

A rumble from the room around us signified the vaults sliding closed once more. The skeletal hands no longer gripped the lip of the wall above us. I turned back to the lich and found the stairwell empty. Damn. He hadn't answered any of my questions. Talking to him had only created new ones.

"Addie?" Rowan whispered.

Thank God. "Hey. You back?"

"I never left." He tried to sit up, but slumped back against me once more. "I wanted to stop him."

"It's all right." I ran my hand over the back of his head. He had the softest hair. "Can you stand?"

"Give me a moment."

"Okay." I wanted to get out of here, but I couldn't carry him. While I waited, my mind returned to some of the things the lich had said. "That mastery of the elements crack—"

"Is true," Rowan cut in. "Era and Donovan adore you. Cora respects you—which is huge coming from her." He fell silent.

"And what of you, Your Grace?" My tone was teasing, but my stomach muscles tensed, anticipating a gut shot. I'd caused him so much trouble.

He straightened, bracing a hand on the wall to keep his balance, and looked me in the eye. His hesitation set my pulse racing.

"I think I'm falling for you," he whispered.

I blinked then jumped as a growl echoed up the stairwell. The lich must have another dog. I gripped Rowan's arm. "We need to go."

Rowan reached up and grabbed the lip of the sarcophagus. He pulled himself up, using my shoulder for support. We were doing well until he tried to use his injured leg. The leg buckled and he fell against me.

"Shit." His expletive came out on a pained grunt.

I caught the lip of the sarcophagus, corralling him in the corner. My back groaned, but I kept him from tumbling down the stairs.

"I'm sorry." He shifted his weight back onto the wall.

"It's okay. With my rapid healing, I'm sure the crushed vertebrae will be fine."

"Not funny." He bowed his head, taking several deep breaths. On the final one, he hoisted himself up onto the wall with the strength of his arms alone. A pause, and he swung his legs over.

The mausoleum looked the same as when we first walked in. No evidence remained that two-dozen zombies had just crawled out of their graves.

I glanced back down the stairwell and froze. Another dog stood at the base of the stairs, this one more bone than fur. Its milky white eyes focused on me, and it raised one paw and set it on the next step up.

That broke me out of my paralysis. I vaulted the wall in a move so coordinated, it earned a startled look from Rowan.

"We have company." I wrapped my arm around his waist. "Let's go."

Rowan accepted my help, letting me take some of his weight each time he had to use his bad leg. He stopped to catch his breath at the door, his free hand braced on the jamb. The lich's now familiar laugh rose from the sarcophagus. I urged Rowan outside and shoved the door closed before securing the hasp.

"Come on." I pulled his arm across my shoulders and helped him toward the nearest streetlight. A low monument made a decent bench, and I encouraged him to sit. I knelt beside him, pulling back his shredded pant leg. Bile rose in my throat at the sight of the nasty wound.

"Oh God, Rowan." The dog had ripped open a wide gash, tearing deeply into the muscle. I didn't know how Rowan had come this far, even with my help.

"It'll heal."

"We need to get you to a hospital." The dark material masked it, but his pant leg was blood soaked. I slipped off my jacket and got out my knife to cut off the sleeves.

"No, I'll be fine. We need to keep moving. If he sends the dog after us, my magic..." He gripped the edge of the monument, his knuckles white. "I'd rather not have to use it right now," he finished in a whisper.

Because of what I'd done or because his injury robbed him of his ability to concentrate? I didn't ask. Instead, I worked on getting my makeshift bandage snuggled around his thigh. He grunted as I pulled it tight.

I got to my feet. "Give me the keys and I'll get the car."

"You killed the engine last time." His reference to the time I'd stolen his car brought color to my cheeks. "Have you ever driven a stick?"

"How would I know?" I held out my hand, but he didn't reach for his keys. "For heaven's sake, it's a damn car. If I destroy the transmission you can buy a new one."

"I don't want you going alone."

I blinked and my cheeks heated, remembering what he'd said inside the mausoleum. "Well, I don't particularly like leaving you here alone either." I put some anger in my tone to hide my confusion. I wiggled my fingers. "Keys?"

He eyed me for one long moment and then wordlessly dug out the keys.

"Be right back," I said.

"Don't destroy my transmission."

"Yes, Your Grace," I called over my shoulder.

It turned out that I could drive a stick, but I was out of practice. I killed the car twice before we were out of the cemetery. Rowan groaned from the passenger seat, but didn't say anything. He dozed off shortly thereafter, but I found the freeway and later the exit I needed. I finally drove up to the manor about thirty minutes after leaving the cemetery.

No sooner did I step out of the car than Cora came running out.

"Where have you been?" She stopped. "Why are you driving?" She didn't wait for an answer before hurrying to the passenger side.

"We met a lich and some of his zombie dogs. Rowan got chewed up."

"A lich?" a familiar voice asked.

I whirled to find James standing behind me.

"You should have called me," he said.

"He was a necromancer."

"Oh."

Cora had Rowan's door open and was shaking his shoulder, trying to wake him.

"Here, Cora, let me." James touched her shoulder and she moved aside.

James lifted Rowan from the car and started for the house. Rowan mumbled something, but I didn't catch the words.

"No," James answered him. "The transmission sounded fine."

I rolled my eyes and followed them inside.

CHAPTER 27

James found me in the kitchen a short time later. I'd done a thorough search of the pantry and was in the process of devising several rudimentary formulas, but I could only do so much with a stovetop and an assortment of kitchen appliances. Rowan refused to go to the hospital and no one gainsaid him. It was up to me to make him well.

James eyed the cluttered island. "He's going to be all right, Ad."

I returned my attention to my notes, scratching out one line to add another. "He was chewed on by dead things. Decayed dead things."

"I helped Cora strip him down. The wounds have already sealed and when she washed away the blood, I saw no evidence of infection."

I stopped writing and looked up. "No way. I saw the wound. It was deep, the muscle torn."

James shrugged. "He's an Element. Aside from me, there's not a whole lot that can hurt him. Still, I wish you two hadn't gone alone. I could have taken care of the dogs."

"There was a necro, remember? It's not good to get you too close to one."

He frowned, though not at me. "I have a will. I'm not a mindless corpse that any common necro can command."

"Are you saying you can resist?"

"The weak ones." He hesitated. "I think."

"That's not good enough. Besides, how do we know which ones are weak?" I hated to shoot him down, but I didn't want him anywhere near a necro. And certainly not that thing in the crypt.

James huffed out a breath. "I don't know." He looked up, his green eyes meeting mine. "I want to help. *I'm* supposed to be your sidekick."

I struggled not to smile. Here was the problem. I reached over and gripped his forearm. "Come on. You're my one and only. I just went along with Rowan to keep him out of trouble. Good thing, huh?"

He snorted. "Did you tell him that?"

"Not yet." I gathered up my notes. "How'd your evening go?"

"Better than yours. The only dead thing involved was me."

"Ha ha." I picked up the lid to the paprika and twisted it in place.

"Anyway, we didn't find much at his PIA office, but we did find several interesting things at his house."

"Like...?" I reached for another lid.

"Copies of PIA registration files for hundreds of magical folks."

"What? Why would he have those?"

"No clue, but you might find the answers on his laptop."

I stopped twisting the lid on the garlic salt. "You have his computer? Here? Can I take a peek?"

"It's in Rowan's office."

"Oh. Well, maybe I could—"

"It's almost one in the morning. Lawson is dead and that computer isn't going anywhere. Let me help you clean up and then you can get some rest."

I didn't realize it was that late. Maybe he was right. "Fine." Rowan may not want me nosing through his office, even if he was falling for me.

"Why are you smiling?" James asked.

I realized that I was. "Just glad to have a lead." I gathered up a handful of spice tins and headed for the pantry.

I COULDN'T SLEEP—NOT WITH THE potential answers Lawson's computer represented sitting on Rowan's desk. My bedside clock read 2:57 a.m. Close enough to dawn for me. I left my rumpled bed and snatched up my robe, not bothering to tie it. Rowan's office wasn't far.

I reconsidered the wisdom of my nocturnal visit when I noticed the dim light beneath his office door. I hesitated, hand on the doorknob. I didn't hear any movement within. Had James left the light on when he dropped off Lawson's computer? I turned the knob and walked in, but stopped on the threshold.

Rowan stood behind his desk, but looked up as I entered. "Addie?"

"What are you doing up?" I blurted, pleased to see him well, but annoyed that he wasn't resting.

"I could ask you the same thing, but I think I know the answer." He waved a hand at the unfamiliar laptop sitting on one corner of his desk. I gave it a glance, but that wasn't what caught my attention. Rowan was dressed for bed, or had just left it. Beneath an open robe, he wore a pair of navy blue pajama bottoms, low on his hips—and nothing else.

"Well?" he prompted, pulling my attention away from his body. "Come in and shut the door. I'm sure it'd be pointless to tell you to go back to bed."

"As pointless as me telling you that you should be resting." I closed the door and started toward his desk.

His eyes flicked over me, but I didn't want to appear self-conscious and pull my robe closed. It wasn't as if my pajamas were indecent. Granted, the silky pants and matching camisole top weren't my usual bedtime wear. But it did look a little better than the stained T-shirt and oversized sweatpants I'd worn while living over the gun shop.

"I'm fine." He sat down in his chair and pulled the laptop closer.

I let the question of his health go and circled around behind his desk. "Find anything?"

"I just turned it on." The screen showed the Windows logo while the system booted up.

I sat down on the arm of his chair and waited. At least it wasn't password protected. Within a few moments, we were staring at Lawson's wallpaper—a mostly naked woman in a vulgar position.

"Nice," I said.

"I agree."

"Perv." I gave him a half-hearted nudge with my elbow. "What kind of person uses a picture like that as his wallpaper? Maybe we should have disinfected the keyboard."

Rowan chuckled. "A girly picture doesn't make him evil."

"Speaking from experience, Your Grace? I trust you don't have one as your wallpaper."

"No."

"They're tucked away in a folder labeled *dull accounting spreadsheets*?"

He laughed again. "I have no porn on my computer."

"You prefer the magazines?"

"Only for the articles." He nudged me back, bumping my ribs with his shoulder.

I grinned and got busy sifting through the various programs and looking for anything personal. I hit the mother lode in the My Documents folder. He had an impressive collection of lengthy Word documents. Most had titles like *Book 1, Draft 3*.

"Lawson was a writer?" I asked.

"Looks that way."

I opened one of the files out of curiosity and began to read. About two paragraphs in, I quickly closed the file, my cheeks flaming.

"I was reading that," Rowan complained.

I didn't look at him, but I could tell he smiled. I selected another file and found more of the same. A quick click and I closed it, too.

"The man wrote erotica?" I asked.

"Apparently."

I grunted, not sure what to say.

"Scroll down," Rowan said. "Are there any other files of interest?"

"Define interest." I did as he requested. Toward the bottom we came across a file entitled, *My Life After Death*. I clicked on it, but a password prompt came up.

"Damn." I didn't know how to get around that. "The guy leaves the other stuff unprotected, but takes the trouble to secure this? I'm not so sure I want to read it."

Rowan chuckled. "I can call Gerald in the morning. He's good with computers."

Morning. Great. I sighed and took my hands from the keyboard. "I hate waiting."

"I've noticed."

I ignored that. "Anything else we can go over? James said there were some registration forms—"

"All minor talents. I don't think Lawson had the clearance for anything else."

Like the Elements.

"Besides, it might have been job related. I can check with Waylon."

I got to my feet, rolling up on my toes to stretch my sore calf. The bullet wound was completely healed, but it was still tender. "Lawson wasn't the one behind this."

The chair creaked as Rowan came to his feet.

"I want to know who Lawson was working for. I don't think it was that lich." I braced my hands to either side of Lawson's laptop. "But Lawson did call him. What's the connection between the two?"

Rowan leaned against the edge of the desk beside me. "We'll find it."

I didn't share his optimism. "What is a lich king?"

"A lich with the ability to make other liches. Only the most powerful necromancers can pull it off, and they usually start with themselves."

I looked over at him. "Why?"

"To give them a sort of immortality."

"As a rotting corpse?"

"They're necromancers." He seemed to think that explained everything.

I sighed and straightened.

"Come here," he said.

Curious, I moved closer and forgot to breathe when he caught me by the hips. "We'll figure this out." He pulled me closer, between his parted knees. "Or rather, you won't let it rest until we do."

I arched a brow. "Is that so?"

"I wish you hadn't given him your blood," he said, ignoring my comment. "A powerful necromancer can do nasty things with blood freely given."

"It wasn't freely given. He held our lives in the balance."

A small smile curled his lips. "Leave it to you to find a loophole."

"I'm not as clueless as you think."

"I've never thought that." He held my gaze with those unusual gray eyes. "You were amazing tonight." He raised a hand, running the back of his fingers over my cheek. "You saved me."

"I nearly killed you," I whispered.

The corner of his mouth twitched. "Your mastery of the Elements could use some work."

"Don't tease me. I was terrified."

"You didn't let it show."

I ducked my head, embarrassed and yet thrilled by the praise. His fingers touched my chin, tipping my face up. He hesitated and then leaned down and kissed me.

I pressed my hands to his stomach. Warm, bare skin met my palms. His hands found the small of my back and pulled me closer. I slid my hands up over the ribbed contours of his stomach, enjoying the freedom to explore. I was lightheaded when he finally let me up for air. His eyes were completely orange and even as I watched, a shimmer of gold flickered through them.

"We shouldn't be doing this." I turned away.

He caught my hips again and pulled me to him—my back to his chest.

"Why not?" His warm breath on my ear gave me chills.

"Your eyes. The fire hurts you."

He nuzzled my neck. "Only if I use it, remember?" He pulled me back tight against him and I gasped. "I want you."

"I noticed," I answered and he chuckled. The thin pajama bottoms we each wore hid nothing.

"Let me touch you?"

"Yes." God, yes.

His hands slid upward to cup my breasts through the light camisole I wore. I couldn't completely muffle my cry as he teased me through the thin material.

My head came to rest against his collarbone and I arched my back. Was I really the sort of woman who did things like this? Emil claimed we'd been lovers, but I didn't remember it. This all felt so new. Maybe I shouldn't be doing this with Rowan, but damn, it felt good. I wanted more. I wanted him.

His right hand slid downward over my stomach and then lower still. I jumped when he found what he was looking for, even though two layers of silky fabric separated me from his fingers. I arched a little more, moving against him.

"Damn," he whispered, his breath hot against my jaw. "I want to strip you bare and get you down on this desk." He moved to my throat as he spoke, tongue and lips working toward my shoulder.

"I think your bed would be more comfortable." Did I say that out loud?

"Would you like to test that hypothesis?"

I shouldn't. I really shouldn't. "Yes, I would."

WE SLIPPED THROUGH THE HOUSE like a pair of ghosts, our bare feet making no sound on the carpet. Hand in hand, he led me to a wing of the house I'd never been in before and opened a door at the end of the hall. I had a moment to take in the large room decorated in rich jewel tones before he pulled me to him. His mouth covered mine, his kiss passionate, promising. Without breaking contact, he shrugged off his robe and then pushed mine back off my shoulders. I let it slide to the floor. Goosebumps rose as he ran his fingers over my bare upper arms, tracing my tattoos.

His hands fell to my waist and found the hem of my camisole.

He took his mouth from mine just long enough to pull my top over my head, then let it fall to the floor. My cheeks heated, and I suddenly didn't know what to do with my hands.

Rowan relieved me of the dilemma when he kissed me again. I wrapped my arms around his neck and my bare chest met his. We groaned in unison. His hands returned to my hips and this time he disrobed me from the waist down. My mind informed me that I was naked, but oddly, I didn't care. Pressed against him, I didn't feel exposed, and the fact that he still wore his pants was strangely…salacious.

Warm fingers trailed from my shoulder blades to the small of my back, and then lower. Without warning, Rowan lifted me. I drew a surprised breath against his lips and gripped his shoulders, wrapping my legs around his waist to keep from falling. His back thumped against the closed door behind him before he regained his balance. Through it all, our lips never broke contact.

He pushed off the door and started across the room. I suspected he headed for the large four-poster bed, but I didn't know for certain until my back pressed against the cool softness of his silk bedding. He released me and straightened. I squirmed against the black sheets, loving the way the silky fabric caressed my bare skin.

"God, you're beautiful," he whispered.

I warmed all the way to my toes. Before I could comment, he shucked off his pants. Dear God. Naked Rowan was a glorious sight—though a bit intimidating. He crawled onto the bed, bracing a hand to either side of my shoulders.

"You're pretty pleasing yourself, Your Grace."

He laughed and gave me the most wicked grin before covering my mouth with his. My lips parted, and I welcomed the hot thrust of his tongue, loving the way he tasted. A quick kiss and then he moved down my body. I cried out when he caught a nipple in his mouth. He moved to the other and then went lower, and lower still.

"Rowan!" I gasped when he reached the inside of my thigh.

"Relax." He exhaled, hot breath against the most sensitive part of my body, and despite my inhibitions, I did eventually relax for him. Well, not relax exactly. Dear Lord, the man had a gifted tongue. And when he raised his orange eyes to watch me, I almost lost it.

The tension built, and I moved closer to sliding over that edge when he stopped. Before I could voice my disappointment, he slid back up my body and covered my mouth with his. His tongue wasn't the only thing he thrust inside me. I cried out against his lips, more in surprise than pain. Although that little twinge did knock the edge off the delicious tension he'd been building.

He froze. "You okay?"

Hyperaware of his presence, I could only nod.

"Why didn't you say something?"

I frowned. What did he want me to say? "Ow?"

"Addie."

And then it hit me. "I was a virgin?" No way.

The annoyance faded from his features. "You didn't know."

"How would I? I didn't even know my name."

He brushed a hand over my forehead, pushing back my hair. "When I find out who did this to you, I'll kill him."

I smiled, touched by his concern. "Can we discuss that later?"

Amusement twinkled in his flame-colored eyes. "Very well." He slid forward and I gasped. "Addie?"

"Wow." I found my voice. "It did fit." Oops. I hadn't meant to say that out loud.

He chuckled and pushed up a little to gaze down our joined bodies. "It seems you were made for me."

"How pretentious, Your Grace." I looped my arms around

his shoulders as his eyes returned to mine. "Perhaps *you* were made for *me*."

He laughed and then he started to move. I decided the argument could wait. Right now, I was far too preoccupied to form a coherent sentence. Within moments, I couldn't even form a coherent thought. He'd brought me back to where I'd been, then pushed me beyond. I almost wanted to pull away from the intensity of it all. Almost.

I watched him watch me, noting the way the gold shimmered outward from his pupils, obscuring more and more of the orange. His eyes were golden by the time I finally let go, then he followed. My breath caught as the air around us ignited. He squeezed his eyes closed and the muscles in his jaw tensed as he gritted his teeth.

The flames died and Rowan pressed his face to my throat. He didn't exactly collapse, but I was certainly aware of his greater weight pressing me into the sheets. His rapid breathing filled the silence.

Concerned, I rubbed his back, aware of how warm his skin was. "You okay there, Hot Stuff?"

A pause, and he pushed himself up on his elbows. The orange had receded to the thin band around his pupils. "You test my control, alchemist."

"Yeah, blame me."

He smiled. Goodness, he was gorgeous, rumpled hair and all. I reached up and touched his cheek. He turned his head and kissed my palm, closing his eyes.

I released a breath. "I think I'm falling for you, too," I whispered.

He opened his eyes and met mine for a heartbeat before he leaned down and kissed me. I felt the heat as the air ignited around us again.

CHAPTER 28

Knocking woke me, and I pried open my eyes to watch Rowan slide from the bed. He grumbled something I didn't catch and headed for the door without a stitch of clothing. Damn, that was nice.

To my surprise, he pulled the door open with no concern for his nudity. I pulled the sheet to my chin, though the bed wasn't visible from the doorway. I could hear the low rumble of Donovan's voice, but I didn't catch the words. Had Rowan known it was his brother Element? I certainly hoped so.

"Already?" Rowan answered. "Tell him I'll be down shortly."

Still clutching the sheet, I sat up to better see the clock—9:24 a.m. Whoa. The door closed, and I made the mistake of watching Rowan return to me. Mmm, even better.

He climbed onto the bed and pulled me close. "Good morning." A long leisurely kiss followed.

"More like mid-morning," I said when I could. "What did Donovan want?"

"Gerald's here. He's working on that file now." His hands were sliding over my bare skin, pushing the sheet away. His mouth found my shoulder and slid downward.

"Um. Didn't you say you'd be right down?" I gasped when his tongue flicked over my breast.

"I'd rather spend the day inside you." The words came out muffled.

"Rowan." I moaned.

"God, I love it when you say my name like that." He licked the other nipple. "Shower with me?"

"I seriously doubt that'll save much time."

He leaned up and grinned, eyes already aglow. "I must confess, that wasn't why I suggested it."

By the time we arrived in Rowan's office, Gerald had commandeered his chair and sat hunched over Lawson's laptop. His sandy-blond hair stuck up in clumps like he'd just rolled out of bed. The glare of the screen reflected off his thick glasses, but I still caught the rapid movement of his eyes as he scanned the screen.

"Be careful what you read there," I said. "Some of it is a little risqué."

Gerald sprang from the chair, almost overturning it in the process. I couldn't decide if I'd startled him, or if I'd caught him partaking of Lawson's literary talents. The flush on his cheeks suggested the latter.

"Your Grace," he said, catching sight of Rowan. He glanced at me and frowned, but if he still considered me a threat to Rowan, he kept those comments to himself.

"Any luck?" Rowan asked, a hint of amusement in his tone.

"It was a simple encryption." Gerald returned to the laptop and hit a few keys. "I also printed a copy." He gestured at the tiny printer on Rowan's desk.

While Rowan joined him at the laptop, I picked up the printed copy. After the security measures, I expected something more substantial than two single-spaced pages. Hoping it wasn't more erotica, I cautiously started reading.

Today I was murdered.

I woke in a crypt, my back pressed against cold stone while I strained to see in the darkness. Flickering light drew my attention, and I turned my head to watch a cloaked man walk into the room. He placed his candle on a table loaded with strange glassware and lab equipment.

"Rise," he commanded.

I didn't want to obey him, but I couldn't resist. In an instant, I was on my feet.

He turned to face me and closed the distance between us. I couldn't see his features in the shadow of his hood, but when he caught my face in one fleshless hand, I was glad.

"Oh God," I whispered, dropping into one of the chairs before Rowan's desk.

"What is it?" Rowan asked.

"Read the file," I muttered, my eyes falling to the next paragraph. "Just read the file."

"You are dead, Robert Allen Lawson. I have bound your soul to your corpse. If you wish to return to the land of the living, you will complete the task I give you. You will bring me the Elixir of Life."

"We were wrong," Rowan said. "The lich is behind it." He leaned over the laptop, a hand braced to either side. His eyes continued to move over the screen.

I stared at the last line. The Elixir of Life. The Final Formula. That made no sense. All the lich wanted was my blood. I continued reading. Lawson went on to describe the days and weeks that followed. How he tried to fulfill his new master's orders, while his body began to decay. He no longer ate or slept. He began to lose sensation in his extremities. His tale ended with his discovery of a new bullet and his plans to visit the manufacturer's gun shop, in hopes of meeting the alchemist.

A thump made me look up, and I noticed that Gerald had backed against the wall behind Rowan's desk. He stared, wide-eyed toward the door and I turned to look. James stood in the doorway, a frown on his face and his narrowed eyes on Gerald.

When I turned back to check Gerald's reaction, he was gone. He'd teleported from the room.

Rowan sighed.

"I didn't do anything," James said.

Ignoring the exchange, I got to my feet and walked over to James. "You won't believe this." I waved the pages I held. "Lawson was a lich."

"What?" James's attention shifted to me.

I passed him the printout. "He was made one—against his will. I'm surprised you didn't notice."

"I see souls. Liches have them."

"Soul or not, he was still dead," Rowan said, straightening. "Lawson would have been susceptible to necromantic control."

"Ian, the lich king. Why didn't he demand I give him the Formula?"

"That is odd," James said.

I rubbed a hand over my face. What was I missing? The lich had me, and all he'd asked for was my blood. He must have known that I didn't have the formula—which meant he knew who did.

I dropped my hand. "Emil." I rose to my feet. "He'll go after Emil." Who lay helpless in the hospital.

"Lawson's dead," James pointed out.

"But there were other men." I thought about how interested they'd been in the outcome of Lawson's actions. "Oh God. Were they liches, too?" I turned to Rowan. "What about those men at the gun shop?" Or the Alchemica.

"We'll go to the hospital now." Rowan started for the door. "Let me grab some flashlights."

"Flashlights?" James asked.

"We're going back to the crypt?" I asked.

"The two of you can watch over your Grand Master while I take care of this lich." He walked out the door without waiting for any input.

"I want to come with you," I called after him. James could stay with Emil and keep him safe while we confronted the lich.

Rowan didn't answer.

I paced while I waited, trying to think of some excuse to tag along to the crypt. What formulas did I have that'd prove useful? The truth serum? Would my formulas even work on a corpse? James had let me experiment on him in the past, but that wasn't an accurate comparison. He might refer to himself as dead, but his body still lived. He had to eat and sleep. He bled—sometimes. Depending on how long Ian had been dead, he might be little more than a well-preserved sack of bones.

"Guess there are worse ways to be dead," James said, finishing Lawson's tale. He returned the printout to Rowan's desk.

"It doesn't sound pleasant." How had Lawson ended up that way? Had he stumbled upon Ian's tomb while working for the PIA? "I wonder how difficult it is to make a lich."

"From what I've read, it can take a day or more."

I glanced over at my buddy. "You've read up on lich making?"

He leaned against the front of Rowan's desk, his hands braced to either side of his hips. "I thought it in my best interest to learn something about necromancy, but I couldn't find much." He shrugged. "I did discover that a lot of the old necros were alchemists."

The faintest stirring of déjà vu tingled across my senses. "Tell me more."

Something in my tone made him glance over. "What is it?"

"That sounds...familiar. What else?" I moved closer, not wanting to miss a word.

"The old necros used alchemy to bolster their ability, though I'm not sure how. It seemed to deal with blood alchemy quite a bit. I tried to learn more, but didn't get far since modern academies won't teach blood alchemy."

The déjà vu hit again. A little harder this time. It kept coming back to blood alchemy.

James gripped my shoulders. "Addie?"

I stood still, not wanting to move for fear the sensation would slip away. "Go on."

"That's about it, except," he hesitated, "my ancestor was supposed to have given a necromancer his blood. I have no way to prove it, but I think that necro used blood alchemy to create the first grim."

The déjà vu hit full force.

I sat in a darkened room, the light of a computer monitor the only illumination. Pudgy fingers typed on the keyboard, and I realized they were my own. The monitor flickered, a status bar slowly filling as a new screen loaded. When it finished, a genealogy record appeared. My eyes traced the line down to the final entry. Forrest Huntsman. A name I'd giggled at the first time I heard it. James's father.

One plump finger rose and tapped the screen over his name. "Found you," I heard myself say.

"Addie?" James's green eyes swam into focus, only inches from my own.

I gasped and jerked back.

"Hey, you with me?" he asked.

I realized that I sat in one of Rowan's guest chairs. I ran my palms over the smooth leather arms, trying to ground myself in this time and place. James knelt in front of me, his brow wrinkled in concern.

"Here." Rowan stopped beside my chair, and I jumped at his sudden appearance. When did he get back? He pressed a tissue into my hand. "Your nose is bleeding."

I dabbed the tissue to my nose and it came away bloodstained.

"The stronger surges of déjà vu give her nose bleeds," James told Rowan.

"I'm sure he can't relate," I muttered, remembering how Rowan's nose had bled the night before. I wiped my nose again, glad to see that the bleeding had almost stopped.

"Did you remember something?" James asked.

I didn't know what the memory meant, but I didn't want to tell him. "Bits and pieces. Nothing coherent." I rose to my feet. "Are we ready?"

"Yes." Rowan picked up the copy of Lawson's tale from the crypt and headed for the door. James and I fell in behind him.

I suddenly remembered a comment George had made the other night at the clinic. Something about James receiving a call from the Alchemica.

"Why were you in Cincinnati the night the Alchemica blew?" I asked James. I knew he'd been on some errand for the gun shop, but I'd never asked for particulars.

"George wanted to get into the magic bullet business. And since I dabbled in alchemy…"

"Why the Alchemica?"

"George got a flier. He told me to set up an appointment."

My stomach dropped. I knew I'd sent the flier.

"Why do you want to know?" he asked. "Something in the memory?"

"Just thinking about your research in necromancy and interest in alchemy," I glanced up at him. "You *were* trying to find a cure."

"There is no cure for death." He met my eyes a moment before he looked away, but in that moment, I caught a glimmer of hope.

"And yet everyone is after the Final Formula," Rowan said, waiting for us at the door. "The Elixir of Life."

"The title's misleading," I stopped beside him. "Maybe I should join you and set the lich straight."

Rowan just smiled and led us from the room.

CHAPTER 29

I climbed into the back seat of Rowan's Camaro, giving James the roomier front passenger seat. My buddy hadn't said anything since leaving Rowan's office. I chided myself for not wondering why he'd been so interested in alchemy, especially after I'd learned about the connection between grims and alchemy. It made sense that an alchemist would be responsible for his family curse.

Rowan slid in behind the wheel, laying Lawson's printed document on the dash before starting the car. "Buckle up."

Rowan and his seatbelt fetish. Smiling, I slid back in my seat. Something bunched behind me, and I reached back, pulling a roll of fabric from beneath my backside. It turned out to be my jacket from the night before—or what was left of it. I wadded it up and the crinkle of paper drew my attention to the pocket. In all the excitement, I had forgotten about the page of alchemy notes I'd taken from the crypt. The thick sheet of paper was yellowed with age and the uneven writing looked like it'd been made with a calligraphy pen—or maybe a quill. How long had the lich been in that tomb?

I leaned back in my seat, reading the paper as Rowan backed the car out of the garage. I expected to see notes on the Final Formula or maybe the lich's attempt to recreate it, but this formula had nothing to do with it. It wasn't even a formula I knew—yet it was familiar. Something I could almost remember. I hadn't bumped up against a formula I didn't know since—

"Oh." I hit my seatbelt release and slid up between the front seats. "Could I see your phone?" I asked Rowan.

He picked it up and passed it back to me. "Who are you going to call?"

"No one." I scrolled through his pictures until I found the one I wanted.

"Addie? What is it?" James leaned to the side to look back at me.

"Just checking…" My voice trailed off as I compared the two formulas. "That's why it looked familiar."

I slid up between the front seats once more and handed James the phone and paper. "Compare those."

"What do you have there?" Rowan put the car in neutral and watched while James compared the pictures on the phone to the paper.

"A sheet of notes I took from the crypt," I said.

"It's the same formula," James said.

"It matches what you found in Xander's basement?" Rowan asked, recognizing the pictures on his phone.

"Yes. Xander's alchemist is working with the lich."

"With or for?" Rowan asked.

"I don't know."

"What does this formula do?" James asked. "It's…odd."

"Archaic," I amended. "I'll need to study it closer, but I can tell you it's blood alchemy."

"They are necromancers." James handed me back the page and phone. "No surprise that they'd know blood alchemy."

"Yeah." I slid back in my seat. And since I was an Alchemica alchemist, I shouldn't have too much trouble figuring it out. Rowan's phone buzzed in my hand, startling me.

"Who is it?" Rowan asked, taking his hand from the gearshift.

I'd started to hand him the phone, but hesitated to read the screen. I recognized the number. "It's Neil."

"How'd he get my number?" Rowan asked.

"Waylon?" I hit the talk icon and brought the phone to my ear. "Neil?"

"Amelia." Neil sounded relieved. "The director suggested I could reach you at this number, though I didn't expect you to answer."

I gave Rowan a nod before turning my attention back to Neil. "What's up?"

"Emil is missing."

I sat up straight. "What?"

"Emil's missing," James whispered to Rowan.

I gripped James's shoulder. "When? Did anyone see something?" I asked Neil. "What's being done?"

"Easy," Neil said. "The PIA is on it."

"The PIA?" How did they know where Emil was? "Did you—?"

"I don't have any other information, but I did visit the scene."

"What did you find?"

"I'd like to show you. Can you meet me at the hospital?"

I agreed and ended the call. "The compass," I said, handing Rowan his phone. "Where is it?"

"Desk drawer in my office."

"I'll get it." James hurried from the car.

Too anxious to sit still, I pushed up his seat and climbed out after him.

"Addie?" Rowan followed me from the car.

"All that trouble and Emil is still taken." I paced to the hedge bordering the drive and back. "Damn it. We should have checked on him this morning."

Rowan caught my wrist on the way past and tugged me over to him. "I rather liked how this morning turned out."

My cheeks warmed. "Yes, but—"

"You would have rather spent the morning searching for the man who claims to be your lover?"

"Rowan."

"You do realize he lied." He pulled me closer. "You were a virgin."

"The Formula has regenerative properties."

He lifted my left hand and traced the wrinkled white line along the second joint of my index finger. "Yet you have a scar."

"That happened after I took the Formula. At the gun shop."

"If you can scar, then your body no longer regenerates. You've been a virgin since you took the Final Formula—if not before."

"I'm forty-two. That's just sad."

"Perhaps." A faint smile curled his lips before he grew serious. "Either way, Emil lied."

"Then I'll confront him about it when we find him. It doesn't matter anyway. That old man in the hospital bed is the man I remember. My mentor, a father figure. He's also the key to getting my memory back."

Rowan studied me. "So, you didn't mind spending the morning with me?"

I bit my lip, touched yet amused by this glimpse of vulnerability in him. I pressed my palms to the solid expanse of his stomach. "I regret nothing. I just feel guilty that I was busy enjoying myself while Emil was being taken."

"Only enjoying?" His hands settled on my hips.

"I'm not stroking your ego."

"Perhaps I could find you something else to stroke?"

"Rowan." Remembering this morning, my cheeks burned. I caught a glimpse of that smug smile before his lips covered mine. He pressed me against the side of the car, giving me nowhere to go—not that I wanted to.

A growl, low and close. "Release her." James stood directly behind Rowan.

I gasped, surprised by his sudden appearance, and tried to slip around Rowan, but he wouldn't move. "Step back." I met his eyes and noted the faint ring of orange around his pupils.

"I said, release her," James repeated. He caught Rowan by the arm and pulled him back. Rowan turned around trying to reach him, but James slung him aside. He didn't even grunt with the effort, yet Rowan cleared the hedge and smacked against the side of the house—a good fifteen feet away.

"James!" I stepped in front of him, pressing my hands to his chest. He didn't even look at me, his glowing eyes focused on Rowan.

"Hey!" I caught James's face between my palms, forcing his attention on me. "Stop it."

"He can't have you." The words came out in a low growl.

"James—"

Without warning and almost too fast to follow, he caught me by the shoulders and turning, pressed me against the car once more. I opened my mouth to protest and his mouth covered mine. For a moment, I was too shocked to do anything. Dear God, James was kissing me. What the hell? I shoved him back.

"James!"

"You said you loved me," he whispered.

What? Abruptly he stumbled back as Rowan pulled him away. James snarled and twisted in his hold. For one heartbeat the pair faced off. Gold shimmered through Rowan's eyes and a hedge bordering the drive went up in a flash of blue-white flame. James didn't even flinch. His lip curled away, exposing teeth that looked more canine than human. I'd never seen him do that.

James sprang at Rowan who ducked and kicked out a leg at the last moment. His foot slammed into James's hip with an audible crunch and James stumbled back.

"Stop!" I stepped between them again, my back to Rowan. "Don't do this."

"Rowan!" Donovan shouted. The side door slammed behind him as he joined us in the driveway.

I didn't turn to watch, confident that the big man could calm his brother Element. I had my hands full.

"James, please." I moved closer and his attention shifted back to me.

"I'm sorry, Addie." His forehead wrinkled, and he reached in his pocket to pull out the shattered compass. It dropped, piece by broken piece, to the cobble drive. "I'll get Emil back for you." Darkness flickered around him.

"James, no!"

A flash of black fur and he was gone. I stared at the spot James had been only an instant before. It had happened so fast, it didn't seem real.

"Walk it off," Donovan said behind me.

I turned and found him standing close to Rowan, one hand on his shoulder.

"What the hell?" I waved a hand at the shattered compass. "How do I find Emil now?"

Rowan frowned at me, the orange still visible in his eyes.

"Go on," Donovan encouraged him. He gave him a small nudge. "You need to cool off first."

Rowan's frown deepened. He gave us a curt nod and then turned on his heel and walked around the side of the house.

"Coward." I glared after him.

Donovan heaved a sigh. "Addie—"

"He lost it." I gestured at the vacant spot where the hedge had been.

"A lesser Fire Element would have taken out most of the first floor." Donovan moved closer, his boots making no sound on the cobbles.

"But..." I didn't know what to say. I pulled in a breath and released it, aware of how it shook. I looked up into those warm hazel eyes. "James kissed me," I whispered.

Donovan pressed his lips together, a sad smile turning up the corners. "He's in love with you, honey."

"What?" I resisted the urge to shake my head. "That's crazy." James was my best buddy, my sidekick. Even considering him having romantic thoughts about me felt so...wrong. "He's like my kid brother."

"Attraction is a strange beast."

Didn't I know that firsthand? I rubbed a hand over my face. "Emil was taken from the hospital. If not by a necro, then by people who work for one. James went after Emil."

"As soon as Rowan gets back, we'll go."

"Why wait? Let's go get him now." I started for the front of the house, unable to bear the thought of James walking into a necro lair.

"Addie, please. You need to give him a moment."

Something in Donovan's tone made me hesitate. I turned to face him. "Why? Can't he cool down while he drives?"

A faint smile curled the big guy's mouth. "The two of you are just alike." He closed the distance between us. "He's a Fire Element, honey. You need to make allowances for—"

"The fact that he's a hot head? A control freak?"

"Exactly."

His easy agreement silenced me.

"He's also the only original Fire Element still alive."

"Original?"

"Those who were adults when the magic returned. Those who became Elements."

I remembered Cora saying something along those lines.

"It takes an iron will to control such a volatile element," Donovan continued. "Emotion is the enemy of control. Did you know that most Fire Elements are celibate?"

"That bad?" I remembered the way the air had ignited around us this morning. Did Donovan know?

"Rowan is unique among his kind."

Heat climbed my cheeks. Yeah, Donovan knew.

"I'm not suggesting you concede to his every whim, but when you see him on edge, give him a moment."

I didn't want to concede, but if what Donovan said was true, I'd have to. "I can try."

"If you need to vent while you're waiting, you're welcome to yell at me."

"I'm not that bad." I looked up to check his expression. "Am I?"

He gave me a wide grin—a flash of white teeth through his beard. If a bear could smile, it'd look exactly like that.

Before I could say more, Rowan walked back around the house. His eyes settled on me. Gray eyes. He didn't even glance at Donovan, but came to stop in front of me. "I'm sorry I lost—"

I pressed a finger to his lips, silencing him. "The fault is mine. I didn't see how he truly felt." I dropped my hand. "God, what a mess." I looked up again. "Will you help me get him back?"

He didn't hesitate. "Of course."

That surprised me. Rowan had been angry. Beyond angry. "You're not pissed? He threw you across the drive."

"That's not what pissed me off."

I couldn't decide if I was annoyed or amused. "So you're a possessive control freak?"

"Yes." He held my gaze.

"Do you want me to come with you?" Donovan asked Rowan.

"I've got it. A couple of necromancers, maybe a lich." He waved away Donovan's offer.

The confidence might be sexy, but I wasn't falling for it. "I'll get my vials."

"Addie." Rowan turned a frown on me.

"If necros are involved and James finds them first, you're going to need me."

Rowan studied me for one long moment and then gave me a stiff nod.

WITH NEITHER THE COMPASS NOR the supplies to make a new one, I hoped Neil had some valuable information to share. I also hoped that James would be unsuccessful in his hunt and would show up at the manor once he came back to his senses.

If Neil's information proved to be nothing, then perhaps I could build a compass to track James. I had access to his hairbrush and closet, but what happened when he was the hound? Would a strand of his human hair track his other form? I needed to get a hair sample from the hound—or better yet, his blood.

Rowan pulled into the hospital parking garage, taking the corners fast and tight. Perhaps I should have given him a little more time to cool down, but instinct told me that I didn't have the luxury of time.

Orange pylons prevented our parking on the first two floors, but Rowan did find a space on the third.

I climbed out, careful not to bump my door against the car beside us. It said something about Rowan's anxiety that he was willing to endanger his paint job. Maybe he sensed that time was running out as well.

A single light hung from the low ceiling about halfway to the elevator, forcing me to trail my fingers along the car to find the aisle.

"Someone forget to buy bulbs?" I asked, meeting Rowan behind the car.

He hit a button on his key fob and the taillights flashed as the locks engaged. "Perhaps a power surge? It wasn't this bad yesterday."

We started toward the elevator and took only a few strides before glass crunched under our feet. Suspicious, I looked up and could just make out the light socket above our heads.

"Or vandals," I suggested. Someone had busted the light bulb. Maybe all the bulbs. Except the one we were about to walk under.

The hair on the back of my neck stood up. "Rowan?"

He abruptly turned and wrapped an arm around my shoulders, but before he could comment, he grunted and fell against me.

"What—"

He righted himself and shoved me toward the parked cars across from us. "Move."

I stumbled forward, but looked back as I did. He hobbled after me, a quarrel buried in his thigh.

A light scrape on the pavement behind me, and I whirled to face the sound. Shadow moved against shadow, before stepping into the low light. Henry grinned at me over the sights of his loaded crossbow.

"Keep those hands where I can see them, alchemist."

Two more forms stepped out of the shadows across the aisle: George and Brian. Both were armed with crossbows and wore black camo and face paint like their brother.

"I told you this wasn't over," George made a show of reloading his bow.

I let Henry herd me back to Rowan's side. "Now would be a good time to ash some weapons," I whispered.

"I can't," Rowan ground out between clenched teeth.

I glanced up, surprised.

George started to laugh. He stepped into the light and held up one of his quarrels. An iridescent sheen coated the razor-sharp tip.

"We're working with a new alchemist now," George said.

"Clarissa's son," I said. "The Deacon's nephew." It couldn't be anyone else.

"He tells me that your name is Amelia Daulton and that you really are an Alchemica alchemist."

How did Clarissa's son know so much about me?

"Where's James?" George demanded.

"I'd say the necros have him now." I prayed that wasn't true, but saw no need to tell George that.

"What?" Henry moved closer.

Rowan shifted to the side and Brian's bow came up.

"Stay where you are." Brian's voice broke on the last syllable. Rowan clearly made him uneasy.

"Explain yourself," George said to me.

"James isn't with me. I have reason to believe the necros have him." I didn't think I could make it any clearer. "Looks like you've been duped."

"No."

"Yes. Let me help you find him."

"You're an Alchemica alchemist," George said. "You can't be trusted."

"I believe it's the necromancers you can't trust."

Something clanked against the asphalt at my feet. Before I could react, a small explosion enveloped us in a thin white cloud. Gas grenade.

I caught the faintest whiff of Knockout Gas and held my breath. My hands fell to my slim fanny pack, struggling to pull open the zipper.

Rowan lunged to the side, but George and Henry caught

him. The cloud thickened around us, spreading across the width of the aisle. I lost sight of Rowan, but the thumps and grunts made it clear that he still fought. Had the Huntsman boys been given the antidote?

I hadn't had a chance to draw a deep breath and already my lungs were burning. My fingers closed over a vial when arms suddenly wrapped around me from behind. Cool hands seized my wrists, preventing me from bringing the antidote to my lips.

"You're right, Amelia," Emil said in my ear. "Necros can't be trusted."

"He's out cold," I heard Henry say.

Unable to hold my breath any longer, I sucked in a lung full of Knockout Gas, and fell into darkness.

I CAME AWAKE IN AN uncomfortable position, my hands bound behind my back. I curled my fingers, running them along the smooth plastic binding my wrists. A cable tie? It had been looped through the rungs of the straight-backed chair I sat on, and judging by the stiffness in my shoulders, I'd been here for a while. I blinked my eyes into focus and wasn't surprised to find myself in Xander's basement laboratory.

A clink of glassware pulled my attention to the bench to my right. Emil didn't look in my direction, busy transferring an orange-green solution to a vial. I half-expected to slip into déjà vu at the sight of the familiar older man in his white lab coat, but it didn't happen.

"So, you work for necros," I said.

He must have realized I was awake because I didn't startle him at all.

"I work for myself, Amelia. I always have."

I puzzled over that, wondering if there was some underlying

meaning to the statement. Something from our joint past that I remembered nothing about.

"I thought you'd been forcibly taken from your hospital room. I came looking for you."

He capped the vial and turned to face me. "I'd claim you've become quite the altruist in the past few months—if I didn't know what you wanted."

"What I wanted?"

"Your memories."

Oh, right. I looked around the room. "Where's...my companion?" I'd almost said Rowan's name, though it was probably a moot point to protect it now.

"You mean the Flame Lord?"

"We'll meet him upstairs," a new voice said.

I turned my head and my jaw fell open. Neil stood on the threshold. Before he could say anything further, Clarissa pushed past him and hurried into the room.

"You said I had to wait until the alchemist arrived," she said over her shoulder. "She's here now."

Neil sighed. "Yes, Mother."

I closed my gaping mouth. Neil was Clarissa's son. The realization left me half sick. He'd been playing me all along.

I glanced between the pair of them. There wasn't a strong family resemblance. She was blonde with those white eyes, while he had dark hair and eyes. Still, there was something in the structure of the face that gave them a similar look.

Clarissa walked past me, her heels clacking on the tile with her brisk pace. Unlike Neil's casual jeans and sport coat, her low-backed red dress looked out of place. She walked to the back wall and stopped before a stainless-steel door I hadn't noticed. A freezer? She pulled open the door and held it wide. "Come, my love."

I knew what I'd see, but I still wanted to sob when James

stepped out of the freezer. He'd wrapped a lab coat around his waist, the sleeves knotted on one hip. Otherwise, he was naked. They'd used the steel box of the freezer to contain him while not under necromantic control. His gaze met mine and then dropped to the floor, his dark hair falling over his forehead when he bowed his head.

"My poor baby," Clarissa cooed, rubbing his shoulder. "You're so cold."

"Amazing find." Neil stopped beside me. "Even more amazing that he jumped right out of the ether and into my lab." He chuckled. "Mother was delighted."

"What about the lich?" I asked. "How does he factor in?"

"Ian Mallory is a family treasure. An old, forgotten family treasure." He gave Clarissa a smile, watching her fuss over James. "We all have them." He glanced at me on that last part, a knowing look in his eye.

Clarissa planted a kiss on James's cheek.

I fisted my hands. "And the phone registered to the lich?"

Neil reached in his pocket and pulled out a cell phone. He chuckled. "Funny how well it worked. Ian wouldn't even know how to turn the thing on, yet none of them doubted that it was him calling."

"Because it was registered with his name and address. So if Lawson had checked…"

Neil gave me a wink before he turned to walk to Emil's side. I glared at his back. He really had been behind it all.

"You have it?" he asked Emil.

Emil offered him the vial he'd just filled.

Neil took it and held it up to the light before tucking it in his coat pocket. "Bring our colleague," he said to Emil, starting back toward the door. "It's time we finish this." He left the room.

"Go on," Clarissa said, her tone cheerful. "Do as my boy asks. He's a brilliant alchemist, you know."

Emil snorted, but didn't comment. He pulled out a pocketknife and walked over to sever my bonds.

"Such a shame my Neil was stunted," Clarissa rattled on, seeming to need no input from us.

Emil closed the blade against his pant leg before returning it to this pocket. So much for hoping he'd leave something sharp within my reach.

"Stunted?" I asked Clarissa.

"He can't touch his power." She shook her head. "Dear Ethan was so disappointed. And then there was Xander." She released a loud sigh.

Emil rolled his eyes and started for the door.

"By power, you mean necromantic power?" I asked. I eyed the bottle of nitric acid on the bench where Emil had been working. If I could reach it…

"Story hour can wait," Emil said from the doorway. "Neil is waiting."

"Oh, yes." Clarissa stared up at James. "Collect her for me and let's go upstairs."

I lunged for the bench, but James caught my wrist, pulling me away with ease. "I'm sorry," he whispered.

"It's okay." I looked up, but he wouldn't meet my eyes. "I'll fix this."

He just sighed and escorted me toward the door.

NEIL WAITED FOR US ON the second floor in an office I suspected belonged to his uncle. The decor was certainly macabre enough for the city's most powerful necromancer. Heavy burgundy drapes covered the windows and pooled on the glossy black tile. Neil sat behind a large cherry desk, feet propped on one polished corner, while he read from a worn book. Across the room, George lounged on a black leather couch, his combat boots crossed at the ankles and resting on the burgundy area rug.

Neil snapped the book closed and rose to his feet. "Grand Master, Amelia, if you would both please join me." He gestured at the nearby table crafted from the same cherry wood as the desk. He gave George a nod, and to my surprise, George wordlessly left the room.

"When did you and the Huntsman boys hook up?"

"I recognized their potential the night we tried to abduct you from the clinic." Neil stopped behind one of the chairs around the table.

"You drove the getaway car." I watched Clarissa walk over to the couch George had vacated, James trailing in her wake. She sat down and he settled at her feet. I turned to glare at Neil, but Emil caught my arm and propelled me toward the table.

"Take a seat, Amelia," Emil said.

I jerked my arm free and glared at my former Grand Master. He'd been lying to me since I stumbled across him at the club, maybe from long before that. "We were never lovers," I whispered.

Emil just smirked and took a seat at the table, as Neil did the same. Each had a notepad and a pen while my place remained empty.

Neil removed the vial of orange-green liquid he'd taken from Emil earlier and set it before my chair. "You're going to drink that."

"I am? And what exactly is that?"

"You don't remember it, but you were given it once before." Emil leaned over to uncap the vial. "But you'll be pleased to know I've made some refinements. There should be fewer nasty side-effects this time."

"What—"

"It still lacks any compulsive elements," Neil said, ignoring me.

"It takes a certain degree of finesse to brew as it is," Emil said. "I wouldn't expect you to understand."

"Give me the formula," I offered. "I'll tweak it for you."

Emil glared, but Neil laughed.

"Ah, Amelia." Neil shook his head. "You always were too confident for your own good." He waved a hand toward the couch. "But I've provided the compulsion. Mother?"

Clarissa leaned forward and whispered in James's ear. A flicker of darkness and an enormous hellhound lay at her feet. She clasped her hands and grinned before leaning down to ruffle his fur. After a brief rub of his ears, she rose to her feet and walked over to open the door.

"Bring him in," she said.

Dread and relief warred within me when Rowan stepped into the room, closely followed by George with his crossbow. The quarrel was no longer embedded in Rowan's thigh, and he didn't appear to be limping. Elemental healing at work or had I been out longer than I realized?

"That's far enough," George said.

Rowan stopped, his hands folded before him, a cable tie cutting into his wrists. His gray eyes settled on Neil. "Let her go."

"Completely at my mercy and he still makes demands." Neil gave me a smile followed by a tsk. "Really, must you make such powerful friends?"

At his mercy? "What was on that quarrel?" I asked, though I suspected I knew. "What did you do?"

"It's what you've done. Brilliant work as always, though I decided to convert it to a paste. What did you call it? Extinguishing Dust?" Neil smirked. "Such quaint names."

I gritted my teeth, realizing that he must have lifted the formula from my journal the day he'd visited me at the clinic.

Neil turned to George. "Thank you, Mr. Huntsman."

"You better keep your word, alchemist," George glared at Neil.

"I believe you'll agree that the reward is worth the price."

George glanced at James, but made no further comment. With a huff, he stepped out into the hall and slammed the door behind him.

I stared at the closed door. George had once stepped in front of Lawson's gun to save James, now he let a necro have him?

Neil picked up Emil's vial and offered it to me. "The grim has been commanded to rip out the Flame Lord's soul if he tries anything—or if you fail to drink this."

Rowan stood near the couch, and as I watched, James rose to his feet. Without hesitation, I took the vial from Neil's fingers and downed it.

"What was that?" Rowan demanded.

"One of Emil's mind fucks," Neil said.

"Quaint names?" Emil frowned at Neil and got a smirk in return.

"How long?" Neil asked him.

"A minute. Probably less since she had it before."

"Ah." Neil turned his attention to me. "Here's the deal. You're going to speak when asked, otherwise His Grace will pay with his soul." He held out a hand to Clarissa, and she walked over to take it.

"And when you're done, the grim is mine?" she asked, ruffling Neil's brown hair.

"To do with as you please."

My stomach twisted at the adoring look Clarissa gave James before she turned and walked back to him.

I opened my mouth to demand that they leave him alone,

but all that came out was a couple of ingredients. I snapped my mouth closed. Oh God, not again.

"Hold up!" Neil picked up his pen. "Is she ready?" he asked Emil.

My former Grand Master smiled. "Tell us the Final Formula, Amelia."

CHAPTER 30

I couldn't think of a way out of it, so I spoke. I wanted to ask questions, make demands, but what came out of my mouth wasn't what I meant to say. It was alchemy. For the next twenty minutes, I recited a formula I'd never heard before. A formula that grew more familiar with each word. I stopped to swallow.

"Finish," Neil said, "and I'll get you some water."

"The quint ingredients," Emil said. "This is where she held out on me before. I'd increased the dose and was waiting for it to take effect when she destroyed the Alchemica."

I sat up straighter and gave him a frown. He blamed that on me? Emil glared right back.

"What are you talking about?" Rowan demanded. The sound of his voice after such a lengthy silence surprised me.

Neil chuckled and our attention shifted to him. "She doesn't remember," Neil told Emil. "I suspect she was trying to frame you for the death of the Elements." He glanced at Rowan before his attention shifted back to Emil. "Good thing you were in her lab trying to brew her formula."

I stared at Neil. Close to forty people had died in that explosion. Neil had to be lying. I wouldn't have done that.

Would I?

"Or could it have been you?" Rowan asked Neil.

"Hmm, yes, I did have a motive," Neil agreed. "But the liches I sent to retrieve her hadn't returned. They might survive an explosion, but I didn't know how well the Formula would protect her."

"How did you know she was the one who found it?" Rowan asked.

"She came to me seeking one of the ingredients, promising me the grim if I got it for her." Neil turned his smile on me. "Remember, Amelia?"

I stared at him, remembering my search of James's family tree. Was that what I'd been searching for? A bargaining chip for Neil's cooperation? And what ingredient did I need a necromancer's help in securing?

"Is that true?" James asked.

I gasped at the sound of his voice and turned my head. The shaggy black hellhound no longer lay at Clarissa's feet. Human now, he knelt beside her, his eyes on me. I took a breath to answer and stopped. If I spoke, it wouldn't be the answer to his question that came out.

"Of course, it's true," Neil answered for me. He rose to his feet and crossed to the desk to retrieve a worn leather-bound journal.

"George was right," James said to me, "you were the one who called to invite me to the Alchemica." He flinched as Clarissa stroked his hair, but it wasn't anger that wrinkled his brow.

Neil chuckled before answering him. "Did you think your alchemical skills warranted the call? The Alchemica doesn't let just anyone in."

"I let *you* in," Emil said to Neil. "I never did figure out how you made master. Some necromantic trick, most likely."

Neil glared at our Grand Master, but didn't try to defend himself.

"I bet you're quite brilliant," Clarissa said to James, still stroking his hair like he was nothing more than a pet.

Neil returned to the table and placed the journal beside his notepad. He smiled at me and patted it with one hand. "This is your journal. The one you kept while researching the Formula. Perhaps you'd like to read it. Later."

I stared at the worn journal. Would reading my own notes return any memories to me?

"Do I need to add a threat to get you to finish?" Neil asked, then looked at Clarissa.

"Baby's breath," I said.

"The flower?"

No, dipshit. A handful of actual baby's breath. "The first blooms, dried and ground," was what I actually said.

Neil and Emil went back to scratching on their notepads. I looked down at the journal beneath Neil's hand.

"Go on," Emil said.

"Spring rain. Three drops."

"Of course," Emil said, chuckling.

Neil looked up, meeting my eyes. "You suspect, but you're not certain." His smile was smug. He opened the journal and thumbed through the pages before turning it to me. I leaned forward and looked down at the words, recognizing my own handwriting. A twinge of déjà vu crept through me.

June 27th

The blood sample resists everything I throw at it, which is more than I can say for the girl. Perhaps I shouldn't have left her in Neil's tender care, but I couldn't chance her being found at the Alchemica. Relations between the magical community and us are strained enough. It's best to let the magical hold her captive for me. He promised to return her when our experiments are finished and tomorrow may be the day. The quintessent ingredients have been added. Tomorrow I will take the Final Formula, and he can return the Air Element to her people.

I gasped and sprang to my feet, overturning my chair in the process. I stared at Neil in wide-eyed horror, but he just laughed. "Now do you remember?"

I shook my head. I really didn't.

"Addie?"

The sound of Rowan's voice froze me where I stood. Oh God, no. If he found out that I was responsible for what had happened to Era...

"Enough games," Emil cut in. "What's the last ingredient?"

"Amelia?" Neil's dark brows rose.

I could feel the tears on my cheeks. I couldn't say it. Not in front of Rowan. I didn't fear the fire. In truth, I'd prefer it to his disapproval, his disgust, his hatred of me.

"This is tiresome," Emil complained.

My attention shifted to my Grand Master. The man who'd been like a father to me for so long. The man who destroyed my mind to achieve his ambition. Destroying lives in the name of alchemy. I must have learned my lesson well.

"Answer, or I'll have Clarissa put your gift to use." Neil gave his mother a smile, but she was too busy petting her new toy to notice. Neil shook his head. "I still can't believe you found the grim, Amelia. You must have necromancy in your ancestry."

Or the astounding ability to use Ancestry.com.

"That true?" Emil demanded. "Are you magical, too?"

Jaw set, I glared at my Grand Master. That's right, attribute my skills to magic, asshole. With an unhurried motion, I gave him the finger.

His face went red and he rose from his chair.

"Sit, both of you," Neil said. "We haven't finished here." He glanced over at Clarissa. "Mother?"

"Sit," she said and Emil immediately dropped back into his chair.

My heart pounded against my breastbone as I suddenly understood why Emil had been so willing to work with Neil. James was wrong. It didn't take days to make a lich. Just a few hours.

I stared at Neil and his brow rose in question. Holding his gaze, I moved closer to the table and gestured at the pen lying beside his notepad. After an amused quirk of the lips, he nodded. I picked up the polished steel pen and pulled his notepad closer.

He's a lich, I wrote in the margin.

Neil smirked. "His interest in the Final Formula is no longer academic."

I clenched my fist around the pen. Once they had the Formula, then what? I glanced at Rowan, noticing that he'd moved a little closer to our table. Powerless, but not helpless, even with his death kneeling a few feet away. Though James wasn't watching him. He had his head bowed while Clarissa trailed her fingers over the back of his neck.

"Let's finish this," Emil said, the words barely understandable through his clenched teeth.

Yes, let's.

I jabbed the pen at Neil's face and he jerked back, eluding my half-hearted jab. He tried to catch my wrist, but I dodged his grasp and dove to the side, landing only feet away from my true target. James's head came up and I lunged at him.

"Mother!" Neil shouted. "Stop her."

I collided with James's chest, sprawling him on his back. One hand braced on his bare shoulder, I met his confused gaze before jabbing the pen between his ribs. I hadn't anticipated the resistance of the muscle surrounding his chest, and the pen only penetrated a few inches.

"James!" Clarissa cried. "Save yourself!"

A muscle ticked in his cheek as he absorbed the command. Jaw clenched, he covered my hand with his and shoved the pen deeper. He was saving himself—from her.

"Addie, his blood!" Rowan shouted. "Don't get it on you!"

James's eyes widened. "No." He caught me by the shoulders.

I lifted my hand from his chest. Blood oozed around the pen, having already slicked my palm.

"Oh no," he whispered and choked on a sob. A second went by and then two. Understanding dawned on his face. "The Final Formula."

I held his gaze and slammed the heel of my hand into the two inches of pen sticking out of his chest, shoving it all the way in. James gasped and then went limp beneath me. A final breath escaped his parted lips and his chest rose no more.

"What have you done?!" Clarissa shoved me aside and dropped to her knees beside him. She sunk her fingers into the wound trying to grab the pen.

"No!" Neil shouted. He took a step toward her and then she started to scream. Cradling her hand, she withered on the floor. Blood coated her fingertips, clashing with her burgundy nail polish. The smell of burning flesh wafted in my direction. Not just flesh, but burning sulfur. Brimstone.

"No," Neil repeated, a whisper now. Clarissa thrashed a few more times and with a final whimper, stilled. I clenched my left hand, hiding my blood-slicked palm.

"Freeze!" Neil yelled.

I jumped and twisted around to face him, but his attention wasn't on me. Nor was the gun he now held in his shaking hands. Rowan stood only a few feet away, having almost reached him in the excitement.

Neil's skin had paled, but he seemed to be regaining control. He glanced at Clarissa's still form and released a breath.

"Emil," he said. "Retrieve our colleague. I will finish this."

I wondered what Neil had in mind. He knew the last ingredient. Why the charade? Did he want me to say it in front of Rowan? Or did he think I'd used another ingredient?

Jaw tight, Emil rose to his feet. He walked over, gripped my upper arm and hauled me to my feet.

"Enough of this," Emil turned me to face him, his grip crushing my upper arm. "You dumb, fat bitch," he whispered, his face only inches from mine. "I bet you're loving this. What he did to me; what I need from you. But the power's not all yours." He leaned closer, his voice lowering further. "The last ingredient for your memories. I can give them back to you."

I looked up into his blue eyes. Mind rape, betrayal. This was my mentor. The man I looked up to and aspired to imitate. How far had I gone down that path? I gave him a smile and reached up to cup his cheek. No more. The dark rumors about the Alchemica alchemists had been true. I had been one of them.

Emil stumbled back and his eyes went wide. He raised a hand to his blood-smeared cheek, but didn't touch it. A tendril of smoke rose from the aged skin, and he started to scream. I didn't flinch or back away. A moment later, he collapsed at my feet, twitched a few times, and then lay still.

"Ruthless as ever," Neil said in the sudden silence.

I turned to look at him.

"You don't need to tell me the last ingredient." He no longer smirked. Clarissa's death had sobered him. "I was there when you discovered it."

I had a thing or two to say to that, but I held my silence. No need to give him the satisfaction of hearing it. Let him wonder. I took a step closer, my hand still wet with James's blood.

"Don't even consider it." Neil trained the gun on me.

I spread my hands and smiled, inviting him to take a shot.

"Addie," Rowan said.

Neil frowned at him before glaring at me. "Your friends are

so loyal. What will they say when they read that journal?" He gestured at the worn book still lying open on the table. "What if I read it to them?"

I sprang and he fired. I saw an explosion of light at the end of the barrel. Suddenly, the light became a fireball. Neil screamed when the gun joined it.

"You're not the alchemist she is," Rowan said, eyes aglow. He gradually began to frown. "Why can't I see in you?"

Neil smiled, but didn't answer.

"A formula?" Rowan asked. He glanced at me, no doubt wondering if it was mine.

I shook my head. Not mine, the lich's. I thought about the page of notes I'd taken, and it all became clear. With the way Rowan had been bleeding, it would have been a simple matter to get a sample of his blood in the tomb. Unlike me, the lich hadn't created a potion to take away Rowan's power; he had created one to make a person immune to Rowan's magic. Impressive. I wondered how long the effect would last.

James growled and the hairs on my arms stood up. He was up on his knees, braced on one hand. He pressed the other hand to his chest, a wisp of smoke leaking from the wound, and gave Rowan a tentative smile. "Thanks." Rowan had ashed the pen.

"It was the Air Element," Neil scooped up the journal and shoved it into Rowan's hands. "She was Amelia's secret ingredient."

"What?" Rowan demanded.

"No," James whispered.

Rowan looked down at the journal in his hands, and James stepped up beside him. Helpless to stop them, I turned on Neil, reaching for him with my blood-smeared hand.

He saw me coming, but instead of backing away, he raised his hands to his eyes. For a moment, I feared he meant to pluck them from his face, then I realized he was removing his contacts.

He tossed them aside and his white eyes met mine. "Remember me now?"

Without warning, the déjà vu hit me. Images flew at me. Visions of Neil in college. The nice guy who had doted on me. Pudgy, geeky me. I would have done anything for him. I kept his secret. Got him into the Alchemica. Kept him close even when Emil learned his secret and kicked him out. I remembered going to him for information on the magical. Asking him to catch an Element. I remembered Era.

A door slammed somewhere close by. Neil escaping? I couldn't do anything about it. I stayed on the floor, fighting the dry heaves as the memories lessened and finally ceased. I pushed up on my knees, hands braced on the polished black tile. I could almost see my reflection in it.

Silence.

I followed a crack between the tiles to a cluster of feet. James and Rowan. A sharp inhale of breath on James's part and the journal snapped closed. I returned my gaze to my dark reflection, watching the occasional tear smack the tile, interspersed with drops of blood from my nose.

"Amelia," Rowan said.

I squeezed my eyes shut and hot tears scalded my cheeks.

"The last ingredient of the Final Formula."

I swallowed and took a breath. "The blood of an Element." My voice broke and I finished in a whisper. "One drop." I fisted my hands against the floor, but kept my head down.

Footsteps approached and those familiar loafers came into view. The flame embossed on the slim metal band winked in the light. The journal smacked the tile in front of me and I jumped.

"Counter what you did to her and I'll spare you." His voice held that deathly calm that always made me so uneasy. Having it used on me turned my insides to ash. I couldn't look up, so I just nodded.

"Rowan, the blood," James said.

A flicker of flame where James had lain, and a sudden searing across my palm. I gasped and clutched my hand to my chest.

I didn't speak. I didn't move. I sat there cradling my hand and listened to them leave the room.

I opened my hand and looked down at my unblemished palm. James's blood was gone. A good precaution. Never leave a blood alchemist with a sample.

EPILOGUE

I STOPPED AND STARED UP AT the stately Victorian house before me. It seemed larger than I remembered, towering over the spot where I stood on the sidewalk. Even the cheerful cream and yellow paint seemed somber this morning—or perhaps it was the leafless trees and overcast sky. I kept expecting it to storm, but the angry gray clouds just swirled and darkened, reserving their gift for a more appropriate moment.

"Hey, lady." The cabbie had rolled down his window to poke out his head. "You know you're still on the meter, right?"

I gave myself a mental shake and the man a smile. At least, I hoped it was a smile. I suspected it was closer to a lunatic's grin and by his concerned expression, I could see he did, too.

"This won't take long," I told him—and myself—and forced my feet to move.

I didn't remember the sidewalk being so long or the porch steps so steep, but I eventually arrived at the front door and let myself in. I stopped two strides into the room and the door closed behind me with a click.

The sound echoed in the empty space, and I took in the unoccupied receptionist's desk and the dimmed lighting. I didn't know why it surprised me. I knew that the Elemental Offices weren't open on Saturdays.

"You're late," a female voice said from behind me.

I turned with a gasp and watched a gray-robed figure rise from one of several leather chairs grouped around the waiting area. Cora. I knew her voice and the graceful way she moved, though I couldn't see her face beneath the hood.

"Traffic," I said.

She ignored the excuse and closed the distance between us. "You have it?"

In answer, I slipped a hand into my jacket pocket and pulled out a vial. The golden liquid caught the dim light and twinkled in my unsteady hand.

Cora studied it in silence for one long moment. She didn't reach for the vial. Instead, she pushed the hood back off her head. She'd pulled her dark hair up in an elegant twist that the hood hadn't disturbed.

"Try anything and I will kill you." Her eyes shifted from navy to black-indigo.

I didn't doubt she meant every word. Even so, I lifted my chin and met her eyes. "Fair enough."

"Cora?" Donovan's deep voice rumbled from the hall.

My heart clenched in my chest, but I didn't turn toward him. I couldn't bear to see the disapproval in his eyes.

"Ah, she's here," his voice grew closer, and I knew he'd stepped into the room. "Are you coming?"

"Come along, Amelia." Cora stepped past me, leading the way to the hall and the offices beyond.

I followed, my eyes locked on her back. Donovan didn't speak as I passed him, but he didn't threaten me either. I couldn't summon the courage to check his expression. Knowing my destination and whom I'd face next, it was an accomplishment not to vomit all over the polished stone tile.

I followed Cora toward those double doors, and Donovan fell in behind us. It'd been sixteen days since I'd seen their brother Element. Sixteen days since the Lord of Flames had granted me a stay of execution.

Cora opened both doors wide and led me inside. Donovan

closed them behind us, the snick of the latch audible in the silence.

"Addie!" Era's shrill voice echoed around the room.

I closed my eyes.

"Where have you been?" She caught me in one of her crushing embraces, momentarily lifting me from my feet. "It's been months!"

Guilt twisted through me at her inability to grasp something as basic as the passage of time. I looked up, meeting her smiling eyes. I'd done this. I'd caused the damage to this incredible girl.

As if reading my thoughts, a frown gradually replaced her grin. "You don't look so good."

Okay. Maybe it wasn't my thoughts she read.

"Have you been sick? You're all pale and skinny."

"Give her a little room, honey," Donovan said. He stopped a few feet away and beckoned her to him. Like Cora, both he and Era wore their gray robes, though neither had pulled up their hoods.

Era gave us each a frown, clearly not understanding, but did as Donovan asked.

A chair scraped near the oblong table that took up half the room. I didn't look over, focusing instead on the floor a few feet ahead of me. Gray robes trimmed in black triangles moved into my line of sight, stopping in that very piece of carpet I'd been so diligently studying.

No one spoke.

I steeled my courage and raised my eyes to Rowan's expressionless face. He looked tired, and I wondered if he'd had another adverse reaction to his gift. Worry washed away my other concerns.

"Rowan—"

"The antidote," he said, cutting me off. But it was his cold gray eyes that silenced me.

I unfisted my hand and held up the vial of golden liquid.

A glimpse of movement to my right, then someone plucked the vial from my fingers. I jumped and took a step in the opposite direction before I realized it was James.

"What is it?" Rowan asked, his attention shifting from me to James.

"Antidotes are typically in shades of blue or green." James eyed the vial.

"It's not an antidote," I said.

James lowered the vial and every eye in the room focused on me.

"Clarify," Rowan said.

"I don't know what formula Neil used. The journal didn't say." I suspected the potion contained properties much like Emil's Identity Crisis. Something to confuse the target and make her unable to use her magic. Neil had either given her too much or not bothered to make the effect temporary. "I can't counter what I don't know."

"Then…"

I took a breath. "That's the Final Formula."

James's eyes widened, and he closed his hand around the vial.

"But she's already immortal," Rowan said.

"The Final Formula has regenerative properties. Powerful properties. It resets the body to its peak."

"I know." Rowan studied me.

I tried not to squirm under the scrutiny. "She's twenty-three. Outwardly it won't change her, but it will repair her mind."

"Then why didn't it fix you?" Cora demanded, joining us.

"Emil got me after I took it."

Her blue eyes narrowed. "Then you could fix yourself. Regain your memories."

"Yes."

"Have you?"

"No."

She frowned. "Why not?"

I shifted my attention to Rowan. "It will work." I just managed to stop myself from adding *trust me*.

"I thought you needed the blood of an Element," he said.

"I do." I didn't look away. "The formula isn't complete."

He considered this a moment then turned to James. Rowan's brow rose a little, questioning. The trust between the pair surprised me. But then, they were no longer competing for the same woman. Neither of them wanted anything to do with me.

James offered Rowan the vial.

"Use mine." Donovan stepped forward.

"I've got it." Rowan turned toward the table, but Donovan gripped his shoulder.

"I need to do this." Donovan's low voice just reached me.

Rowan frowned, but didn't comment. Clearly a story existed behind the exchange. Did Donovan feel responsible for what happened to Era, or something else?

The two men moved to the table, shielding Era from what they did. I watched their backs, keenly aware that James still stood beside me.

"One drop," Rowan said.

I didn't see what Donovan used to prick his finger, but a moment later, Rowan capped and shook the vial.

"Era."

She bounded across the room to his side. "What is it, Roe?"

He removed the cap from the vial. "Drink this, honey."

She looked at the vial he offered her. "Why?"

James stepped up beside her. "Addie made it for you, Er. It'll help you remember things."

"Like where I left my camera?"

"Yes. Exactly."

She gave him a grin and plucked the vial from Rowan's fingers. "Cool." She drained it without further comment.

"It might be—" I didn't get to finish.

Era cried out, her hands pressed to her temples. Rowan stepped forward and caught her before she dropped to the floor.

"I knew it!" Cora grabbed me by the front of my jacket. She shoved me back, slamming me into one of the straight-backed chairs encircling the table.

I grunted on impact and tried to grab her wrists, but discovered I couldn't move.

"What did you do to her?" Cora demanded.

I tried to speak, but my body didn't respond. She'd done something to the liquids inside me.

"Cora, let her go," Donovan said. "She can't tell us what's wrong if she can't speak."

Suddenly, I could breathe again. I gripped the chair behind me and drew in a deep breath. Era whimpered in Rowan's arms.

"Speak," Cora demanded.

"The regenerative process is uncomfortable," I said. "But it doesn't last long."

"How would you know?" she asked. "Emil took your memories after you took the Final Formula."

She didn't miss much, I had to give her that. I'd done an experiment with the Formula before giving it to Era, but I didn't want to elaborate on that.

"Rowan?" Era's voice drew our attention back to her. She straightened, stepping out of his arms, and rubbed her temples. "Damn. That must have been some party."

A light breeze kicked up around the room, lifting my hair and ruffling some loose papers on the table.

"Easy." Rowan gripped her shoulders, his brow wrinkled in concern, though a hint of a smile teased the corner of his mouth.

"What happened?" Era raised her head and frowned at him. "I remember…" Her voice trailed off.

"What do you remember?" James asked.

I cringed at the question. Please don't make her go there. Not with me in the room.

Era stared at James. "I remember you," she told him. "James, the grim." Her cheeks pinkened and she pressed her palms to them. "Oh my God. I've been flirting with a dead man." Her laugh sounded forced.

My guilt took a back seat to the urge to smack her upside the head. But she seemed to notice that her words were unkind—or maybe it was James's strained smile.

"Oh, I'm sorry," she said. "That was rude as hell."

James shrugged. "I am dead."

"But hot."

He smiled. "I'm part hellhound."

Era laughed and the pair exchanged a grin. It appeared their friendship would survive.

"Era?" Cora stepped up beside her and then pulled her into an embrace. "You are back," she said against Era's spiky blonde hair.

"I was gone?" Era looked up at Donovan who had moved over beside them. "Where did I go?"

Donovan just smiled and touched her cheek. He blinked several times, but didn't answer.

"You were abducted," Rowan said. "Your mind was damaged during your confinement."

I glanced at him, surprised by the answer. He hadn't lied, but I had expected some finger pointing.

Era pulled away from Cora and slowly turned to face me. "Addie."

I froze. Now she would remember me, and my role in her abduction. She started toward me, but I stood still. I wouldn't run. I'd face whatever she did to me. I certainly deserved it—and more.

"Oh my God," she whispered and abruptly pulled me into another rib-crushing embrace. "You saved me!"

"Huh?"

She'd caught my arms in the hug so I couldn't return the gesture even if I wanted to.

"That sparkly potion." A final squeeze and she released me. "Everything was so...hazy before. Now I can think."

I released a breath, hoping she wouldn't notice the way it shook. "That's good."

"And you feel okay?" Cora asked her.

Era laughed, turning to face her. "Right as rain. Even the headache is gone now."

"And your element?" Rowan asked. "You'd regressed."

A wind kicked up, whipping around the room and catching the neatly stacked papers on the table, whirling them into a small tornado.

"Era," Rowan complained.

She laughed and gave me a wink. Her amber eyes had taken on a metallic sheen.

"Everything seems to be working, Roe."

He shook his head and pulled her into a hug. His eyes caught mine, but I couldn't read his expression. A moment later, Cora and Donovan joined the embrace.

Feeling like an intruder, I thought it a good time to leave. I'd done what I'd come to do, and aside from Era, none of them wanted me here. I crossed to the door and when no one seemed to notice, slipped out into the hall.

I shoved my fists into my jacket pockets and willed them to stop shaking. Once again, my potion was a success. I should be celebrating, but all I wanted to do was cry.

The shadowed foyer hadn't changed, and I could still see

the cab waiting at the curb. It didn't seem too much time had passed.

"Addie?" James's voice stopped me with my hand on the door.

I turned to face him. His silent tread had carried him halfway across the room, but he stopped when I turned. Silence stretched.

"I need to go," I finally said. "I have a cab waiting." I hooked a thumb toward the front door and the car beyond the glass.

"You said the Final Formula regenerates the body. Resets it."

I swallowed, painfully aware of the hope burning in his eyes. "You're already in your prime and immortal." But that wasn't what he was asking. "It doesn't restore life," I added, my voice softening.

"James?" Rowan stood in the doorway.

My heart lodged in my throat, and I tried to swallow it back down. "I'm sorry," I whispered to James. "About everything."

I didn't wait for a response, but turned and hurried toward the door. My fingers closed over the cold knob.

"Wait." To my surprise, it wasn't James, but Rowan who spoke.

I slowly turned to face him, hopeful, yet fearful at the same time.

Rowan walked to the receptionist's desk and laid a manila folder on the surface. "I need your signature." He sifted through the pages, but didn't look up.

Disappointed yet curious, I moved over to the desk. The overhead lights were off, but the multitude of windows let in enough light that I could make out the official-looking forms he thumbed through. I stepped closer and read *Amelia Daulton* at the top of the first page.

"What do you need me to sign?"

"Your PIA registration forms."

"What?" Lawson had once told me that Rowan had begun

the registration process. I hadn't believed that anything would come of it. "I'm not magical."

Gray eyes rose to mine. "You wield magic better than the majority of those registered."

Sixteen days ago, a comment like that would have made my heart sing. Now it just ached.

"And the PIA bought that?" I asked.

He pulled open the desk drawer. "They agreed that it's best to keep tabs on you."

"Agreed? As in agreed with you?"

He found a pen and laid it beside the papers. "Yes."

His casual indifference hit a nerve, and suddenly I was angry. No, not angry, furious.

"Look, I'm not making excuses. Between the journal and Neil, I remember enough to know that he spoke the truth, mostly, but I am not that person." I jabbed a finger at the name on the forms. "My name is Addie, not Amelia. And I right my wrongs."

"Your wrongs? You didn't run a stop sign; you brain-damaged my little sister." A slim band of fire ignited around his pupils.

"I fixed that." My voice came out as a harsh whisper.

A muscle ticked in his jaw. "Do you expect me to thank you?"

"Rowan." James stepped up beside him.

"No, I don't expect gratitude." I stood my ground, determined to make him understand. To make *them* understand. "But I do expect..." Forgiveness? No, I didn't expect that either. "The opportunity to redeem myself without you and your PIA cronies standing over me." I waved at the paperwork.

Rowan frowned, but didn't immediately speak. Abruptly, he turned back to the desk, picking up the pen, and scratched a few lines on a Post-It pad. He pulled off the top sheet and offered it to me. "If redemption is what you seek, here."

I took the paper. It contained a name and a phone number.

"Dr. Albright?"

"He works in the Burn Center. I'll see that he's expecting your call."

The Burn Center. "My salve."

"He's not magical, but he'll listen to me. You'll have one shot at this."

"My formulas don't fail."

He gave me a flat stare, though the fire had faded from his eyes. "Is that a yes?"

"That's a yes."

"Good, but I still need you to sign." He laid the pen beside the papers again.

"Why?"

"I claimed you before the director."

"Please. You run the show, not him."

"Still, it makes my job easier to let him think he does."

I fisted my hands, crinkling the slip of paper he'd given me. "As a member of the non-magical community, that really pisses me off."

"Are you going to sign or not?"

"No."

He held my gaze for a moment, then closed the folder. "I told Waylon you wouldn't."

"Then why ask?" God, he was exasperating.

He picked up the folder. "This doesn't matter. You're still mine, Addie. Don't make me regret it."

He'd called me Addie. For the first time in weeks, something loosened in my chest. But I didn't want him to see it. I crossed my arms. "You won't."

Another moment's silent study, and just when I thought he'd speak, he turned and headed back toward the hall. "James, the car is here," he said over his shoulder.

I watched him walk away, my emotions a roiling mess I couldn't begin to sort out. I turned and found James watching me.

"The flier that came to the gun shop," he said. "Did you send it?"

The sudden change of topic threw me, and it took me a moment to gather my thoughts. "I remember researching your family, learning where you lived, but beyond that…" I spread my arms and then let them fall. "I don't know."

"So, you did intend to give me to Neil."

"I don't know," I whispered.

"Then why don't you take the Final Formula and find out?" He fisted his hands. "Recovering your memory is what you wanted. All you wanted for the past three months."

"That's not what I want anymore." I wanted to hug him, to reassure him that I'd never betray him, but perhaps I already had. "I don't want to know what I was."

"You think if you don't know, it never happened?"

"No."

"Then what?" His voice broke on the last syllable, but it wasn't truly anger that colored his tone.

"I…I want to try again. Alchemy can be so much more. It shouldn't be hoarded and hidden."

He crossed his arms and frowned at the far wall.

Uncertain, I reached out and gripped his wrist. "Rowan's giving me another chance. Won't you?"

He continued to study the wall, but he didn't pull away. "You worked with necromancers."

"Just one, and apparently, he's stunted."

Intense green eyes bored into my own. Not a good time to joke, I guess.

I pulled my hand from his wrist. "How do I make it right?"

"I don't know." He glanced toward the hall. "I need to go."

"Here." I reached in my pocket and pulled out a pair of vials.

"What is it?" He frowned at my hand, making no move to take the vials.

"It's the last of Rowan's antidote. I can make more, but…"

"You'll need his blood."

"Yes."

He plucked the vials from my hand. "I'll give him these."

"Thanks."

We dropped into silence. God, this hurt. "James?"

"I need to go."

I nodded.

He met my eyes for an instant, and like Rowan, I thought he might speak. Unlike Rowan, I could watch the play of emotion across his face as he firmed his resolve. He returned my nod, then walked away.

I'd hurt him badly, and there didn't seem to be anything I could say to make it better. Not now. Maybe in time. Meanwhile, I'd make a new name for alchemy and in the process, maybe redeem mine as well.

I crossed the silent room and pulled open the front door. Sunlight was trying to break through the overcast skies, the dark clouds moving off toward the horizon. It looked like the storm had missed us. Perhaps it would turn out to be a nice day after all.

THE END

THE FINAL FORMULA SERIES READING ORDER:

The Final Formula
The Element of Death
The Blood Alchemist
The Necromancer's Betrayal
The Alchemist's Flame
The Heir of Death
The Catalyst of Corruption
Blood Gifts
The Bonds of Blood
The Fifth Essence

For more details on the series, please visit:
http://beccaandre.com/the-final-formula-series/

AFTERWORD

THANK YOU FOR READING THE Final Formula Series! I hope you've enjoyed the story so far. If you liked it well enough to leave a review; that would be awesome! If you want me to notify you when I have a new release, all you need to do is subscribe to my newsletter at http://beccaandre.com. As an added bonus, you'll also receive an alternate POV scene from one of my novels when you sign up.

ACKNOWLEDGEMENTS

Writing might be done in solitude, but publishing certainly isn't. Allow me to take a moment to acknowledge all those people who helped me get Addie and the gang off my hard drive and out into the world. I'd like to thank:

My parents, who told me I could do and be anything I wanted. I heard it so many times that I actually believed them.

My husband and children, who gave me the freedom to chase my dream. Thanks for all those evenings you settled for a bowl of cereal instead of a home-cooked meal.

My editor, Shelley Holloway, who kept me on the grammatical straight and narrow, and made the experience fun.

Glendon Haddix and the team at Streetlight Graphics for the cool cover art, website design, and technical support.

The writers I met at the Online Writers' Workshop for Science Fiction, Fantasy and Horror. Those of you who helped me get started down this road and followed my novel along from start to finish: Ashley, Lindy, Jules, Marc, Gail, Amy, Lisa, and Bill.

My beta readers: Kelly Crawley and Maria McConnaughy. Thanks for giving this story a final look before I sent it on its way.

And finally, my awesome critique partners: Lindsay Buroker, Beth Cato, and Kendra Highley. I wouldn't have made it this far without your help, encouragement, and um…prodding. You ladies rock!

ABOUT THE AUTHOR

Becca Andre lives in southern Ohio with her husband, two children, and an elderly Jack Russell Terrier. A love of science and math (yes, she's weird like that), led to a career as a chemist where she blows things up far more infrequently than you'd expect. Other interests include: chocolate, hard rock, and slaying things on the Xbox. She also finds writing about herself in third person a bit strange.

For more on the world of the *Final Formula*, upcoming releases, and random ramblings, stop by www.beccaandre.com

Twitter: https://twitter.com/AddledAlchemist
Facebook: https://www.facebook.com/AuthorBeccaAndre

THE MATT ARCHER SERIES
BY KENDRA C. HIGHLEY

Fourteen-year-old Matt Archer spends his days studying algebra, hanging out with his best friend and crushing on the Goddess of Greenhill High. To be honest, he thinks his life is pretty lame until he discovers something terrifying on a weekend camping trip at the local state park.

Monsters are real…and he's been chosen to hunt them.

So begins Matt's new life as a monster hunter. Serving with a top-secret paranormal military unit, and armed with a sentient, spirit-inhabited knife, Matt suddenly has a lot more to worry about than pop quizzes and hoping Ella Mitchell will notice him.

The series follows Matt as he grows—in some cases, literally—into the monster hunter, the soldier and the man he's destined to become.

Join the hunt!

Made in United States
Orlando, FL
22 December 2023